The Geology of Northern New Mexico's Parks, Monuments, and Public Lands

The Geology of Northern New Mexico's Parks, Monuments, and Public Lands

Edited by L. Greer Price

New Mexico Bureau of Geology and Mineral Resources
A division of New Mexico Institute of Mining and Technology
Socorro, New Mexico
2010

The Geology of Northern New Mexico's Parks, Monuments, and Public Lands

Edited by L. Greer Price

Peter A. Scholle, *Director and State Geologist*

A division of New Mexico Institute of Mining and Technology
Daniel H. López, *President*
801 Leroy Place
Socorro, NM 87801-4796
(575) 835-5420
www.geoinfo.nmt.edu

ISBN 978-1-883905-25-5

We gratefully acknowledge the generous support of the National Park Service in helping to make this volume a reality.

DESIGN & LAYOUT: Christina Watkins and Gina D'Ambrosio
CARTOGRAPHY & GRAPHICS: Leo Gabaldon, Tom Kaus, and Phil Miller
GIS & CARTOGRAPHIC SUPPORT: Kathy Glesener, David J. McCraw, Brigitte Felix, Mark Mansell
EDITING: L. Greer Price, Gina D'Ambrosio, Nancy Gilson, Jane Love, Joseph Friedman, Julie Hicks
COVER PHOTOGRAPHS: Front cover: Rio Grande Gorge © George H. H. Huey. Back cover: Bandelier National Monument © George H. H. Huey (upper left); Pueblo Bonito, Chaco Culture National Historical Park © George H. H. Huey (lower right).

First Edition 2010

Preface

New Mexico is triply blessed: glorious landscapes, an extraordinary diversity of geologic features, and an abundance of public lands. Nearly a third of New Mexico is federally managed public land. That figure doesn't include state parks, state monuments, or a host of other locally administered public lands. Given that, New Mexico seems the ideal place to talk about geology on public lands.

To make it a little less daunting, we decided to tackle the state in two volumes. This volume is the first of those, and it focuses primarily on northern New Mexico north of Interstate 40. We've included all of the (nine) National Park Service units in northern New Mexico, most of the state parks, and as many of the U.S. Forest Service and Bureau of Land Management lands as we could. Our goal was to provide a broad overview of the geologic features and the geologic history of New Mexico, concentrating on those places that are most frequently visited, most accessible, and most geologically significant. Certainly there are other features that are equally significant but far less accessible. We specifically tried not to include those places where access is limited: private lands, Indian reservations, and military bases, to name a few. Even on public lands, we tried to focus on places and features that are most accessible by car on paved roads. But there is information here for those who would venture on foot into the less accessible areas, as well.

Most parks emphasize their recreational and scenic assets, focusing their interpretive efforts on archaeological and biological features. Yet underlying all of these are geologic controls. Lakes and rivers commonly are related to faults, folds, or other structural features; archaeological sites were located where geologic features provided shelter and water, fertile soils, or topography that allowed the trapping and harvesting of wildlife; and what most people think of simply as scenery really consists of mountains, rocky cliffs, vast plains, or verdant valleys whose existence is the result of complex geologic histories of uplift and erosion. So the geologic information provided in this volume is useful not only to those interested in the study of geology, but also to those who care about the environmental context it provides for a wide variety of disciplines.

The chapters are divided into sections by geologic province. The exception to that is Part II, on the Jemez Mountains. Although not strictly speaking a formal geologic province, the Jemez Mountains are significant enough, both geologically and in terms of the public lands they encompass, that we felt they merited a section of their own. They are superimposed on and sit astride the boundaries between the Southern Rocky Mountains, the Rio Grande rift, and the Colorado Plateau.

We wanted this book to appeal to as broad an audience as possible, but our intended audience was primarily the general public. To that end, we tried hard to avoid technical terms and to keep it accessible to the general reader. Having said that: Geology is a science that is full of jargon and based on complex concepts that have evolved over time. But wherever possible, we tried to focus on the concepts themselves, and to provide a broad outline of the geologic story. There's a glossary at the end of the book, which includes many of the technical terms we felt needed some explanation. Although we did not intend this to be a comprehensive guide to visitor facilities, at the end of each chapter we've provided additional sources of information.

Our goal was not to provide a forum for new, original, unpublished research. Rather, we wanted to provide a compilation for the layperson of the basic geologic framework of each of these areas, paying particular attention to the rock that is exposed at the surface and the geologic features that are most conspicuous. Much of this information has traditionally been buried in the more technical scientific literature; our goal was to present visitors with a summary of what we currently know about these places, in a format that is inviting and easy to understand.

For most of the chapters, we've provided generalized geologic maps of the immediate area. These simplified maps show the bedrock that is exposed at the surface. Such maps are one of the most fundamental tools of the geologist. Most of these maps are overlaid on a digital shaded relief base. In most cases, for simplicity and readability, we've included only major faults or none at all. In a few chapters, we've provided generalized cross sections in order to give readers an idea of the nature of the subsurface. Geologists begin by determining what's exposed at the surface, but ultimately it is an understanding of the subsurface, in all of its complexity, that proves most valuable. Whether one is looking for sources of water, oil and gas, seismic hazards, mineral resources, or simply a fuller knowledge of the geologic history of a given place, an understanding of the subsurface is vital.

When one generalizes about a subject as complex and comprehensive as this one, it's difficult not to introduce a measure of uncertainty. Our goal was to focus on the major stories themselves and not worry as much about the minute details. So by design we occasionally stray from the rules. Some of our authors call it the Dakota Sandstone, others refer to it as the Dakota Group; some geologists have abandoned the use of the term "Tertiary" altogether, but in the interest of clarity, we have not. Fifteen different authors contributed to this volume. Although we tried to achieve a certain amount of consistency in how each chapter was developed, we also tried to allow each author his or her individual voice, and a certain amount of discretion in how they approached the subject. We have tried to use the latest radiometric dates, where they were available to us, and all of these chapters have been reviewed by other geologists. But this is a volume that was written first and foremost for the interested layperson, the general public, and we kept their interest foremost. Our understanding of many of the finer details is subject to change; it's one of the things that keep geology interesting. To the best of our ability, we've presented the highlights of these stories as they are currently understood.

As the geologic survey for the state of New Mexico, the New Mexico Bureau of Geology and Mineral Resources has been researching and gathering data on the geology of the state for more than 80 years. Much of that information is available in our print publications and (increasingly) on our Web site, at www.geoinfo.nmt.edu. I would encourage you to begin there, if you are looking for more detailed, technical information on the geology of New Mexico. We also offer for sale topographic and geologic maps for much of the state, and digital copies of many of our geologic maps are available free on our Web site.

For those of you looking for additional information on recreational opportunities in this part of the country, there is no better place to begin than the Public Lands Interpretive Association in Albuquerque. Visit their Public Lands Information Center in Santa Fe (at 301 Dinosaur Trail, just south of Santa Fe at Exit 278 off I-25). Better yet, visit their Web site at www.publiclands.org.

Finally, in the interest of all of us who visit and enjoy and learn from these public lands: Tread lightly. They are ours to care for, but they are also our legacy for the next generation. Be aware of restrictions and regulations on the lands that you visit. Most land management agencies either prohibit or severely limit collecting of specimens, even those that seem abundant to the casual visitor. All of these agencies cooperated with us in the creation of this volume; we ask that you cooperate with them when visiting these places. The state's geologic resources are covered with a thin (but rich) veneer of archaeological resources, and these are all protected by law. To the best of your ability, leave these places as you find them, so that others may share the experience.

Contents

PART 4 THE SOUTHERN ROCKY MOUNTAINS...219

PART 5 THE GREAT PLAINS...309

EON	ERA	PERIOD/EPOCH		ROCK UNITS	EVENTS	PLACES	Age (millions of years)
Phanerozoic	Cenozoic	Quaternary	Holocene				0
			Pleistocene	Bandelier Tuff		Bandelier Nat'l. Mon.	2.8
		Tertiary	Pliocene	Late Tertiary volcanics			5.3
			Miocene	Zuni–Bandera volcanics			23.0
			Oligocene		Mid-Tertiary volcanism; Rio Grande rifting begins		33.9
			Eocene	San Jose Fm.		Navajo Lake State Park	55.8
			Paleocene	Nacimiento Fm.			65.5
		K/T boundary			Laramide orogeny		
	Mesozoic	Cretaceous	Upper			Bisti Badlands Fort Union Nat. Mon. Chaco Canyon	
			Lower	Dakota Sandstone		Clayton Lake State Park	145.5
		Jurassic	Upper Middle Lower	Morrison Fm. Bluff Sst. Summerville Fm. Todilto Fm. Entrada Sst.		Ghost Ranch El Morro Red Rock State Park	199.6
		Triassic	Upper Middle Lower	Chinle Group Santa Rosa Fm. Moenkopi Fm.		Mills Canyon Bluewater Lake State Park	251
	Paleozoic	Permian		Artesia Fm. Yeso Fm. Glorieta Sst. San Andres Fm.			299
		Pennsylvanian		Madera Lst.	Ancestral Rocky Mtn. orogeny (320–290)		318.1
		Mississippian				Isolated exposures on the flanks of the Sangre de Cristo Mts.	359.2
		Devonian		Strata of this age not exposed in northern New Mexico (present only in the subsurface)			416
		Silurian					443.7
		Ordovician					488.0
		Cambrian					542.0
Proterozoic		(Late Precambrian)		Sandia granite 1.75–1.45 billion years: Precambrian rock of the Sangre de Cristos Mts. Oldest rock in New Mexico	Grenville orogeny Mazatzal orogeny	Southern Rocky Mts.	1,750

A Brief Introduction to the Geology of Northern New Mexico

Northern New Mexico encompasses portions of four geologic provinces: the Colorado Plateau, the Rocky Mountains, the Rio Grande rift, and the Great Plains. This unique location on the North American continent gives the state its enormous diversity of landscape. It also makes it challenging to decipher the complex geologic history of the state. In order to do that, geologists work with what they have—the rocks themselves, their relationship to one another, and the structural features that reveal so much about their history. Today radiometric dating techniques allow us to determine numerical ages for many of these rocks. These geologic provinces, however, are divided largely on the basis of events that occurred only in the past 70 million years. The origin of the rocks themselves and the evolution of this part of North America is a much older story.

Much of the history of the North American continent (and the surface of the earth in general) can be understood in the light of plate tectonics, that unifying theory that was developed in the last half of the twentieth century thanks to our increased understanding of both the continents and the oceans. We now know that the surface of our planet is divided into a series of rigid but mobile plates that float on a semi-molten layer of the earth's interior. The interaction of these plates as they move across the surface of our globe is responsible for much of the geologic activity that occurs, including uplift, earthquakes, and volcanic activity. The early continents bore little resemblance to today's continents; they have changed size and shape, and have grown through the accretion of crustal material at convergent plate boundaries and the eruption of new crustal material along divergent plate boundaries. As the continents have moved toward or away from the equator, their climate has changed in response to their location on the earth's surface. We recognize that oceanic plates are quite different from continental plates—in composition, density, thickness, and origin. The precise nature of the plate boundaries and their interactions have been directly or indirectly responsible for shaping much of our geologic history.

Our planet is 4.5 billion years old, but the oldest rocks we can find anywhere on the planet are about 4 billion years old. One of the interesting features of plate tectonics is that much of the older crust is continually recycled, as oceanic crust is subducted beneath continental crust and older continental crust is subjected to uplift and erosion. This makes the early history of our planet more difficult to decipher.

OPPOSITE: Generalized geologic time scale for New Mexico, showing major divisions and timing of major events (in red). Ages (in millions of years) are shown at right. Selected rock units are identified in black. Shown in blue are selected places where these strata can be seen; the list is by no means comprehensive. The Phanerozoic, which is shown in the most detail here, occupies but a small fraction of the geologic history of our 4.5-billion-year-old planet. Ages are from the Geological Society of America's *2009 Geologic Time Scale*.

OPPOSITE: Toward the end of the Precambrian, 650 million years ago, Rodinia had broken apart. By 306 million years ago, the continents were once again moving together, to form the supercontinent of Pangea. North America had collided by this time with the southern continents of Gondwanaland. New Mexico lay close to the equator, and the Ancestral Rockies were taking shape.

Toward the end of the Paleozoic (255 million years ago), Pangea had come together. Vast deserts covered the western part of North America. In the Cretaceous Pangea began to break apart; North America broke away from Europe at this time. By Late Cretaceous (94 million years ago), the Atlantic Ocean had opened, and the continents had begun to move toward the positions they occupy today. The Western Interior Seaway, which reached its greatest extent about 90 million years ago, already occupied an enormous portion of western North America. The subduction zone off the west coast of North America was well established by this time.

Precambrian rocks include only a fraction of the exposed rocks in New Mexico. Where we do find them, often the details of their history have been obscured; however, much of that story has emerged intact.

The oldest rocks in New Mexico—about 1.75 billion years old—are Precambrian igneous and metamorphic rocks that can be found in the heart of the Sangre de Cristo Mountains, the southernmost stretch of the Rocky Mountains, and elsewhere, including the Zuni Mountains and the Sierra Nacimiento. These later Precambrian (or Proterozoic) rocks in New Mexico record at least two major events or orogenies, the term geologists use to describe major episodes of deformation, faulting, and uplift that occur on a grand scale. The older event (1.67 to 1.65 billion years ago) we recognize as the Mazatzal orogeny. This event records the collision of ancient volcanic islands with the southern edge of the continent of Laurentia, an early piece of what would become the North American continent. This process of accretion is how continents grow, as pieces of crust rafted across the face of the globe become welded onto the active margins of continental crust. A younger tectonic event (1.48 to 1.35 billion years ago) can also be identified, an event that culminated in the Grenville orogeny 1.1 billion years ago. Emplacement of the Sandia granite, which now looms above the city of Albuquerque, is associated with this younger event.

Most geologists now believe that toward the end of Precambrian time (1,100 million to 750 million years ago) the earth's continents were united in a single supercontinent that we refer to as Rodinia. The exact construction and location of this landmass are open to interpretation, but the coming together of these older continental landmasses into a single supercontinent, and the subsequent breakup of that landmass, explains a number of the events we see evidence of in the Proterozoic rocks of New Mexico, including both the Mazatzal and Grenville orogenies. The breakup of this landmass occurred about 750 million years ago. Within a few hundred million years, these early continents would come back together again, to form a second supercontinent, Pangea, toward the end of the Paleozoic. This is how the surface of our planet has evolved, as denser oceanic plates tend to be subducted beneath continental plates, and continental plates are subject to uplift and erosion, providing the raw materials for the sedimentary rock record.

The Paleozoic Era

By the beginning of the Paleozoic, the pieces of fragmented continental crust were moving toward one another once again. This would ultimately result in a series of plate collisions that would characterize the late Paleozoic and shape much of North America. However, the first few hundred million years of the Paleozoic in this part of the world were relatively quiet. The Cambrian was marked by worldwide transgressions, incursions of marine waters that accompanied a worldwide rise in sea level. The explosion of invertebrate life that began in the late Precambrian continued, and these early Paleozoic seas were home to a rich variety of invertebrate faunas.

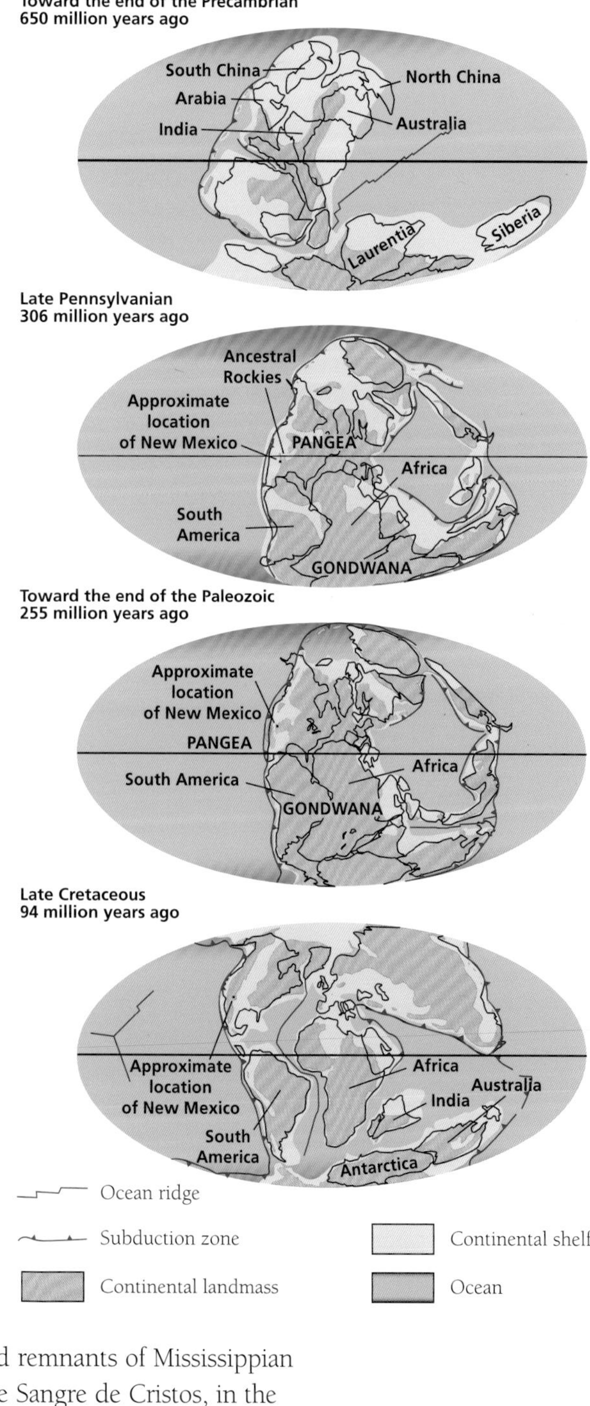

The record for much of the Paleozoic is missing in northern New Mexico, or is buried in the subsurface. Northern New Mexico remained above sea level for much of this time, at least until the Mississippian. This was in part due to the influence of the Transcontinental Arch, a broad, northeast/southwest-trending uplift or series of topographic highs that stretched across the midcontinent region of North America. There is a gap in the geologic record between the Precambrian igneous and metamorphic rocks and the Paleozoic strata directly above them—from about 1,400 million years ago until 330 million years ago where we see it in New Mexico—known as the Great Unconformity. It is perhaps best known from the bottom of the Grand Canyon in Arizona, where it was first recognized and named, but it is exposed here in New Mexico as well, perhaps nowhere better than on the crest of the Sandia Mountains.

By the Mississippian the seas had once again invaded portions of New Mexico, but in northern New Mexico much of the Mississippian rock record is either not exposed or has been lost to erosion. Scattered remnants of Mississippian sediments can be found in the foothills of the Sangre de Cristos, in the Sandias, in the southern Jemez Mountains, and at Gilman Tunnels. By Pennsylvanian time, as much as 80 percent of New Mexico was submerged beneath warm, shallow, equatorial marine waters (New Mexico lay close to the equator at that time). In northern New Mexico remnants of these Pennsylvanian strata (limestones of the Madera Group) can be seen on the crest of the Sandias, in the Jemez Mountains, and in the Sangre de Cristo Mountains. The Pennsylvanian was a time of cyclical fluctuations in sea level, and growing aridity; we see evidence of both of these in the Pennsylvanian sediments that remain.

During Late Pennsylvanian–Early Permian time, the major continents would come together in the single landmass we call Pangea. The final assembly of Pangea involved the collision of Laurentia (North America) and Gondwanaland (Africa and South America). This event was responsible for enormous upheavels in what is now the eastern part of North America and gave rise to the Appalachian Mountains. Here in western North America we see evidence of those upheavals in the Ancestral Rocky Mountain orogeny (320–290 million years ago), which began in the Late Mississippian and extended into the Early Permian, with the most intense uplift occurring in the Middle Pennsylvanian. The Ancestral Rockies provided the raw material for Pennsylvanian and Permian sediments in this part of the continent. By the end of the Permian, the Ancestral Rockies were largely eroded away and were subsequently buried by younger sediments.

The Permian record in New Mexico is rich. In southern New Mexico and Texas, world-class exposures of the Permian reef complex tell a story of marine and marginal marine sedimentation on the edge of the continent. Permian strata in the subsurface of southeast New Mexico and Texas have provided both source rocks and reservoir rocks for one of the most important oil and gas provinces in North America. In northern New Mexico Permian strata are well represented at Glorieta Mesa (not far from Pecos National Historical Park), in the Sangre de Cristo Mountains, and on the flanks of the Zuni Mountain uplift. The end of the Permian in this part of New Mexico was generally a time of increasing aridity, as the ocean retreated from New Mexico. By the beginning of the Mesozoic, most of New Mexico was dry, and the earliest Mesozoic sediments are largely terrestrial.

The Mesozoic Era

At the beginning of the Mesozoic the continent of Pangea was intact. Terrestrial environments dominated both the Triassic and the Jurassic in northern New Mexico. The multi-colored beds of the Chinle Group (Late Triassic) were deposited at this time and represent a variety of nonmarine sands, silts, and clays, including stream and lake sediments and eolian (windblown) sands. Triassic sediments are well represented in east-central New Mexico and in the vicinity of Ghost Ranch. The

Jurassic saw the development of broad, vast, intercontinental deserts of windblown sand. The Entrada Sandstone, beautifully exposed at Red Rock State Park and in the vicinity of Ghost Ranch, is a remnant of one of these extensive dune fields. The overlying Morrison sandstones, largely floodplain and stream deposits, have produced some of the most famous dinosaur remains in the Southwest. Jurassic strata in northern New Mexico, particularly near Grants, are host to some of the richest uranium deposits in the U.S.

By the Early Cretaceous, Pangea had begun to break apart. North America broke away from Europe. By Late Cretaceous time (94 million years ago) the Atlantic Ocean had opened, and the continents began to move toward the positions we see them in today. The subduction zone off the west coast of North America, which would later play such an important role in the evolution of western North America, was well established by this time.

The Late Cretaceous, at the end of the Mesozoic, was a time of rising sea levels throughout the world. In North America this resulted in the growth of one of the greatest inland seas of all time, as marine waters invaded the interior of the continent. Stretching across the midcontinent region, the Western Interior Seaway prevailed from 100 million years ago until about 70 million years ago, reaching its greatest extent about 90 million years ago. In New Mexico the Dakota Sandstone represents the initial transgression of marine waters across this part of the continent. Over a thousand feet deep in places, the Western Interior Seaway divided the continent from north to south. Marginal marine sediments that accumulated on western edge of the seaway are well exposed in Chaco Canyon, and Cretaceous marine sediments are found in many places in northern New Mexico. It was not until the uplift associated with the Laramide orogeny that the Western Interior Seaway retreated to the east and dwindled out of existence.

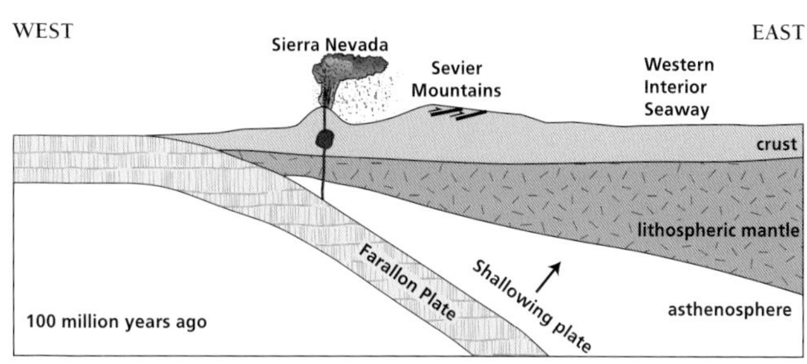

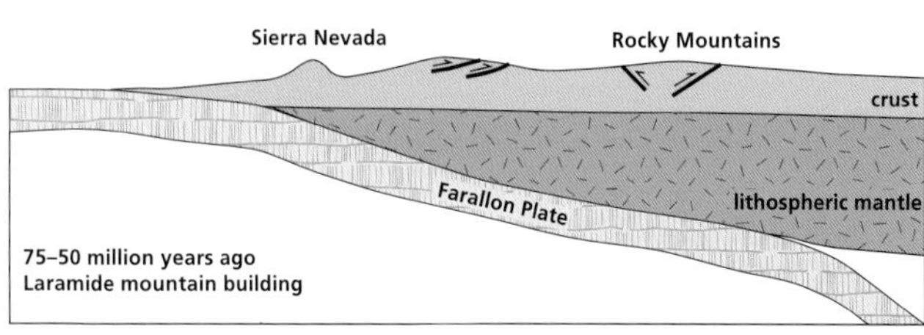

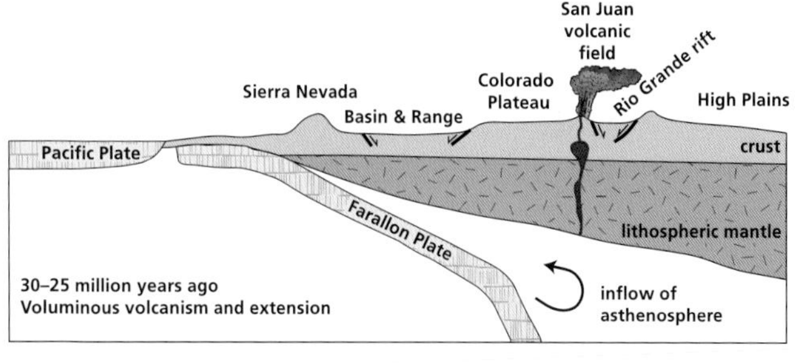

Most geologists now associate the Laramide orogeny with the increasingly shallow subduction of the Farallon oceanic plate, off the west coast of North America. The results of this event included compressive deformation, uplift, and volcanism.

The Laramide Orogeny

Much of the geologic structure of the American West is related to that massive mountain-building event known as the Laramide orogeny, which occurred at the end of the Mesozoic and continued into the Cenozoic. Compressive deformation associated with the Laramide orogeny was responsible for much of the uplift that occurred at the time, including the Rocky Mountains, as well as limited episodes of volcanism. Many of the structural features in New Mexico are Laramide in origin, including the Colorado Plateau, the San Juan Basin, the Chama Basin, and the Zuni Mountains. Beginning about 70 million years ago, the Laramide orogeny lasted for about 30 million years. Although not everyone agrees on the details, many geologists believe that Laramide deformation is related to the subduction of the shallow-dipping Farallon plate, off the west coast, beneath North America. Laramide deformation was in no way limited to New Mexico; in fact, the Laramide orogeny was felt broadly throughout the American West, from Alaska to Mexico, and from the west coast to the Great Plains.

The end of the Cretaceous is marked throughout the world by one of the largest extinction events in the geologic record. This is the event that saw the extinction of the dinosaurs, who had dominated Mesozoic landscapes. Most geologists now think that this event was precipitated by the collision of our planet with an asteroid or comet, an event that occurred in the vicinity of the Yucatan Peninsula some 65 million years ago at the Cretaceous/Tertiary boundary. The "K/T boundary" is recognized worldwide and has been identified in northeastern New Mexico in the vicinity of Raton.

Cenozoic Volcanism and the Rio Grande Rift

The Cenozoic opened in New Mexico with much of the state above sea level. It was a time of widespread erosion, as uplift associated with the Laramide orogeny continued. The Western Interior Seaway had withdrawn to the east, and the Laramide highlands shed sediments into the basins below. With the dinosaurs out of the way, early mammals evolved quickly, occupying the terrestrial niches that were left behind. Remains of many of these early mammals can be found in the Paleocene and Eocene strata—terrestrial silts, sands, and gravels—in the San Juan Basin of northwestern New Mexico.

The Cenozoic in New Mexico is characterized by two major periods of volcanic activity: a period of mid-Tertiary volcanism from 40 to 20 million years ago, and a much younger period that stretched from 10 million years ago to the present. Remnants of that mid-Tertiary volcanic activity are best seen in the southwestern quadrant of the state, particularly in the Mogollon–Datil volcanic field. But perhaps the most significant mid-Tertiary event was the inception of the Rio Grande rift.

The Rio Grande rift is the single most striking topographic feature of New Mexico. This deep-seated crustal feature stretches from Colorado to Texas and Mexico and is considerably wider (and older) in the south. It represents an ongoing episode of east-west extension or rifting that began 36 million years ago in the southern part of the state. In northern New Mexico rifting began 30 to 22 million years ago, depending upon the exact location. The very fabric of the continent has been torn apart along the Rio Grande rift, where the Colorado Plateau has pulled away from the Great Plains. This extension has resulted in a thinning of the earth's crust. The volcanism that is associated with the Rio Grande rift occurred as the upper mantle moved closer to the earth's surface. The rift is considered an extension of the Basin and Range province, a broader zone of lateral stretching that covers portions of the western interior.

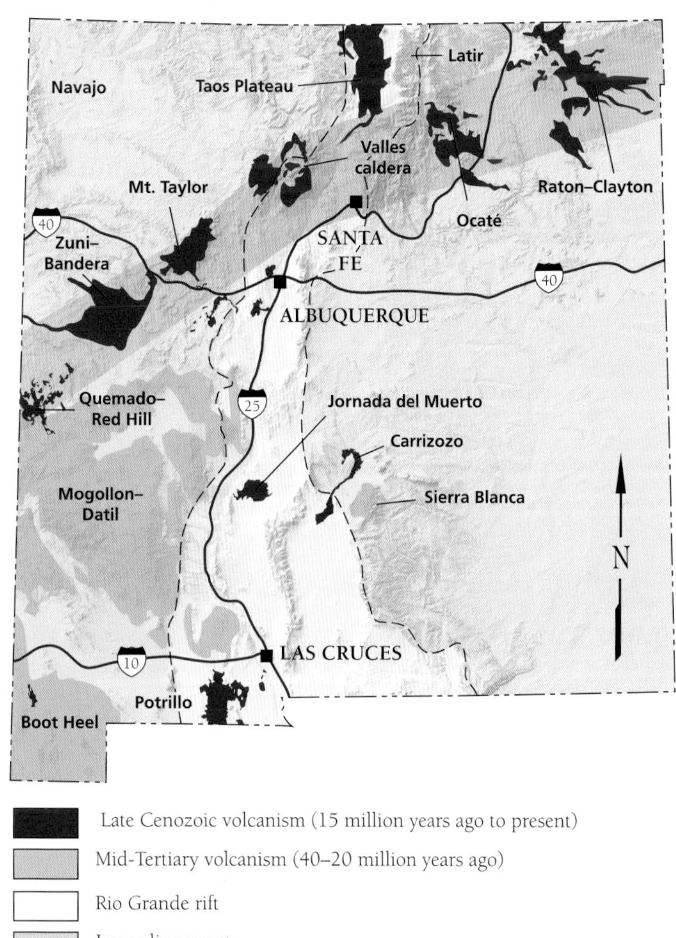

The major volcanic fields in New Mexico. In northern New Mexico late Cenozoic volcanism tends to follow the Jemez lineament, a zone of crustal weakness considered by some to be the remnant of a Precambrian suture zone, where two pieces of the earth's crust were welded onto one another. Note that the Valles caldera and the Jemez Mountains are at the junction of the Jemez lineament with the Rio Grande rift.

The Rio Grande rift is bounded on the east and west by rift-flank uplifts (the Sandia Mountains are a good example), which today are partially buried in sediment that has been carried into the basins of the rift. The growth of the rift has determined the course of the Rio Grande, which is carved into these thick, alluvial sediments.

Late Cenozoic Volcanism

The more recent episode of volcanism occurred toward the end of the Cenozoic, beginning in the Pliocene and extending into the Pleistocene. This episode of volcanic activity is concentrated in

FEATURE	WHERE BEST TO SEE	AGE (YEARS)
Capulin Mountain	Capulin Volcano National Monument	56,000
Albuquerque volcanic field	Petroglyph National Monument	210,000–155,000
Zuni–Bandera volcanic field	El Malpais National Monument	700,000 (but mostly last 60,000)
Bandelier Tuff	Bandelier National Monument Fenton Lake State Park	1.6–1.2 million
Valles caldera	Valles Caldera National Preserve Battleship Rock	1.6 million–50,000
Mt. Taylor volcanic field	Mt. Taylor Cabezon Peak	4 million–1.5 million
Taos Plateau volcanic field	Rio Grande Gorge Wild Rivers Recreation Area	6 million–1 million
Peralta Tuff	Tent Rocks National Monument	7 million
Ocaté volcanic field	Fort Union National Monument Coyote Creek State Park	8.2 million–800,000
Raton–Clayton volcanic field	Capulin Volcano National Monument	9 million–13,000
Jemez Mountains	Valles Caldera National Preserve Fenton Lake State Park	15 million–50,000
Latir volcanic field (including the Amalia Tuff)	Latir Peak Wilderness	25 million–15 million
Cimarron pluton	Cimarron Canyon State Park	25 million
Navajo volcanic field	Ship Rock	30 million–18 million

A summary of some of the significant volcanic features and events in northern New Mexico.

northern and central New Mexico, where it largely follows the trace of the Jemez lineament, a zone of weakness in the earth's crust. It includes Mt. Taylor, the Zuni–Bandera volcanic field (including the very young lavas at El Malpais National Monument), the Taos Plateau volcanic field (including the lavas exposed in the Rio Grande Gorge), the Albuquerque volcanoes (including the lavas at Petroglyph National Monument), and the Raton–Clayton volcanic field. The most spectacular volcanic activity has occurred in the Jemez Mountains, at the intersection of the Rio Grande rift and the Jemez lineament. Although this activity began some 15 million years ago, the most violent (and voluminous) eruptions were those associated with the Bandelier Tuff and the creation of the Valles caldera, 1.6–1.2 million years ago. Since that time, volcanic activity has continued in the Jemez Mountains and elsewhere in northern New Mexico, including the Albuquerque volcanoes, the extensive lavas in the vicinity of El Malpais National Monument, and the volcanoes and lavas in northeastern New Mexico (Capulin Mountain, for example).

The geologic processes responsible for the evolution of the New Mexican landscape are ongoing, of course, and geologic history continues in the making. The continents and oceans continue to move across the face of the globe, at about the rate that our fingernails grow.

The forces of uplift and erosion continue, as well, and although we live in a landscape that looks timeless and eternal to us, it is continually shaped by the very forces that have dominated our geologic history since the beginning. In the brief period of time that humans have been making an impact on this planet, we've managed to alter the face of the land in significant (and not altogether positive) ways. But one is tempted to take some comfort in the fact that ultimately, when our time has come and gone, the planet will reclaim itself through the very same processes that have brought us to this point. In that regard, geology is one of the most humbling of sciences.

—L. Greer Price

Additional Reading

For more detailed information on the geologic evolution of New Mexico, I recommend two very fine volumes, both of which are up-to-date and provide a great deal more detail than is possible here:

Geology of the American Southwest by W. Scott Baldridge. Cambridge University Press, 2004. An excellent comprehensive overview of the geologic history of the Southwest.

The Geology of New Mexico: A Geologic History, edited by Greg H. Mack and Katherine A. Giles. New Mexico Geological Society Special Publication 11, 2004. A more technical and detailed look at selected topics in the geologic history of New Mexico, but an invaluable source of current data.

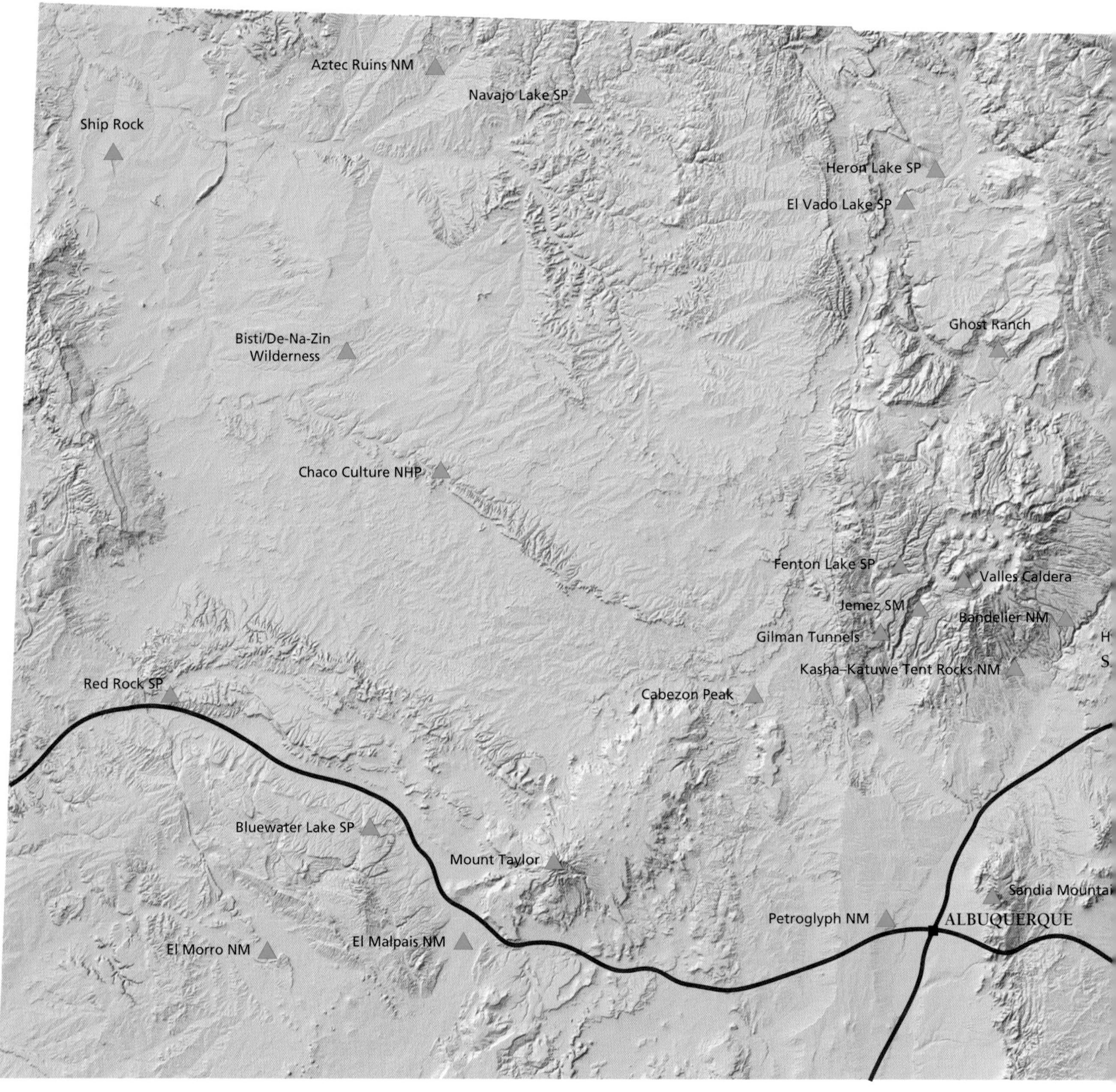
Aztec Ruins NM
Navajo Lake SP
Ship Rock
Heron Lake SP
El Vado Lake SP
Ghost Ranch
Bisti/De-Na-Zin
Wilderness
Chaco Culture NHP
Fenton Lake SP
Valles Caldera
Jemez SM
Bandelier NM
Gilman Tunnels
Kasha–Katuwe Tent Rocks NM
Red Rock SP
Cabezon Peak
Bluewater Lake SP
Mount Taylor
Petroglyph NM
ALBUQUERQUE
El Morro NM
El Malpais NM

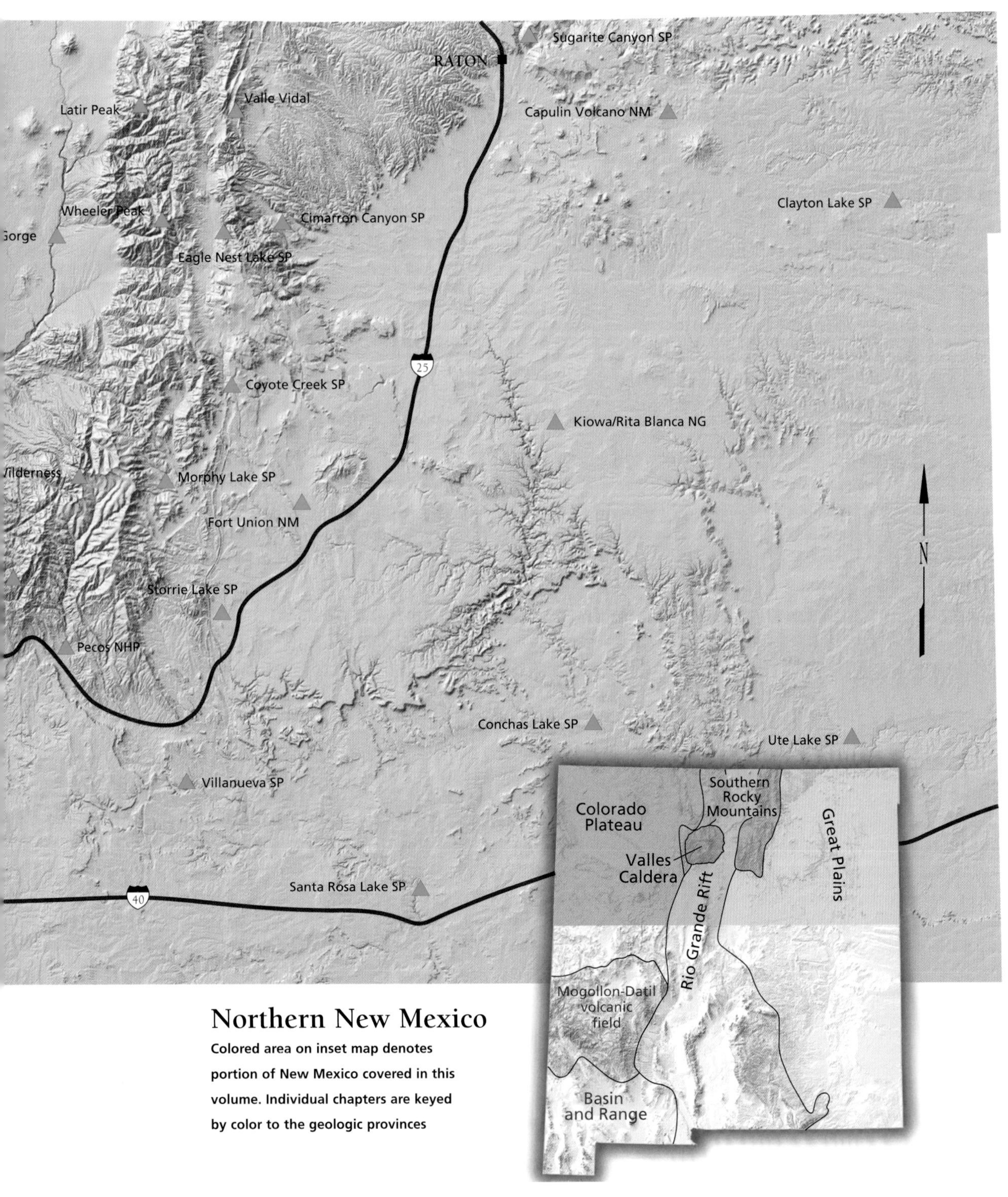

Northern New Mexico

Colored area on inset map denotes portion of New Mexico covered in this volume. Individual chapters are keyed by color to the geologic provinces

PART 1

The Colorado Plateau

OPPOSITE: **The Sierra Nacimiento marks the eastern edge of the San Juan Basin and the Colorado Plateau in New Mexico.**

The phrase "Colorado Plateau" conjures up images of multihued earth-toned cliffs of flat-lying strata, broad mesas, steep-sided canyons, and stark badlands sculpted by erosion. Although such landscapes generally characterize the Colorado Plateau, this physiographic province is geologically quite diverse, encompassing the Grand Canyon of Arizona, the High Plateaus, Uinta Basin, and Canyonlands of Utah, and the Navajo country of the Four Corners region. Three key features define the Colorado Plateau. The continental crust that underlies the plateau is 25 miles thick—much thicker than the crust of the adjacent Basin and Range Province and the Rio Grande rift. The area is relatively undeformed compared to the surrounding Basin and Range, Rio Grande rift, and southern Rocky Mountain province; the Colorado Plateau was tectonically stable for nearly 600 million years, with shallow marine and continental deposition dominating its geologic history prior to 75 million years ago. Finally, this broad, semi-arid region stands high above sea level, with an average elevation of 6,200 feet. Elevations range from 2,000 feet in the western Grand Canyon to 12,000 feet in the High Plateaus of Utah. Topographically, the Colorado Plateau is bowl-shaped, rimmed by highlands and youthful volcanic fields.

The Colorado Plateau of New Mexico

The Colorado Plateau of northwestern New Mexico may be divided into three distinct subdivisions. The Navajo Section is the largest and includes portions of Arizona, Utah, and Colorado. Escarpments, mesas, and canyons of moderate relief are developed on strata of the San Juan Basin, a Laramide structural depression. Badlands are more common in the predominantly fine-grained deposits in the northern and eastern parts of the San Juan Basin. The Chuska Mountains along the New Mexico–Arizona state line are in the Navajo Section.

The Acoma–Zuni Section includes the young (less than 5 million years old) volcanic rocks of Mt. Taylor, the Rio Puerco volcanic necks, and the Zuni–Bandera volcanic field near Grants, as well as the northwest-striking Zuni Mountains. The Datil–Mogollon Section is a transitional zone between the Basin and Range province and the southeastern margin of the plateau, which is partially covered by the Mogollon–Datil volcanic field. The Continental Divide passes through the Colorado Plateau of northwestern New Mexico, separating the San Juan River and Chaco Canyon drainages of the Colorado River system from the Rio Chama, Rio San Jose, and Rio Puerco drainages of the Rio Grande.

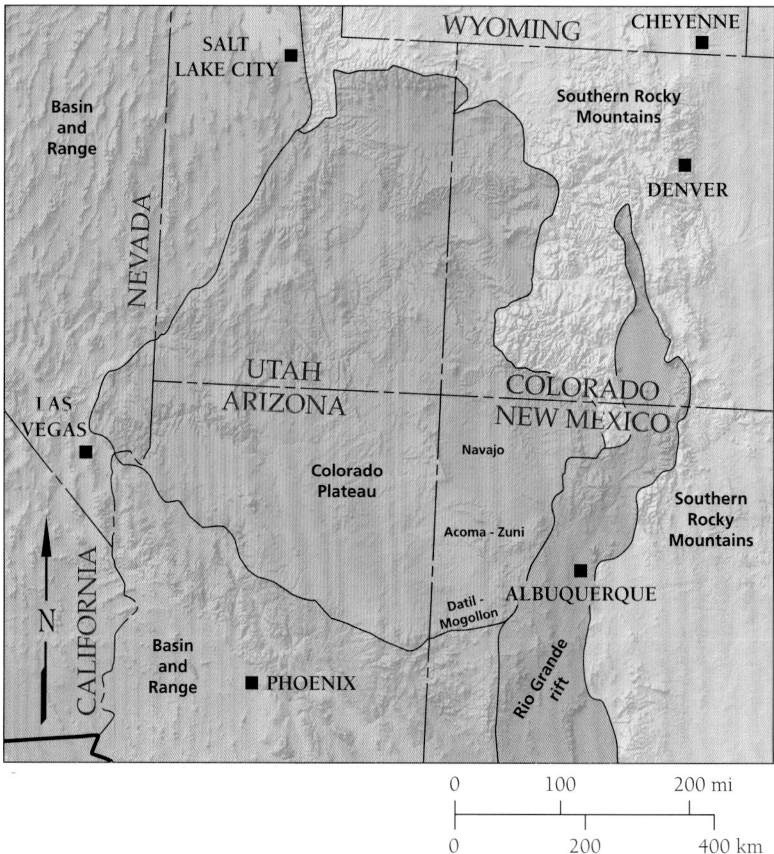

Geologic History

Sandstone, shale, mudstone, coal, limestone, and gypsum are exposed in mesas, mountains, and canyons of northwestern New Mexico. These rocks preserve a rich late Paleozoic-to-Mesozoic depositional and deformational history. The subtle forested hills of the Zuni Mountains uplift southwest of Grants record two episodes of mountain building. Ancestral Rocky Mountain deformation more that 270 million years ago is associated with the assembly of Pangea. Proterozoic granites and associated metamorphosed volcanic rocks that are 1.7 to 1.4 billion year old were uplifted, eroded, and then buried by Permian and younger Mesozoic strata. The Permian rocks include the fluvial Abo Formation, marginal marine Glorieta Sandstone, and marine San Andres Formation. These rocks can be viewed near Bluewater Lake State Park.

The ocean retreated from northwestern New Mexico near the end of Permian time, and during Triassic and Jurassic time the area was above sea level. Triassic fluvial Moenkopi Formation and Chinle Group beds rest unconformably on the karsted top of the San Andres Formation.

Jurassic rocks include the eolian Entrada Formation, Todilto Formation limestone and gypsum (deposited in saline water), coastal plain deposits of the Summerville Formation, eolian and fluvial Bluff Sandstone, and eolian Zuni Sandstone. The Jurassic eolian and evaporitic rocks record arid conditions during Middle Jurassic time. The younger, fluvial Morrison Formation marks a shift to a moister climate in the Jurassic. These strata are particularly well exposed at Red Rock State Park and near Ghost Ranch.

Starting 95 to 100 million years ago, the western shoreline of the Western Interior Seaway moved southwestward and westward across the Colorado Plateau. The shoreline migrated back and forth across the area for 30 million years, depositing 6,500 feet of nearshore and marine sandstone, shale, mudstone, coal, and some limestone and conglomerate. Upper Jurassic and Lower Cretaceous rocks are exposed at El Morro National Monument, Heron Lake State Park, and El Vado Lake State Park. Cretaceous marginal marine deposits are preserved at Chaco Culture National Historic Park.

The sedimentary strata of the Colorado Plateau were broadly warped 75 to 40 million years ago during compressive deformation associated with the Laramide orogeny. The sea retreated from this part of New Mexico 65 million years ago, as deformation raised the land surface above sea level. The Zuni Mountains uplift is the result of this later episode of deformation. The Zuni Mountains provide a rare opportunity to examine the Proterozoic rocks that underlie the Colorado Plateau in this region. Small outcrops of Proterozoic rocks are also exposed in the Defiance uplift near Farmington. The San Juan Basin was downwarped north of the Zuni Mountains uplift, preserving more that 2.5 miles of sediment, and the smaller Gallup–Zuni basin formed to the southwest of the uplift.

Another Laramide basin located in the vicinity of Ghost Ranch, known as the Chama Basin, is separated from the San Juan Basin by the north-striking Gallina–Archuleta arch. Elsewhere on the Colorado Plateau near Gallup and Farmington, sharp flexures called monoclines formed as a result of Laramide compression, locally tilting the gently warped strata to steeply-dipping orientations. Erosion of highlands (in the vicinity of the modern San Juan Mountains in southwestern Colorado) associated with Laramide uplift shed sediments into the San Juan Basin until about 40 million years ago. Classic examples of latest Cretaceous to Early Tertiary deposits associated with the erosion of these highlands are found at Bisti/De-Na-Zin Wilderness, Navajo Lake, Angel Peak, and Aztec Ruins National Monument.

Sediments continued to accumulate on the Colorado Plateau until 25 million years ago. A thick sandstone deposit, the Chuska Sandstone,

OPPOSITE: The Colorado Plateau is roughly centered on the Four Corners region. In northwestern New Mexico it is divided into three sections (the Navajo, Acoma–Zuni, and Datil–Mogollon) and is bounded on the east by the Basin and Range province (toward the south), the Rio Grande rift, and the Southern Rocky Mountains.

located high in the Chuska Mountains, is a remnant of what may have been an extensive dune field that blanketed the south-central Colorado Plateau 37 to 25 million years ago. Ship Rock and dozens of volcanoes in the Navajo volcanic field erupted near the center of the Colorado Plateau 27 to 21 million years ago. The dikes, diatremes, and maars in northwestern New Mexico are remnants of this activity. The Ship Rock diatreme west of Farmington is one of New Mexico's most famous landmarks. Rio Grande rift extension began 25 to 30 million years ago along the eastern margin of the Colorado Plateau in the vicinity of Ghost Ranch and Abiquiu, setting the stage for the spectacular scenery sculpted into now exhumed early rift-fill deposits that we see near Abiquiu today.

The Chuska Mountains

Starting about 10 million years ago, a line of volcanoes formed near the southeastern margin of the plateau, along a regional trend we refer to as the Jemez lineament. The Zuni–Bandera volcanic field (including El Malpais and the McCartys flow), Mt. Taylor, the Lucero volcanic field, and Cabazon Peak and the Rio Puerco volcanic necks are associated with this episode of volcanism.

There is quite a lot of debate on the timing of uplift of the Colorado Plateau. We know that the Colorado Plateau was at sea level 65 million years ago, and part of it, including the Grand Canyon region, was uplifted above sea level during Laramide deformation. The plateau likely was raised to its current average elevation of 6,200 feet above sea level starting in middle Cenozoic time (25-to-30 million years ago), coincident with the timing of regional scale volcanism in the San Juan volcanic field to the north and the Mogollon-Datil volcanic field to the south. The dramatic incised landscape of the Colorado Plateau today is the result of the integration of the Colorado River system, including the San Juan River in northwestern New Mexico, approximately 5 to 6 million years ago, and ongoing regional uplift.

Economic Resources

The San Juan Basin is the source of much of the state's coal, natural gas, and oil, resources that are essential to the economy of New Mexico. The Fruitland Formation, one of the youngest of the Cretaceous strata, was deposited on a swampy coastal plain; thus this unit contains abundant coal. This coal powers the Four Corners and San Juan electric generating plants west of Farmington. The Cretaceous rocks preserved in the San Juan Basin contain thick, organic-rich shale beds that serve as source rocks for oil and gas. The overlying Cretaceous sandstones are good oil and gas reservoirs. New Mexico's first commercial oil well was drilled west of Farmington in 1922. The petroleum industry continues to produce large quantities of natural gas from the San Juan Basin of northwestern New Mexico today.

The Jurassic Morrison Formation sandstone and Todilto Formation limestone contain economic deposits of uranium in the Grants region. Between 1951 and 1989, 97 percent of New Mexico's production (and nearly 38 percent of uranium production in the United States) came from the Grants uranium district. Smaller economic deposits occur in the Morrison Formation near Ship Rock. Uranium is concentrated by organic material to form lenses of uranium oxide in sandstone bodies or irregular bodies in folds of the Todilto Formation limestone.

—Shari A. Kelley

El Malpais National Monument

NATIONAL PARK SERVICE

El Malpais National Monument is part of the Zuni–Bandera volcanic field in west-central New Mexico. It is one of the best places in the lower forty-eight United States to view young, Hawaiian-style volcanic deposits. There are over one hundred individual volcanoes in this volcanic field, as well as the many associated lava flows, cinder cones, shield volcanoes, and lava tubes. The young age of the volcanism (the youngest eruption occurred just 3,000–4,000 years ago) along with the dry local climate means that the rocks and their volcanic features are beautifully preserved.

The name El Malpais comes from early Spanish explorers and translates literally to "the bad country," so named because of the extreme roughness of the lava flow surfaces. The Zuni–Bandera volcanic field was recognized as an important geological feature as early as the 1930s, when the area was first proposed as a national monument. However, El Malpais National Monument and the associated El Malpais National Conservation Area weren't formally established until 1987.

OPPOSITE: Aerial view of the McCartys Flow along NM-117 (visible at left). The view is to the south, with Las Ventanas Ridge at upper left, and the main expanse of El Malpais National Conservation Area in the distance. This lava flow extends 36 miles from its source vent.

Regional Setting

The Zuni–Bandera volcanic field is located in a large, broad valley south of Grants, New Mexico. The volcanic field is on the southeast edge of the Colorado Plateau, which is a thick block of old continental crust that forms a physiographic high region in the area where Colorado, Utah, Arizona, and New Mexico meet. The interior of the Colorado Plateau is characterized by a lack of volcanism, but the Zuni–Bandera volcanic field and several other areas of volcanism are located along the edge of the Colorado Plateau. The Zuni–Bandera volcanic rocks erupted in a transition zone between the Colorado Plateau, where the earth's crust is over 25 miles thick, and the Rio Grande rift, where the crust is much thinner. The Zuni–Bandera volcanic field also falls on the Jemez lineament, a zone of apparent crustal weakness defined by a concentration of late Cenozoic volcanism. The Jemez lineament is a subtle crustal feature but is expressed as an alignment of volcanic vents, including but not limited to the Zuni–Bandera volcanic field, Mount Taylor, and the Jemez Mountains volcanic field. This zone may be the expression of a weakness formed where two very old blocks of the earth's crust were pressed together. Although the Zuni–Bandera lava flows are geographically close to, and fall on the same crustal lineament as the well-known Mount Taylor volcano, the two volcanic areas are not related to each other.

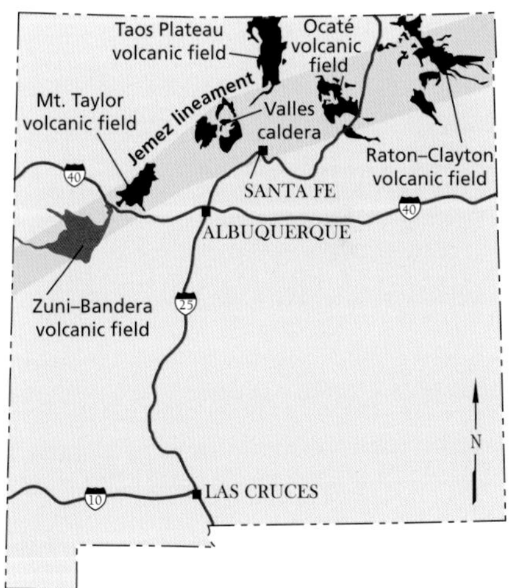

The Zuni–Bandera volcanic field is one of a series of late Cenozoic volcanic fields in northern New Mexico (including Mt. Taylor and the Jemez Mountains) that are aligned along a zone of apparent crustal weakness geologists call the Jemez lineament.

OPPOSITE: **Generalized geologic map showing major volcanic units and underlying bedrock at El Malpais National Monument and vicinity. Source vents for younger flows are shown.**

The Rock Record

There are three main rock types visible at El Malpais National Monument and the adjacent conservation area: very old metamorphic rocks of Precambrian age, sedimentary rocks approximately 100–300 million years old, and young volcanic rocks, which erupted mostly in the past million years. The Precambrian metamorphic rocks typically form smooth hills and can be seen in the El Calderon area north of NM–53. These rocks, which are 1.4 billion years old (or older), have a complex geologic history and have been subjected to intense temperature and pressure deep in the earth's crust. The sedimentary rocks can be seen to the west of NM–53, where the road heads south from I–40, and also to the east of NM–117. These rocks include Permian-through-Cretaceous strata that were deposited when New Mexico was an area of shallow inland seas, rivers, and beaches, although some were formed at times when vast sand sheets covered large parts of the western U.S. Primarily limestone, shales, and sandstones, they exhibit distinctive gray, buff, and yellow colors and form ridges and cliffs. The Sandstone Bluffs Overlook is Dakota Sandstone (Cretaceous); La Ventana Natural Arch is in Zuni Sandstone.

The third rock type found is young volcanic lava flows and cinder cones. These rocks dominate much of the landscape in the national monument. They are typically dark-colored basalts high in iron and magnesium, which formed from very fluid lavas. The youngest lava flows, the McCartys and Bandera Crater flows, have very rough surfaces that are poorly vegetated. Some of the older lava flows have smooth, more heavily vegetated surfaces, but are still distinctly black in road cuts. Many of the conical hills in the area, such as El Calderon, La Tetra, Lost Woman, and Bandera, all visible from NM–53, are cinder cones.

Geologic History

The pre-volcanic history of the region is long and complex, involving mountain building, erosion, invasion by shallow inland seas, regression of the seas, and finally stretching of the crust and erosion to form the non-volcanic part of the landscape that we see today. The Precambrian metamorphic rocks in the area formed when the continents were in a different configuration than they are today, and the metamorphism which transformed these rocks into the form we see today took place during continental collision events. The sediments that are found between the older metamorphic rocks and the young volcanic rocks formed during a long period of several hundred million years in which shallow seas invaded and withdrew from the area. Within the

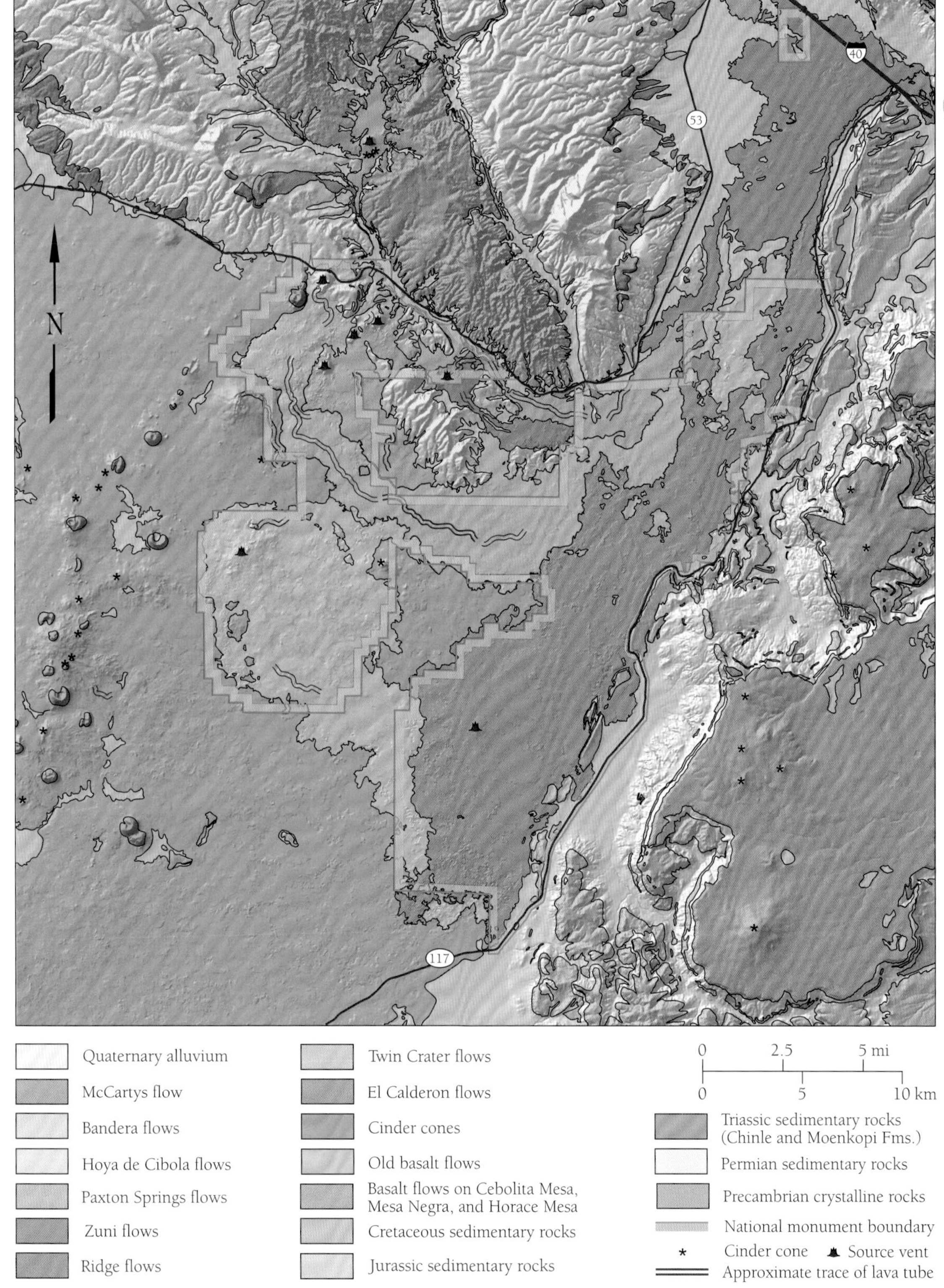

40
53
117
N
Quaternary alluvium
McCartys flow
Bandera flows
Hoya de Cibola flows
Paxton Springs flows
Zuni flows
Ridge flows
Twin Crater flows
El Calderon flows
Cinder cones
Old basalt flows
Basalt flows on Cebolita Mesa, Mesa Negra, and Horace Mesa
Cretaceous sedimentary rocks
Jurassic sedimentary rocks
0 2.5 5 mi
0 5 10 km
Triassic sedimentary rocks (Chinle and Moenkopi Fms.)
Permian sedimentary rocks
Precambrian crystalline rocks
National monument boundary
* Cinder cone
Source vent
Approximate trace of lava tube

package of sedimentary rocks in this area, some formed in deep water (limestones and shales), some in shallow water, beach or river environments (sandstones). Careful study of these rocks allows reconstruction of the history of shallow inland seas in this area.

However, much of the visible landscape in El Malpais National Monument is volcanic and formed in the last million years, which is a very short time, geologically speaking. At least a hundred vents have been recognized in the volcanic field, which covers an area of nearly 1,000 square miles. In many places flows are stacked one on top of another, making a combined flow thickness of as much as 50 feet. The total volume of all flows is at least 18 cubic miles.

The history of volcanism in the Zuni–Bandera volcanic field has been well-studied, in part because the volcanic rocks are so young and well-preserved. Although there are some flows that are over a million years old, much of the eruptive activity has taken place in the past 700,000 years. A pulse of activity over the past 60,000 years produced a number of lava flows, and these are some of the best preserved and most visible lava flows in the region. Determining the exact timing of all of the many eruptions in the youngest pulse of volcanism has been difficult, because many conventional dating techniques do not work well for young basaltic lavas. However, recent advances in geochronological techniques, particularly the development of cosmogenic techniques, which rely on measuring the length of time that a rock has been exposed to cosmic rays, has helped pin down the ages of these very young volcanic events. These techniques have shown that the youngest Zuni–Bandera lava flows are some of the youngest in the lower forty-eight states.

FLOW	AGE (YEARS)
McCartys flow	3,900
Bandera Crater flow	11,200
South Paxton Springs flow	15,000
Twin Craters flow	18,000
North Paxton Springs flow	20,700
El Calderon flow	< 60,000
Bluewater flow	< 60,000

The Zuni–Bandera volcanic field has been active for at least a million years, but the major flows we see today are younger than 60,000 years old.

One interesting aspect of the geochronology work on the young lavas is that two flows, the North and South Paxton Springs flows, which were previously thought to be the same age, actually erupted 5,700 years apart. These data suggest that the Paxton Springs vent area actually produced two separate eruptive events, which is very unusual for a cinder cone vent.

A detailed understanding of the chronology of basaltic lava flows within New Mexico is critical to understanding the potential volcanic hazards that could impact the state. Statistical estimates of volcanic hazards are critically reliant on time of past volcanism as a key to future volcanic activity. The dates of young eruptions from the Zuni–Bandera volcanic field, plus a date from the Valley of Fires area near Carrizozo indicate recurrence intervals of between 1,000 and 4,000 years. Given that the last eruption occurred at 3,900 years ago, another episode of basaltic volcanism could currently be expected in New Mexico. Although there has been no evidence of renewal of volcanism in the Zuni–Bandera volcanic field or the Carrizozo area, there are other areas in the state that could be plausible sites for renewed volcanism.

Geologic Features

Internal structure of a typical cinder cone.

The Zuni–Bandera volcanic field exhibits two main volcanic features: cinder cones and lava flows. These features are typical of Hawaiian-style basaltic volcanism. The cinder cones form around vents from which magma issues onto the earth's surface. The formation of these cones is typically spectacular, with fire fountains jetting up to 3,000 feet above the ground. The fire fountaining process disrupts the magma, forming small, *vesicular* (bubbly) fragments of rock called cinders. The deposition of cinders from the fire fountain is strongly affected by wind, so the shape of cinder cones can give some insight into the dominant wind direction at the time that the cones formed. The cones in the Zuni–Bandera volcanic field indicate a dominant southwesterly wind direction at the time of eruption, similar to the dominant wind direction in this area today.

Cinder cone vents can also produce lava flows. There are two main types of lava flows present in the Zuni–Bandera volcanic field. The first is called *pahoehoe*. This type of flow is formed from fluid lava that flows easily across the landscape. Pahoehoe flows typically have smooth, ropey surfaces, as well as deep fissures and collapse features. The McCartys flow is a good example of a pahoehoe flow. The other type of flow, represented by the flow that issues from Bandera Crater, is called *aa*, and these flows form from more viscous lava. Aa flows typically have very rough, blocky surfaces, because the lava moves along like a bulldozer tread, rather than flowing smoothly along the ground. The surface features allowing one to distinguish between pahoehoe and aa lava flows are very obvious for young flows. As flows age, the surface fills in with windblown dust. The result of this infilling is that many older flows, such as the El Calderon flow in the Junction Cave area, are virtually flat. The features that would allow distinction between the two flow types are still present but are obscured by the dust infilling. The level of dust infilling is one way of determining the relative ages of lava flows.

The formation of cinder cones typically begins with the eruption of a lava fountain, such as this one in Hawaii, which can rise thousands of feet above the ground surface. Coarse cinders from the fire fountain settle around the vent, forming the cone. Fine ash is transported away from the vent and deposited downwind.

The more fluid pahoehoe lava (left) hardens to form a ropey surface like the one shown below. The more viscous aa lava (right) moves more slowly and produces a rough, blocky surface like the flows associated with Bandera Crater. Both of the photos at right were taken during an active eruption on Hawaii.

MCCARTYS LAVA FLOW—The McCartys lava flow is one of the best examples of young, basaltic, pahoehoe volcanism that, short of a trip to Hawaii, most people are ever likely to see. It can be seen in a number of places, including out of the car window on I–40, in overview from the Sandstone Bluffs Overlook, and up close at a number of places along NM–117. Some of the many interesting features that can be observed on the surface of this young lava flow include pahoehoe ropes, deep fissures in the lava, places where the surface of the lava flow was stretched by lava pushing up from below, and some of the lava flow's original glassy rind, preserved in some sheltered areas. You can also observe the small amount of windblown soil that has accumulated on this flow in the past 3,900 years, as well as the amount of vegetation that has developed during that time. Toward the southern end of the flow, at the Lava Falls area, is a particularly good place to observe dramatic pahoehoe lava features.

Ropey pahoehoe lava. Note keys at center of photo for scale.

Hiking the Zuni–Acoma trail offers a good opportunity to view and compare lava flows of different ages. This trail is 7 miles long and is a difficult hike, but as hiked from east to west, each successive flow is slightly older than the last, and the differences can be observed in the surface features of the flows. The first flow is the very young McCartys flow, around 3,900 years old. The next flow encountered is the well-dated Bandera Crater flow (11,200 years old), which issues from Bandera Crater. The next flow is one of similar age to the Twin Craters flow (18,000 years) and finally, the trail ends on the El Calderon flow (less than 60,000 years old, probably in the 30,000–40,000 year range).

Lost Woman Crater

EL CALDERON AND OTHER CINDER CONES—A number of cinder cones are present in the El Malpais National Monument, as well as in nearby private areas. One of the most spectacular, Bandera Crater, is privately owned, but others, such as El Calderon, Lava Crater, Twin Craters, and Lost Woman Crater are within the national monument. El Calderon can be seen from the El Calderon visitor's area. These cinder cones represent the vents from which the magma that formed the lava flows was erupted, and at the time of eruption, red-hot fire fountains would have issued high into the air from the centers of the cones, raining cinders down in layers to build up the cone shape. The original shapes of the cinder cones are well preserved, in original cinder layers, or bedding can be seen in places where erosion has cut into a cone's side.

An interesting feature of cinder cones in the Zuni–Bandera volcanic field is that many are aligned. This alignment is the result of zones of weakness in the earth's crust that make it easier for magmas to rise to the earth's surface. This type of linear alignment is observed in many Hawaiian-style volcanic fields, including the Hawaiian islands. In the Zuni–Bandera volcanic field, the "Chain of Craters" feature is the result of this vent alignment.

JUNCTION CAVE, FOUR WINDOWS CAVE, BRAIDED CAVE, BIG TUBES—Lava tubes are the features that allow basaltic lava flows to travel long distances. Open lava flows can become covered with a crust of cooled magma, forming a tube (diagram). Once a tube has formed, the lava inside is thermally insulated, and is able to stay hot, and therefore fluid, for a much longer time. When the eruption begins to wane, and less lava is being issued from the vent, the tubes can empty out, leaving cave-like tunnels behind. These tunnels can be large enough to walk through, and although many collapse when emptied, others remain intact for long distances and can provide an exciting caving experience. Microclimates often exist within lava tube caves, allowing moss and other moisture-loving plants to flourish even when outside temperatures

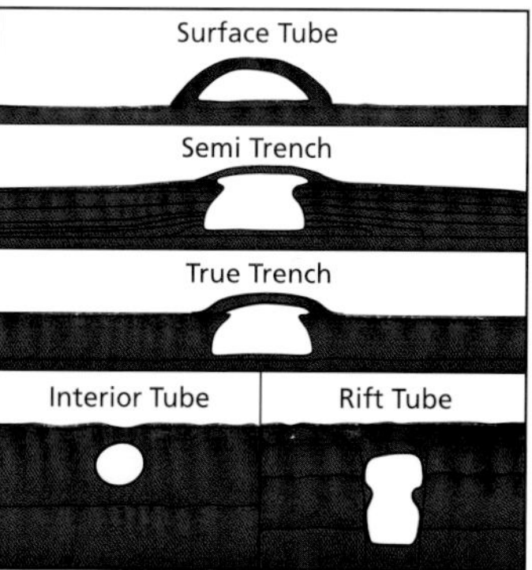

Lava tubes can form in several different ways, with several different morphologies. All involve fluid, hot lava insulated by solidified lava from the same flow.

Braided Cave

are very hot. A few lava tubes in the Zuni–Bandera volcanic field also contain perennial ice deposits.

A number of lava tubes in the Zuni–Bandera volcanic field can be visited. The most easily accessible is Junction Cave, which is in the El Calderon area. Other tube systems, such as Braided Cave, the Big Tubes area, and Four Windows Cave can also be visited, but they are more difficult to access. We recommend consulting with a ranger at the El Malpais Visitor Center for up-to-date information about cave accessibility.

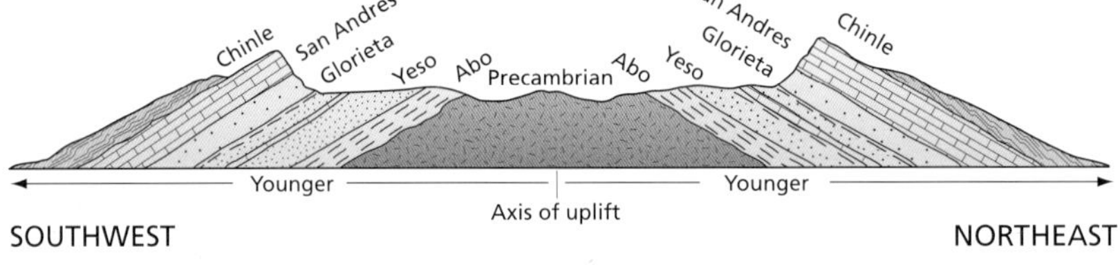

The Zuni Canyon Road crosses the southern flanks of the Zuni Mountains. Precambrian granites are exposed in the core of the Zuni uplift, flanked by younger sedimentary rocks on either side.

ZUNI CANYON ROAD—For those who have seen enough volcanic features and would like a better look at some of the sedimentary strata in the region, the Zuni Canyon Road offers a spectacular route back to Grants from the park. Just a few miles west of the El Malpais Information Center, this well-maintained dirt road heads north from NM–53 and crosses the axis of the Zuni Mountains, exposing Permian through Mesozoic rocks on the flanks of the uplift and granite along the axis. Crossing the continental divide several times before returning through Zuni Canyon to Grants, the scenic drive through the Cibola National Forest across the southern edge of the Zuni Mountains is a highlight of the region.

LA VENTANA NATURAL ARCH—La Ventana Natural Arch is located in the El Malpais National Conservation Area, adjacent to El Malpais National Monument on the eastern boundary. The arch is visible from the road and accessible via a short trail from the parking area on NM–117, just 18 miles south of I–40 (Exit 89). La Ventana Arch is carved in Jurassic Zuni Sandstone.

La Ventana Arch

SANDSTONE BLUFFS OVERLOOK—Sandstone Bluffs Overlook is located just south of the BLM ranger station along NM–117, just 10 miles south of I–40. The panoramic view of the surrounding countryside (including the surrounding lava flows) from this ridge of Dakota Sandstone (Cretaceous) is well worth the short drive.

—Nelia W. Dunbar

Additional Reading

Natural History of El Malpais National Monument compiled by Ken Mabery. Bulletin 156, New Mexico Bureau of Geology and Mineral Resources, 1997.

The Volcanic Eruptions of El Malpais: A Guide to the Volcanic History and Formations of the El Malpais National Monument by Marilyn Mabery, Richard Moore, and Kenneth Hon. Ancient City Press, 1999.

If You Plan to Visit

El Malpais National Monument is located in west-central New Mexico, just south of I–40 in the vicinity of Grants, New Mexico. The Northwest New Mexico Visitor Center just south of I–40 at Exit 85 is a good source of information. Access to the monument is by way of NM–53 or via NM–117. For more information about El Malpais National Monument, contact:

El Malpais National Monument
123 E. Roosevelt Avenue
Grants, NM 87020
(505) 285-4641 Headquarters
(505) 783-4774 Visitor Information
(505) 876-2783 Visitor Information
www.nps.gov/elma/home.htm

The adjacent El Malpais National Conservation Area is managed by the Bureau of Land Management and includes La Ventana Arch, the Cebolla Wilderness, and the Chain of Craters Back Country Byway. For information about El Malpais National Conservation Area, contact:

Bureau of Land Management
Rio Puerco Field Office
435 Montano NE
Albuquerque, NM 87107
(505) 761-8700
or
Grants Field Station
P.O. Box 846
Grants, NM 87020
(505) 287-7911
(505) 280-2918
www.nm.blm.gov/recreation/albuquerque/el_malpais_nca.htm

Bluewater Lake State Park

Bluewater Lake State Park lies at an elevation of 7,400 feet in Las Tuces Valley, near the Continental Divide, in the Zuni Mountains. French settler Martin Boure created the lake in 1850 to irrigate his farm. The original dam failed during a rare, torrential rain, one of only a few such occurrences recorded in the Zuni Mountains. In 1884–85 more French settlers arrived and built a dam at the junction of Cottonwood (or Azul) and Bluewater Creeks. That dam also failed. In 1894 a Mormon named Ernst Tietjen formed a partnership with local businessmen and built another

dam at the confluence of Bluewater and Cottonwood Creeks. Over the next few decades, dams were breached at least three or four times and then rebuilt at various places along Bluewater Creek. In 1930 sportsmen, with the help of the Game Protective Association, opened Bluewater Lake for recreational use. In 1936 the lake was stocked with trout, bass, perch, and crappie, and in 1937 the state of New Mexico purchased 160 acres along the lakeshore for recreational development. In 1955 Bluewater Lake, with a total acreage of nearly 2,200 acres, became a state park.

Permian and Triassic sedimentary rocks are exposed along the lake shore, in the steep-walled canyon of Bluewater Creek and in the hills surrounding the lake. Crossbedded sandstones, fossiliferous limestones, and the brightly colored shales of the Chinle Group are the main draw. A forest of cottonwoods, piñon pine, and juniper surrounds the lake.

An overlook at the end of the road from the Visitor Center offers an excellent view of the dam and canyon. A primitive hiking trail leads down into the canyon below the dam.

Regional Setting

Bluewater Lake State Park lies in the Zuni Mountains, which form the southern edge of the Colorado Plateau. The Zuni Mountains are considered the southern boundary of the San Juan Basin, a basin on the Colorado Plateau known for oil, natural gas, uranium, and coal production. In contrast to the relatively stable Colorado Plateau, the Zuni Mountains form the core of an elongated structural dome or uplift created by regional compression during the Cretaceous and Early Tertiary periods. During the Cretaceous and Early Tertiary, the denser oceanic Farallon plate was subducted, overridden by the continental North American plate. This collision of plates resulted in the Laramide orogeny, which caused widespread uplift throughout the Rocky Mountains. Cretaceous and Early Tertiary volcanic rocks are not exposed on the Colorado Plateau, but they are common in southwestern New Mexico and southeastern Arizona.

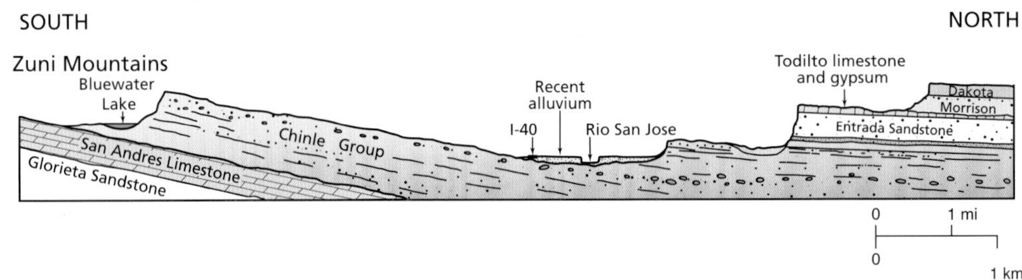

Generalized cross section showing the regional geology in the vicinity of Bluewater Lake.

The Rock Record/Geologic History

The Zuni Mountains are one of the areas that show Laramide deformation along the edge of the Colorado Plateau during Cretaceous and Early Tertiary times. Rocks ranging in age from Proterozoic through Recent are exposed in and around the Zuni Mountains, but only Permian and Triassic strata are exposed near Bluewater Lake. Thin veneers of Quaternary alluvium fill valleys draining into the lake. Similar rocks underlie much of the Colorado Plateau and are exposed only along the edges of the plateau.

The oldest rocks exposed at Bluewater Lake State Park are Glorieta Sandstone, deposited during the middle Permian 268–245 million years ago. The Glorieta Sandstone consists of massive, white-to-buff-to-yellow quartz sandstones. These erosion-resistant sandstones form steep cliffs and hillslopes. They are typically crossbedded, indicating deposition as eolian dunes and in local stream channels along the shore of the Permian sea that extended across New Mexico at that time.

Overlying the Glorieta Sandstone are limestones, dolomites, shales, siltstones, and (locally) gypsum of the Permian San Andres Formation. The San Andres Formation was deposited along the bottom of the shallow epicontinental Permian sea that covered much of New Mexico. At the end of the middle Permian, the seas retreated and erosion occurred. During this period *karst* features began to form on the exposed surface of San Andres limestone. The term karst refers to a type of topography that forms on exposed surfaces of limestone (and other soluble rocks), mainly through dissolution of the rock by slightly acidic rain water and ground water. Such erosional topography is characterized by sinkholes, caves, and underground drainage.

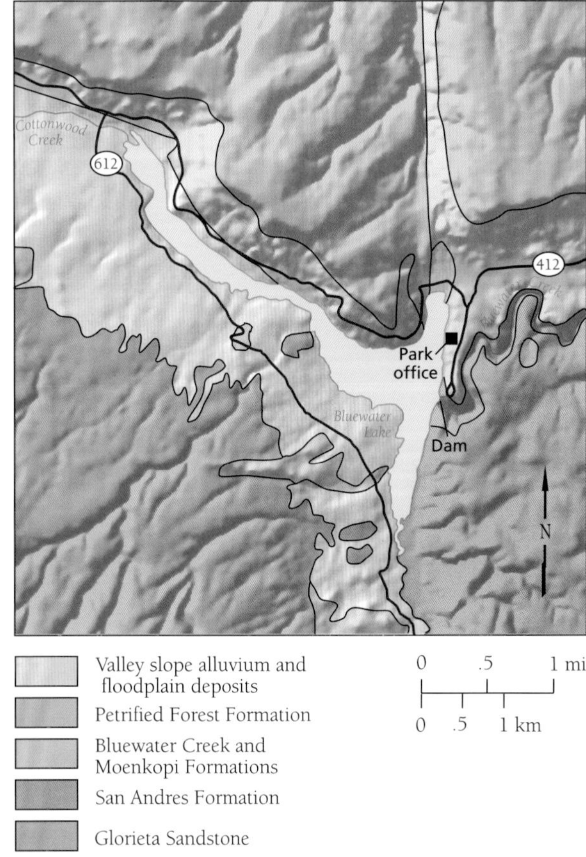

Generalized geologic map of the area surrounding Bluewater Lake State Park.

By Triassic time small rivers had formed a broad floodplain where Bluewater Lake State Park now lies. It was at this time that the colorful sediments of the Chinle Group were deposited. Many of the collapse features and sinkholes that formed on the erosional San Andres surface are now filled with some of these younger, Triassic rocks. The Bluewater Creek Formation (the oldest of the Chinle Group strata exposed here) is exposed along Bluewater Lake and Cottonwood Creek, upstream of the lake. It consists of grayish-red and reddish-brown sandstones, siltstones, and variegated red, gray, and brown mudstones. This unit is well known to local residents; when it's wet, it becomes slick and muddy, and uninformed drivers sometimes get their vehicles stuck in the mud bogs along the lake. The Petrified Forest Formation overlies the Bluewater Creek Formation and forms the upper slopes north of Bluewater Lake. It consists of grayish-white, crossbedded sandstones and red siltstones and mudstones. Rocks in both formations were deposited in continental fluvial and floodplain environments. Crossbedded sandstones were deposited in rivers or streams. Siltstones and mudstones were deposited in floodplains adjacent to rivers and streams. Mudcracks indicate that sometimes the sandstones and mudstones were

Glorieta Sandstone cliffs along Bluewater Creek just below the dam. The Glorieta Sandstone (Permian) is the oldest unit in the park.

exposed to drying. The red color is produced by the oxidation of iron in the minerals forming the sandstone. The climate during deposition of the Chinle Group was warm and seasonally humid as evidenced by plant fossils preserved in the unit.

There is no evidence of a former natural lake in Las Tuces Valley. It contains a thin veneer of Quaternary alluvium and finer-grained valley fill deposits formed by ancient rivers or streams. Quaternary alluvium fills the bottom of the canyons and arroyos that drain into the lake and along the lakeshore. Most of this alluvium consists of sand, silt, and clay, derived from erosion of the surrounding Bluewater Creek and Petrified Forest Formation outcrops.

Geologic Features

The Glorieta Sandstone crops out along the canyon bottom of Bluewater Creek and along the hill slopes south of Bluewater Lake. In Bluewater Creek well-exposed crossbeds are found throughout the unit. The upper San Andres limestone beds contain fossil brachiopods, gastropods, and bryozoa in places. Rocks belonging to the Chinle Group form most of the hills surrounding Bluewater Lake. Plant fossils including leaves, petrified wood, leafy shoots, stems, pollen, and woody debris are locally common in the Chinle Group.

The rugged, irregular surfaces seen in the San Andres limestone along Bluewater Creek represent sinkholes, small caves, and other collapse features that formed on top of the exposed surface of San Andres limestone prior to the deposition of the younger Triassic rocks. Bluewater Lake State Park is the only park in northern New Mexico that has examples of karst (although karst features are very prominent in southern New Mexico, at Bottomless Lakes and Brantley Dam State Parks, and Carlsbad Caverns National Park).

The poorly exposed Bluewater fault zone strikes north-south and locally separates Bluewater Creek and Petrified Forest beds from older

San Andres beds. The Bluewater fault has a vertical displacement of 100–400 feet (down to the west). The age of the fault is uncertain. The dam is built along the west-facing fault scarp. The lake conceals portions of the fault pattern.

—Virginia T. McLemore

Additional Reading

El Malpais, Mt. Taylor, and the Zuni Mountains: A Hiking Guide and History by S. Robinson. University of New Mexico Press, 1994.

If You Plan to Visit

Bluewater Lake is in the Zuni Mountains, just a few miles south of I–40 between Grants and Gallup. It is accessible from I–40 via NM–612 (Exit 53) or NM–412 (Exit 63). For more information:

Bluewater Lake State Park
P.O. Box 3419
Prewitt, NM 87045
(505) 876-2391
www.emnrd.state.nm.us/nmparks

El Morro National Monument

NATIONAL PARK SERVICE

Inscription Rock, most of which is Jurassic Zuni Sandstone.

El Morro National Monument is located south of Gallup in west-central New Mexico, 40 miles from the New Mexico–Arizona border. The name refers to the shape of the prominent sandstone cliff at the monument (in Spanish, a "morro" is a snout or nose). Known today as Inscription Rock, the cliff contains petroglyphs and more than 2,000 carved signatures, some dating back to Spanish explorers of the late 1500s. The oldest authenticated "autograph" is that of the famous Spanish colonizer Don Juan de Oñate, dated 16 April 1605. The sandstone that forms the bulk of the cliff formed near the southwestern edge of a vast Jurassic desert (sand sea) that covered much of the Southwest 160 million years ago.

Regional Setting

El Morro is located in the Acoma–Zuni section of the Colorado Plateau province. Located south of the Zuni Mountains and near the southern edge of the Colorado Plateau, the nearly flat-lying sandstone layers at El Morro are part of a landscape of low mesas, cuestas, and

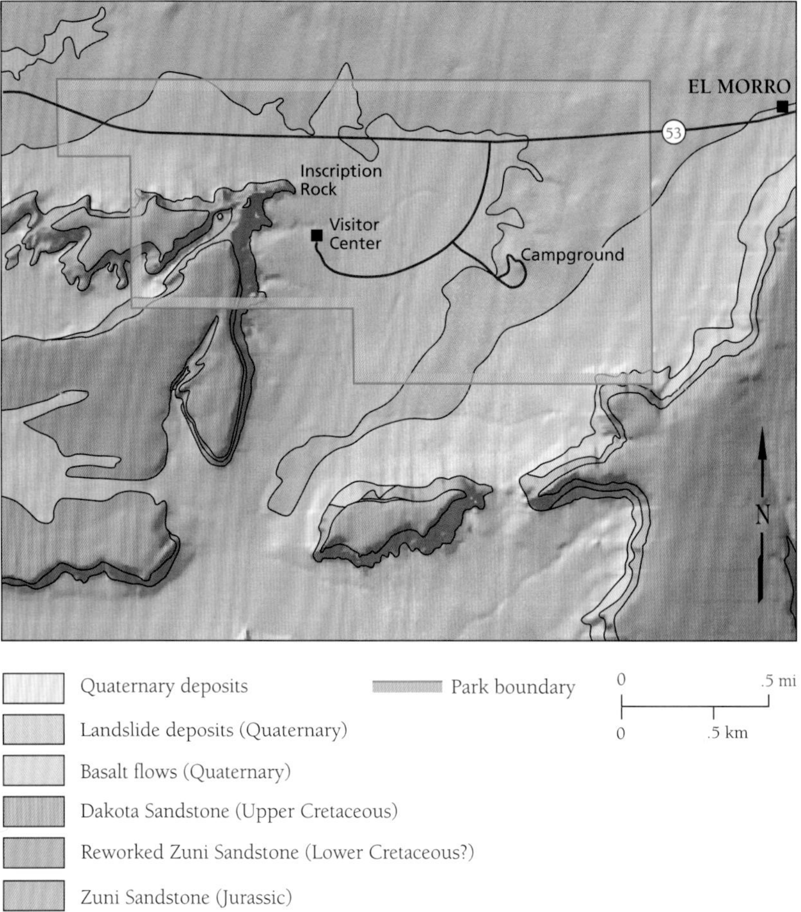

Generalized geologic map for El Morro and vicinity.

broad, dissected river valleys dotted by piñon-juniper forest. The flat-lying rocks are sandstones of Jurassic age, overlain by layers of Cretaceous sandstone and shale.

The monument is located near the western edge of the Zuni–Bandera volcanic field, an extensive, geologically young volcanic field centered just south of Grants. For more information on the Zuni–Bandera volcanic field, see the chapter in this book on El Malpais National Monument.

The Rock Record

El Morro is a cliff of Middle Jurassic sandstone that geologists refer to as the Zuni Sandstone. This sandstone is not very coarse, though its grains are evident to the eye and touch. It has flat layering as well as crossbeds, indicative of deposition by wind. The cliff at El Morro is about 200 feet thick.

The top of the cliff has a thin veneer of Cretaceous Dakota Sandstone (this rock formation extends northward into what was once the Dakota Territory). On the northern face of the cliff, windblown sand has been accumulating for the last few thousand years, piling up soft slopes of yellow sand against the hard cliff of Jurassic sandstone.

Basaltic lava flows from the Zuni–Bandera volcanic field to the east fill some of the valleys. The road to the campground crosses one of the lava flows from this field. This particular flow is thought to be as young as 115,000 years old (and perhaps younger).

Geologic History

Historic Spanish record of the re-conquest in 1692, following the Pueblo Revolt, on the south side of Inscription Rock. The photo was taken in 1873 by T. H. O'Sullivan of the Wheeler Survey.

About 160 million years ago, northern New Mexico was approximately 20 degrees north of the equator (it is now about 35 degrees north) and at the southern edge of a vast desert or sand sea that covered much of the Southwest. Winds blew primarily toward the southwest at that time, and sand accumulated in dunes and as sand sheets. This sand eventually became the sandstone cliffs at El Morro.

The desert persisted for a few million years, and during that time—about 40,000 years (a geological instant)—a vast salt lake developed in the desert. It extended from the Four Corners across most of northern New Mexico to Santa Rosa on the east. But the lake did not reach the site of El Morro.

After the desert disappeared, the site of El Morro must have been a stable and eroding landscape for nearly 60 million years. No rocks were formed until 90 million years ago, when the shore of a seaway that encroached from the east reached the site of El Morro. The Cretaceous Dakota Sandstone on top of the Jurassic sandstone cliff at El Morro is the remnant of that shoreline.

Younger rock layers deposited after that shoreline can be seen to the north of El Morro but have been eroded away here. Today, only windblown sand accumulating at El Morro has the potential to become part of the rock record.

Geologic Features

The cliff at El Morro is the central geological feature of the park. Ironically, none who carved their names there knew just how old the sandstone is.

Regionally, the cliff at El Morro is but one geologic feature developed in this Middle Jurassic sandstone. La Ventana Arch at El Malpais National Monument is another. Acoma Pueblo (the fabled "sky city"), 45 miles east of El Morro, is built on top of a 200-foot-high mesa of Zuni Sandstone capped by a thin veneer of Cretaceous Dakota Sandstone.

Acoma Pueblo is built atop a mesa of Zuni Sandstone capped by a thin veneer of Dakota Sandstone.

—*Spencer G. Lucas*

If You Plan to Visit

El Morro National Monument, in Cibola County, is located 56 miles southeast of Gallup and 42 miles southwest of Grants. From Gallup, the monument may be reached by taking NM–602 south of Gallup to NM–53, then following NM–53 east to the monument. Coming from the west, it may be reached by exiting I–40 at Exit 81, following NM–53 south and west to El Morro. For more information:

El Morro National Monument
HC 61 Box 43
Ramah, NM 87321-9603
(575) 738-4226
www.nps.gov/elmo

Red Rock State Park

CITY OF GALLUP

Red Rock State Park is a unique attraction blending spectacular views of bold red sandstone cliffs with an impressive array of public facilities, including a rodeo arena, a trading post, and a museum. The 640-acre park offers excellent scenery for balloonists, hikers, campers, and other visitors. Red Rock State Park opened in 1972 as a state park; in 1989 the park was turned over to the Navajo Indian Tribe. The park is currently managed by the city of Gallup. Church Rock (more properly known as Navajo Church) is the notable landmark that can be seen north of the park.

Massive red cliffs of Entrada Sandstone provide a colorful backdrop for the facilities at Red Rock State Park.

Regional Setting

Red Rock State Park is on the Chaco Slope, a gently north-dipping slope between the Zuni Mountains to the south and the San Juan Basin to the north. Both the Zuni Mountain uplift and the San Juan Basin depression formed during Laramide-age compression of the southeastern Colorado Plateau. The gentle northward tilting of the rocks in this part of the Colorado Plateau and subsequent exhumation has revealed a colorful series of Triassic-to-Cretaceous strata that have been sculpted by erosion into striking spires and prominent cliffs.

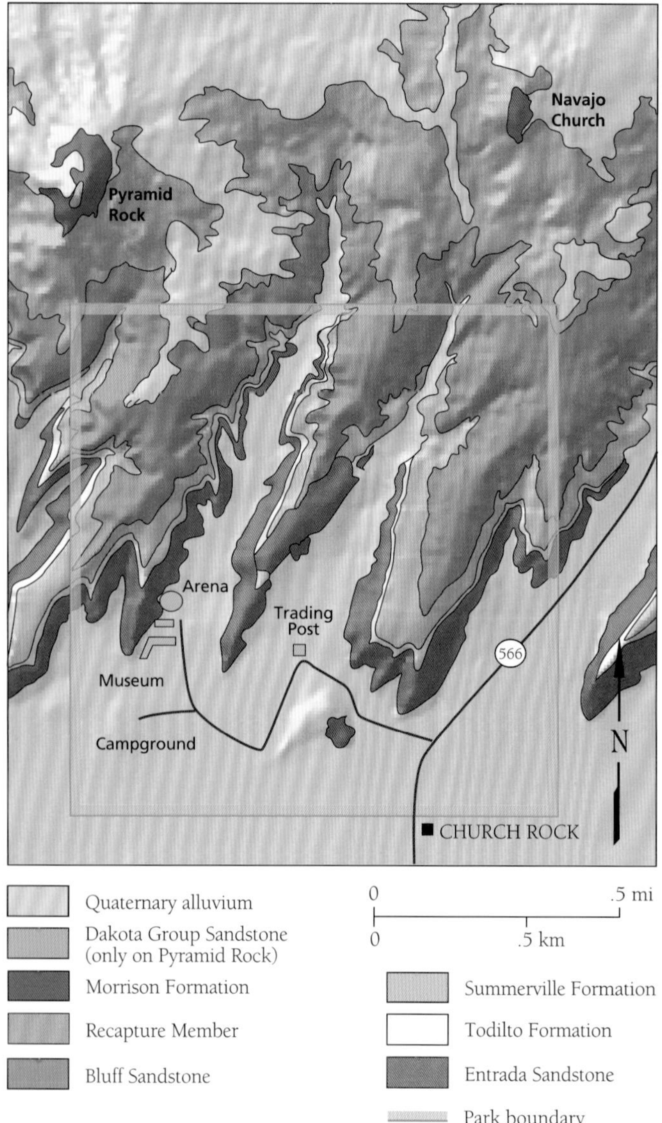

Generalized geologic map of Red Rock State Park and vicinity. Navajo Church and Pyramid Rock are the two most prominent topographic features visible from the park.

The San Juan Basin is an important oil and gas province in New Mexico. It is also noted for its deposits of coal and uranium.

The Rock Record

The oldest rocks are poorly exposed brick-red mudstones underlying the plains to the south of the park. These mudstones form the upper part of the Triassic river deposits of the Chinle Group. The impressive cliffs that provide a background for the public facilities in the park belong mostly to the Jurassic Entrada Sandstone, which lies unconformably on the Chinle Group mudstone. The Entrada Sandstone includes a basal silty unit overlain by massive sandstone with high-angle crossbeds and well-rounded sand grains. The upper part of the Entrada Sandstone was deposited in an eolian dune field. The Jurassic Todilto Formation forms the thin, gray, resistant limestone cap on top of the Entrada Sandstone. The laminated limestone of the Todilto Formation was deposited in a saline body of water. Interbedded white, pink, and reddish-brown sandstone, siltstone, and shale belonging to the Summerville Formation form the slopes above the Entrada and Todilto cliffs. The Summerville Formation was deposited in a shallow-water coastal plain.

The Jurassic Bluff Sandstone overlies the Summerville Formation. The Bluff Sandstone is a greenish-gray-to-reddish brown sandstone with rounded sand grains that was deposited in damp, eolian dunes. The Recapture Member above it consists of reddish-brown to brick-red siltstone interbedded with white-to-green-to-yellow sandstone. Some workers place the Recapture Member in the Bluff Sandstone, while others include it in the Morrison Formation. The Recapture Member is well exposed at the base of Navajo Church, as seen from the Outlaw Trading Post. The Recapture Member was deposited in both fluvial and eolian environments and includes the prominent eolian sandstone with east-dipping crossbeds that forms the shoulders of Church Rock.

The spire on top of Navajo Church and atop Pyramid Rock to the west is red-to-orange sandstone with thin lenses of siltstone and shale belonging to the Morrison Formation. This unit was deposited in a fluvial environment and is host to most of the uranium resources in the Gallup-Grants area.

The Upper Cretaceous Dakota Sandstone on White Rock Mesa and on Pyramid Rock can been seen in the distance to the north and west of Navajo Church. The Dakota Group consists of sandstone and interbedded shales and coal, deposited in swamps and rivers adjacent to the Western Interior Seaway.

Geologic History

The mudstones of the Triassic Chinle Group were deposited along the banks of large Mississippi River-scale fluvial systems flowing from central Texas toward the northwest to Nevada between 228 and 205 million years ago, when the Red Rock area was located about 10° north of the equator. A significant gap in the rock record (unconformity) spanning tens of millions of years occurs between the late Triassic rocks and the middle Jurassic rocks at Red Rock. The oldest of the middle Jurassic rocks, the Entrada Sandstone, was deposited in a vast sand dune field that covered much of Four Corners region from 161 to 165 million years ago.

The contact between the Entrada Sandstone and limestone of the Todilto Formation gently undulates and is gradational, which has led some scientists to speculate that the Entrada dune field was flooded catastrophically by sea water, with very little reworking of the sand dunes. The Todilto Formation was most likely deposited in a *salina*, which is a moderately deep, oxygen-poor body of saline water. A subtle barrier separated the salina from the Jurassic ocean (the Sundance Sea), which was located to the northwest in east-central Utah. The Todilto Formation, based on fossil evidence, is 159–160 million years old. The Todilto Formation grades up into the Summerville Formation. Alternating alluvial flat deposition and eolian deposition is recorded in the Summerville Formation (alluvial flat), Bluff Sandstone (eolian), Recapture Member (alluvial flat and eolian).

The contact between the Recapture Member and the overlying Morrison Formation marks a shift from an arid to a more humid environment in this region. The Morrison Formation was deposited by

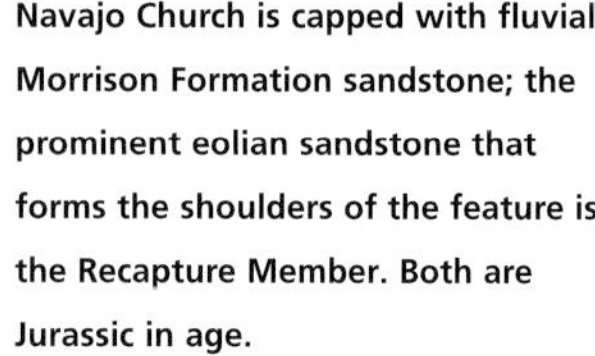

Navajo Church is capped with fluvial Morrison Formation sandstone; the prominent eolian sandstone that forms the shoulders of the feature is the Recapture Member. Both are Jurassic in age.

rivers flowing northeast across a broad, fairly low-gradient muddy floodplain that dipped toward the north-to-northeast away from the developing Mogollon highlands in southwestern New Mexico and southeastern Arizona.

The unconformity between the Morrison Formation and the Dakota Group on White Rock Mesa north of the park represents a 50-million-year gap in the sediment record. The Dakota Sandstone records the alternating rise (shale) and fall (sandstones) of sea level as the shoreline moved back and forth across the area 98 to 100 million years ago.

Geologic Features

NAVAJO CHURCH is the official name of the most prominent feature visible from the park (though it is outside the park). It is also known as Church Rock. The uppermost unit is fluvial sandstone of the Morrison Formation. Below that unit are the eolian (windblown) sands of the Recapture Member, easily identified by the east-dipping crossbeds.

THE ENTRADA SANDSTONE forms the spectacular massive red cliffs that provide the background for the public facilities in the park, specifically the upper sandstone member of the Entrada. High-angle crossbeds are visible in the sandstone. Close examination with a hand lens reveals that the sandstone consists predominantly of well-rounded quartz grains of uniform size. These characteristics lead geologists to believe the sandstones were once large sand dunes, which have since been cemented by silica and calcite from ground water and compacted to form the strata we see today.

THE GRANTS AND SHIPROCK URANIUM DISTRICTS in the San Juan Basin are well known for large resources of sandstone-hosted uranium deposits in the Morrison Formation. More than 340 million pounds of uranium oxide were produced from these uranium deposits from 1948 through 2002, accounting for 97 percent of the total uranium production in New Mexico to date. New Mexico ranks second in uranium resources in the U.S. Most of New Mexico's uranium resources are currently in the Morrison Formation in the San Juan Basin. Uranium ore bodies are found mostly in the West Water Canyon, Brushy Basin, and Jackpile Sandstone Members of the Morrison Formation. Typically, the ore bodies are lenticular, tabular masses of complex uranium and organic compounds that form roughly parallel trends; beds of fine-to-medium-grained barren sandstone lie between the ore bodies.

—Virginia T. McLemore and Shari A. Kelley

If You Plan to Visit

Red Rock State Park is located 10 miles east of Gallup, north of I–40. It is accessible via NM–566. There's a wide variety of day-use facilities in the park, including a rodeo arena, museum, and convention center. There is also a campground. For more information, contact:

Red Rock State Park
P.O. Box 10
Churchrock, NM 87311
(505) 722-3839
www.ci.gallup.nm.us/rrp/00182_redrock.html

Mount Taylor

CIBOLA NATIONAL FOREST

If you compare the sizes all of the young volcanoes in New Mexico, Mount Taylor volcano is second in size after the Valles Caldera. Because of its size and elevation, Mount Taylor and its surrounding concentration of smaller volcanoes and lava flows, known as the Mount Taylor volcanic field, are prominent parts of the landscape in western New Mexico. And together with Mesa Chivato, the plateau of smaller volcanoes extending northward, they dominate Albuquerque's sunset views to the west.

Mount Taylor has the classic low, upward-sweeping profile of a composite volcano. This view from the south is from the Sandstone Bluffs Overlook at El Malpais National Monument. From this angle and in the winter sunset lighting deep canyons are visible on the upper slopes. The top of the volcano appears to be missing, probably because of erosion in the 2 million years since it last erupted.

There are several young volcanic fields similar to the Mount Taylor volcanic field distributed around the margins of the Colorado Plateau where it adjoins the lower elevations of the Basin and Range province on the south and west and the Rio Grande rift on the east. In addition to the main cone, the Mount Taylor volcanic field includes Mesa Chivato, a broad plateau of volcanic cones, craters, and lava flows that lies at an elevation over 8,000 feet above sea level and extends for 37 miles north and east of Mount Taylor. Surrounded by high desert, the Mount Taylor volcanic field is an isolated plateau that hosts pines, junipers, grasses, and a variety of wild life, including mountain lions,

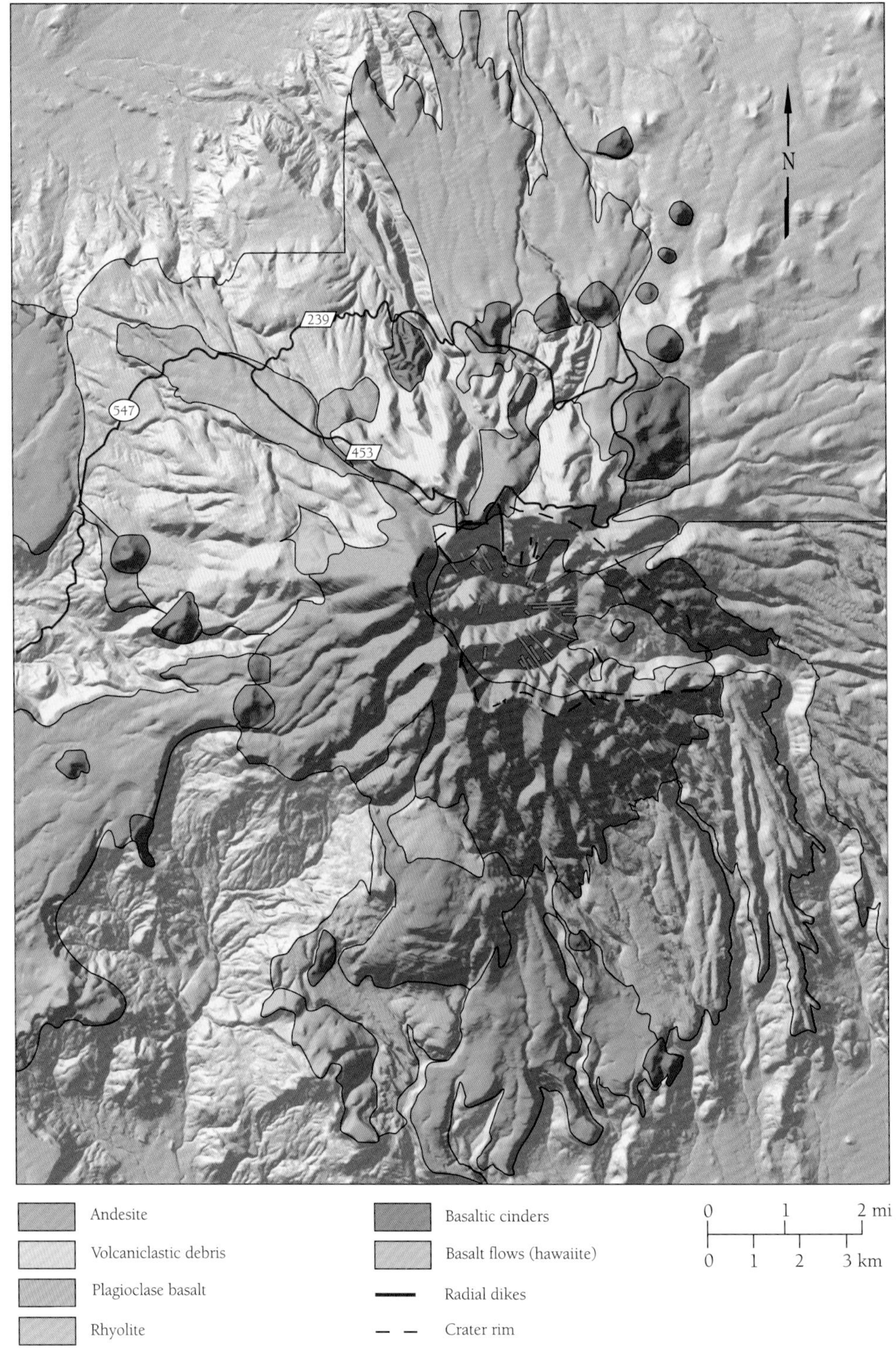
N
239
547
453
Andesite
Volcaniclastic debris
Plagioclase basalt
Rhyolite
Basaltic cinders
Basalt flows (hawaiite)
Radial dikes
Crater rim
0 1 2 mi
0 1 2 3 km

bears, deer, and elk. The plateau is the remnant of a Pleistocene volcanic landscape that developed by erosion of the surrounding landscape since the last eruptions 1.5 million years ago. The erosion that has isolated the plateau has exposed numerous dissected cones and volcanic necks, including the Rio Puerco volcanic necks, the best known of which is Cabezon Peak, a large dark plug-like mass of rock that is visible for miles throughout the region.

OPPOSITE: Generalized geologic map of Mount Taylor volcano. Most of the upper part of the volcano consists of thick lava flows with so many large crystals that the rocks resemble granite. The lower slopes consist of ash from eruptions and debris shed from flows on the steep upper slopes, now mostly eroded away. Among these deposits are smaller cinder cones and dark basaltic lava flows.

The Rock Record

The earliest rocks of the Mount Taylor volcanic field erupted onto an eroded surface of mostly Cretaceous sedimentary rocks of the Mesaverde Group. During the events that formed the Rocky Mountains, these sediments were warped slightly in a broad down sag that exists today beneath the Mount Taylor field. The surface onto which the lavas and cones erupted appears to have been graded toward the east, as there were many streams flowing in that direction before the development of the modern drainages of the Rio Puerco and the Rio San Jose that today wrap around the north and south margins of the field.

Geologic History

Mount Taylor volcano is a composite volcano. Such volcanoes consist of alternating layers of lava and ash and are frequently composed of an aggregation of many volcanic centers around a small area, with many different magma compositions and eruption styles. The earliest eruptions of Mount Taylor were overlapping domes of viscous thick rhyolitic lavas that were subsequently draped with later pyroclastic ash sheets (tuff) and lavas of more intermediate compositions. These later eruptions were entirely different from the initial ones. In fact, the large-scale symmetry of the final volcano is largely a result of these later eruptions. Mount Taylor volcano and the surrounding volcanic vents were active from approximately 4 million years ago to 1.5 million years ago—a relatively long-lived volcano compared with many composite cones such as those in the Pacific Northwest, where entire volcanoes have been built and have gone dormant within the space of several hundred thousand years.

East Grants Ridge rhyolite domes. The earliest eruption from Mount Taylor consisted of rhyolite somewhat like that which now forms East Grants Ridge. The part exposed is partly a result of extrusions that filled the shallow, near-surface vents areas. The thick, viscous lavas flowed onto the surface to form much of East Grants Ridge. Intermixed with these are ignimbrite deposits, which formed as parts of the dome and the steep margins of flows collapsed and cascaded as hot debris onto the surrounding landscape.

The earliest eruptions elsewhere within the volcanic field, especially Mesa Chivato to the north, consisted of white to light gray viscous rhyolite (East Grants Ridge), trachyte lava domes and ash (Mesa Chivato), and dark, very *mafic* lava flows of a type known as basanite.

Even as far north as the very northern tip of Mesa Chivato, rhyolite ash layers may be seen at the base of the overlying lava flows, demonstrating that the rhyolite eruptions of the Mount Taylor field were among the earliest eruptions. White pumice layers and ash are exposed in many roadcuts along the southern part of the volcanic field and in canyons around the base of Mount Taylor. In some outcrops, large chunks of pumice contain fragments of the granitic deep crust, suggesting that the rhyolite is the result of melting of rocks from the lower crust. These granitic *xenoliths* also provide geologists with an opportunity to examine rocks from the lower crust.

Aerial view of Mount Taylor and the summit crater, also known as Water Canyon. The bald upper slopes are areas where the massive lava flows of the upper volcano and intermixed ash deposits have been eroded to crumbly, porous outcrops of dense but broken rock that support little in the way of soils and vegetation. Below the tree line, the surface consists mostly of lavas and debris flows.

Mount Taylor is truly a composite of many eruptions and types of volcanic rocks. Basaltic lava flows, thick and viscous crystal-rich andesitic lavas, ash falls, and mudflows all contribute to various layers that make up the volcano. These eruptions occurred in an intermingled fashion, so that one may see darker basalts here and there on the sides of the volcano that erupted from cinder cones now buried by later thick andesitic lavas farther up the flanks of the volcano. At the top of the volcano there is a broad, crater-like valley that opens toward the east in the shape of a giant amphitheater. This may have formed by erosion alone acting on the weaker ash and debris layers of the inner parts of the cones, or it may have developed from erosional widening of an original Mount St. Helens-like lateral blast crater.

Much of the latest volcanic history of Mount Taylor involved emplacement of these thick, viscous lava flows and associated debris flows that formed from collapsing domes of the viscous lavas near the summit. These debris flows moved down valleys towards the lower flanks. The flows and domes are composed of brownish-to-dark gray lava, containing big crystals of white plagioclase and assorted darker minerals. It looks like granite to the untrained eye, but it is really just a crystal-rich type of lava flow. Most of these viscous late flows were truncated by erosion on the upper slopes above approximately 9,500 feet, so in many cases thick sections of the crystal-rich lavas appear on the lower slopes with no apparent source. In these cases the upper portions of the flows have been removed by erosion. The extent to which a summit pyroclastic cone occupied the center of the volcano is not known, but outcrops of intermediate-composition ash and scoria in the amphitheater walls suggest that at various stages in the volcano's

growth, such a cone existed. Late explosive modification followed by more extensive erosion may have played a role in reducing the cone to its current lower profile.

The more viscous trachydacitic domes tended to be extruded high up on the accumulated volcanic mass. Their precarious perch on the higher elevations, together with the abundance of snow or water in the upper volcano, resulted in frequent collapse and avalanching of the hot and/or muddy debris down the flanks of the growing volcano, and the accumulation of a considerable volume of what to the casual visitor appears to be boulder conglomerate around the base of Mount Taylor. This debris has the appearance of loose cobbles and soils along the road on top of the mesa north of where the pavement ends at the head of Lobo Canyon. While much of the avalanched material formed blocky debris aprons around the volcano, avalanches from growing domes, thick viscous lavas high on the volcano, and collapsing lava domes yielded masses of highly comminuted and low density material that partially welded into solid masses when it stopped moving. Today these remain as buff-colored cliff-forming rock that is exposed particularly well on the north side of the volcano in an area known as "Spud Patch." A summit cinder, ash, and lava cone may have existed near the center of this extrusive activity and would have contributed fine light-colored ash and large house-size blocks of trachydacite to the abundant loose,

The "Spud Patch" on the north side of Mount Taylor is an area where erosion has incised the irregularities in welded debris flows that originally filled valleys. The debris flows formed when steep crumbly hot masses of viscous lavas and domes on the upper flanks of the volcano collapsed. The hot debris raced down the valleys on the lower slopes, sometimes burying the tops of the lava flows that erupted from the same vent, sometimes flowing in the lows on either side of the lava flows.

muddy materials that now litter the lower flanks of the volcano. Radial dikes of trachydacite, some of which may be seen in the summit amphitheater, were probably feeder dikes for many of the viscous extrusions that populated the summit in between more explosive eruptions. Extrusion and collapse of viscous flows along with occasional basaltic lava flows contributed to the final growth of the volcano.

Mount Taylor is characterized by the classic low, upward-sweeping profile of a composite volcano. This view from the south is from the Sandstone Bluffs Overlook at El Malpais National Monument.

Geologic Features

MOUNT TAYLOR—The current morphology of Mount Taylor is that of a truncated cone, centered on a point located at the western end and head of Water Canyon. The outlines of lava flows and debris flows that make up much of the volcano are still preserved at elevations below approximately 9,500 feet as sinuous ridges and valleys. Above this elevation, few lava flow-like shapes or outlines are apparent, the lava flows coating the volcano appear more eroded, and the dominant volcanic rock type is brown and very granular, with large white crystals of feldspar (plagioclase).

This sequence of volcanic rocks and their arrangement around the volcano give rise to a systematic geology that is notable as one ascends from the lower flanks of Mount Taylor to the upper elevations. Near the base of the volcanic pile one encounters abundant loose debris consisting of boulders and fine silt and sand-sized material. The boulders are generally well rounded and consist of dark brown granular-appearing trachydacitic lavas. Ascending, one moves into a zone on the mid flanks of the volcano consisting of various lava flows that are largely in place. These include thick viscous lavas and some distinct basaltic lava flows and scoria cones. It is in this zone that one may see vesicular (gas bubble-rich) lava, scoria, and similar materials that are representative of the surface or near surface of volcanoes and lava flows. At about 9,500 feet one crosses a bench that appears to be the up-flank termination of these lavas and then ascends into the upper flanks, where outcrops are largely massive occurrences of dark brown, granular and crystal-rich lavas, with some dikes radial to the main cone. This pattern varies in elevation from place to place, but it characterizes most of the general ascent routes along trails and roads. This is particularly evident on the drive up FR 239 and FR 453 to La Mosca Peak.

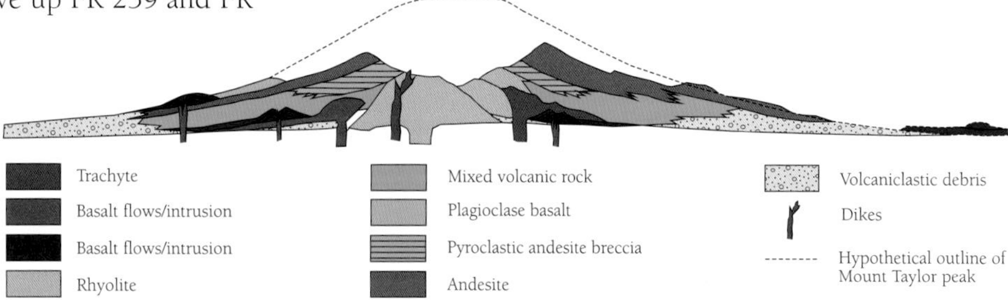

Generalized cross-section of Mount Taylor showing the major volcanic units and the hypothetical outline of Mount Taylor peak prior to erosion of the upper slopes. Areas above 9,500 feet elevation tend to be deeply eroded. Below that, the surface of lava flows and debris flows are only slightly dissected. Like all composite volcanoes, Mount Taylor is really just a collection of many types of lavas and ash, especially the viscous and explosive types, all surrounded by collapse and outwashed debris.

The transition from lava shapes at lower elevations to the more massive morphology in the upper part of the volcano begs the question of how much of the top of the volcano has been eroded and what the original height of the volcano may have been. Estimates of the original height are, at best, just that. The uncertainty results largely from the extreme individuality of most volcanoes. Based on what we know about long-lived volcanoes similar to Mount Taylor, erosion continually worries away the steep and loosely consolidated summits, even while the volcano is active. As a result, not all the material erupted by a large, long-lived volcano remains on the summit; limited erosion removes it before the next eruption. If the summit pyroclastic cone was well developed, an estimate of 13,000–14,000 feet in height for the original cone is within reason. Many cones evolve through several stages of growth and collapse, as well as multiple summits, rather than a single conical mass, resulting in a more rounded and "lumpy" summit. If the near-terminal morphology attained this form, then 12,000–13,000 feet may be a better estimate of the original height. San Francisco Mountain, in the San Francisco Peaks near Flagstaff, Arizona, probably gives us a good idea of what Mount Taylor looked like 500,000–1,000,000 years ago. There is good evidence that collapse of the east flank occurred late at San Francisco Mountain. A similar event could well have occurred at Mount Taylor volcano during the late stages of its development.

MESA CHIVATO—North-northeast of Mount Taylor, is a remote plateau in the northern Mount Taylor volcanic field. As one drives across Mesa Chivato on one of the many maintained forest service roads, one is

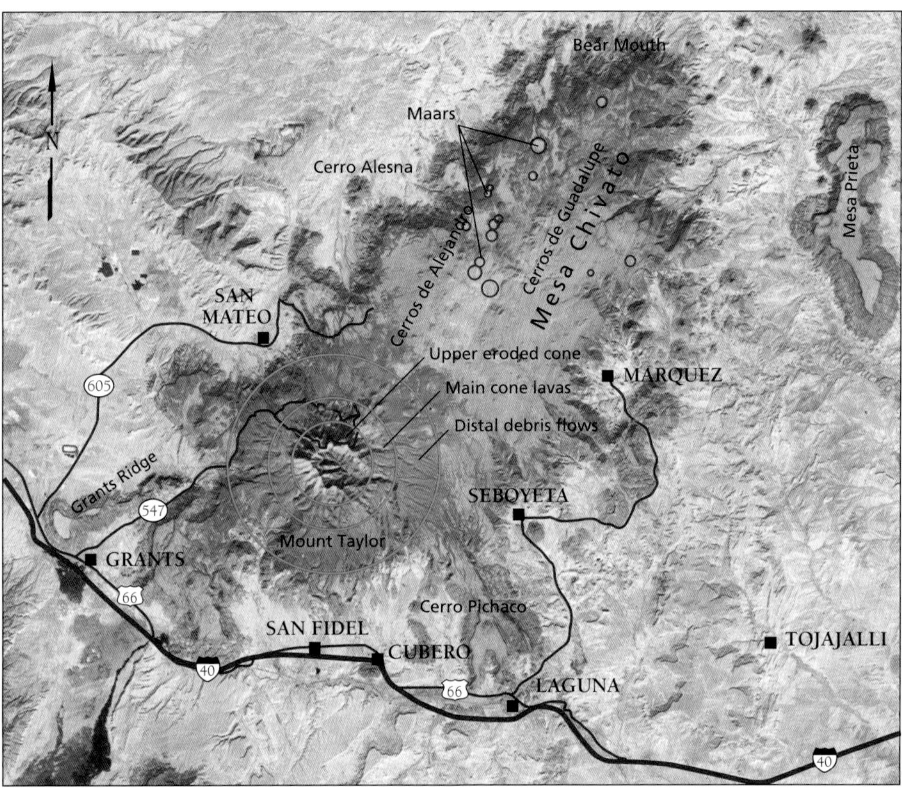

Mount Taylor, the mesa to its northeast (Mesa Chivato), and Mesa Prieta, now on the east side of the Rio Puerco, were at one time all part of one surface before erosion dissected the surrounding landscape. Exposure of some of the small volcanoes in the landscape where the Rio Puerco valley lies now, and corresponding back wasting around the margins of Mount Taylor and Mesa Chivato, have exposed the interiors of many small volcanoes. Today these make up the Rio Puerco volcanic necks and deeply exposed small volcanoes like the East Grants Ridge plug and Cubero volcano.

surrounded by a landscape of old pine-covered volcanic landforms that are relatively well preserved, given the general age of most of the volcanic eruptions (over 3.5 million years old and 2.5 million years old). It is a classic volcanic field composed mostly of individual scoria cones, numerous hydromagmatic explosion craters (see the discussion of *maars* elsewhere in this volume), basalt flows, and viscous lava flows of unusual composition. The volcanic rocks of the Mount Taylor region include some types of volcanic rocks that are uncommon on the North American continent (with names such as hawaiite, mugearite, benmoreite, and trachyte). Rocks with these compositions are typically seen in oceanic islands and in the major rifts and hot spots on our planet. Most unusual perhaps are lava flows of mugearite and benmorite and the domes of silvery white trachyte that constitute the central range of hills, the Cerros de Guadalupe, within the interior of Mesa Chivato. These unusual rocks were erupted early in the history of the field and were followed by more basaltic lava flows that developed some of the larger scoria cones that dominant the landscape of the plateau.

In contrast to the older lavas from the early eruptions, which are fine grained in texture, many of the more basaltic lava flows that erupted after the trachytes contain abundant crystals of olivine, pyroxene (mostly augite) and white-to-translucent plagioclase. One cone on the east flank of the Cerros de Guadalupe has an abundance of large, centimeter-size augite crystals littering its slopes, many of which are so large that they may be mistaken on first glance as small lumps of obsidian. Elsewhere distinct nodules of material from the mantle may be found, with mineralogy similar to the large crystals in the flows on Mesa Chivato, suggesting that the large crystals in many flows may in fact be fragmented mantle materials caught up in the erupted lavas.

Scarps and swells, many of which are the margins of various lava flows that can be traced back to their source cones, are a characteristic of the landscape. Many of the hills and peaks that dot the landscape are more familiar scoria cones. Many of these cones are frequently arranged in long rows oriented north-northeast and south-southwest. This is typical of fissure-fed eruptions, where an initial linear fissure eruption develops into a series of vents that ultimately build individual cones. Fissure eruptions are better developed in the northern Mount Taylor volcanic field than in many other fields in the Southwest, perhaps because of the active extension that was occurring along the Rio Grande rift just to the east at the time of eruption.

Two of the many maars or steam explosion craters on Mesa Chivato. Maars are evidence of a very wet environment at the time that much of the Mount Taylor volcanic field was erupting. In this oblique air photo of Laguna de Alejandro, two maars overlap and are aligned along one of the many northeast/southwest-trending fissures that characterize the smaller vents of the field north of Mount Taylor.

Throughout the northern field there are also long nearly linear scarps that cut across both lava flows and cones, generally in northeast-southwest directions. These are fault scarps, and they illustrate how the forces that stretched this landscape, causing faulting and earthquakes, were intimately allied with the development of fissure vents and volcanic eruptions. Faulting was concurrent with much of the volcanism, and several long fault scarps are parallel to fissures and cut across individual cones. Several cones are distinctly elongated along the general northeast-southwest trend of faulting and fissures. Maar craters and collapse craters are also common along this same trend. Also unusual is the abundance of almond- or spindle-shaped volcanic bombs.

Large circular craters, or maars, geologically similar to the much younger Zuni Salt Lake crater located near Quemado, were formed by steam-blast eruptions and are numerous. These have the appearance of meteor impact craters, with raised rims of debris consisting in part of large blocks of older country rock and earlier lava flows.

Most of the cones are at a stage of erosion typical of cones older than a few hundred thousand years: Erosion has removed the loose cinders and ash on the outer flanks, exposing the near-surface structure of the cone interiors. In addition, many cones are naturally half-sectioned along the margins of Mesa Chivato. These exposures provide a wealth of information about scoria cone interiors and are among the best examples in the world.

–Larry S. Crumpler

Additional Reading

Volcanoes of North America, Charles Arthur Wood and Jürgen Kienle, editors. Cambridge University Press, 1990.

Volcanoes of Northern Arizona by Wendell A. Duffield. Grand Canyon Association, 1997.

Also see *Volcanoes of New Mexico* on the New Mexico Museum of Natural History and Science Web site at:
www.nmnaturalhistory.org/sci_volcanoes.html

If You Plan to Visit

Mount Taylor is in the Cibola National Forest. Access to trailheads and U.S. Forest Service lands is primarily along unpaved Forest Service roads. Roads may be closed from time to time due to fire or other restrictions. Always inquire in advance of your visit, and go armed with a map of the Cibola National Forest, Mount Taylor Ranger District. For more information, contact the district office at the address below. Information is also available at the Interagency Visitor Center on I–40 at Grants (Exit 85).

U.S. Forest Service
Mount Taylor Ranger District
1800 Lobo Canyon Road
Grants, NM 87020
(505) 287-8833
(505) 287-4924 (Fax)
www.fs.fed.us/r3/cibola/districts/mttaylor.shtml

Cabezon Peak and the Rio Puerco Volcanic Necks

BUREAU OF LAND MANAGEMENT

Cabezon Peak, viewed from the north. In the background is Cerro Guadalupe. Farther in the distance is Mesa Chivato, the northern part of the Mt. Taylor volcanic field. The field extended as far east as Cabezon, and a little beyond, but erosion by the ancestral Rio Puerco has back-wasted the edges of Mesa Chivato and exposed the insides of former volcanoes like Cabezon Peak and Cerro Guadalupe.

Cabezon Peak is one of many massive, dark peaks known as volcanic necks that are scattered throughout the Rio Puerco valley between Mesa Chivato to the west and Mesa Prieta to the south. These are among the best examples of volcanic necks in the world. The Rio Puerco necks are one of New Mexico's greatest volcanological treasures and would deserve attention in their own right even if they were not also set in a natural landscape of buttes and mesas that makes the Rio Puerco Valley so appealing to the visitor. Although another volcanic neck, Ship Rock, is more widely known, the Rio Puerco volcanic necks, including Cabezon, are in many ways more interesting geologically. They are of particular interest because they represent one of the best places to see the interior structure of one of the most common types of volcano on Earth, the cinder (or scoria) cone.

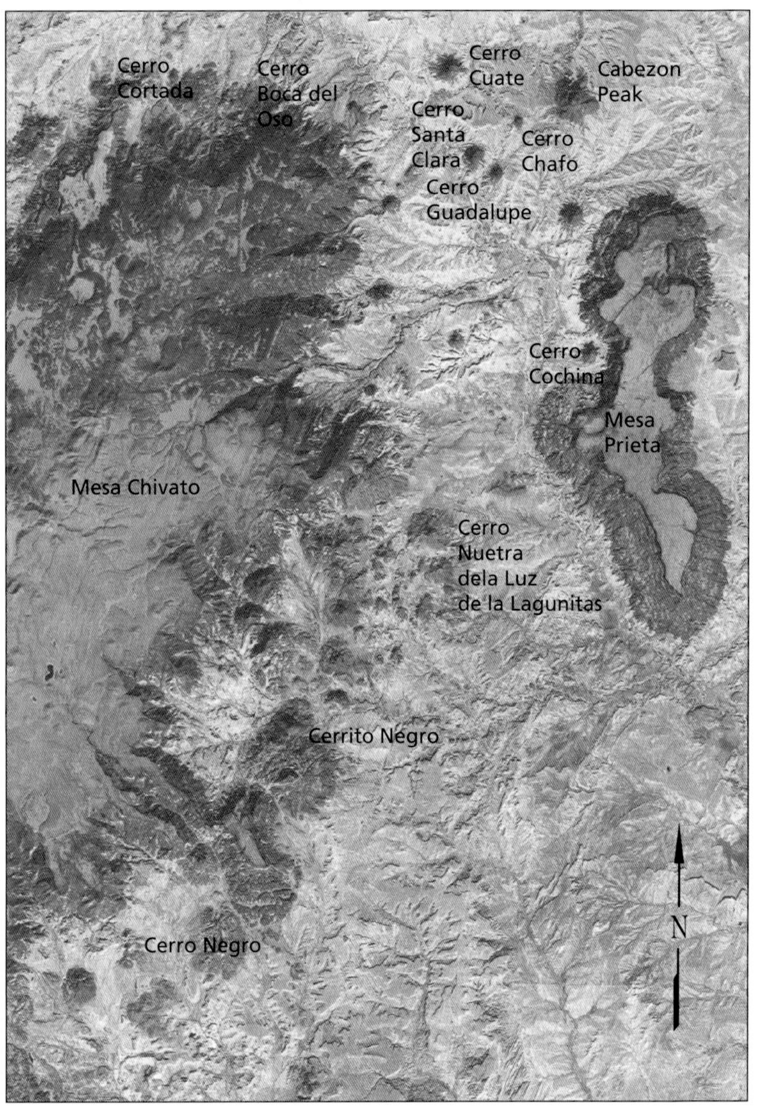

Many of the Rio Puerco volcanic necks lie between Mesa Chivato and Mesa Prieta. On this satellite image the volcanic features (dark) stand out strikingly in contrast to the sedimentary rocks (pink) that surround them. Note the crater shapes on Mesa Chivato. Many of the Rio Puerco necks are probably the eroded interiors of craters and small cinder cones like those on Mesa Chivato.

Regional Setting

Together with Mesa Chivato and Mesa Prieta the volcanic necks of the Rio Puerco Valley are part of the Mount Taylor volcanic field, a cluster of several hundred small volcanoes associated with the broad area of volcanism around the Mount Taylor composite volcano. A few volcanic necks, including Cerro Alesna, are found on the west side of Mesa Chivato. Other examples may be found around the south margin of the Mount Taylor field and include half-sectioned volcanoes (such as the one exposed on the flanks of East Grants Ridge) and deeply dissected volcanoes (such as Cubero volcano).

The volcanic necks of the Rio Puerco and Mount Taylor fields are all the eroded near-surface interiors of small volcanoes and are geologically young. They were deeply dissected when the Rio Puerco and other drainages surrounding the Mount Taylor field incised the softer Mesozoic sediments surrounding the field. Similar back wasting around the margins of Mesa Chivato has exposed the complex interiors of many of the small volcanoes in the Mount Taylor field in general, but the most significant concentration occurs in the Rio Puerco Valley.

Unlike simple sandstone buttes and mesas, volcanic necks are intriguing because one is actually seeing inside a volcano where the violent events associated with the eruption process are recorded in their complex structure. The eruptions were similar to those that form small cinder cones, such as Capulin or Bandera volcanoes, and in some cases are similar to the steam blast (hydromagmatic) eruptions that formed Zuni

Salt Lake or Kilbourne Hole. More importantly, volcanoes of the same general age and type are preserved in the interior of the Mount Taylor field in a way that offers an opportunity to see what the original volcanoes were like before erosion. Both cinder cones and hydromagmatic craters are preserved on the surface of Mesa Chivato and are probably good analogs for the original morphologies of the volcanoes that produced the volcanic necks.

Although most of the necks occurring within the Rio Puerco Valley are at a similar stage in erosion, others scattered around the margins capture the process of erosion and evolution of the landforms from original cones to the deeply exposed cores typical of the Rio Puerco Valley. Some, like Cabezon and those throughout the Rio Puerco Valley, are isolated and completely denuded of the overlying former volcanoes. Others, like the half-section cone in Lobo Canyon north of Grants, are "caught in the act" as the cones are being sliced in half by erosion around the margin of the plateau-like Mount Taylor volcanic field. Others, like Cubero volcano south of I–40 between Exits 102 and 104, are denuded in place so that the interiors of the craters are being exposed.

Cubero volcano, visible south of I–40 between Exits 102 and 104. The east side is nearly denuded to the point at which the interior crater fill is exposed along the valley on its east side.

Cabezon Peak is the largest of the Rio Puerco volcanic necks. The main mass of the volcanic neck is nearly 1,000 feet in diameter and close to 600 feet from the base of the cliffs to the top of the peak. The cliffs along its sides consist of striking columnar basalts that grade upward into more scoriaceous materials that are probably residual fragments of the original volcanic cone that once surrounded the basalt.

The large diameter and vertical height of volcanic necks throughout the valley give the impression that they are the exposed tips of masses that plunge straight down as massive cylinders of basalt. In reality, there are many lines of evidence that most of the necks are simply large masses of basalt that rapidly narrow downward to feeder dikes measuring less than a few feet wide. One drilling experiment bored almost horizontally beneath Cerro Negro, a small double-topped neck near the village of Seboyeta on the east side of Mesa Chivato. The results showed that the massive structure of the neck is in fact a simple dike a few yards wide immediately below. Likewise, one can walk along the base of the massive plug of basalt in the interior of the half-sectioned volcano visible in Lobo Canyon north of Grants and actually see that the

Half-sectioned volcano exposed on East Grants Ridge in Lobo Canyon, north of Grants. On the left is a reconstruction of the cone that resulted in the plug we see today.

massive plug rests on underlying sediments and volcanic debris. It too narrows down to less than 6 feet wide before disappearing into the loose scree at its base.

All of these observations imply that if one were to remove the upper 300 to 600 feet of most of the necks all that would remain would be a narrow little feeder dike. So most of the necks are really just large ponds of deep lava and scoria that have filled in former craters in the original cones into which they originally erupted. Their mass and greater hardness compared to the softer enclosing scoria and sandstone have made them resistant to erosion, resulting in their preservation; erosion of the surrounding rocks has isolated these more resistant features.

Not all of the Rio Puerco necks are masses of basalt. Some are clearly layered masses of scoria and blocks of surrounding country rock, apparently the debris of many explosions that fell back into the vents and accumulated along with later injections of magmas that in turn fed further eruptions. As a result some necks, like Cerrito Negro south of the village of Marquez, are complex structures from which we can infer how the eruptions actually occurred.

Cerrito Negro, a small volcanic neck south of Marquez. The margins are complexly layered with volcanic blocks, scoria, ash, and sandstone blocks that were deposited in the original vents during violent explosions.

Geologic History

Most scoria cones start out as eruptions from short fissures, where magma rising along a crack breaks through to the surface. Initial eruptions of pyroclastic materials accumulate first as low, circular mounds of layered ash, scoria, and spatter. As the cone continues to build, the accumulation of scoria on the slopes eventually exceeds the angle of repose of loose material (usually about 33 degrees for scoria cones), and subsequent layers are deposited as long straight slopes that cover the earlier more gently sloping cone flanks. The vent area is a funnel of pyroclastic material that is either deposited on the crater walls or collapses from the loose material of walls. These in turn re-enter the vent and are often reworked by subsuquent explosions. During the eruptions, the walls of the crater may become very steep because the materials deposited near the vent may be welded together more firmly than materials farther out on the flanks of the cone. As the explosions become less violent, often as a result of decreasing gas content of the ascending magma, the crater may be filled with lava or loose pyroclastic material. Because the final eruptions can be relatively free of the gases that are responsible for explosions earlier in the eruption of the cone, the final event can sometimes be a filling of the crater with lava forming a deep lava pool covered with loose pyroclastic material cascading off the steep crater walls or local pyroclastic bursts. Or the lava can break through the wall and flow out through a gap in the crater, leaving behind a lava pool connected to a flow that expands outward onto the surrounding

Reconstruction of the original cone that ultimately resulted in the Cabezon volcanic neck. The dashed white line represents the original ground surface. Dark lines show the possible layers deposited ballistically during initial eruptions (ballistic cone); straight dark lines show the probable slope and dimensions of the mature cone when the accumulations exceeded the angle of repose, and a deep crater formed through explosive excavation and collapse of the vent walls.

countryside. Ultimately the eruption ceases, the interior lava ponds and feeder dikes congeal as hard basalt, and the cone begins to erode with time. Erosion occurs relatively quickly due to the loose nature of scoria cones in general. Eventually the crater is filled with loose rubble eroded from the crater walls, and the flanks are worn down. By the time a cone is 2 million years old, like the ones on the surface of Mesa Chivato, as much as half of the cone height may have been lost. In the case of Cabezon the erosion occurred as the Rio Puerco etched out the surrounding valley. In the case of the half-sectioned volcano in Lobo Canyon, the plug was exposed as the canyon widened.

The columns that characterize many of the volcanic necks arise because of contraction and cracking of the lava ponds as the basalt solidifies. A peculiar characteristic of basalt is that once cracks form they tend to propagate inward as the interior of the basalt mass cools from the surface downward, or from the walls of the crater inward. Cracks tend to be spaced laterally with remarkable uniformity, resulting in the hexagonal pattern of cracks and forming columns as the cracks propagate inward along the same plane. Another peculiarity is that cracks tend to develop perpendicular to cooling surfaces. As a result, near the surface of the lava ponds cracks tend to be vertical, while inside the lava ponds cracks develop perpendicular to the closest cooling surface, which often is the crater walls. This accounts for the appearance of vertical columns near the tops of many necks when the surrounding volcano is eroded away, while the lower sides of the necks

Cerro Alesna, a large volcanic neck located on the west side of the Mount Taylor volcanic field. It has unusually large and long columnar joints and is somewhat different from most of the volcanic necks on the east side of the volcanic field.

may have columns that are variously oriented, but commonly near horizontal. Later injections of magma during the cooling process can alter the cooling surfaces in complex ways, resulting in all sorts of variations in the most prominent crack orientations. The scoriaceous materials often encountered near the tops of many necks are probably remnants of the crater floor, where loose scoria accumulated either during the last stages of the eruption, burying the lava ponds, or later, as erosion produced the accumulation of loose scoriaceous scree.

—Larry S. Crumpler

If You Plan to Visit

Cabezon Peak is on land managed by the Bureau of Land Management. It is accessible by dirt roads only. The best way is via CR 279, which heads west from US 550 about 20 miles northwest of San Ysidro, then south on BLM Road 1114. A dirt road heads east from BLM 1114 to Cabezon Peak. At the end of the road a trailhead provides access to the summit, but it is a moderate-to-difficult 4–6 hour climb for most and requires some climbing and route-finding skills. These roads may be impassable during wet weather; always check with the BLM office before undertaking a trip to Cabezon Peak. For more information, including more detailed instructions regarding access, contact:

Bureau of Land Management
Rio Puerco Field Office
435 Montano Road NE
Albuquerque, NM 87107-4935
(505) 761-8700
(505) 761-8911 (Fax)
www.nm.blm.gov/aufo/aufo_home.html

Chaco Culture National Historical Park

NATIONAL PARK SERVICE

Visitors to Chaco Canyon, having crossed corrugated expanses of the San Juan Basin to get there, wonder that such a striking canyon exists at all in a landscape otherwise dominated by rolling sand-covered uplands, small mesas, bluffs, and badland-bordered shallow valleys. The canyon's size (500 feet deep, 2,100 feet wide, 15 miles long), elevation (6,100 feet), orientation (northwest), and noticeable differences in layered rock sequences and landforms on either side arouse further curiosity. How could the current tiny ephemeral stream cut such a canyon unless past climate was different from present semiarid conditions? Moreover, how could prehistoric peoples, let alone park visitors and personnel, live in this remote area with few obvious resources?

OPPOSITE: Aerial view of Chaco Canyon, looking west, with Pueblo Bonito prominent in the foreground.

Regional Setting

Chaco Canyon is in the Navajo Section of the southeastern Colorado Plateau physiographic province. It arises 16 miles northwest of the Continental Divide, which crosses the San Juan Basin diagonally northeastward from the Zuni to the Nacimiento Mountains. The Chaco River runs from the divide through the canyon, then west to the Great Bend, then north and northwest to the San Juan River, a distance of more than 125 miles. The northward-dipping erosion-resistant Cretaceous rocks in the canyon are part of a larger stratigraphic succession exposed across the southern structural margin of the San Juan Basin known as the Chaco Slope. Precambrian rocks of the Zuni Mountains form the base of the Chaco Slope, with progressively younger Permian, Triassic, Jurassic, Cretaceous, and lower Cenozoic sedimentary rocks exposed northward toward the center of the asymmetric basin (particularly near Angel Peak). The deepest, doubly plunging axis of the basin lies north

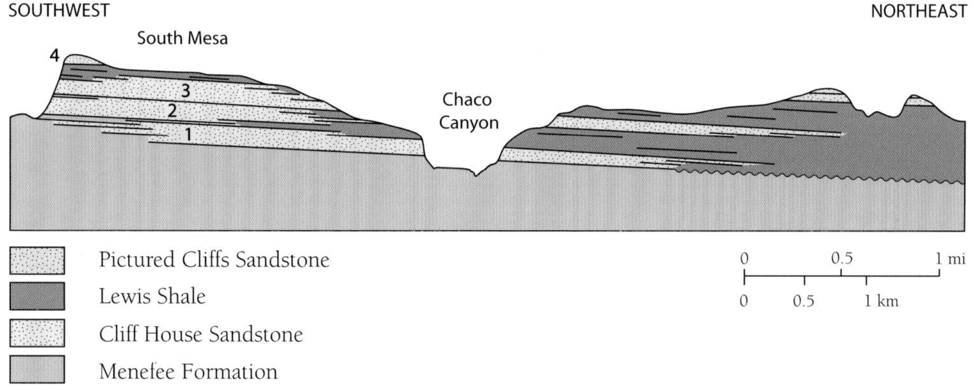

Generalized southwest/northeast cross section showing bedrock geology across Chaco Canyon.

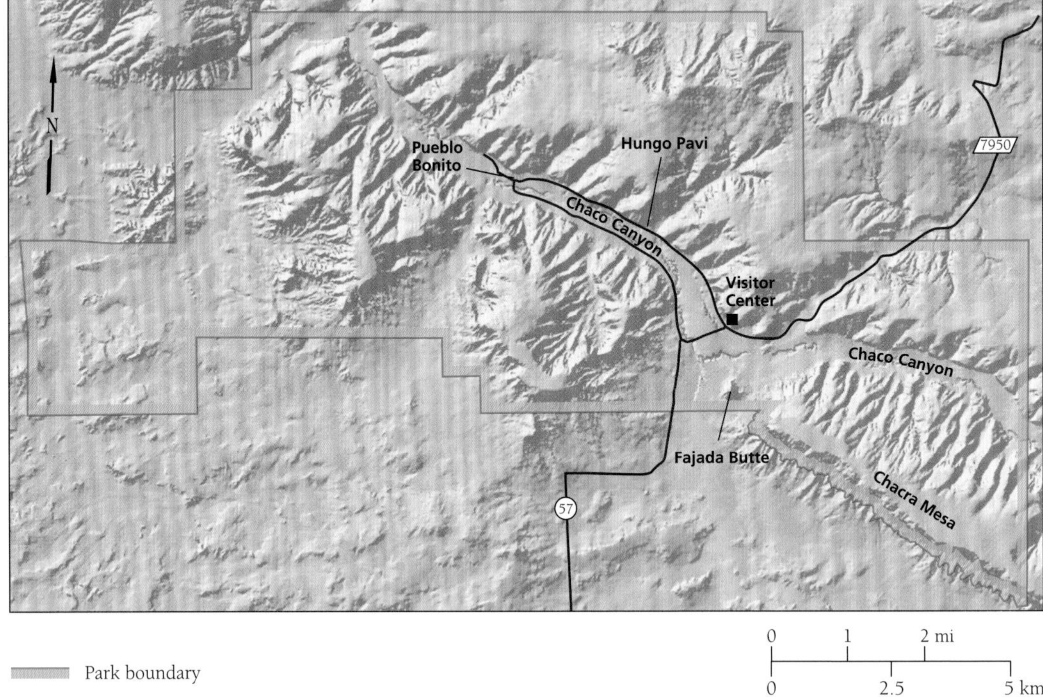

Major topographic features in the vicinity of Chaco Culture National Historical Park.

of Aztec Ruins National Monument, closer to the New Mexico–Colorado state line where Precambrian rocks are more than 3 miles below the surface. Landforms across the San Juan Basin reflect differential erosion of less resistant mudrocks versus more resistant sandstones and igneous intrusions, coupled with geologically temporary storage of eroded sediments in valleys, paleovalleys, and eolian sand sheets.

The Rock Record and Geologic History

Chaco Canyon is cut along a slightly sinuous path nearly parallel to the northwesterly trend of slightly northeastward-tilted alternating sandstones and shales of Cretaceous coastline deposits exposed in this part of the San Juan Basin. Here the preserved coastline recorded minor shifts in the position of the western shoreline of a vast inland sea that stretched from the Arctic to the Gulf of Mexico across the middle of the North American continent. Multiple northeast-southwest shifts in position of the northwest-trending shoreline over several miles were caused by minor changes in sediment transport and deposition, sea-level rise, offshore subsidence, and persistence of depositional features such as barrier islands, lagoons, tidal inlets, stream deltas, estuaries, and swamps.

The lowest exposed bedrock within the canyon and to the south is the Menefee Formation of Late Cretaceous age. It preserves abundant

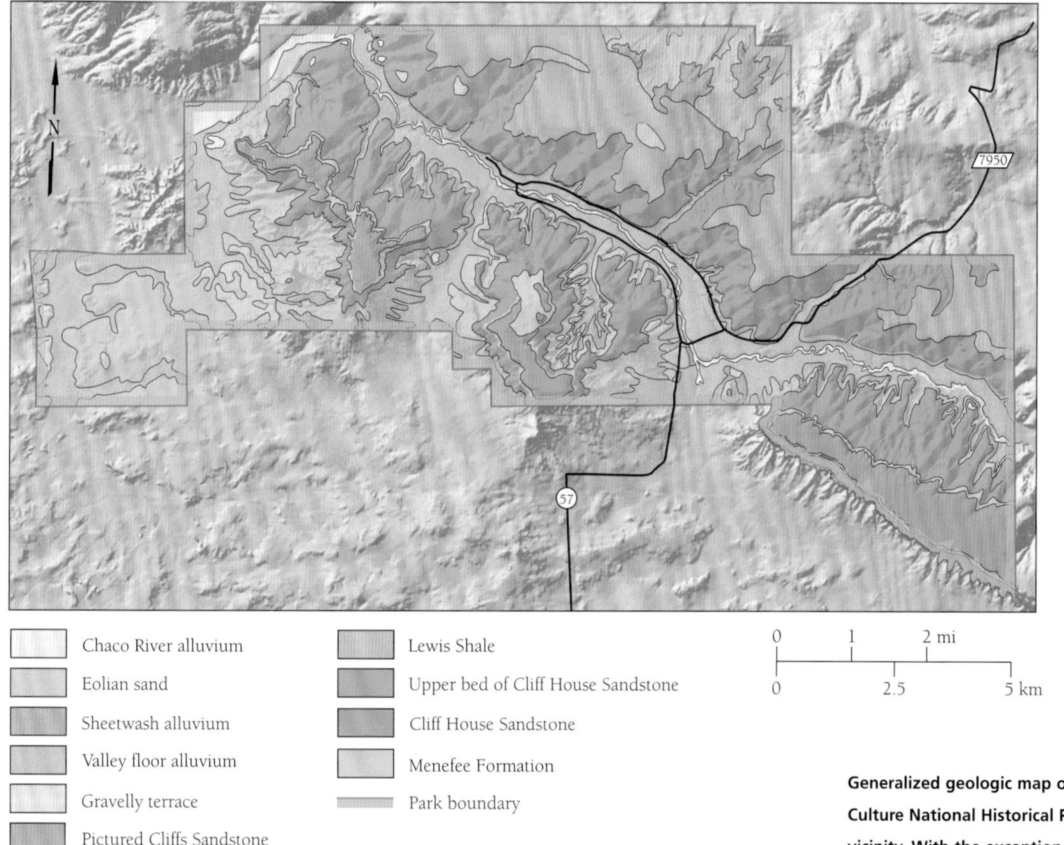

Generalized geologic map of Chaco Culture National Historical Park and vicinity. With the exception of the (Quaternary) alluvial deposits, all of the units shown here are Cretaceous in age (76–80 million years old).

evidence of its origins as coastal lowland swamps, streams, and lagoons that became coal seams, sinuous sandstone ledges, and mudstones with abundant fossil vegetation and brackish water microfossils. The overlying Cliff House Sandstone forms as many as four vertical cliffs and intervening slopes within Chaco Canyon and its tributaries. Preserved crossbedding, laminations, fossils, biological disturbances, and cross-canyon changes within the sandstones show that these alternating cliffs and slopes are the vertically stacked remains of four separate barrier-island complexes with shoreward lagoons to the southwest and offshore marine muds to the northeast. Each barrier-island sand deposit is about 3 miles

The Cliff House Sandstone was deposited during the Cretaceous as a series of four separate barrier-island complexes with shoreward lagoons to the southwest and offshore marine muds to the northeast.

wide and up to 70 feet thick. Positions of the barrier-island complexes shifted back and forth during sediment accumulation so that cliffs now exposed vary in height and record different depositional environments across Chaco Canyon and adjacent mesas. After the sandstone and shale sequence exposed in Chaco Canyon was deposited, the Cretaceous sea retreated to the northeast, more coal swamps and coastal plains covered the area, and ultimately the whole region was downwarped by tectonic and volcanic forces that created the sag in the earth's crust called the San Juan Basin. More than 3,000 feet of Paleocene through Oligocene (65–25 million years old) sediments covered the future site of Chaco Canyon before erosion began to develop the present drainages in the last few million years.

Geoarchaeology and Use of Resources

Chaco Canyon is the New World birthplace of the scientific study of the relation between prehistoric human lifeways and the affected environment. This scientific discipline is called "geoarchaeology." Early chroniclers of Chaco Canyon (following visits by J. H. Simpson in 1849 and W. H. Jackson in 1877) noticed the contrast between the big prehistoric pueblos and the stark environment and speculated about environmental changes during or following occupation of the structures. W. H. Jackson methodically described a prehistoric filled-in gully with potsherds at the bottom of it adjacent to Pueblo del Arroyo, compared it with the modern arroyo, and found the remains of a prehistoric occupant. Dr. W. J. Hoffman, the physician who examined the prehistoric cranium, set the speculative theme of prehistoric environmental degradation by humans that persists a century and a quarter later:

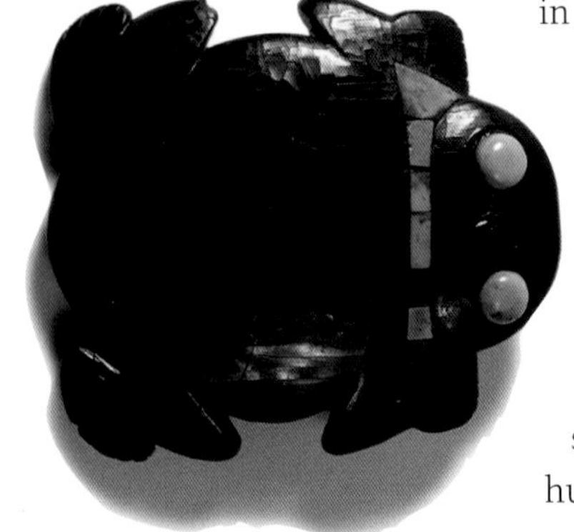

Frog of highly polished jet inlaid with turquoise.

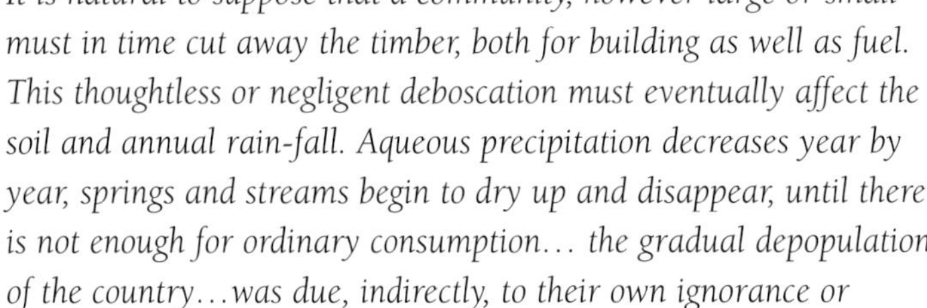

> *It is natural to suppose that a community, however large or small must in time cut away the timber, both for building as well as fuel. This thoughtless or negligent deboscation must eventually affect the soil and annual rain-fall. Aqueous precipitation decreases year by year, springs and streams begin to dry up and disappear, until there is not enough for ordinary consumption… the gradual depopulation of the country…was due, indirectly, to their own ignorance or thoughtlessness….*

Later archaeologists have continued to enlist geologists to describe, date, and interpret the stratigraphy of that buried arroyo and the preexisting sediments. For example, in the 1920s Dr. Kirk Bryan, Harvard

Pueblo Bonito and (in the distance) the south wall of Chaco Canyon, viewed from the cliffs above. The large bouldery debris covering the far end of the pueblo close to the cliff is what remains of Threatening Rock, which collapsed in 1941.

professor, geomorphologist, and native New Mexican traced the pottery-bearing channel a few miles along the floor of Chaco Canyon and speculated that the gully was the result of human-caused environmental degradation that finally forced the inhabitants to move away. During the Chaco Project of the 1970s and 1980s, geologists studied the canyon floor and archaeological stratigraphy, sedimentology, and paleobiology to extend interpretations of environmental changes over several thousand years. These workers suggest that the pottery-bearing channel formed earlier in the occupation of Chaco Canyon and kept Chaco River waters from flooding newly constructed pueblos on the canyon floor.

The attraction of Chaco Canyon for researchers has continued for more than a century and a half, including early applications of tree-ring dating and biogeochemistry, palynology, physical and chemical anthropology, remote sensing, archaeological stratigraphy, and millennial-scale environmental reconstructions via pack-rat midden preservation.

Archaeologists noted that prehistoric inhabitants had engineered an earth and masonry berm to support a large (100 feet high, 30 feet in diameter, 150 feet long) sandstone monolith known as "Threatening Rock" just north of Pueblo Bonito. Before measurements began in 1935, the monolith had moved between three and twelve feet away from the cliff and had settled eight inches. National Park Service custodians made nearly monthly measurements of the movements of Threatening Rock before it finally fell on January 22, 1941, during a particularly wet winter. Witnesses about 300 feet south of the rock "heard the rock groan and looked up to see dust shooting out of the cracks in it. The slab leaned out about 30 or 40 feet from plumb, settled sharply, and when it hit solid bottom, rocks from the top of it were broken loose and propelled into the ruin. The lower two-thirds then pivoted on its outer edge and fell down the slope toward the ruin. The whole mass broke into many fragments and an avalanche of rocks catapulted down the slope and into the walls of the back portion of Pueblo Bonito."

Comparisons of resource use between modern and prehistoric living conditions cannot be made quantitatively yet. Obviously, both modern and prehistoric occupants require water, food, shelter, cooking/warming facilities, waste-disposal procedures, tools, and other cultural amenities. Prehistoric occupants are thought to have gotten their daily requirements for water from small seeps and springs along the canyon margins

Fajada Butte, an erosional remnant of Cliff House Sandstone and Menefee Formation (at the base).

and possibly from shallow hand-dug wells in the prehistoric arroyo bottom. Historic analyses of the shallow water suggest that it was potable but relatively high in sulfate. Modern occupants get their water from a well tapping an aquifer 3,095 feet deep. Water from this deep modern well is high in total dissolved solids and must be treated using reverse osmosis to remove high levels of fluoride, sodium, sulfate, and other constituents to make the water potable. Waste water from the 90,000 visitors and from the 18 housing-unit residents is processed through a sewage treatment plant (maximum 7,000 gallons per day) and returned to shallow ground water and the atmosphere.

Modern occupants import almost all food, clothing, and building materials into Chaco Canyon. In 2003 geobiochemists analyzing prehistoric corn kernels demonstrated that most maize was transported to Chaco Canyon from the surrounding region, as were the large trees used for building the pueblos. Local rodents were also used for food, however. The millions of tons of rocks to build the pueblos were obtained locally, although not from known, centrally located quarries.

Modern roads in Chaco Canyon are built with gravel hauled from the San Juan River drainage 60 miles away. Prehistoric roads were built from local materials.

Prehistoric Puebloans discarded their trash locally, whereas all waste is now transported out of the park in 30-cubic-yard amounts and disposed of in a landfill near Farmington, New Mexico.

Tools, other arts/crafts, and items of religious significance were primarily imported in the prehistoric past, although some local materials were used where appropriate. For example, baked and opalized red argillite and clinker adjacent to burned-coal seams, locally known as "red dog," were used to make tools and red beads. Under modern conditions, similar "red dog" is used to make muddy unpaved roads more passable during wet weather. Modern tools, crafts, and religious items are all imported to Chaco Canyon.

Hungo Pavi, an unexcavated Chacoan great house, against the Cliff House Sandstone cliffs that form the northeast wall of Chaco Canyon.

Geologic Features

Chaco Canyon itself is an unavoidable geologic feature, as are the cliffs of Cliff House Sandstone along the canyon sides and at Fajada Butte, Chacra, South, and West Mesas. The large bouldery debris covering the northeastern edge of Pueblo Bonito is the result of the fall of Threatening Rock in 1941. Chaco Arroyo is best seen from Pueblo Del Arroyo and from the loop road bridges south of Pueblo Bonito and the Visitor Center. Visitors should ask at the Visitor Center for guidance regarding features off designated trails. These might include looking at Cretaceous *Ophiomorpha* burrows or the Bonito paleochannel near Pueblo del Arroyo.

Erosional features in Chaco Canyon include the canyon itself, other tributary canyons, Fajada Butte, Chacra Mesa, and other mesas and buttes along the course of the Chaco River formed by erosion during the past couple of million years. Beds of sandstone resisted erosion much more than intervening mudrocks, so sandstones formed cliffs and mesas, whereas mudrocks were reduced to slopes and valleys. The Chaco River arises along the Continental Divide east of Chaco Canyon at elevations of 6,660–7,400 feet and establishes a slightly sinuous course on northward-tilted mudrocks overlying the Cliff House Sandstone near Pueblo Pintado. From this unentrenched reach of the river, one can envision the meandering river cutting into the mudrocks and encountering the less erodible underlying tilted sandstones. Rather than cut into the sandstones immediately, the river erodes northward down the regional slope of the sandstone before entrenching some of its meanders. Tributaries from sandstone-dominated Chacra Mesa to the south are already established and entrenched whereas tributaries draining mudrocks from the north are shallow and primarily flow southwestward, parallel to wind-blown sand dunes, but transporting sands in the opposite direction. Ultimately, the resistant Cliff House Sandstone holds the meanders of the river and courses of its tributaries in place as erosion continues, forming the sinuous canyon and deep tributary canyons the park visitor encounters today farther northwest.

The present floor of Chaco Wash is deeply gullied with arroyo channels like this one. Channels like these are cut and filled in climate-related cycles of a few hundred years.

Remnant patches of gravel derived from the headwaters are stranded on sandstone ledges within Chaco Canyon, marking former higher positions of the river. Tributary canyons from the south are various lengths, deep, dendritic, broader where erodible mudrock is encountered, and oriented north-northeast. Tributary canyons from the north are fewer, mostly short and steep, and oriented southwest.

Along the canyon walls there are vertical cracks in the sandstone cliffs. Some cracks parallel the canyon walls, reflecting release of stress into the open space provided by erosion. In other areas, the canyon walls cut across fractures, suggesting that the fractures formed before the canyon eroded. Overall, the landforms along the canyon sides reflect the dip and fracture network of underlying bedrock, the uneven stacking of erosion-resistant and non-resistant sandstones and shales, the erosional history of ancestral river and tributaries, and the canyon's erosional fate far into the future.

The canyon preserves subtle geologic clues to past cyclic alternations of climate. For example, the canyon used to be more than 100 feet deeper than it is now. It has been partially filled with deposits of sand, silt, and clay washed to the canyon floor from the sides and headwaters of the canyon. This tells us that under present climatic conditions the ephemeral Chaco River cannot wash all the fine-grained sediment out of the canyon to the San Juan River. Yet, higher gravel terraces stranded along the canyon margins and farther downstream demonstrate that the river was able to transport quantities of coarse-grained sediments in the past. Several different levels of widespread, coarse- and fine-grained deposits within Chaco Canyon show that the river has alternated between low-transport and high-transport conditions over hundreds of thousands of years as the canyon was cut.

On smaller time and spatial scales more important to humans, the present valley floor has alternated between being deeply gullied with arroyo channels, as it is currently, and having no gullies. The past arroyo channels cut and filled in climate-related cycles of a few hundred years.

—David W. Love

If You Plan to Visit

Chaco Canyon is located in northwestern New Mexico and is administered by the National Park Service. The preferred access route to the park is from the north, via US 550 (formerly NM–44), County Road (CR) 7900, and CR 7950. Turn off US 550 at CR 7900, 3 miles southeast of Nageezi and approximately 50 miles west of Cuba (at mile 112.5). This route is clearly marked from US 550 to the park boundary (21 miles). The route includes 5 miles of paved road (CR 7900) and 16 miles of rough dirt road (CR 7950).

From the south, two routes access Chaco from NM–9, which runs between Crownpoint, Pueblo Pintado, and Cuba. Both routes can vary from very rough to impassable, including 20 miles of rough dirt road, and are not recommended for RVs. If you are traveling from the south, please call ahead for the latest conditions. For more information:

Chaco Culture National Historical Park
P.O. Box 220
Nageezi, NM 87037-0220
(505) 786-7014
(505) 786-7061 (Fax)
www.nps.gov/chcu/

Aztec Ruins National Monument

NATIONAL PARK SERVICE

Aztec Ruins National Monument was established in 1923 to preserve the remarkable remains of an ancestral Puebloan farming community, including a twelfth-century Chacoan great house. The settlement flourished from A.D. 1050–1150, at which time it was one of the largest Puebloan settlements in the Southwest, strategically situated between Mesa Verde to the north and Chaco Canyon to the south. Culturally it is considered a Chacoan outlier, at the northern terminus of one of the prehistoric roads that emanated from Chaco. Later occupants (in the 1200s) are thought to have had closer ties to Mesa Verde.

One of the earliest written eyewitness accounts of Aztec Ruins was provided by geologist John Newberry in 1859, who reported at that time that the walls stood 25 feet high. Both the ruins and the setting are spectacular, but the park is perhaps best known for the reconstructed Great Kiva, which was excavated in 1921 and reconstructed by Earl Morris in the 1930s. It is the only restored great kiva in the Southwest and is accessible to visitors; stepping inside provides a unique glimpse of what these ceremonial structures might have been like when they were intact. The park is now a World Heritage Site.

Regional Setting

The monument is located within the San Juan Basin, a structural depression that formed during Laramide time. The basin is bounded on the north by the San Juan uplift and the San Juan volcanic field, whose remnants may be seen today in the San Juan Mountains of southwestern Colorado. To the east it is bounded by the Nacimiento uplift. To the south lie the Mt. Taylor volcanic field and the Zuni uplift; to the west lies the Defiance uplift. The Hogback monocline, visible on US 64 between Shiprock and Farmington, forms the northwest boundary of the San Juan Basin.

The Rock Record

An enormous thickness of sediments (close to 15,000 feet in places) is preserved in the San Juan Basin. This thick accumulation of sediments ranges in age from Pennsylvanian to Tertiary; these are underlain by Precambrian crystalline rocks (1,400–1,750 million years old). As is the case in structural basins, the youngest strata are exposed near the center, and it is here that the thickest accumulations of sediment are found. Progressively older strata are exposed as one approaches the edge of the basin. The oldest strata and the Precambrian crystalline rocks that underlie them are exposed in uplifts along the edge of the basin—the Nacimiento and Zuni uplifts in New Mexico and the San Juan uplift in Colorado.

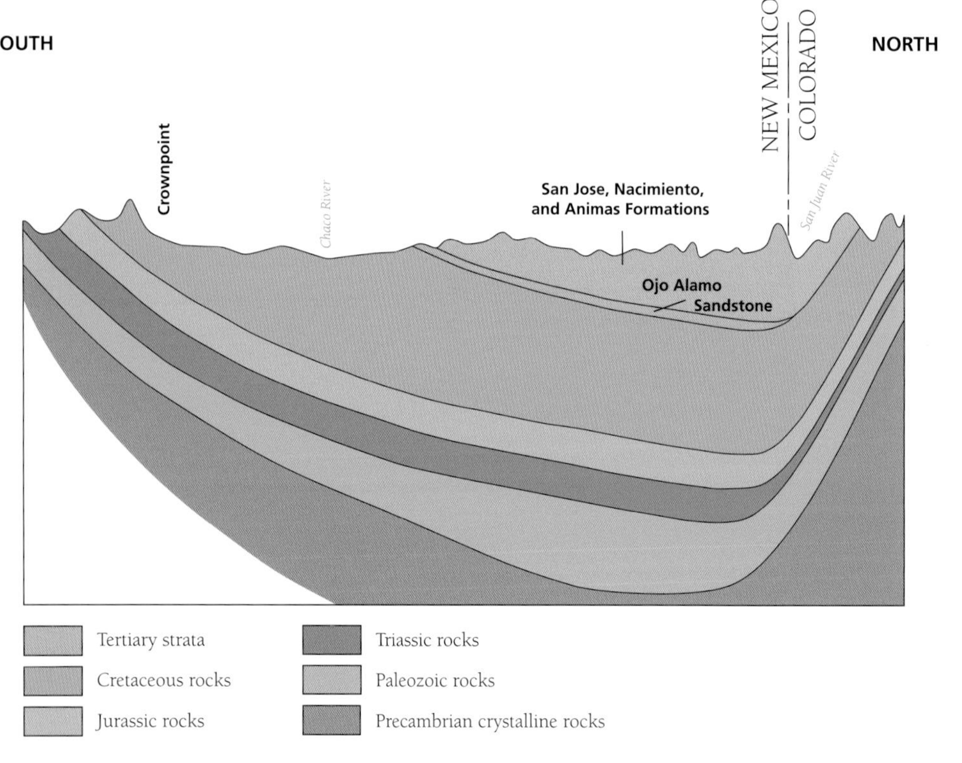

Generalized north–south cross section of the San Juan Basin, from the Colorado–New Mexico border to south of Crownpoint. The thickest accumulation of sediments is close to the center of the basin.

The bedrock within the monument is entirely Paleocene Nacimiento Formation (64.5–61 million years old). These sediments are primarily nonmarine continental sandstones and shales. They represent floodplain, river, swamp, and lake deposits. The sediments were carried into the basin from the San Juan uplift to the north and the Brazos-Sangre de Cristo uplift to the east. Outside the monument there are exposures of the younger, largely fluvial San Jose Formation, which was deposited on top of the Nacimiento.

There is a single outcrop of Nacimiento sandstone in the park. Blocks of Nacimiento sandstone are incorporated into the ruins. Other materials were used as well (the limestone disks found in the Great Kiva, for instance), some of which must have been transported some distance by the builders. Elsewhere in the San Juan Basin, the Nacimiento Formation has yielded a wealth of vertebrate fossils, as well as petrified wood, but no fossils have been found in the Nacimiento within the national monument to date.

The ruins themselves sit on Quaternary alluvial terrace deposits of the Animas River. The complex recent history of the river valley is recorded in these terraces and reworked alluvium, but the details are difficult to decipher with the untrained eye.

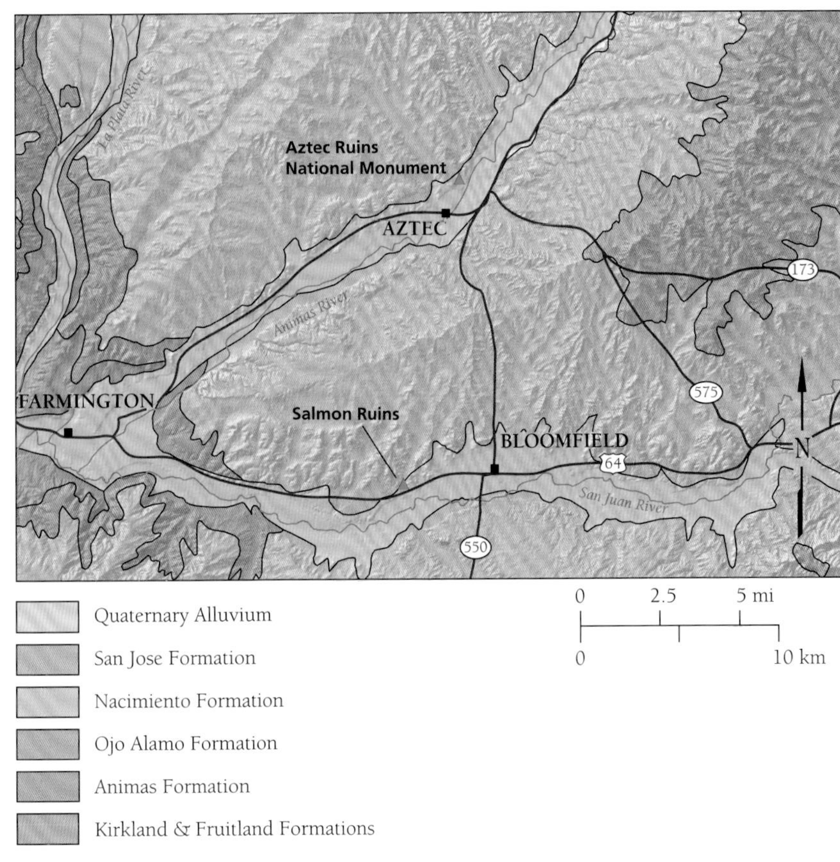

Generalized geologic map of the region surrounding Aztec Ruins National Monument. Salmon Ruins to the south, just west of Bloomfield, are the remains of another eleventh-century Chacoan great house. Salmon Ruins is managed by the San Juan County Museum Association.

Geologic History

The San Juan Basin is primarily a Laramide feature (late Cretaceous to Eocene). Prior to the Laramide orogeny, the San Juan Basin occupied a small part of the Western Interior Basin, at the western edge of the Western Interior Seaway. During the late Cretaceous and on into the Tertiary, the basin subsided, and thousands of feet of additional sediment accumulated. These sediments were deposited in an array of marginal marine, nonmarine, and terrestrial environments and include coal deposits and petroleum source rocks. The late Cretaceous strata in the San Juan Basin have proven to be a rich source of oil and gas, coal, and coalbed methane. These strata represent a transition from the older, primarily marine sediments (deposited on the edge of the Western Interior Seaway) and the predominantly nonmarine strata that dominate the Tertiary record here.

The end of the Cretaceous, here and elsewhere throughout the world, is marked by major extinctions. The creatures that survived into the Paleocene inhabited a world of new possibilities, new ecologic niches. Dinosaurs are notably absent from these early Paleocene terrestrial faunas. For the first time, mammals became the dominant terrestrial vertebrates. These mammals evolved rapidly throughout the Tertiary, producing an array of diverse mammals. The Nacimiento Formation in many places has produced fossils of many of the vertebrates that did survive into the Paleocene, giving us an important glimpse of the world as it existed soon after the cataclysmic events that occurred at the Cretaceous/Tertiary boundary.

Decorative bands of green sandstone from the Nacimiento Formation were incorporated into the ruins. These were quarried near Tucker Canyon, about three miles from the monument. At the time of occupation these walls would likely have been plastered with mud, so these would have been invisible to the occupants.

The region was further affected by an episode of mid-Tertiary volcanism 35–18 million years ago, with the eruption of the San Juan volcanic field to the north. In fact, mid-Tertiary volcanism was widespread and affected much of the Southwest, including enormous portions of southwest New Mexico. The episode of volcanism in the San Juan volcanic field began with the eruption of a series of lava flows. Later eruptions produced widespread, thick blankets of volcanic debris (ash-flow sheets or *ignimbrites*) that likely extended far enough south to cover the Aztec area, but much of that has since been eroded away.

The Animas Valley is the largest glaciated valley on the margin of the Colorado Plateau. Late Pleistocene glaciers covered about 20 percent of the Animas River basin and about half of the river's length. During the Pleistocene the upper Animas Valley contained one of the largest glaciers in the Rocky Mountains in the U.S., the Animas Glacier. This was one of many glaciers that issued from an ice field in the San Juan Mountains. The Animas Valley contains moraines of middle and late Pleistocene age that have been identified as far south as Durango. In the vicinity of the national monument, three distinct river terraces have been identified. Such terraces provide insight into Quaternary glacial-interglacial cycles. The ruins are situated on outwash from the Animas Glacier, since reworked into terrace deposits by the Animas River.

Geologic Features

THE ANIMAS RIVER is one of the primary reasons that the prehistoric settlement at Aztec was situated here. The river runs along the eastern boundary of the park and provides a (nearly) perennial source of water, as it must have during the eleventh and twelfth century. This source of water allowed for the development of these fertile bottomlands during prehistoric times. The first European visitors to the area reported seeing signs of prehistoric irrigation features.

THE SAN JUAN BASIN is one of the richest and most productive oil and gas provinces in North America and has been producing since the 1920s. The monument is on the edge of the Blanco Mesaverde gas pool. There are currently three gas wells operating within the boundaries of the park, producing from Cretaceous sandstones at a depth of 4,300 feet below the surface. The San Juan Basin of New Mexico and Colorado is also one of the most prolific coalbed methane-producing areas in the U.S.

—*L. Greer Price*

Additional Reading

Aztec Ruins on the Animas: Excavated, Preserved, and Interpreted by Robert H. Lister and Florence C. Lister. Revised edition, Western National Parks Association, 1996.

The House of the Great Kiva at the Aztec Ruin by Earl H. Morris. Originally published in 1921, reissued by Western National Parks Association, 1996.

If You Plan to Visit

Aztec Ruins National Monument is located within the city limits of Aztec (the city was in fact named for the ruins, which were well known before the city was founded in the late nineteenth century), on Ruins Road (County Road 2900), about a half mile north of NM–516. The park is about 9 miles from Bloomfield and 11 miles from Farmington. For more information:

Aztec Ruins National Monument
Visitor Services
84 County Road 2900
Aztec, NM 87410
(505) 334-6174
(505) 334-6372 (Fax)
www.nps.gov/azru/

Ship Rock and the Navajo Volcanic Field

NAVAJO NATION

Perhaps the most distinctive and classic landforms of the Colorado Plateau of New Mexico and the adjoining Four Corners states are the monoliths and ramparts of dark igneous rock that the *Diné* (Navajo) people call *Tsézhiin 'íí 'áhí*, "Black Rocks Protruding Up." Geologists refer to them collectively as the Navajo volcanic field, an array of more than 80 individual volcanic and intrusive landforms that extends in a roughly crescent-shaped pattern for about 265 miles across the Colorado Plateau: from the vicinity of Zuñi Pueblo northward along the western edge of the San Juan Basin and the Chuska Mountains, to Mesa Verde in southwestern Colorado, and then west along the Arizona–Utah border to Monument Valley. Most prominent of these is the Rock With Wings, *Tsé bit'á'í*, known more widely as Ship Rock, which is visible for miles in all directions. The majority of these landforms are found on or near the lands of the Navajo Nation, *Diné bikéyah*, and nearly all of them have been so deeply eroded that their volcanic origin may not be readily apparent to the casual observer.

OPPOSITE: Aerial view of Ship Rock from the southwest. This monolith was originally formed more than a half mile below the surface and gradually exhumed by erosion. The light-colored rock is breccia, formed of ash and fragments welded explosively. Concave beds in the breccia near the summit indicate where it slumped partway back into the volcano after the explosions ceased. Later, in a more quiet eruptive phase, additional magma penetrated the breccia from below, resulting in the two dark plugs visible on the left and at lower right.

Regional Setting

The landscape of the surrounding Colorado Plateau is characterized by a thick stack of earth-toned sedimentary rock layers draped over structural highs and lows in the deeper crust: the San Juan and Blanding Basins, the East Defiance and Monument uplifts, and the Four Corners platform. These basins and uplifts are separated by major regional monoclines: the Hogback, which bounds the San Juan Basin on the west and northwest; the East Defiance monocline, which extends along the east side of the Chuska Mountains; and toothy Comb Ridge, on the eastern and southern flanks of the Monument uplift. Most of the landforms of the Navajo volcanic field occur along these monoclines, and they protrude vertically through older, flat-lying or gently folded sedimentary rocks of the Colorado Plateau.

The Rock Record

The igneous rocks of the Navajo volcanic field range in age from 30 to 18 million years old. Analyses of Navajo volcanic rocks indicate that the magmas that formed these features were of a composition similar to basalt, but comparatively richer in potassium and poorer in aluminum. The major type of rock that occurs is called *minette*, a name that originated with miners who encountered the same rock far away in France.

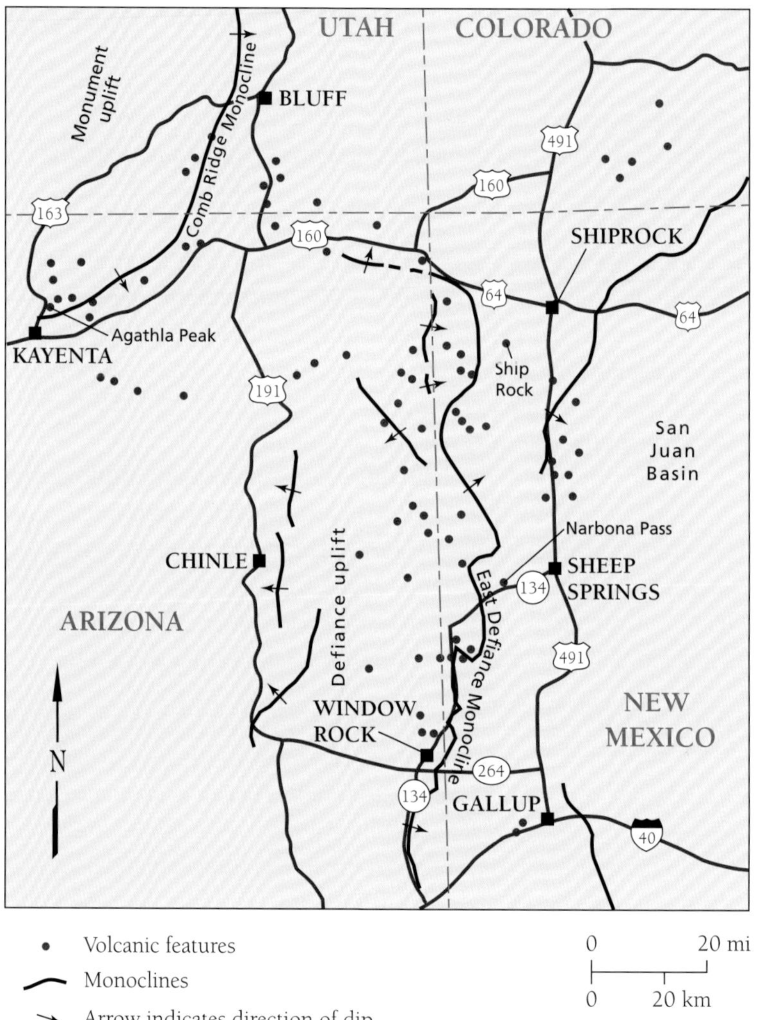

Volcanic and structural features of the cenral Navajo volcanic field.

It is characterized by a dark-grey to greenish-grey color and usually contains visible crystals or *phenocrysts* of shiny black or gold-tinted *phlogopite* mica, green olivine, and needlelike black pyroxene set in a fine-grained matrix. Its composition places minette in a class of unusual alkali-rich, low-silica igneous rocks called *lamprophyres*.

The rocks exposed here are predominantly sedimentary, representing different levels of the miles-thick sequence of Colorado Plateau strata. The level of exposure in different places depends in part on whether the layers were locally uplifted or downdropped by folding, and how deeply they have been eroded. In and near the San Juan Basin, Navajo volcanic landforms protrude through Cretaceous rocks. At the other end of the volcanic field, in the Monument uplift, once-deeper layers of Pennsylvanian to Triassic age are exposed. None of these layers represents the original surface upon which the Navajo volcanoes erupted; these features now stand well above their surroundings.

Geologic History

The igneous rocks of the Navajo volcanic field formed during the middle Tertiary Period, following the Laramide orogeny, a regional mountain-building event that locally folded the crust of the Colorado Plateau into uplifts, basins, and *monoclines*. The Laramide orogeny is thought to be the result of a somewhat unusual episode of the process of subduction, in which the southwestern edge of the North American continent rode over a shallowly-dipping segment of Pacific oceanic lithosphere. After the Laramide orogeny ended and the oceanic plate dropped back into the mantle, volcanoes began to erupt voluminously across much of the Southwest, building great complexes such as the San Juan volcanic field in southwest Colorado. But on the Colorado Plateau, only the less voluminous and more widely-scattered Navajo volcanoes emerged, perhaps because the lower crust of the Colorado Plateau acted as a filter against more effusive eruptions. How did the Navajo volcanic field magmas get through? These volcanic landforms today are found mostly clustered along the Hogback, East Defiance, and Comb Ridge monoclines, which formed above faults in the deep crust. Although these faults do not reach the surface, at depth they may have facilitated the upward transport of Navajo volcanic field magmas through the Colorado Plateau.

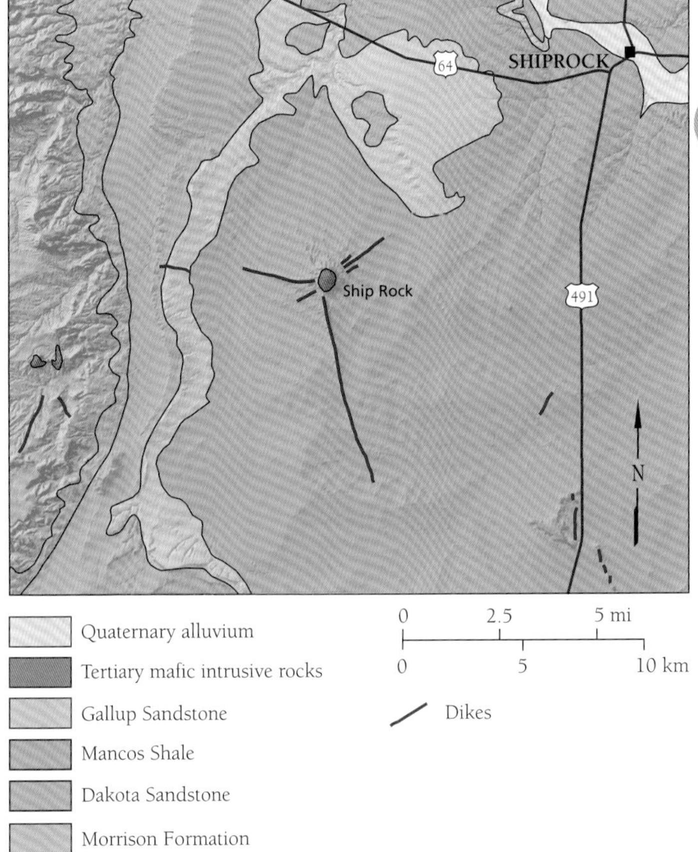

Generalized geologic map of Ship Rock and vicinity.

Across their beautiful semi-arid homeland, *Diné bikéyah*, and in its climate, flora, and fauna, Diné people view natural processes as the collaborative work of the Earth and Sky. Internal processes of the Earth uplift mountains and create volcanoes, whereas external processes of the Sky sculpt away at the landscape. Ship Rock and its kin are exemplars of this principle. Nearly all of the rock visible in the Navajo volcanic field today represents the exhumed magmatic "plumbing" deep beneath Tertiary-age volcanoes that have been completely erased by erosion, along with about a half-mile or more of sedimentary rock layers that covered the surface. Imagine a sink in a kitchen cabinet, and what it would look like if you pulled out the sink and removed the cabinet but left all the pipes sticking out. Such is most of the Navajo volcanic field today, but with one important distinction: the volcanoes were fed at depth not by cylindrical pipes but by *dikes*, which are sheet-like flows of magma ascending near-vertically through minor fractures

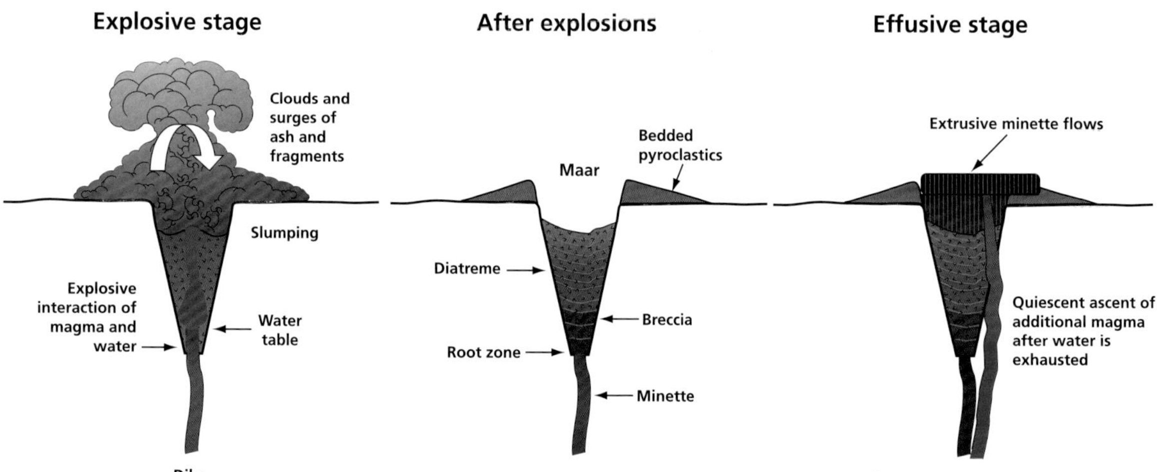

A hydrovolcanic eruptive sequence. In the explosive stage, magma in a dike vaporizes subsurface water in a series of powerful explosions. When the water is depleted and explosions end, a broad, shallow maar remains at the surface, surrounded by ejected pyroclastic material and overlying the welded breccia diatreme. An effusive stage may follow, in which magma ascends more quiescently to the surface.

in the crust. Remnants of these (sheet-like, vertical) dikes are clearly visible extending outward from Ship Rock and other large monoliths of the volcanic field.

As the dikes gradually penetrated the layered sediments of the central Colorado Plateau, they encountered *aquifers*: porous and permeable layers of sandstone and similar sedimentary rocks that can hold about 30 percent ground water by volume. The heat of the magma flashed some of this ground water to rapidly expanding steam, resulting in a violent eruption that blasted hot, wet fragments of minette and surrounding sedimentary rocks upward in a conical conduit known as a *diatreme*, and out onto the surface through a broad, shallow explosion crater called a *maar*. These dynamic events thus resulted from the interaction of magma, rising from the upper mantle of the earth, with water infiltrating down from precipitation in the (mid-Tertiary) sky. Geologists call them *hydrovolcanic* eruptions. One of the maars in the Navajo volcanic field remains today almost in its entirety, at Narbona Pass in the Chuska Mountains.

Similar maar craters probably formed above the Black Rocks Protruding Up from the basins on either side of the Chuskas, but post-eruptive uplift of the Colorado Plateau (another dynamic interaction of Earth and Sky) likely facilitated their exhumation, through regional incision of the landscape by the Colorado River drainage system. At the time the Navajo volcanoes erupted, the San Juan Basin and environs may have been covered by an additional half mile or more of layered rocks and sediments. In other words, a maar above Ship Rock would have sat twice as high as the present-day monolith, which is an exposed segment of the middle part of the diatreme. Beneath its uniform grayish-brown patina, the monolith, termed a *volcanic neck* by geologists, is composed of *breccia*, a welded composite of rock fragments and ash. Breccia superficially resembles concrete, but in this case it was formed by the explosive fragmentation and mixing that occurred in the diatreme eruption. Ship Rock and the other diatremes also incorporated larger intact pieces of crustal rock, termed *xenoliths*, some of which are as large as houses.

Ship Rock, with a clear view of one of the large, radial dikes or "wings."

The volcanic necks and dikes of the Navajo volcanic field stand tall today because the textures and mineral compositions of minette and breccia render them more resistant to weathering and erosion, under the semi-arid Colorado Plateau climate, than the mudstones and sandstones through which they erupted. This same phenomenon of differential erosion accounts for the "stairstep" mesas and buttes that characterize much of the regional landscape. The magnificence of the landforms of the Navajo volcanic field is a direct consequence of the interaction of Earth and Sky over tens of millions of years.

Geologic Features

SHIP ROCK *Tsé bit'á'í*, The Rock With Wings, is an icon of the Four Corners region about 1,600 feet (500 meters) tall. The "wings" are three large dikes and several smaller ones, each composed of non-fragmented (massive) minette that solidified within the fractures underlying the volcano. The extensive south dike is almost 6 miles (10 kilometers) in length and nearly 100 feet high in some places, yet it is only a few feet thick. This dike may have supplied magma to the Ship Rock diatreme, in which case the point where the diatreme budded off of the dike is still buried. Each of the smaller dikes on the northeast flank of Ship

Rock intersects its own minor neck of massive minette. These smaller necks may have channeled magma upward to quiescent lava flows after the sequence of explosive hydrovolcanic eruptions, such as occurred at Narbona Pass.

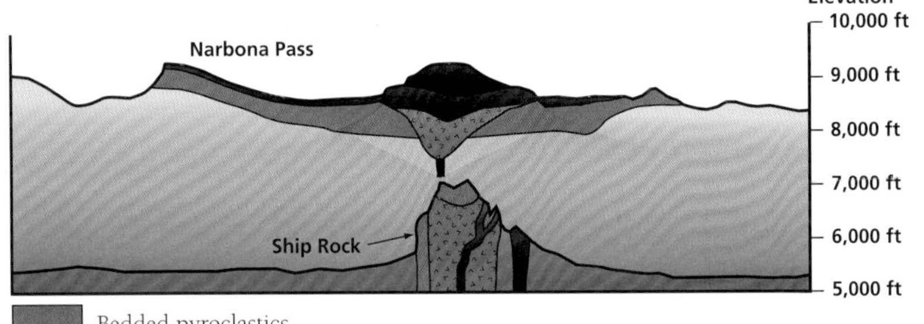

Cross-sectional comparison of the Ship Rock and Narbona Pass volcanoes. The Narbona Pass maar, which likely covers its own buried diatreme, has remained almost intact, whereas at Ship Rock erosion has removed all of the surface features and cut deeply into the diatreme.

NARBONA PASS In the Chuska Mountains, on NM–134 southeast of Sheep Springs, is the well-preserved remnant of a maar. The maar at Narbona Pass (previously known as Washington Pass) is an elliptical crater about 1 by 1.25 miles in size, surrouned by a high rim built of welded, layered *pyroclastic* materials that were blasted both vertically and laterally out of the volcanic vent, which is now covered. Layers of pyroclastic material are particularly well-exposed in the impressive ramparts at the east portal of Narbona Pass. Within the crater and along its southwestern flanks, the pyroclastic materials are covered by minette lava flows, indicating that once the initial violence siphoned all the ground water from the surrounding rocks, magma continued to erupt for a time, now more quiescently. The present floor of the Narbona Pass maar is at an elevation of about 8,600 feet, and its original rugged profile has been smoothed considerably by erosion and mountain vegetation, but the maar crater, rim, and lava flows will still be apparent to the geologically aware traveler crossing the pass on NM–134.

A columnar-jointed minette lava flow caps a tree-covered slope of bedded pyroclastics near the west portal of Narbona Pass, on NM–134 near the Arizona border.

OTHER FEATURES Other impressive kin to Ship Rock include Mitten Rock, about 7 miles to the southwest, near the Arizona border; Bennett Peak and Ford Butte, which flank US 491 near Newcomb; and Agathla Peak, which is located at the southern edge of Monument Valley, along US 163 north of Kayenta, Arizona.

—*Steven Semken*

Additional Reading

Monster Birds, a Navajo Folktale by Vee Browne and Baje Whitethorne. Northland Publishing, 1993.

Ship Rock, New Mexico: The Vent of a Violent Volcanic Eruption by P. T. Delaney. In: Geological Society of America, Centennial Field Guide, Rocky Mountain Section. Geological Society of America, 1987.

Black Rocks Protruding Up: The Navajo Volcanic Field by Steven Semken. In: *Geology of the Zuni Plateau*, New Mexico Geological Society Guidebook 54. New Mexico Geological Society, 2003.

Agathla Peak, near Monument Valley, Arizona.

If You Plan To Visit

Ship Rock is just southwest of the town of Shiprock, in the northwest corner of New Mexico. It is most easily viewed heading west from the town of Shiprock on US 64, or heading south from the town of Shiprock along US 491 (previously US 666). Narbona Pass is accessible via NM-134, which leads southwest from US 491 at Sheep Springs, about 45 miles south of Shiprock.

Please be aware that the Navajo Nation is neither a park nor public land, and there are specific regulations regarding access. Many of the most spectacular features of the Navajo volcanic field can be observed and photographed at a distance, from the major highways crossing the Four Corners region. However, features located on lands of the Navajo Nation must not be accessed without a permit obtained in advance from the Navajo Nation Minerals Department in Window Rock, Arizona. Collection of rock, mineral, paleontological, and archaeological specimens on Navajo Nation land is expressly prohibited. In some places Navajo families live in close proximity to Navajo volcanic field landforms. Please respect their privacy and do not photograph their homes or activities. Even while traveling public highways here, you are a guest of the Diné people. For permits, contact:

Navajo Nation Minerals Department
P.O. Box 1910
Window Rock, Navajo Nation, AZ 86515

Bisti/De-Na-Zin Wilderness

BUREAU OF LAND MANAGEMENT

The country in northwestern New Mexico between Cuba and Farmington is a land of contrast. Flat grassy plains are cut by valleys that expose the multi-colored moonscapes that we call badlands. The largest area of badlands in the region that is readily accessible to the public is the Bisti/De-Na-Zin Wilderness, popularly known as the Bisti Badlands. The badlands are generally exposed in a series of east-west-trending valleys formed by the tributaries that feed the south-north-flowing Chaco River.

The many fossils preserved in this region make this one of the best places on Earth to study the fascinating story of the end of the age of dinosaurs and the beginning of the age of mammals. These fossils will not be obvious to casual visitors, but visitors will be instantly struck by the spectacular scenery of this area, which has been featured in books, magazines, calendars, and Web sites.

The Bisti Badlands is one of the most striking landscapes in northwestern New Mexico. The prominent dark bed is a coal seam.

Regional Setting

Northwestern New Mexico is on the edge of the Colorado Plateau, which includes most of northeastern Arizona, most of eastern Utah, and western Colorado. The Colorado Plateau is a part of North America that has stayed relatively rigid while the areas around it (such as the Rocky Mountains) have crumpled as the continent has collided with other parts of the earth's crust. In general the Colorado Plateau is characterized by high plateaus of flat-lying rocks that are spectacularly dissected by enormous canyons such as at Grand Canyon National Park or Canyonlands National Park. The edges of the Colorado Plateau are characterized by a series of saucer-shaped geological basins where the rocks slant towards the center of a depression. The San Juan Basin is one such saucer; it includes most of northwestern New Mexico and a portion of southwestern Colorado that extends nearly to Durango. The rocks of the Bisti area are on the western side of the basin, so they are tilted to the east at about 5 degrees.

The current San Juan Basin formed at the end of the Laramide orogeny, the mountain-building event that formed the Rocky Mountains. A geologic basin looks like a bull's eye from above, with concentric rings of rocks that are younger toward the center. The older rocks on the edges of the San Juan Basin are from the beginning of the

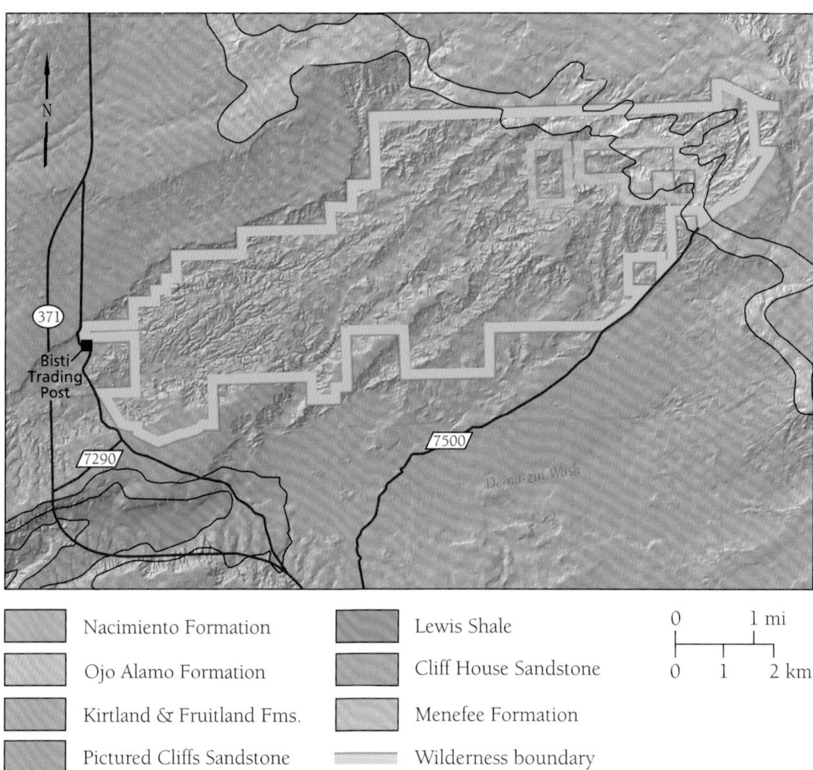

Generalized geologic map of the Bisti/De-Na-Zin Wilderness and vicinity. The Cretaceous Kirtland and Fruitland Formations are commonly mapped as a single unit, because they are difficult to tell apart.

age of dinosaurs (Triassic) and are about 220 million years old. Going toward the center we find rocks from the middle of dinosaur time (Jurassic) and the end of dinosaur time (Cretaceous). Finally, at the center of the bull's eye we have rocks from the two time intervals that followed the extinction of the dinosaurs (Paleocene and Eocene). The Bisti Badlands expose rocks from the end of the Cretaceous and the Paleocene—from just before to just after the great dying that occurred at the Cretaceous/Tertiary boundary.

The San Juan Basin also includes younger volcanic rocks, and it has a rich archeological record, particularly of the prehistoric Puebloans (the people we have for years referred to as the Anasazi), who built large stone complexes, including those at Chaco Canyon National Historical Park and Aztec Ruins National Monument.

The Rock Record

The hoodoos that are characteristic of the Bisti Badlands are eroded from sandstones of the Kirtland Formation. The softer white sandstones that form the stalks are often capped with the harder, more resistant brown sandstones of the Bisti Member of the Kirtland Formation.

Geologists divide the thick sequence of rocks exposed in the Bisti Badlands into four main intervals or formations, which, starting from the oldest, are: (1) Fruitland Formation; (2) Kirtland Formation; (3) Ojo Alamo Formation; and (4) Nacimiento Formation. The oldest rocks occur in the west part of the Bisti Badlands and the layers become progressively younger to the east.

The Fruitland Formation is the most easily visible and forms arguably the most scenic, and certainly the most photographed, badlands close to NM–371. The Fruitland represents swamps and rivers that formed close to the Cretaceous shoreline about 74 million years ago. The rocks that formed in swamps and other poorly-drained areas are black coals and gray shales. The river channels are represented by white sandstones that provide a stark contrast to the drab colors of the other rocks. The sandstones are more resistant to erosion than the soft coals and shales, so they form resistant cliffs and ridges that are often sculpted by nature into exotic shapes including those mushroom-shaped rocks commonly referred to as hoodoos. The other very hard rocks in the Fruitland are layers or concretions of iron minerals (mainly siderite) that vary in color from brown to purple.

The Fruitland is divided into a lower Ne-nah-ne-zad Member, which has most of the thick coal and all of the thick seams, and an upper Fossil Forest Member, which has less coal and concretions and (as the name suggests) many fossils. The name derives from an area south of the Bisti Badlands where there are remnants of a large buried forest represented by petrified stumps. Similar layers of stumps can be found at Bisti.

Coal burns not only in fireplaces but also naturally. Whole seams of coal may catch fire and burn, baking the surrounding shales into a hard, red rock. Stripes of this "clinker" or "red dog" provide the only bright colors in the Fruitland Formation.

The overlying Kirtland Formation is also Cretaceous in age, although it is a little younger than the Fruitland. The Kirtland is easy to spot because it consists of thick sequences of shales and siltstones that are primarily shades of green in contrast to the grays of the Fruitland. The Kirtland only has a few very thin coals, less than a foot thick. The Kirtland does have a few white sandstones, but they are thinner than those in the Fruitland.

The Kirtland can be divided into three sequences: (1) a lower Hunter Wash Member that has a basal sandstone layer with a white base and a brown top (Bisti Bed) and consists mainly of drab green siltstones; (2) a middle Farmington Sandstone Member that includes sheet-like sandstones, many of which have brown tops; and (3) an upper De-na-zin Member that is similar to the Hunter Wash Member but includes purple beds near its top. Dinosaur and other fossil bones are scattered through the Kirtland.

Fossil tree, from Alamo Wash area.

The Ojo Alamo Sandstone is on top of the Kirtland and is mostly Cretaceous in age, although it may extend into the lowest part of the Paleocene. The Ojo Alamo includes two starkly contrasting layers. The lower Naashoibito Member is a colorful interplay of purple mudstones and white sandstones, whereas the upper Kimbetoh Member is a massive, cliff-forming brown sandstone. Fossils are abundant in the Ojo Alamo. The Naashoibito includes many bones of dinosaurs and other land animals (including turtles and crocodiles), whereas the Kimbetoh contains only a few dinosaur bones but spectacular fossil logs.

It is probable that the end of the Cretaceous and the extinction of the dinosaurs occurred somewhere in the upper Ojo Alamo, at what we have come to know as "the K/T Boundary" (or the Cretaceous/Tertiary Boundary). The upper part of the Kimbetoh Member is inter-layered with the Paleocene Nacimiento Formation, which contains remains of mammals who survived the great dying.

The Nacimiento Formation is a candy-striped unit of rock with whites, blacks and red. These rocks are mainly shales and sandstones with some thin coaly beds. Most of the rocks in the Bisti Badlands represent the Arroyo Chijuillita Member. The Nacimiento has yielded the youngest animals in the Paleocene, which are globally important. The two earliest ages in the Paleocene are based on these mammals and are named the Puercoan and Torrejonian for the Rio Puerco and Torrejon Wash in the San Juan Basin.

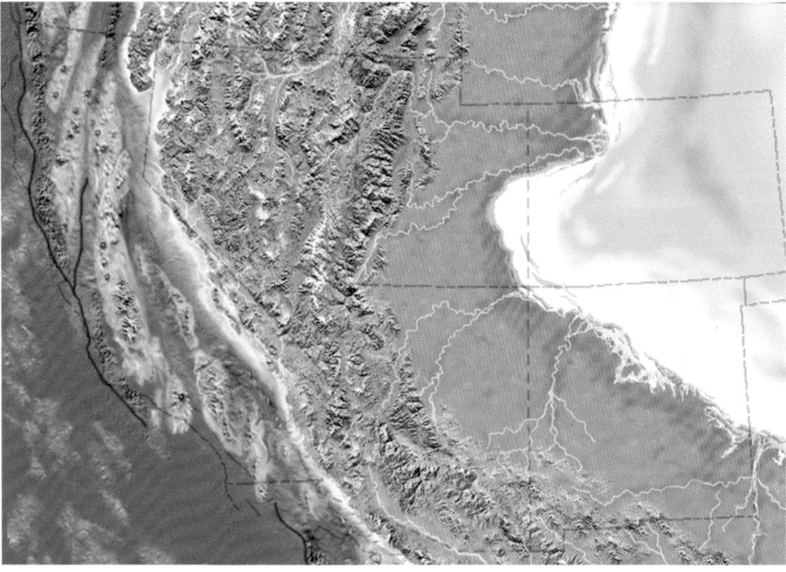

Paleogeographic map of the southwestern U.S. during the Late Cretaceous, approximately 75 million years ago. New Mexico at that time was characterized by predominantly terrestrial environments—rivers, floodplains, and swamps.

Geologic History

The rocks of the Bisti Badlands tell two dramatic and parallel stories: the final retreat of the ocean from New Mexico, and the extinction of the dinosaurs at the end of the Mesozoic. During much of the Cretaceous a narrow strip of sea split North America into two land masses. The western shoreline moved backward and forward through what are now the western states of New Mexico, Colorado, Wyoming, Arizona, Utah, and Montana. As the shoreline shifted, parts of New Mexico were (alternately) underwater, beach front properties, or dry land. Finally, as the Cretaceous drew to a close, the sea retreated northeastward out of New Mexico, leaving the northeastern corner last.

Coal forms from peat, which forms in swamps. Therefore, the coal-rich Fruitland Formation obviously represents an environment close to the shore, much like areas in the modern southeastern United States—the Mississippi delta and the Okefenokee Swamp, for example. As you go upward through the layers of Cretaceous rock there is less and less coal. This reflects the fact that the sea was retreating and that the Bisti area was getting farther and farther from the swampy coast. The Kirtland Formation represents flat river plains. The white and brown sandstones formed in the rivers and streams, and the green shales represent floods that dumped mud between them.

There are two intervals in the rock sequence that contain very high percentages of sandstone: the middle Farmington Member of the Kirtland Formation and the upper Kimbetoh Member of the Ojo Alamo Sandstone. There are several ways that rivers can produce thick layers of sandstone with very little shale. The easiest explanation is that mountains were being pushed up and heavily eroded, which produced lots of sand. This is the explanation for the Kimbetoh Member; there was mountain building and volcanism occurring in southwest Colorado

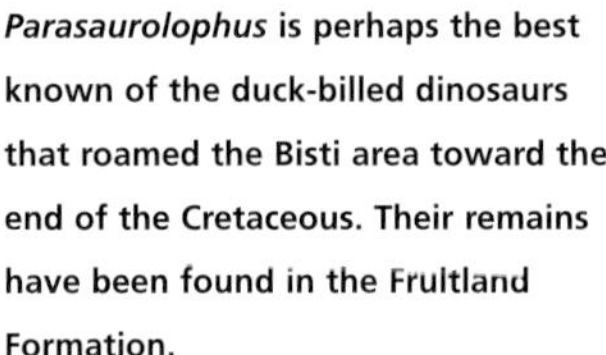

Parasaurolophus **is perhaps the best known of the duck-billed dinosaurs that roamed the Bisti area toward the end of the Cretaceous. Their remains have been found in the Fruitland Formation.**

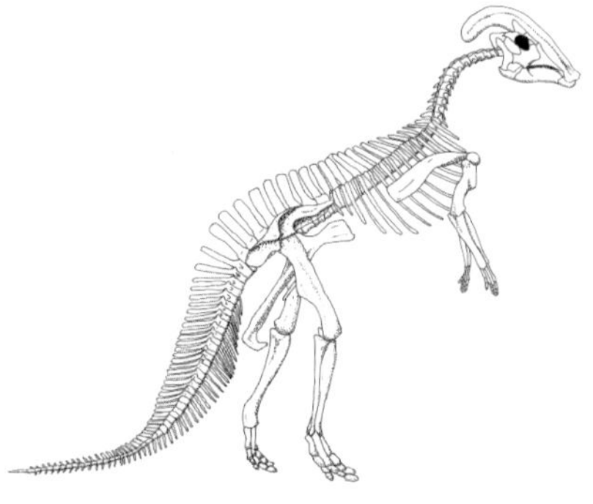

at the time it was deposited. The Farmington Member contains a lot more shale than the Kimbetoh Member, but it has the same general origin.

The Kimbetoh Member of the Ojo Alamo Sandstone contains fossil logs in excess of 100 feet long, so it must represent fast-flowing rivers. As these rivers were flowing, a major catastrophe struck the Earth. A large meteorite several miles in diameter crashed into the sea near what is now the Yucatan Peninsula of Mexico resulting in a large hole called the Chicxulub Crater. Enormous quantities of dust were thrown into the air, and the surface of the earth was covered by huge fires. The meteoritic dust eventually settled and created a thin (2–4 inch) layer of fine, whitish clay that is rich in elements that are common in meteorites but rare on the surface of the earth, such as iridium. In the Bisti area the dust never had a chance to settle in the torrential rivers that were carrying enormous trees downstream. In northeast New Mexico the dust settled in quiet swamps and the iridium-rich layer can be found in several places around Raton including Sugarite Canyon State Park. The dust may not have settled on the Bisti area, but the devastation of life that resulted in the extinction of the dinosaurs affected this area.

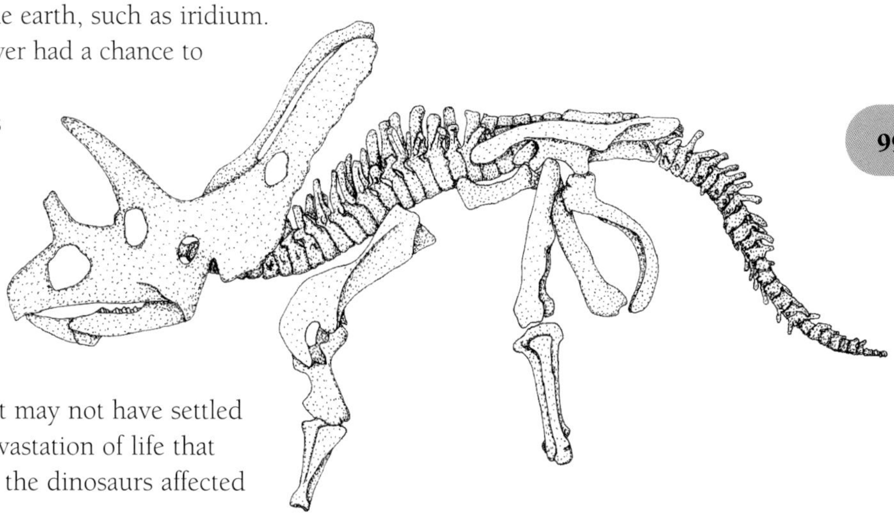

Triceratops

The dinosaurs that inhabited this area were dominated by two groups of herbivores. The most common animals were duck-billed dinosaurs or hadrosaurs, the most famous of which was *Parasaurolophus*. This bizarre animal looked as though it had a boomerang protruding from the back of its head. The other main group of herbivores was the horned dinosaurs. The most famous dinosaur of this type is the three-horned Triceratops, but it doesn't occur any further south than Denver. In New Mexico we have a unique relative called *Pentaceratops* that has five horns. Other plant-eating dinosaurs include the armored dinosaurs or ankylosaurs, which include *Nodocephalosaurus* and bone-headed or pachycephalosaur dinosaurs such as *Prenocephale*. Meat-eating dinosaurs include *Tyrannosaurus*, *Daspletosaurus*, and *Ornithomimus*. The Cretaceous fauna also includes a variety of turtles, crocodiles, lizards, and mammals.

Collecting an *Ankylosaurid* pelvis in the Ah-shi-sle-pah Wash area of the San Juan Basin.

After the extinction of the dinosaurs the landscape was dominated by a variety of small mammals. Mammals had evolved at about the same time as dinosaurs during the Late Triassic (about 225 million years ago). Mammals living at the end of the Cretaceous included an extinct group of rodent-like animals called multituberculates, pouched-marsupials, and a lesser number of placental mammals including our ancestors. Mammals did not suffer a major extinction at the end of the Cretaceous, but the relative numbers of groups changed. Paleocene faunas were dominated by placental mammals and marsupials, and multituberculates were much less common. Turtles, crocodiles, and lizards continued through the great dying with little change. The Nacimiento Formation that contains these Paleocene faunas represents flat, river plains with a climate that was cooler and drier than during the Cretaceous.

—*Adrian P. Hunt*

If You Plan to Visit

The main access to the Bisti/De-Na-Zin Wilderness is 36 miles south of Farmington on NM–371. The turnoff is to the east on CR 7297 and is marked. Follow the gravel road for 2 miles to reach the dirt parking lot. You will intersect with a north-south dirt road (CR 7000). Cross this road and follow a track to the boundary fence. The most scenic area is now about a mile southeast of you. The most interesting geological features are the eroded white sandstones. There are many hoodoos or mushroom rocks where resistant rocks are preserved on pinnacles of softer rock that have been eroded back to form the "mushroom stalks." The very hard, brown sandstones of the Bisti Member of the Kirtland Formation often cap very high pinnacles and sharp ridges in this area. Some of the highest brown peaks are used for nesting areas by ferruginous hawks.

Alternatively, turn west off US 550 at Huerfano Trading Post. This route is entirely on dirt roads (CR 7500 and CR 7023), which can be hard to follow and are impassable in wet weather. There are many unmarked turnoffs; the best advice is to follow the most heavily traveled dirt road.

The Bisti/De-na-zin Wilderness originally consisted of two separate wildernesses. The former Bisti Wilderness at the western end near NM–371 includes the strangely sculpted landscapes that are the favorites of both photographers and hikers. The Bisti/De-Na-Zin Wilderness includes 45,000 acres managed by the U.S. Bureau of Land Management. The Wilderness boundaries enclose three parcels of private Navajo land. For more information contact:

Farmington Field Office
Bureau of Land Management
1235 La Plata Highway, Suite A
Farmington, NM 87401
(505) 599-8900
(505) 599-8998 (Fax)
www.nm.blm.gov/ffo/ffo_home.html

The Bisti Badlands are featured on many other Web sites, including:
www.publiclands.org
www.recreation.gov
www.americansouthwest.net
www.wilderness.net
www.bistibadlands.com

Navajo Lake State Park

NEW MEXICO STATE PARKS

Located near the Four Corners, Navajo Lake is the reservoir behind Navajo Dam, which was built by the U.S. Bureau of Reclamation in 1958–62. The lake covers more than 15,000 acres and is the second-largest lake in New Mexico. The dam impounds water from the San Juan River and adjacent tributaries, including the Piedra and Los Pinos

Rivers and La Jara and Sambrito Creeks. Bedrock exposed in the park belongs to the lower Eocene San Jose Formation. During the early Eocene, about 50–55 million years ago, large rivers flowing to the south deposited the San Jose Formation in the San Juan Basin. This rock formation contains a world-famous fossil record of early mammals and associated plants, fishes, and reptiles.

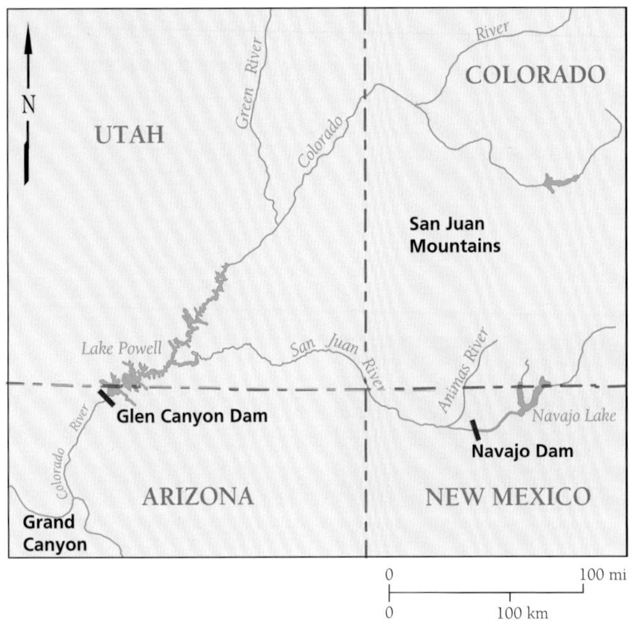

The San Juan River, a tributary of the Colorado River, originates in the San Juan Mountains of Colorado. Today it empties into Lake Powell in southern Utah.

Regional Setting

Navajo Lake is in the San Juan Basin, in the southeastern portion of the Colorado Plateau. The San Juan Basin is a depression in the crust that preserves more than 12,000 feet of strata that range in age from Cambrian to Pleistocene. During the Late Cretaceous through Eocene, the San Juan Basin was a particularly active site of sediment accumulation.

The Rock Record

The cliffs and hills around Navajo Lake expose ledges and cliffs of sandstone between slopes of mudstone and siltstone. These rocks of the lower Eocene San Jose Formation are deposits of ancient rivers and their floodplains. The sandstones are yellow, tan, or gray, and their coarse grains are visible to the naked eye. Beds of pebbles are also present in some of the sandstones, and most display crossbeds, which are formed by flowing water. The mudstones and siltstones are more difficult to examine because they form slopes mantled by soil and vegetation. Where exposed, these rocks are color-banded gray, yellow, pink, purple, and lavender.

A thin veneer of Pleistocene sand and gravel is present locally at Navajo Lake State Park. These unconsolidated sediments are mostly covered by soil and vegetation.

The San Juan River canyon below Navajo Dam is cut in siltstones and sandstones of the Eocene San Jose Formation and Paleocene Nacimiento Formation. This stretch of river offers some of the best trout fishing in New Mexico.

Geologic History

A seaway covered most of the central United States during the Late Cretaceous, and its shoreline passed through the area of Navajo Lake State Park. A thick section of shale and sandstone deposited by the seaway underlies the rocks exposed at the park. At the end of the Cretaceous, the uplift of mountains north and east of the San Juan Basin drove the sea out. Rivers flowed from these mountains during the Paleocene and early Eocene and

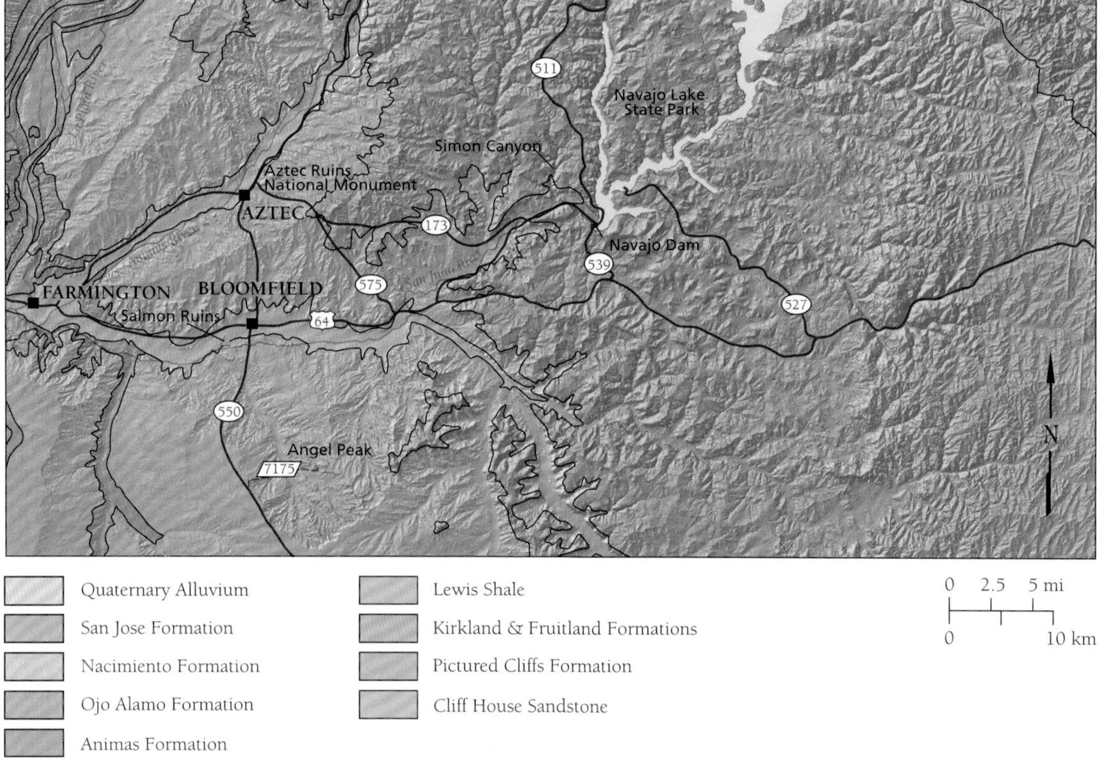

Generalized geologic map of northwestern New Mexico.

deposited the sandstones, mudstones, and siltstones that are the bedrock around Navajo Lake State Park.

Today, Navajo Lake sits at an elevation of 6,100 feet, and nearby mountain peaks reach heights of more than 10,000 feet. But, during the early Eocene, the present location of Navajo Lake State Park was only a few hundred feet above sea level. Ancient mountains to the north and east towered no more than a couple of thousand feet in elevation. Large rivers flowed from these mountains, heading southward toward the present location of Cuba, New Mexico. Sand and gravel accumulated in the river channels and on river bars and levees. During floods, muds and silts washed out of the river channels onto the adjacent river floodplains. Over a few million years, repeated times of river flow and interspersed floods built up more than 2,500 feet of rock that geologists call the San Jose Formation.

The early Eocene river floodplains were forested, mostly by palms and other tropical plants. Garfish, soft-shelled turtles, and alligators were among the inhabitants of those ancient rivers. On land and in the trees, primitive mammals prospered, including some of the earliest primates.

After the early Eocene, the San Juan Basin was uplifted. Some sedimentary and volcanic rocks accumulated, but they were subsequently

The Angel Peak Scenic Area, 25 miles southeast of Navajo Lake State Park. These badlands are mostly in Paleocene mudstones and siltstones of the Nacimiento Formation.

eroded away, mostly during the last few million years. Most of the uplift of the San Juan Basin to its present elevation took place during the last 25 million years.

Geologic Features

Sims Mesa, the main recreation area in the park, is a tableland underlain by sandstones of the San Jose Formation. Simon Canyon, 3 miles downstream of Navajo Dam, exposes Paleocene rocks of the Nacimiento Formation that are directly beneath the San Jose Formation. The San Jose Formation is mostly sandstone at Navajo Lake, but the Nacimiento Formation is dominantly mudstone and siltstone. It forms slopes that are color banded gray, red and white beneath ledges of brown sandstone of the San Jose Formation.

Eocene rocks at Navajo Lake State Park contain fossil logs and pieces of petrified wood. They may also contain some fragments of fossil bones and teeth, but almost all of the known fossil localities in the San Jose Formation are farther south in the San Juan Basin.

An outstanding geologic feature near Navajo Lake State Park is Angel Peak, a pinnacle of Eocene sandstone, the cliffs of which resemble the outspread wings of an angel. Located 25 miles southwest of the park, Angel Peak is at the head of Kutz Canyon, a vast amphitheater of badlands eroded out of the Paleocene Nacimiento Formation, the rock formation just beneath the San Jose Formation. The peak is a block of sandstone at the base of the San Jose Formation that stands as an erosional remnant above slopes of siltstone and mudstone. Today it is part of Angel Peak Scenic Area, administered by the Bureau of Land Management.

—*Spencer G. Lucas*

If You Plan to Visit

Navajo Lake State Park is 25 miles east of Bloomfield, in the northwest corner of New Mexico. It is reached via US 64 and NM–511. Sims Mesa includes a visitor center with interpretive exhibits, developed campgrounds and a full service marina. The San Juan River area below the dam is world renowned for excellent trout fishing and includes wheelchair-accessible fishing facilities on the river, Cottonwood Campground, seven day-use areas, and several hiking trails. For more information:

View of the mouth of Simon Canyon, a tributary on the north side of the San Juan River three miles below Navajo Dam.

Navajo Lake State Park
1448 NM–511 #1
Navajo Dam, New Mexico 87419
(505) 632-2278
(888) 451-2541
www.emnrd.state.nm.us/nmparks/pages/parks/navajo/navajo.htm

The Simon Canyon Area of Critical Environmental Concern includes 3,900 acres of land adjacent to Navajo Lake State Park. The Angel Peak Scenic Area is off US 550, 15 miles south of Bloomfield on CR 7175. Both are administered by the Bureau of Land Management through the Farmington field office. For more information:

Bureau of Land Management
Farmington Field Office
1235 La Plata Highway, Suite A
Farmington, NM 87401
(505) 599-8900
www.nm.blm.gov/recreation/farmington/farmington_rec_home.htm

Heron Lake and El Vado Lake State Parks

Heron Lake

El Vado Lake State Park and Heron Lake State Park are within a few miles of each other along the Rio Chama. Heron Lake lies on Willow Creek, upstream of the confluence of Willow Creek with the Rio Chama. The U.S. Bureau of Reclamation built Heron Dam in 1967–1971 as part of the San Juan–Chama Project, a massive project designed to move water from the San Juan River Basin to the Rio Grande Basin. The Middle Rio Grande Conservancy District built El Vado Dam, downstream, as a work relief project in 1935 during the Depression. In 1955 the Bureau of Reclamation took control of the operation of El Vado Dam. The County of Los Alamos currently operates an 8.8-megawatt hydroelectric power plant at El Vado Dam. The Rio Chama downstream of the dam is part of the Chama River Canyon Wilderness, administered by the U.S. Forest Service.

The possibility of diverting water from the San Juan River into the Rio Grande was examined soon after World War I but wasn't authorized until 1962, when the U.S. Congress amended the Colorado River Storage Act of 1956, creating the San Juan–Chama Project. This project allows diversion of Colorado River basin water into the Rio Grande. Under the San Juan–Chama Project authorization and the Rio Grande and Colorado compacts, only water imported from the San Juan–Chama Project may be stored in Heron Reservoir. None of the native

Rio Grande water can be stored but is released to the river below Heron Dam.

Water comes to the project from several sources. Water from the Rio Blanco is diverted by tunnel to the Little Navajo River. Water from the Little Navajo River and the Little Oso Diversion Dam goes into the Navajo River, where the 12.8-mile Azotea Tunnel diverts a portion over the Continental Divide. After the underground trip, the water enters Azotea Creek, which flows into Willow Creek and then into Heron Lake. The water in Heron Lake is released into the Rio Chama, into El Vado Lake, and continues downstream via the Rio Chama into the Rio Grande.

Water from the project supplies numerous municipal, industrial, and domestic needs, including drinking water, for the cities of Albuquerque, Santa Fe, Los Alamos, Los Lunas, Espanola, Taos, Bernalillo, and Belen. Water is also supplied to the Twining Water and Sanitation District, the Jicarilla Apaches, the Middle Rio Grande Conservancy District (for irrigation), the Pojoaque Valley Irrigation District, and to Cochiti Reservoir.

El Vado Lake was named after the village of El Vado ("the crossing"), which was established in the late nineteenth century and named for a ford across the Rio Chama. In the early 1900s the town of El Vado was a noisy, bustling railroad and lumber center and the largest town in the county. Railroad spurs of the Rio Grande and Southwestern Railroad branched out from El Vado through the numerous canyons and mesa tops to transport timber to markets. El Vado also was home to a large sawmill, box factory, drying kilns, roundhouse, machine shop, and the usual salons, school, churches, and houses. By 1923 the timber became logged out, the railroad spurs were removed, and El Vado diminished as a viable town. In 1933–1935 the dam was built, which flooded the original town site. Only the cemetery and foundations of a water tower remain above the lake level. A small settlement called El Vado now lies near the entrance to El Vado State Park.

Regional Setting

Both parks lie on the eastern margin of the San Juan Basin in the Colorado Plateau province. Relatively little folding, faulting, or deformation have affected the Colorado Plateau in most places. However, folding and faulting have occurred along the edges of the plateau, including the Heron–El Vado area, which was subjected to regional compression during the Cretaceous and Early Tertiary periods, as a result of the subduction of the oceanic Farallon plate. The area was uplifted during the Laramide orogeny, forming the Sierra Nacimiento, Brazos Mountains, and Rocky Mountains. Heron and El Vado Lakes lie

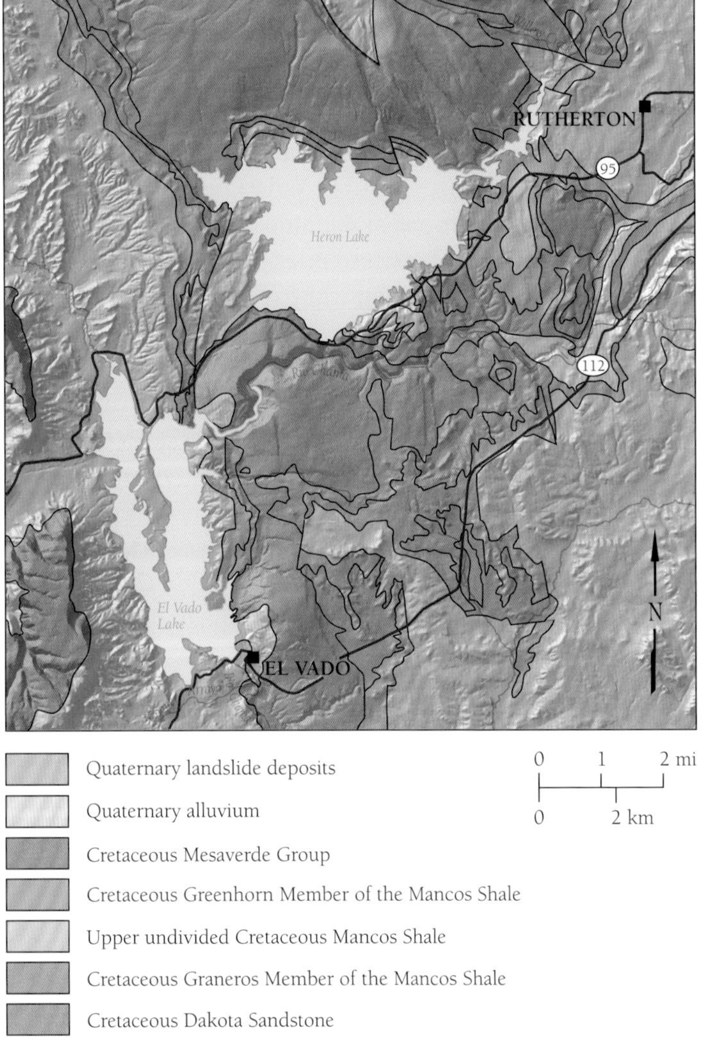

Generalized geologic map of the area surrounding Heron and El Vado Lakes.

along a portion of the Archuleta anticline (also called the Gallina–Archuleta arch), which is the northern extension of the Nacimiento uplift and separates the San Juan Basin to the west from the Chama Basin and Rio Grande valley to the east. The Archuleta anticline was formed during the Eocene after the area was uplifted and the San Juan Basin began to subside, 70–80 million years ago.

Another structural feature that formed during Laramide uplift is El Vado dome. Cretaceous rocks on El Vado dome are visible dipping westward into El Vado Lake. These structural features in the subsurface provide natural traps for the accumulation of oil and natural gas, which have been produced nearby from fractured Cretaceous rocks. The Brazos Mountains of the Southern Rocky Mountain province form the eastern skyline.

The Rock Record

The oldest rocks exposed at both lakes are Cretaceous in age. However, older Jurassic rocks (about 180–140 million years old) are exposed in the bottom of Rio Chama Canyon between Heron and El Vado Lakes and downstream of El Vado Dam. The Jurassic rocks include the upper portions of the Morrison Formation and consist predominantly of reddish-brown to brick-red shale with minor white to green to yellow sandstone and white to gray limestone that were deposited in fluvial and alluvial fan environments.

The Cretaceous Dakota Sandstone (about 100–95 million years ago), 180–210 feet thick, consists of beach and lagoonal sandstone, shale, and conglomeratic sandstone deposited as the shallow Cretaceous sea advanced across New Mexico. Sand, mud, and organic remains were deposited in swamps and fluvial (rivers or streams) environments marginal to the seas, later forming sandstone, shale, and coal. The Dakota Sandstone caps the cliffs and mesas forming Rio Chama Canyon. Overlying the Dakota Sandstone are intertonguing marine shale and nonmarine shale, sandstone, and coal deposits of the Mesaverde Group and Mancos Group, deposited as the Cretaceous seas migrated back and forth across New Mexico. Geologists call this advancement of the marine shoreline with time a transgression. Meandering rivers and streams deposited sand, whereas mud was deposited in the adjacent floodplains. Peat was deposited in poorly drained swamps. Southeast of Tierra Amarilla lies the Tierra Amarilla coal field, representing one of these peat swamps.

The Mancos Group consists of 500–600 feet of shale and interbedded limestone and sandstone that were deposited in shallow marine seas. It is divided into four formations (in ascending order): the Graneros Shale, Greenhorn Limestone, Carlile Shale, and Niobrara Formation. The Greenhorn Limestone is exposed throughout the area and can be seen in road cuts. The Mesaverde Group overlies the Mancos Group and forms the tops of some of the mesas.

Geologic History

The Rio Chama has been cutting into the older rocks for at least the past 4 million years, as a result of regional uplift of the Jemez Mountains and the Sierra Nacimiento. Two million years ago a change in climate took place that increased the flow of the Rio Chama and the downcutting of the river into the older rocks. More recent climatic changes have decreased the water flow.

Small earthquakes went unnoticed in the Heron–El Vado region until 1962 when seismograph stations were established throughout New Mexico. Several earthquakes have been felt in the area, with the largest occurring on January 22, 1966, when a magnitude 5.5 earthquake occurred in the vicinity of Dulce. The greatest damage—broken windows and cracked masonry—was to the Bureau of Indian Affairs office and Dulce schools. The Dulce earthquake was a result of earth movement along a north-trending normal fault approximately 1.8 mile deep. This was the beginning of a series of earthquakes that affected the area. Los Alamos scientists recorded 264 earthquakes between 1976 and 1984. Some studies suggest that these earthquakes may have been enhanced as a result of loading by the reservoir.

—Virginia T. McLemore

If You Plan to Visit

El Vado Lake State Park and Heron Lake State Park are within a few miles of each other along the Rio Chama, 9 miles southwest of Tierra Amarilla and 13 miles southeast of Chama. Heron Lake State Park has been designated a "no wake lake" or "quiet lake" and boats operate at no-wake speeds only. Heron Lake State Park has a visitor center, developed and primitive camping sites, group shelter, restrooms, marina, and nature trail. El Vado State Park facilities include developed and primitive camping sites, group shelter, and restrooms.

NM–96 connects Heron and El Vado Lakes through the Rio Chama Canyon. A 5.5-mile hiking and fishing trail (the Rio Chama Trail) along the Rio Chama from the caprock stairway near Heron Dam crosses the river by a suspension bridge and affords panoramic views and an adventurous route to neighboring El Vado Lake. The trail is open to foot, mountain bike, and horse travel. A shorter hiking trail from Willow Creek campground at Heron Lake leads to a bluff overlooking Heron Lake. For more information:

New Mexico State Parks
1220 South St. Francis Drive
Santa Fe, NM 87505
P.O. Box 1147
Santa Fe, NM 87504
(505) 476-3355
(888) 667-2757
(505) 476-3361 (Fax)
www.emnrd.state.nm.us/PRD/heron.htm
www.emnrd.state.nm.us/PRD/elvado.htm

Ghost Ranch and Vicinity

CARSON NATIONAL FOREST

The area around Abiquiu and Tierra Amarilla preserves a wide variety of geologic features and vistas in a small geographic area. The majestic multihued cliffs near Ghost Ranch inspired the artistry of Georgia O'Keefe, and the stark, bare cliffs of the Brazos Box near Tierra Amarilla are the focus of many photographs. Flat-topped Cerro Pedernal is a landmark that can be seen for miles. Although much of this area is not public land, many of the most spectacular features are visible from US 84 and NM–96.

OPPOSITE: The Rio Chama, at the boundary between the Colorado Plateau and the Rio Grande rift. Capping the hills on the skyline are volcanic deposits from the Jemez volcanic field. The colorful sediments of the Chinle Group are visible at the base of those hills.

Regional Setting

The Abiquiu–Tierra Amarilla area is geologically complex. It sits at the boundary between the Rio Grande rift (to the east) and the Colorado Plateau (to the west). The middle part of the area includes the Chama Basin, which roughly follows the valley of the Rio Chama. This basin is a geological depression that formed during the Laramide orogeny, a compressional basin-forming and mountain-building event. To the west is the San Juan Basin, a bigger version of the Chama Basin, which also formed during the Laramide orogeny. The Chama and San Juan Basins are on the Colorado Plateau, which has been a relatively stable block in the earth's crust for at least 600 million years. Consequently, the rocks around Ghost Ranch are relatively flat-lying and are only mildly deformed by broad-scale folding and localized faulting with offsets of less than 120 feet. To the east and south is the Española Basin, which is part of the Rio Grande rift, a large and complex trench of Tertiary age that runs down the center of New Mexico. To the south is the enormous volcanic complex of the Jemez Mountains and the Valles caldera. To the north and east are the Tusas Mountains, a mass of ancient Precambrian rocks with a veneer of Tertiary volcanic rocks. To the west is the Sierra Nacimiento, which is also composed of Precambrian rocks partially covered with Pennsylvanian to Permian sedimentary rocks. These mountainous areas formed partly during Laramide time and partly at the same time as the Rio Grande rift.

The Rock Record

The Tusas Mountains include a variety of Precambrian rocks that were deposited or emplaced 1,760 to 1,650 million years ago. These rocks include quartzite, a low-grade metamorphic rock that is made up primarily of quartz sand grains that were later recrystallized as the rock

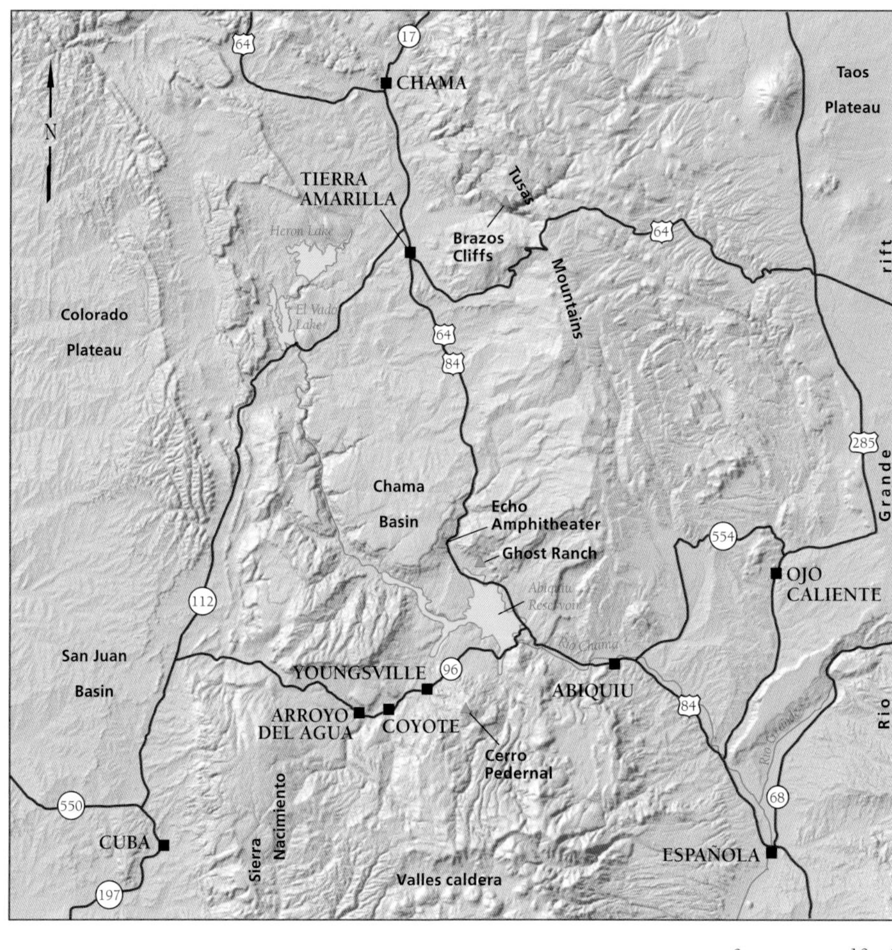

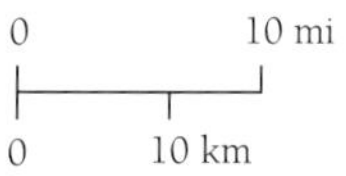

Geographic overview of the Abiquiu region.

was buried and heated. The distinctive grayish-white Ortega Quartzite forms the bold cliffs of the Brazos Box. There is also a range of ancient sedimentary rocks that were metamorphosed in the middle of the crust to form schist and phyllite, as well as basaltic-to-rhyolitic volcanic rocks that were metamorphosed to form amphibolite and metarhyolite.

The scenic red rocks that surround Abiquiu Reservoir and extend off to the west toward Arroyo del Agua and Gallina are sedimentary rocks of Permian and Triassic age. These rocks include the Permian Cutler Group and the Triassic Chinle Group, both of which formed by rivers flowing during times of semi-arid climate. Both of these rock units are well known throughout the Southwest. The Permian Cutler Group is well exposed at Canyonlands National Park in Utah. The Chinle Group is the unit that forms the Painted Desert in Arizona. Both units consist

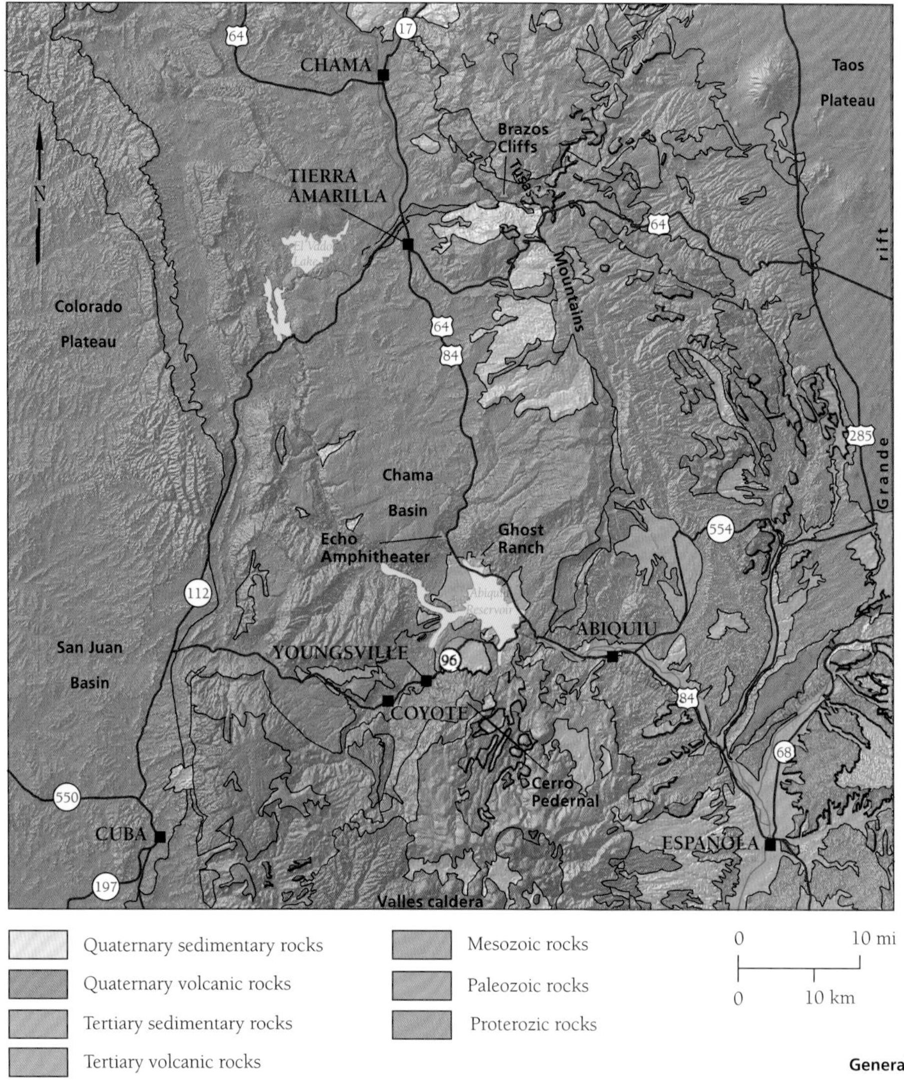

Generalized geologic map of the Abiquiu region.

of thick packages of red siltstone and mudstone and white-to-tan sandstone and conglomerate. These rocks have yielded significant fossils that document the rise of primitive reptiles and subsequently dinosaurs. The most famous are *Limnoscelis*, which is close to being the ancestor of reptiles, found in the 1870s near Abiquiu, and *Coelophysis*, a small meat-eating dinosaur that is the state fossil of New Mexico. The first pieces of *Coelophysis* were found in 1876, but the animal did not become well known until Edwin Colbert of the American Museum of Natural History found a mother lode of hundreds of skeletons at Ghost Ranch in 1947.

The cliffs above Ghost Ranch and the rocks visible along US 84 as it climbs north of Abiquiu Reservoir represent younger Mesozoic rocks, including a sequence of Jurassic and Cretaceous strata. The most prominent Jurassic rocks are the massive red, white, and yellow cliffs of Entrada Sandstone, which formed in a large desert during middle Jurassic time. The Entrada Sandstone contains impressive crossbeds that are several feet high. On top of these cliffs is a thin interval of limestone and a thick pile of soft white gypsum, both part of the Todilto Formation that formed in a large shallow body of saline water that once covered northern New Mexico. Colorful slopes of the maroon Summerville Formation and green Morrison Formation are above the Entrada/Todilto cliffs. The basal 25-to-40 feet of the Summerville Formation is laminated white-to-tan sandstone with ripple marks and casts of gypsum crystals, interbedded with green-to-red mudstone and shale. The basal sandstone unit is overlain by a thick section of maroon mudstone and pinkish-tan, poorly cemented, crossbedded sandstone (Bluff Sandstone) deposited in an arid environment. The Brushy Basin Member, the only member of the Morrison Formation present at Ghost Ranch, consists of pistachio green-to-salmon pink mudstone with a few interbedded tan and green sandstone beds deposited in a slightly more humid setting. Rounded, highly polished stones often interpreted to be *gastroliths* from the digestive tracts of dinosaurs are common in the Morrison Formation in this region.

Jurassic bivalves (in cross section) from basal sandstones of the Summerville Formation on Kitchen Mesa at Ghost Ranch.

Cretaceous rocks, including the Burro Canyon Formation, the Dakota Sandstone, and the Mancos Shale, cap the tall cliffs behind Ghost Ranch and are easily visible as US 84 snakes up past Echo Amphitheater. The Burro Canyon Formation consists of crossbedded medium-to-fine-grained sandstone, quartz and chert pebble conglomerate, and pale-green to pale-red mudstones. The Dakota Sandstone is composed of tan-to-yellow-brown sandstone and interbedded dark gray carbonaceous shale and siltstone (Mancos Shale). Ripple marks on tops of sandstone beds are common. The Cretaceous rocks all formed close to or in the Western Interior Seaway, a shallow sea that split North America north to south during this time period.

Younger strata including basal conglomerates of the Eocene El Rito Formation are visible in a road cut on the north side of US 84 between Abiquiu and Abiquiu Reservoir just as the highway starts to climb out of the white to tan sedimentary rocks deposited in the Rio Grande rift onto the red Permian and Triassic rocks of the Colorado Plateau. The basal conglomerate consists of well-rounded Ortega Quartzite boulders and cobbles derived from the Tusas Mountains to the north during

AGE	UNIT	ROCK TYPE	ENVIRONMENT OF DEPOSITION OR DEFORMATION	BEST SEEN
Pleistocene	Bandelier Tuff	Tuff	Caldera eruption	South of Coyote
Pliocene	Jemez volcanic field lava flows	Andesite basalt dacite	Volcanic eruption	Cerro Pedernal
Miocene	Ojo Caliente Sandstone (Sante Fe Group)	Crossbedded sandstone	Dune field	Abiquiu
	Chama-El Rito Member (Sante Fe Group)	Sandstone, siltstone, conglomerate	River	
	Abiquiu Formation	Sandstone, conglomerate	Braided streams	Abiquiu
Oligocene	Pedernal Chert	Chert, limestone	Silica-rich groundwater	Cerro Pedernal
	Ritito Conglomerate	Conglomerate, Sandstone	River	Abiquiu
Eocene	El Rito Formation	Sandstone, conglomerate	River	West of Abiquiu
Cretaceous	Mancos Shale	Shale, siltstone	Marine	US 84 west of Ghost Ranch
	Dakota Sandstone	Sandstone, shale	Marine to marginal marine	
	Burro Canyon Member	Conglomerate, Sandstone	River	
Jurassic	Morrison Formation (Brushy Basin Member)	Siltstone, sandstone	River and floodplain	Ghost Ranch
	Bluff Sandstone	Crossbedded sandstone	Dune field	
	Summerville Formation	Siltstone, sandstone	Alluvial flat	
	Todilto Formation	Gypsum, limestone	Salina	
	Entrada Sandstone	Crossbedded sandstone	Dune field	
Triassic	Chinle Group	Mudstone, sandstone conglomerate	River	
Permian	Yeso Formation	Crossbedded sandstone	Dune field	South of Coyote
Pennsylvanian	Cutler Group	Sandstone, siltstone	River	Arroyo del Agua
	Madera Group	Limestone, shale, sandstone	Marine	Southern Sierra Nacimiento
Precambrian	Igneous and metamorphic rocks	Quartzite, schist, metavolcanics, amphibolite	Island arc caught up in mountain building	Brazos Cliffs

Generalized stratigraphic record in the vicinity of Ghost Ranch (not to scale).

Laramide uplift of that mountain range. The basal unit is overlain by reddish-orange fine-grained sandstone.

An early Rio Grande rift conglomerate, which contains cobbles of a variety of Precambrian rock types derived from the Tusas Mountains, forms low hills near the village of Abiquiu. The conglomerate is overlain by the Abiquiu Formation, a very distinctive unit that contains volcanic rock fragments and thin beds of volcanic ash derived from the Latir volcanic field north of Taos. The Abiquiu Formation forms the dazzling white ribbed cliffs just west of the town of Abiquiu on both sides of US 84. The Abiquiu Formation is also exposed on Cerro

Pedernal and on highlands as far west as the Sierra Nacimiento. One interesting unit just below the base and within the Abiquiu Formation on the flanks of Cerro Pedernal and on nearby highlands is the Pedernal Chert. Chert is a hard, fine-grained silica-rich rock, often called flint when it is black or dark gray. Prehistoric arrowheads, spear points, and hand axes made from Pedernal Chert have been found hundreds of miles away, and there are several ancient quarries high on Cerro Pedernal.

The prominent cliffs on the west edge of the village of Abiquiu are composed of the Miocene Chama–El Rito Member and the Ojo Caliente Sandstone of the Santa Fe Group. Normally these units are quite soft and form slopes, but fluids that came up along a major fault on the west side of the village, the Cerrito Blanca fault, provided abundant calcium carbonate to cement the rocks. The Chama–El Rito Member is an ancestral Rio Chama deposit containing small rounded pebbles of volcanic rocks derived from San Juan volcanic field near the New Mexico–Colorado state line to the north. The crossbedded Ojo Caliente Sandstone formed a sand dune field that once covered the area between the Sierra Nacimineto and Española.

The majority of younger rocks are volcanic in origin, or are sedimentary rocks eroded from volcanoes. Cerro Pedernal, the high mountain with a distinctive flat top just south of Abiquiu Reservoir, is capped by 8-million-year-old andesite flows from the Jemez volcanic field. The mesas south and west of Abiquiu are also capped by basaltic-to-andesitic rocks from the Jemez volcanic field that are as young as 3 million years old.

Geologic History

The geologic history of the area is delightfully complicated. The oldest Precambrian rocks in the Tusas Mountains are 1,693 to 1,760 million-year-old basaltic-to-rhyolitic volcanic rocks and associated intrusions that formed in a volcanic arc setting. These rocks were buried, deformed, and then eroded to be exposed at the earth's surface. Sedimentary rocks of the Vadito Group and the Ortega Quartzite overlie these deformed volcanic rocks. Although deposition of sediment continued until 1,650 million years ago, this whole package was buried and deformed starting 1,690 million years ago. The Precambrian rocks did not come back up to the earth's surface until middle Pennsylvanian time, 315 million years ago during Ancestral Rocky Mountain deformation, when the Tusas Mountains were part of the Uncompahgre/San Luis uplift that occupied much of north-central New Mexico.

Rocks with ages between 1,650 and 300 million years are not exposed in the immediate vicinity of Ghost Ranch, although the Madera Limestone of Pennsylvanian age is present in the subsurface and is exposed on the flanks of Sierra Nacimiento to the west. Starting 300 million years ago, the ocean shoreline retreated toward the south, and a south-flowing river system drained the region. The lower part of the Cutler Group contains abundant cobbles and pebbles of Proterozoic quartzite and granite likely derived from areas to the northeast, off of the Ancestral Rocky Mountain Uncompahgre/San Luis uplift. As time went on we know the climate started to dry out because channel sandstones in the upper part of the Cutler Group are much less common that they are in the older part.

Seventy-two million years of geologic history is missing at the contact between the Cutler Group and the Chinle Group. The Late Triassic Chinle Group was deposited by large Mississippi River-scale river systems flowing from central Texas toward the northwest between 205 and 228 million years ago. At that time the Ghost Ranch area was located about 10 degrees north of the equator.

A significant unconformity representing a gap of 44 million years is present between the late Triassic rocks and the middle Jurassic rocks at Ghost Ranch. The eroded, muddy top of the Chinle Group was desiccated when sands of the Entrada first moved across this region, as evidenced by the sand-filled mud cracks on top of the Chinle Group. The Entrada Sandstone deposits at Ghost Ranch are remnants of a vast sand dune field that covered much of northern New Mexico, southwestern Colorado, southeastern Utah, and northeastern Arizona. The dip of crossbeds in the Entrada Sandstone has been used to determine that the sand was transported by wind blowing toward the south to southwest.

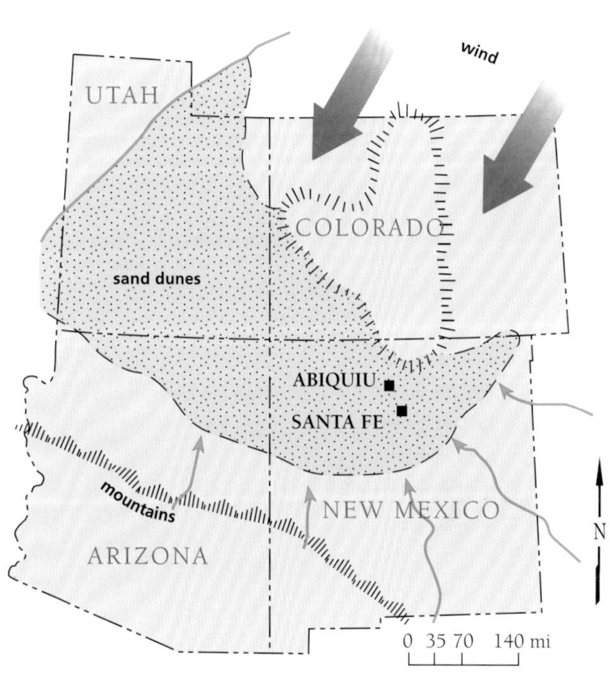

The Jurassic Entrada Sandstone dune field extended hundreds of miles to the northwest.

The Entrada dune field may have been flooded catastrophically, with very little reworking of the sand dunes, by an arm of the Jurassic Sundance Sea, which was in east-central Utah during this time period. The resulting Todilto Formation was most likely deposited during evaporation of a *salina*, a moderately deep, oxygen-poor, body of saline water that was isolated from the main body of the Jurassic ocean by a

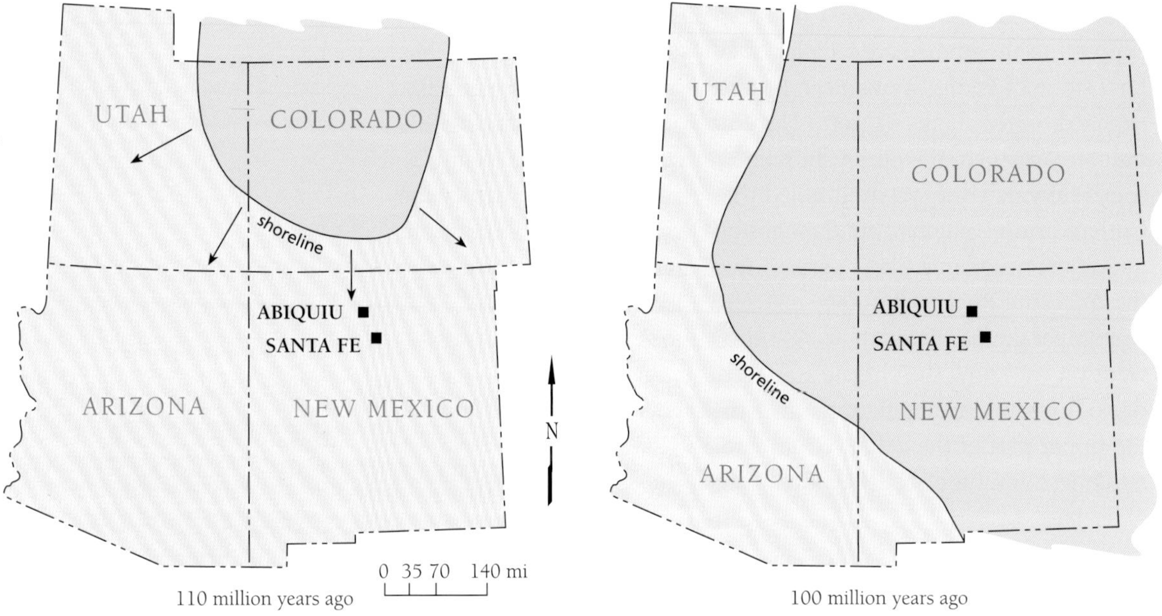

The Dakota Sandstone was deposited as seas advanced from the north/northwest in the late Cretaceous in response to worldwide changes in sea level. This was the first advance of the Western Interior Seaway.

barrier. The Todilto grades into the Summerville Formation, which was deposited on an arid coastal plain. The Bluff Sandstone, exposed near the top of the Summerville Formation, represents a return to eolian deposition in this area. Crossbeds in the Bluff Sandstone record winds blowing toward the east during this time interval.

An unconformity between the Summerville Formation and the overlying Morrison Formation marks a major plate tectonic reorganization of the southwestern United States and a shift from an arid to a more humid environment in this region. The Jurassic Morrison Formation was deposited by rivers flowing northeast across a broad, low-gradient muddy floodplain that dipped toward the north to northeast away from the developing Mogollon highlands in southwestern New Mexico and southeastern Arizona. Radiometric dating of ash beds in the Brushy Basin Member in Utah and Colorado yields ages of 148 to 150 million years for this unit.

Burrows of marine organisms on the base of a block of Dakota Sandstone near Ghost Ranch.

The mesas around Ghost Ranch are capped by Cretaceous coastal plain, shoreline, and marine units that were deposited along the western edge of the Western Interior Seaway 93 to 125 million years ago. Twenty-five million years of earth history is missing across the contact between the Late Jurassic Morrison Formation and the Early Cretaceous Burro Canyon Formation, deposited by braided streams flowing north/northeast across a coastal plain. This unit is 100 to 125 million years old. The Dakota Sandstone records the alternating rise (shale) and fall (sandstones) of sea level as the shoreline moved back and forth across the area 98 to 100 million years ago. The sandstones of the

Dakota Sandstone are locally crossbedded, but in general the sandstones were intensely burrowed by marine organisms living in the shallow water along the shores of the Western Interior Seaway. A gradual, long-term rise in sea level deposited rocks of the Mancos Shale on a shallow ocean floor 98 million years ago.

Starting 75 million years ago, compressional Laramide deformation delineated the major basins (Chama and San Juan) and uplifts (Tusas and Sierra Nacimiento) of the region. Several small monoclines, including those visible from NM–96 north of Coyote and near Arroyo del Agua, formed during this time frame. The Eocene El Rito Formation was deposited in the low spot between the Tusas Mountains and Sierra Nacimiento.

Triassic and Jurassic sedimentary rocks form this cliff near the Box Canyon trail at Ghost Ranch. The brick-red Chinle Group at the base of the cliff is overlain by red, white, and yellow-banded Jurassic Entrada Formation. The banding is caused by variable chemical reactions with iron within the sandstone. The cliff is capped by gray Todilto Formation.

A broad basin developed between the Sierra Nacimiento and the Sangre de Cristo Mountains starting 30 to 35 million years ago and accumulated first sediments of the Abiquiu Formation and later Santa Fe Group sediments. Normal faulting associated with the Rio Grande rift began to disrupt the basin 25 million years ago. The basaltic dikes that can be seen along US 84 west of Abiquiu were emplaced 18 to 20 million years ago, signaling the onset of volcanic activity in the vicinity of the Jemez Mountains. The main phase of volcanism in the Jemez Mountains started at about ten million years ago. The Rio Grande rift, accommodated by normal faults with hundreds of feet of displacement, mainly formed in this area between 13 and 3 million years ago.

The youngest units around Ghost Ranch and Abiquiu are Quaternary terrace and pediment gravels exposed along the drainages, especially the Rio Chama, and extensive landslide and colluvial deposits along the escarpments. Many of the terrace gravels contain quartzite that is likely derived from the Tusas Mountains to the northeast of Ghost Ranch, either directly from the Precambrian Ortega Quartzite, or from quartzite clasts recycled from the Eocene El Rito Formation on the west flank of the mountain range.

Geologic Features

GHOST RANCH—Privately owned and run by the Presbyterian Church, Ghost Ranch includes two public museums. The Ruth Hall Museum of

Paleontology focuses on the Triassic fossils of the area, notably *Coelophysis*. There is a trail up to the quarry where the skeletons of this dinosaur were excavated. The scenic red cliffs behind Ghost Ranch and Georgia O'Keefe's house, which is adjacent to the ranch, are formed by the uppermost part of the Chinle Group, capped by the Entrada Sandstone and the prominent white gypsum of the Todilto Formation. Several trails, including the Chimney Rock, the Kitchen Mesa, and the Box Canyon trails, allow visitors to more closely examine the upper parts of the Triassic and lower portions of the Jurassic sections at Ghost Ranch. The lower part of the Chinle Group can be seen a few miles away at Abiquiu Dam.

Cerro Pedernal on the horizon, with Triassic Chinle sandstone and siltstone along the shore of Abiquiu Reservoir in the foreground.

CERRO PEDERNAL—Located in the Santa Fe National Forest, Cerro Pedernal is a popular climbing destination. Late Triassic to Early Cretaceous sedimentary rocks are exposed around the northern and eastern base of Cerro Pedernal, while younger Cenozoic basin fill sediments underlie the shoulders of the peak. The Pedernal Chert occurs just below the base of the Abiquiu Formation, where it is locally interlayered with thin beds of the underlying arkosic sandstone and conglomerate. The unit, a conspicuous ledge former, can be massive chert, limey chert, or limestone containing nodular chert. The chert can be red, yellow, black, white, gray, or bluish gray. Cerro Pedernal, which means "flint mountain," derives its name from this unit. South and west of Cerro Pedernal, the Pedernal Chert is present at several intervals within the Abiquiu Formation, and the chert is totally absent near the village of Abiquiu. The distribution of the unit indicates that it formed sometime after the Abiquiu Formation was deposited and is likely a diagenetic unit that formed as silica-enriched ground water moved through and precipitated in the sediment. The andesite flows capping Cerro Pedernal give the mountain its distinctive flat top and were erupted from the northern Jemez volcanic field about 8 million years ago.

ECHO AMPHITHEATER—A few miles north of Ghost Ranch on US 84 is the Echo Amphitheater, on the Carson National Forest. Here high cliffs of Entrada Sandstone form a natural amphitheater. Look closely at the Entrada Sandstone and you can see inclined lines of stratification running at angles to one another through the cliffs. These are called crossbeds, and they outline the faces of ancient sand dunes. The red rocks at

Echo Amphitheater is cut into the Jurassic Entrada Formation. This rock unit is underlain by brick-red Chinle (lower right) and overlain by Todilto Formation.

the base of the cliff are the Triassic Chinle Group. The thinly bedded gray rocks and white soft rocks on top of the Entrada Sandstone cliffs are the Todilto Formation.

THE BRAZOS BOX—East of Tierra Amarilla on US 64 there are great views to the north of the feature known as the Brazos Box. Here extremely tall cliffs of Precambrian Ortega Quartzite rise above the trees. The Rio Brazos has cut a 2,000-feet-deep gorge through the quartzite. Rivers do not cut slots through rocks unless the rock slowly rises. Raise a piece of cheese up through a cheese wire and you will end up with a slot. Imagine the wire is the Rio Brazos and the cheese is the quartzite, to get some idea of how the Brazos Box formed.

The Ortega Quartzite exposed in the Brazos Box was deposited along the ancient southern margin of the North American continent 1.7 billion years ago.

HOPEWELL LAKE—Traveling farther east on US 64 you will reach Hopewell Lake on the Carson National Forest. If you hike around this area you will see Precambrian rocks. The rocks in this area are metamorphosed igneous rocks and include altered volcanic rocks that are now hornblende schist as well as a 1.7 billion-year-old intrusive granodiorite. Placer gold mining is part of the history of the Hopewell Lake area. Modern-day gold panners still work the main drainage below the lake.

—Adrian P. Hunt and Shari A. Kelley

Additional Reading

The Little Dinosaurs of Ghost Ranch by E. H. Colbert. Columbia University Press, 1995.

Ghost Ranch by Lesley Poling-Kempes. University of Arizona Press, 2005.

Geology of the Chama Basin edited by Spencer Lucas, Kate Zeigler, Virgil Lueth, and Donald Owen. New Mexico Geological Society 56th Annual Field Conference Guidebook, 2005.

If You Plan to Visit

The Abiquiu–Tierra Amarilla area is most easily accessed by taking US 84 north from Española. An alternate, more scenic route is by way of NM–96 west from US 550 just north of Cuba. Not all of this is public land, although much of the geology is visible from the highway. Portions of it are included in the Carson National Forest, including Hopewell Lake. Abiquiu Reservoir is managed by the U.S. Army Corps of Engineers. Ghost Ranch is privately owned, though the museums and trails there are open to the public.

Cerro Pedernal can be accessed by driving 27 miles northwest from Española on US 84, then turning west (left) onto NM–96 toward Youngsville. Travel 11.5 miles west and watch carefully for a small brown sign marking Forest Road 100, a gravel road on the south side of the highway, and turn left. The left turn into Temoline Canyon (Forest Road 160) on the south side of Cerro Pedernal is located 5.7 miles south along Forest Road 100. You can park your car here and walk about 3 miles up the road to an open meadow at the base of the steep slope near the top of Cerro Pedernal, or you can drive a high clearance four-wheel-drive vehicle to the meadow. For more information:

Carson National Forest
208 Cruz Alta Road
Taos, NM 87571
(575) 758-6200
www.fs.fed.us/r3/carson/

Ghost Ranch Conference Center
HC 77, Box 11
Abiquiu, NM 87510-9601
(505) 685-4333
www.ghostranch.org

PART 2

THE JEMEZ MOUNTAINS AND THE VALLES CALDERA

The Jemez Mountains in north-central New Mexico are the geographic expression of a series of volcanic eruptions that occurred over the past 15 million years. The two largest of these eruptions, which occurred 1.6 and 1.2 million years ago, produced the rock seen in the distinctive white-to-salmon-colored cliffs that form a spectacular backdrop around much of the area, including Bandelier National Monument. These two very explosive eruptions poured hundreds of cubic miles of hot ash, pumice, and gas over the landscape. Since then erosion has shaped these rocks into the beautiful landscape characteristic of the area. These eruptions also formed the large volcanic crater or *caldera* that is now part of the Valles Caldera National Preserve. Bandelier National Monument, Kasha-Katuwe Tent Rocks National Monument, Jemez State Monument, Battleship Rock and Soda Dam, the Jemez Wild and Scenic River, and Fenton Lake State Park are all within the Jemez Mountains.

OPPOSITE: **View of the caldera floor as seen from the eastern rim.**

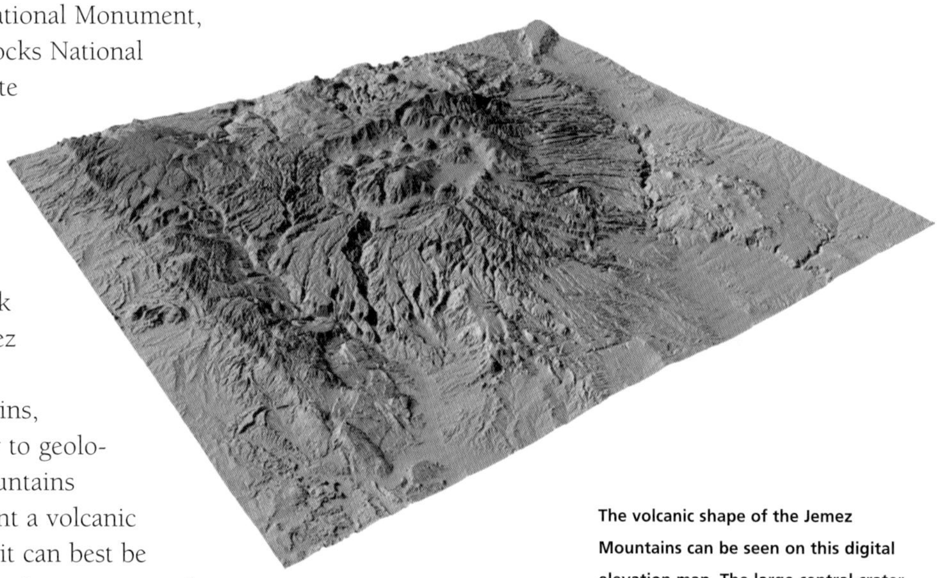

The Jemez Mountains, known more precisely to geologists as the Jemez Mountains volcanic field, represent a volcanic complex so large that it can best be recognized from space. As you approach the Jemez Mountains, it is difficult to perceive the volcanic form because it is on such a large scale. However, on a digital elevation map of the mountains, the volcanic shape, particularly the large central caldera, becomes evident.

The volcanic shape of the Jemez Mountains can be seen on this digital elevation map. The large central crater or caldera, nearly 15 miles in diameter, can be seen in the middle of the broader accumulation of volcanic rocks.

The Jemez Mountains are one of the three largest volcanic centers in the United States that have been active over the past 2 million years. The other two are Yellowstone volcano, in Wyoming, and the Long Valley caldera in California. These three "supervolcanoes" all have produced large, highly explosive eruptions that resulted first in widespread ash and pumice deposits, followed by the eruption of *pyroclastic flows*, which produced much of the cliff-forming rock in the Jemez Mountains. This style of eruption is so explosive that during the last

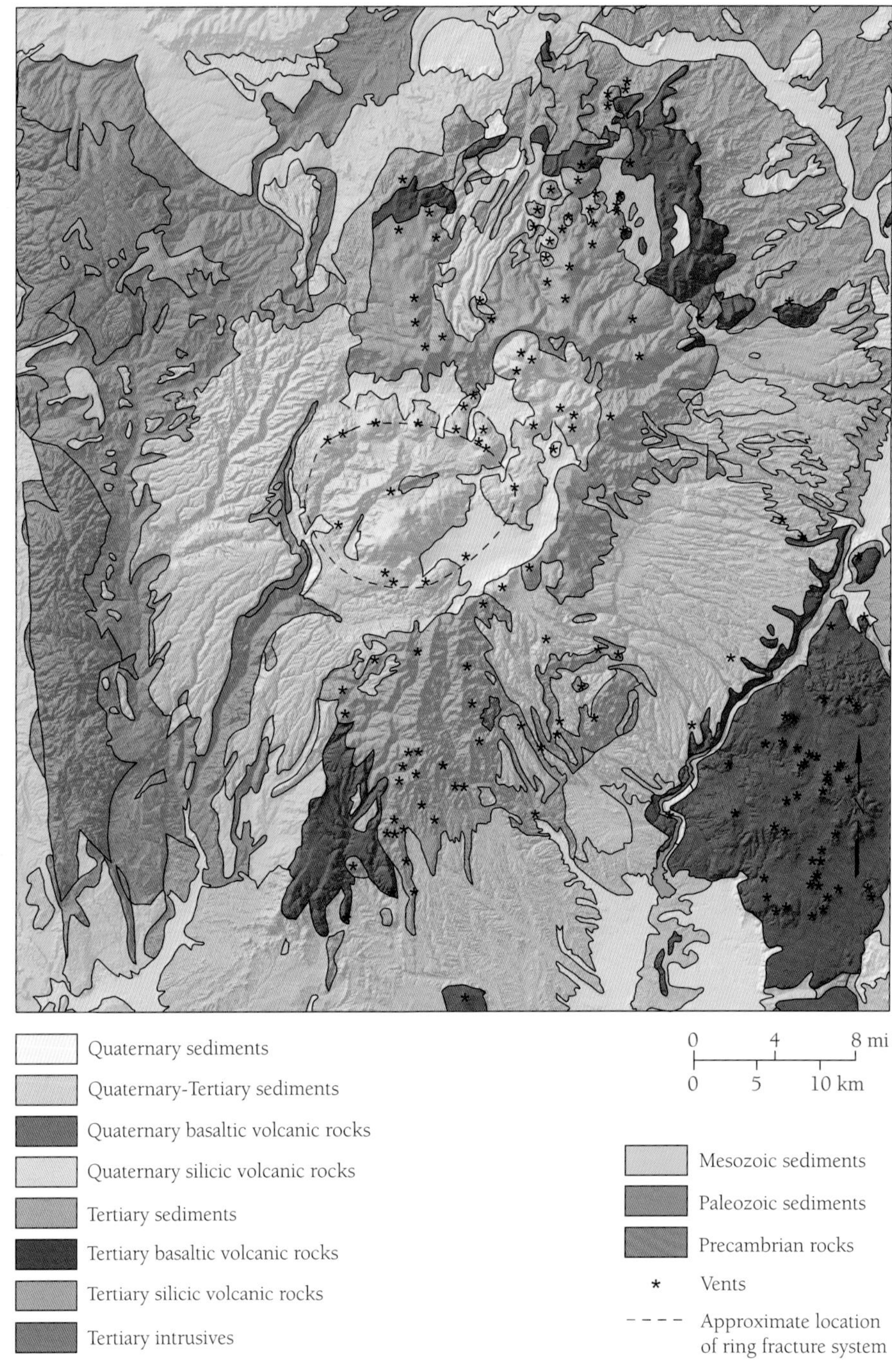

Generalized geologic map of the Jemez Mountains.

major eruption of Yellowstone volcano, as much as 5 inches of ash was deposited in parts of New Mexico.

The Jemez Mountains volcanic field is at the intersection of two zones of crustal weakness: the Rio Grande rift and the Jemez lineament. These zones of weakness in the earth's crust and underlying mantle allow magma to rise from deep within the earth to the earth's surface, at which point a volcano can form. The Rio Grande rift is a major zone of crustal weakness that runs north-south through New Mexico. It formed in the last 35 million years or so in order to accommodate stretching of the crust in this part of North America in an east-to-west direction. The surface expression of the Rio Grande rift today is a broad, shallow valley caused by down dropping of blocks of the crust along a series of rift-bounding faults. The Rio Grande flows through a series of broad valleys created by this stretching process. The Jemez lineament is a more subtle crustal feature; it is expressed as an alignment of volcanic vents of late Cenozoic age, including (but not limited to) the Zuni–Bandera volcanic field, Mount Taylor, and the Jemez Mountains volcanic field. This zone may be the expression of a weakness formed

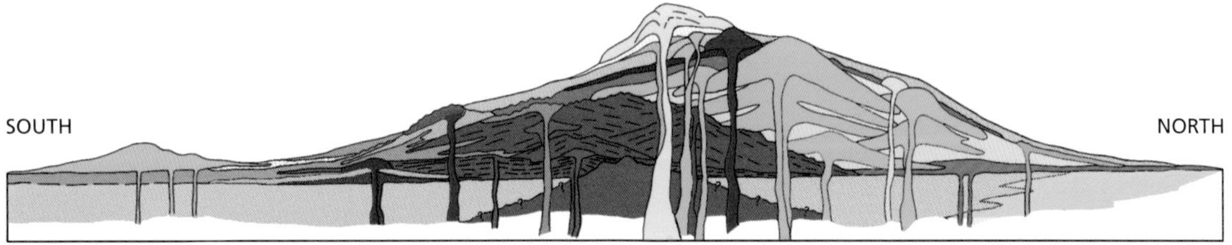

This schematic cross section of the Jemez Mountains volcanic field illustrates the complex history of the field and the gradual accumulation of volcanic material of different ages and types. The yellow represents the eruptive domes that appeared following the collapse of the caldera.

where two very old blocks of the earth's crust were pressed together billions of years ago, or it may be the result of anomalies in the underlying mantle. The exact nature of the Jemez lineament is still not fully understood.

Building the Foundation of the Jemez Mountains

The Jemez Mountains volcanic field's large size is due in part to the very long time over which it has been active. The first eruptions of the volcanic field took place around 15 million years ago, and eruptions have been occurring on and off ever since. Between 15 and 1.6 million years ago the eruptions were relatively small and occurred over a wide geographic area of roughly 40 miles by 40 miles. No large central crater or caldera developed at this time, but many small vents were formed. These many, small eruptions created deposits that are the foundation of the present Jemez Mountains and may be seen in many areas on the flanks of the volcanic complex. The eruptive style of these many small eruptions varied widely, from passive, Hawaiian-style basaltic eruptions (see discussion of this type of volcanism in the El Malpais National Monument chapter of this book) to more explosive eruptive styles. This was due in part to the chemical composition of the magma at the time of eruption. The chemical composition varied widely, from basaltic to rhyolitic, with the dominant rock type being andesite. After these small volcanic deposits formed, they were eroded by rivers or rain, resulting in thick sequences of sediment formed largely from volcanic material. These sedimentary sequences, called *volcaniclastic*, can be observed interbedded with lava flows in many parts of the Jemez Mountains volcanic field. This phase of eruptive activity, between 15 and 1.6 million years ago, produced about 500 cubic miles of volcanic rock, more than half of the total volume of the entire volcanic field.

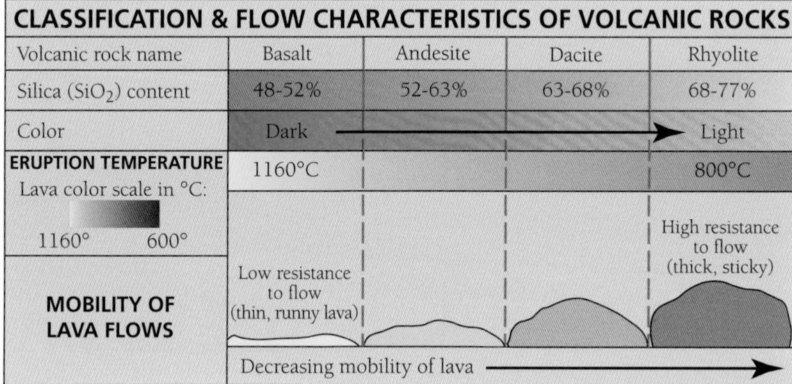

CLASSIFICATION & FLOW CHARACTERISTICS OF VOLCANIC ROCKS				
Volcanic rock name	Basalt	Andesite	Dacite	Rhyolite
Silica (SiO_2) content	48-52%	52-63%	63-68%	68-77%
Color	Dark →			Light
ERUPTION TEMPERATURE Lava color scale in °C: 1160° 600°	1160°C			800°C
MOBILITY OF LAVA FLOWS	Low resistance to flow (thin, runny lava)			High resistance to flow (thick, sticky)
	Decreasing mobility of lava →			

A wide range of volcanic rock types are represented in the Jemez Mountains. Characteristics of the rocks and the lavas from which they formed are closely related to composition.

The Big Events—Eruption of the Bandelier Tuff

Approximately 1.6 million years ago the most spectacular eruptive activity of the Jemez Mountain volcanic field began. Two major explosive eruptions took place at 1.6 and 1.2 million years ago, releasing at least 150 cubic miles of magma. These eruptions ultimately resulted in the formation of the 15-mile-diameter crater known as the Valles caldera. Because no eruption of this size has ever been witnessed or documented, geologists can't know exactly what the eruption looked like. However, study of the volcanic deposits has provided information about the likely sequence of events. Both eruptions probably followed a similar eruption pattern, beginning with a very explosive stage that ejected ash high into the stratosphere. The eruption column probably would have been around 30 miles high, composed of pumice, fine-grained ashy dust, and hot gas. This material then would have been transported away from the volcano by the wind in an eruption cloud. As the cloud traveled, pumice and ash would have rained on the landscape, resulting in a type of deposit called an *ash fall* (stage 1 in the illustration to the right). The ash fall would have blanketed the area around the volcano like hot, dusty snow, and would have been thickest downwind of the volcano.

Ash from this phase of the eruptions was distributed widely throughout New Mexico and has been identified as far away as Lubbock, Texas. As much as 10 feet of ash have been measured as far as 10 miles from the vent. Ash layers 5 inches thick have been identified in Socorro, 180 miles south of the main vent. The pattern of ash deposition reveals information about the wind direction at the time of the eruptions. During one of the eruptive phases, the winds appear to have been blowing strongly from the west. During another eruptive phase, the winds appear to have been calmer and coming from the southeast. The ash fall from the Bandelier eruptions can be observed in roadcuts on the east side of the Jemez Mountains as a white, layered deposit composed entirely of pumice.

The next phase of these large eruptions was very different from the ash fall phase, and represents a far more dangerous type of eruption. This type of eruption is called an ash flow or *ignimbrite* eruption, and typically occurs associated with but following an ash fall eruption. The ash component of the eruption takes place when the volcanic vent or conduit is narrow, allowing the volcanic column to be projected upward to great height. An analogy to this is what occurs when you shake up a bottle of carbonated water and take off the cap. The narrow neck of the bottle will direct the jet of water upward to considerable height. However, as a volcanic eruption proceeds and magma is removed from the underlying chamber, the conduit may begin to break down. When this happens, the formerly high and distinct eruption column collapses, generating a hot mass of ash, pumice, gas, and crystals (mostly quartz and feldspar) that flows across the surrounding terrain at speeds up to the speed of sound (stages 2 and 3). This hot mass eventually comes to rest, forming a deposit called an *ignimbrite*. Whereas deposition of the ash fall

Stage 1—Ash fall

Stage 2—Beginning of column collapse

Stage 3—Full column collapse

Stage 4—Formation of caldera

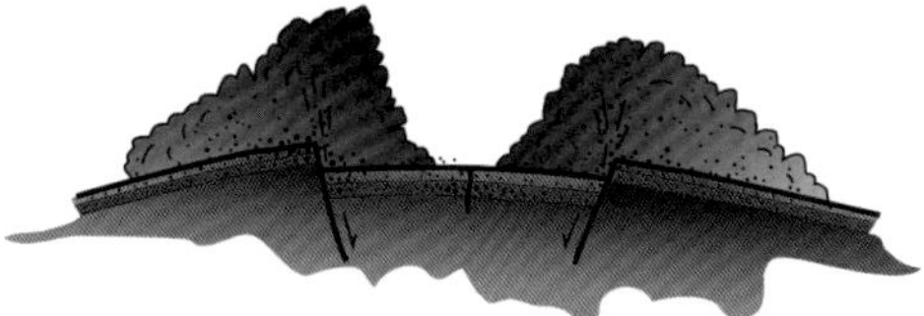

Stage 5—Final stage of ignimbrite eruption

Stages of eruption that produced the Bandelier Tuff. Stage numbers are keyed to references in text.

component of the eruption is controlled in part by wind direction at the time of the eruption, the ignimbrite components of the eruption are distributed more or less evenly around the vent.

Two large ignimbrites erupted from the caldera at 1.6 and 1.2 million years ago and formed the white-to-salmon-colored cliffs found

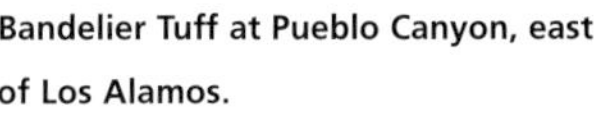

Bandelier Tuff at Pueblo Canyon, east of Los Alamos.

in many canyons around the Jemez Mountains. The maximum thicknesses of these two deposits (collectively known as the Bandelier Tuff) are 600 feet for the older (the lower Bandelier Tuff) and 800 feet for the younger (the upper Bandelier Tuff). The total volume of magma erupted during the ignimbrite phase of these eruptions was around 90 cubic miles and 55 cubic miles respectively. As magma was removed from the magma chamber during the eruptions, the roof of the chamber progressively collapsed, resulting in a large, circular crater or caldera, which partially filled with material from the final eruptive stage (stage 5). The second of these eruptions produced the Valles caldera.

Between the two large eruptions that produced the lower and upper Bandlier Tuff, a series of much smaller eruptions occurred, resulting in a set of rocks called the Cerro Toledo rhyolites. The Cerro Toledo rhyolites comprise a series of small ash fall deposits, as well as a series of volcanic domes and lava flows. The high viscosity rhyolite lava doesn't flow as readily as basaltic lava and tends to accumulate around the vent, forming a dome-shaped pile of lava. One example of a Cerro Toledo dome is Rabbit Mountain. A number of young rhyolite domes are present within the Valles caldera. The Cerro Toledo domes and ashes erupted from along the fractured edge of the caldera left by the 1.6-million-year-old eruption of lower Bandelier Tuff. The first of the Cerro Toledo eruptions began about 100,000 years after the 1.6 million-year-old Bandelier Tuff eruption, and the eruptions continued until just before 1.2 million years. Although the Cerro Toledo rhyolite eruptions are small in volume, study of the geochemical composition of the deposits from these eruptions has allowed researchers to understand the chemical processes that took place as the magma chamber under the caldera refilled between the two large eruptions.

Activity Since 1.2 Million Years Ago

After the second large eruption that took place 1.2 million years ago, the Valles caldera filled with a shallow lake. The lake was disrupted by a non-eruptive event that created a landform that dominates the landscape of the Valles caldera today. The process is called *resurgence*. Although the exact geologic mechanisms that cause resurgence are not well understood, the result is that the floor of the very large crater formed by the 1.2 million-year-old eruption of the upper Bandelier Tuff was bowed upward, forming the topographic dome called Redondo Peak. The formation of Redondo Peak may have occurred in as little as 40,000 years following the 1.2 million-year-old eruption. Following the formation of the resurgent dome of Redondo Peak, a number of volcanic domes and lava flows formed around the margins of the crater. These eruptions began shortly after the resurgence of Redondo Peak and continued until about half a million years ago, forming a set of well-defined landforms that can be seen in the Valles Caldera National Preserve. The domes and flows are concentrated along an arcuate ring fracture, and there is an age progression in the domes, with the oldest being on the eastern side of the caldera, the others becoming progressively younger in a counterclockwise direction.

The Most Recent Activity

The most recent eruptive activity in the Jemez Mountains volcanic field is represented by deposits from a relatively small set of eruptions. These eruptions are thought to have occurred 50,000 to 60,000 years ago. Some of the material from these eruptions can be seen as tuff at Battleship Rock and in roadcuts of pumice and obsidian along NM–4. Deposits from these eruptions include the El Cajete ash fall deposit, the Banco Bonito lava dome, and the Battleship Rock ignimbrite. Reseachers have shown that these three deposits are chemically different from the older Valles rhyolites and are thought to be part of a distinct batch of new magma. The presence of the new magma seen in these deposits suggests that the Jemez Mountains volcanic field may be entering a new phase of activity. These small eruptions may be the precursors to further eruptive activity. The Jemez Mountains volcanic field is likely to erupt again, but the next eruption may not take place for thousands, or even tens of thousands of years.

—Nelia W. Dunbar

Valles Caldera National Preserve

VALLES CALDERA TRUST

The Valles Caldera National Preserve is one of the most geologically unique and significant areas in North America. The preserve encompasses much of the Valles caldera, a huge volcanic crater that formed 1.2 million years ago during an enormous volcanic eruption that spread ash over large parts of New Mexico. The caldera is located near the summit of the Jemez Mountains, a large volcanic complex in north-central New Mexico. The Valles caldera exhibits world-class examples of the landforms produced by a very large, explosive volcano, and the preservation and exposure of geological features within the Valles is spectacular. Much of what geologists know about large-scale explosive volcanism began with detailed studies of the rocks in the Valles caldera and Jemez Mountains, and the area continues to draw geologists from around the world. Since the eruption 1.2 million years ago, there has been uplift of the crater floor, followed by the eruption of smaller, younger volcanoes called "domes" within the crater left by the large eruption. Since then, the caldera has from time to time been home to a series of large lakes. This dynamic geological history is responsible for the beautiful and unique landscape that we see in the region today.

Movie set on the caldera floor, with Cerro La Jara dome in background. Cerro La Jara is one of a series of domes that erupted following the explosive eruptions of Bandelier Tuff.

Regional Setting

The Jemez Mountains, in which the Valles Caldera National Preserve is located, are situated at the intersection of the Rio Grande rift, a major zone of crustal weakness formed by stretching of the continental crust, and the Jemez lineament, which is a second, more poorly defined crustal zone along which volcanism has occurred. The large and long-lived nature of the Jemez Mountains volcanic field may be related to its location at the intersection of these two major crustal anomalies.

EVENT	AGE (YEARS)
Banco Bonito lava dome	60,000–50,000
Battleship Rock tuff & ignimbrite	60,000–50,000
El Cajete ash fall	60,000–50,000
Valles rhyolites	1.2–0.5 million
Upper Bandelier Tuff	1.2 million
Cerro Toledo Rhyolite	1.52–1.43 million
Lower Bandelier Tuff	1.6 million

Major Jemez Mountains and Valles caldera eruptive events.

The Rock Record

Three main packages of rocks are present in the Valles Caldera National Preserve. The first group includes rocks related to the eruption of the upper member of the Bandelier Tuff, which occurred 1.2 million years ago and formed the large volcanic crater that frames the preserve. These rocks are mainly exposed in the area around Redondo Peak, which is a part of the crater floor that was uplifted following the major eruption of the Bandelier Tuff. These rocks are dense and hard, and typically grayish to purple. They contain small glassy-looking crystals of quartz and feldspar and in some cases exhibit faint layering, which is caused by the rock being compressed while still hot after eruption.

The second package of rocks in the preserve is formed by the eruption of a number of volcanic domes which form the rounded hills around the periphery of the preserve. These domes include Cerro Del Medio, Cerro Abrigo, Cerro Santa Rosa, Cerro La Jara, and South Mountain. These volcanic domes, which consist of several rock types, erupted after the large 1.2 million year old eruption. Most of the domes are composed primarily of a fine-grained, gray-to-pinkish crystalline rhyolite. A second, very notable rock type associated with the domes is rhyolitic obsidian. This black, glassy rock is present in parts of some of the domes, and represents the same chemical rock composition as the crystalline rhyolite. The obsidian cooled quickly upon eruption, producing the glassy texture, whereas the crystalline rhyolite cooled more slowly, allowing time for the crystals to grow. Obsidian is typically found on the outer part or "carapace" of the domes. Obsidian from the Valles caldera domes was widely used as tool-making material by local prehistoric Puebloan cultures, and a number of quarries and tool-making sites have been identified on the flanks of the volcanic domes.

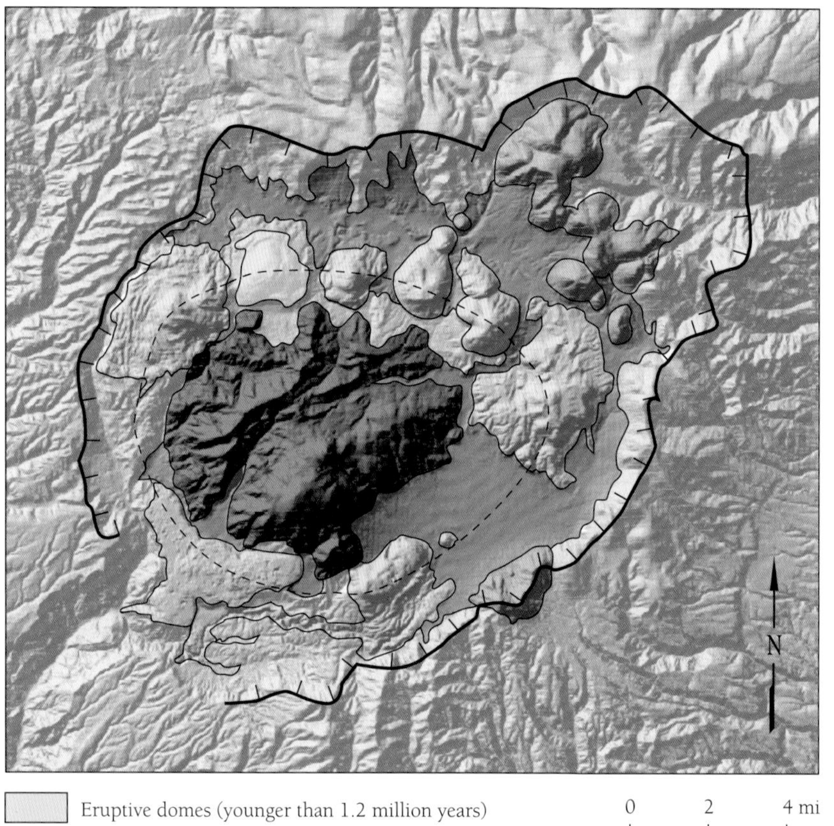

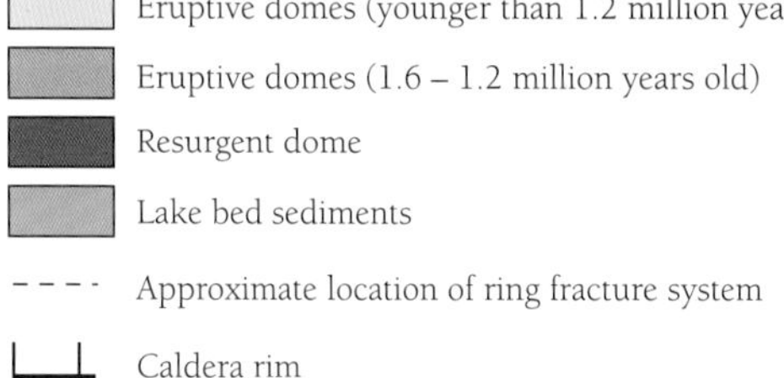

Detailed map of the Valles caldera, showing the resurgent dome (Redondo Peak) and the younger eruptive domes that surround it.

Another rock type associated with the Valles caldera domes is rhyolitic pumice. The whitish-colored, frothy rock can best be observed around South Mountain. Thick roadcuts of pumice can be seen along NM–4 on the western approach to the Valles Caldera National Preserve.

The third package of rocks found in the Valles caldera is the most difficult to see and includes remnants of lakes that once occupied the floor of the caldera. These lake sediments are being studied to help us understand the climate history during the time that they were deposited. Although the sediments are exposed only in a few places, the evidence of these lakes is clearly visible in the notable flatness of the caldera floor between the volcanic domes. Additional evidence for the presence of lakes in the caldera includes wave-cut terraces and the presence of water-deposited gravels on the flanks of some of the volcanic domes.

In addition to these three main packages of rocks, older rocks are exposed in a few places in the preserve. On the northern wall of the caldera, older volcanic rocks and sediments associated with the Jemez Mountains volcanic field can be seen. In several places on the Redondo Peak resurgent dome, large blocks of much older, Permian sedimentary rocks and older volcanic andesites are found. These rocks are thought to have slid off the crater walls during the final phase of the 1.2-million-year-old eruption of Bandelier Tuff.

Geologic History

Thanks to many years of geological mapping, aided by geochemical and geochronological analysis, the fascinating geologic history of the Valles Caldera National Preserve is well understood. The formation of the large crater or caldera that dominates the preserve occurred 1.2 million years ago with the enormous volcanic eruption that produced the upper member of the Bandelier Tuff (stages 1 and 2 in the illustration on this page). This eruption was an order of magnitude larger than any eruption that has ever been witnessed by humans, and ejected at least 50 cubic miles of magma, most of which was deposited outside the caldera. This material may be seen today in the buff-to-salmon-colored cliffs in many parts of the Jemez Mountains. The caldera formed roughly on top of the crater that formed during the previous large eruption, 1.6 million years ago. Calderas form during these huge eruptions when such a large amount of magma is withdrawn from the chamber during the eruption that the overlying crust can no longer support itself, and it collapses into the magma chamber below. The eruption of the upper Bandelier Tuff would have caused total devastation in a large area around the Jemez Mountains, as well as a moderate amount of destruction further afield. Volcanic ash 5 inches thick from this eruption is found 180 miles to the south, in Socorro. This ash is found interbedded with river sediments, which indicates to geologists that the ancestral Rio Grande was well established 1.2 million year ago.

Following eruption of the upper member of the Bandelier Tuff, the crater filled with a shallow lake (stage 3). Shortly thereafter, a structural upheaval of the crater floor occurred, resulting in formation of Redondo Peak. Redondo Peak is a *resurgent dome* (stage 4), very distinct in origin from the other hills inside the caldera, which are volcanic domes (stage 5). The volcanic domes form by eruptive processes, whereas a structural dome forms by being pushed up from below, by processes that although not fully understood are probably related to the presence of magma at depth. Redondo Peak is largely composed of Bandelier Tuff, which formed the floor of the caldera after the 1.2-million-year-old eruption (which produced the Bandelier Tuff) and prior to the uplift of Redondo Peak. The type of resurgent dome represented by Redondo Peak is present on many other large volcanoes around the world, but few are as well exposed or preserved as Redondo Peak. Recent detailed geochronological investigations within the Valles caldera suggest that the uplift of Redondo Peak may have occurred in as little as 40,000 years.

Shortly after the formation of the Redondo Peak resurgent dome, the eruption of the family of volcanic domes inside the Valles caldera began. These eruptive domes are quite different in nature from Redondo Peak. The first dome that erupted, 1.2 million years ago, was Cerro del Medio, which is also one of the largest of the volcanic domes. This dome is visible as a series of low hills in the eastern part of the Valles Caldera National Preserve. Following the eruption of Cerro del Medio, eruption of the domes continued in an orderly, counter-clockwise, pattern, ending with the eruption of the tiny Cerro La Jara approximately half a million years ago. Cerro La Jara is the very small, tree-covered hill that is visible to the north of NM–4 and to the west of the main access road to the Valles Caldera National Preserve headquarters. The volcanic domes within the caldera would have been formed by passive eruptions that squeezed the viscous magma out of the magma chamber, allowing it to accumulate near the volcanic vent. These eruptions would have been similar to the eruption of the Mt. St. Helens dome that began building shortly after the explosive 1980 eruption. Each dome probably took many tens of years to accumulate, and some, particularly Cerro del Medio, show evidence of having formed in a series of eruptive events, each forming a distinct lobe. Some of the dome eruptions may have begun with an explosive phase that formed pumice beds underlying the dome lavas, but these are not well exposed in most of the Valles caldera domes. Some of that pumice ended up in Los Alamos, many miles to the east. The distinctive arrangement of the domes along an apparently circular trace is probably due to the presence of a large fault or ring fracture that formed when the crater floor collapsed to form the caldera. The dome-forming magma rose along this fractured, weakened area on the crater floor.

Stage 1—Final stage of eruption

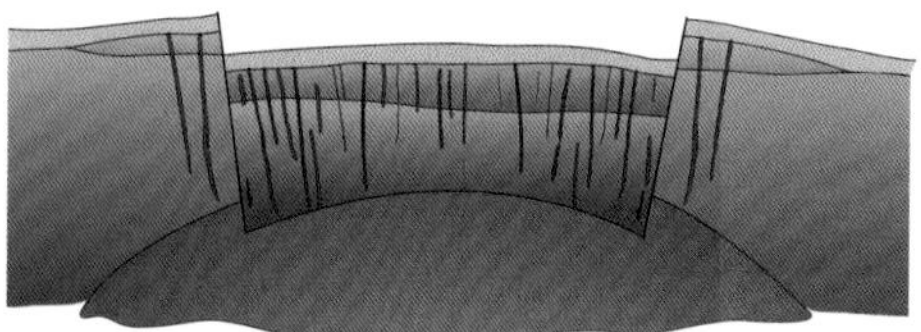

Stage 2—Post-eruption (caldera collapse)

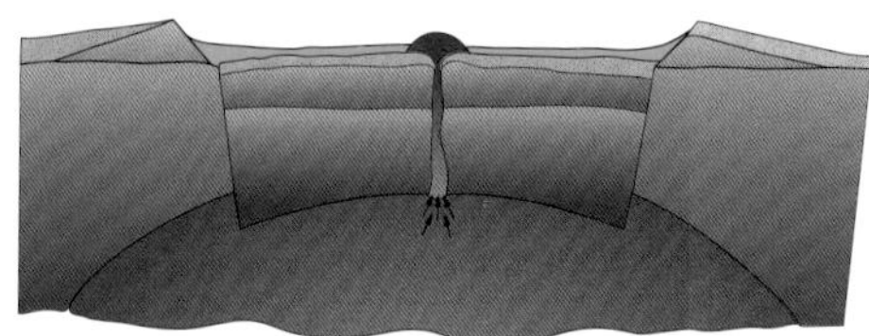

Stage 3—Eruptive domes & lakes

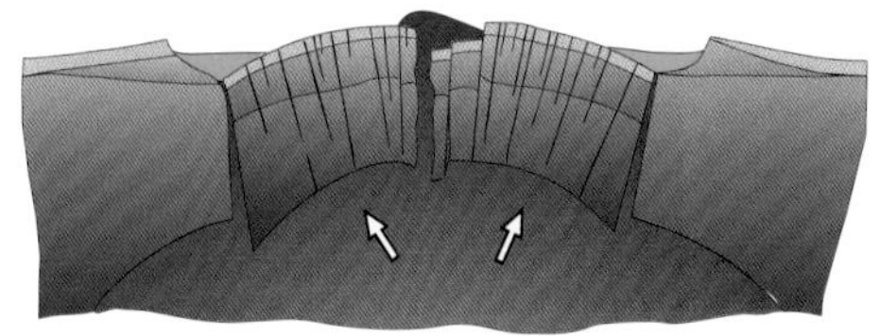

Stage 4—Structural resurgence (resurgent dome)

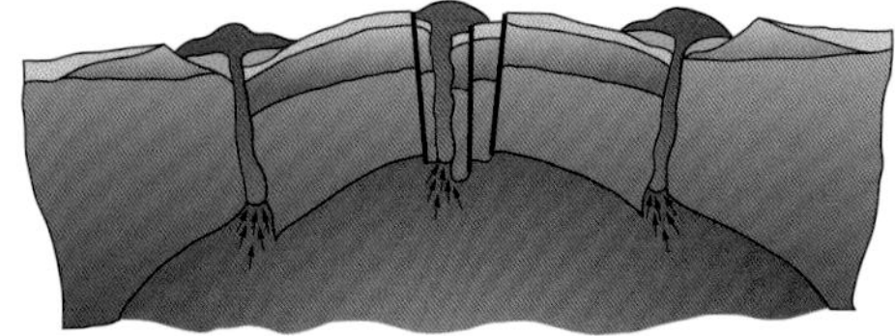

Stage 5—Post-resurgent eruptive domes

Following the eruption of Cerro La Jara peak approximately half a million years ago, there was a long period of quiescence in eruptive activity. Then 60,000 years ago the volcano came back to life, producing a series of small, rhyolitic eruptions. The one of these that can be seen within the Valles Caldera National Preserve is the El Cajete pumice deposit, formed

The Valles caldera: View from the South Rim (Rabbit Ridge). Cerro La Jara is the isolated peak on the crater floor.

by an explosive eruption. El Cajete pumice can be seen in the southernmost part of the preserve, to the west of and overlying the 0.5 million-year-old South Mountain dome. The crater from which the pumice was erupted formed a distinctive, flat, circular meadow in which the previous owners of the Valles caldera used to hold Fourth of July celebrations. Some geologists who have studied the El Cajete pumice suggest that this eruption represents the beginning of a new phase of eruptive activity in the Valles caldera.

The large, circular depression of the Valles caldera has, from time to time, been filled by large lakes. The history of these lakes in not well known, but they were probably best developed during glacial times, when the climate of New Mexico was cooler and wetter than it is today. In these lakes accumulated the sediment that underlies the relatively flat areas seen between the volcanic domes. There may have been several episodes of lake formation and emptying in the 1.2-million-year life of the caldera. Some of these events may have been related to water flow out of the caldera being dammed by eruption of domes, and there is evidence that episodes of damming followed by dam failure may have occurred. A recent scientific drilling project in the Valles caldera indicates that a lake formed around 0.5 million years ago, probably as a result of obstruction of drainage through San Diego Canyon. Lake sedimentation probably occurred for several tens of thousands of years following that damming event. A number of areas of the caldera floor today are distinctly marshy, and some small lakes exist, even in today's warm, dry climate.

Geologic Features

The most remarkable geological aspect of the Valles Caldera National Preserve is the enormous, well-preserved crater itself. Among the many fascinating geological features of the preserve is the beautifully exposed example of a resurgent, structural dome (Redondo Peak) as well as the series of distinctive volcanic domes arrayed around the outer edge of the caldera. Of these, the small, and very visible Cerro La Jara offers a good opportunity to observe an entire volcanic dome at a scale that is easily interpretable. The geometry of the other, larger domes, although more difficult to observe directly, is basically the same as Cerro La Jara, although the shape of some, particularly Cerro del Medio and South Mountain, has been complicated by multiple eruptive events.

Another geological feature of interest within the Valles caldera is the presence of beautiful, black, glassy obsidian associated with formation of the domes. This material is not only geologically interesting but also has cultural significance because of its value to the prehistoric Puebloan societies who frequented the Valles caldera.

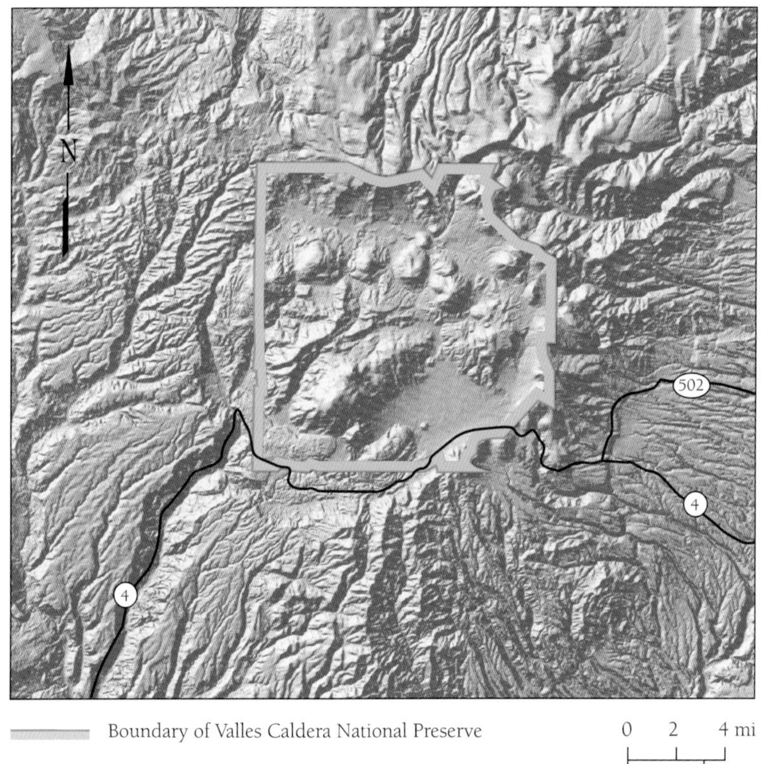

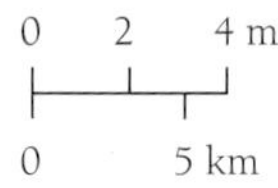

Although access to the preserve is limited, NM–4 skirts the south end of the caldera and provides spectacular views of the caldera floor and Redondo Peak.

The Valles obsidian was likely a valuable commodity that was not only used to form tools but probably also widely traded throughout the region. Obsidian, as well as white pumice deposits, can be seen along several miles of NM–4 just west of where the road crosses the East Fork of the Jemez River. Other obsidian deposits and quarries are present on the flanks of the intracaldera domes.

—Nelia W. Dunbar

Redondo Peak

If You Plan to Visit

The Valles Caldera National Preserve has only recently become public land. It was created when Congress purchased the 89,000-acre Baca Ranch in 2000. The preserve is currently managed by the Valles Caldera Trust, a non-profit consortium of land managers. Access is limited, and many areas may be visited only through prior arrangement. NM–4 skirts the southern edge of the preserve and offers spectacular views of the Valle Grande (the floor of the caldera) and Redondo Peak. For more information on the wide variety of activities that are available, their Web site is a great place to start.

Valles Caldera National Preserve
18161 Highway 4
P.O. Box 359
Jemez Springs, NM 87025
(505) 661-3333
(866) 382-5537 for reservations and information
www.vallescaldera.gov

Bandelier National Monument

NATIONAL PARK SERVICE

OPPOSITE: **Long House Ruin in Frijoles Canyon, Bandelier National Monument. The cliffs in the background are composed entirely of Bandelier Tuff.**

Bandelier National Monument, best known for its cultural significance and well-preserved cliff dwellings, also offers visitors a chance to observe the volcanic geology that made the area so well-suited for prehistoric Puebloan civilization. The rock in most of the monument is Bandelier Tuff, a light-colored, soft volcanic rock that formed during two very large, explosive volcanic events that occurred 1.6 and 1.2 million years ago. These two large eruptions, which together produced hundreds of cubic miles of rock, created the thick sheets of white-to-pink volcanic ash and ignimbrite seen in cliffs in many parts of the Jemez Mountains. This rock, composed of pumice, ash, and volcanic crystals, is not very strongly cemented, and, in many places, has a chalky texture. The soft and easily eroded nature of this rock allowed the deep Frijoles Canyon to be incised by Frijoles Creek, and then provided the perfect setting for the prehistoric Puebloan civilization. These people carved cliff dwellings and building blocks for structures from the volcanic rocks. They occupied this idyllic setting until around A.D. 1,100, when climate change or a combination of factors forced them to abandon the dwellings, the remains of which we see today.

Black basaltic rock is exposed elsewhere in the monument and is particularly apparent on the lower Frijoles Canyon Trail. This rock formed as a result of relatively passive, Hawaiian-style volcanism. Dense lava flows from this volcanic activity, resistant to erosion, form the topographic steps over which the Frijoles Canyon waterfalls flow. In some places, particularly interesting volcanic deposits formed where the basaltic lavas interacted explosively with water from the ancestral Rio Grande.

Regional Setting

Bandelier National Monument is located on the flanks of the Jemez Mountains, in north-central New Mexico. These mountains are a large, long-lived volcanic complex situated at the intersection of the Rio Grande rift, a major zone of crustal weakness formed by stretching of the continental crust, and the Jemez lineament, which is a second, more poorly defined crustal zone along which volcanism has occurred. The large and long-lived nature of the Jemez Mountains volcanic field may be related to its location at the intersection of these two major crustal anomalies. The Jemez Mountains volcanic field has been active for the past 15 million years. It was formed by a sequence of many smaller volcanic eruptions, which produced lavas with a range of chemical compo-

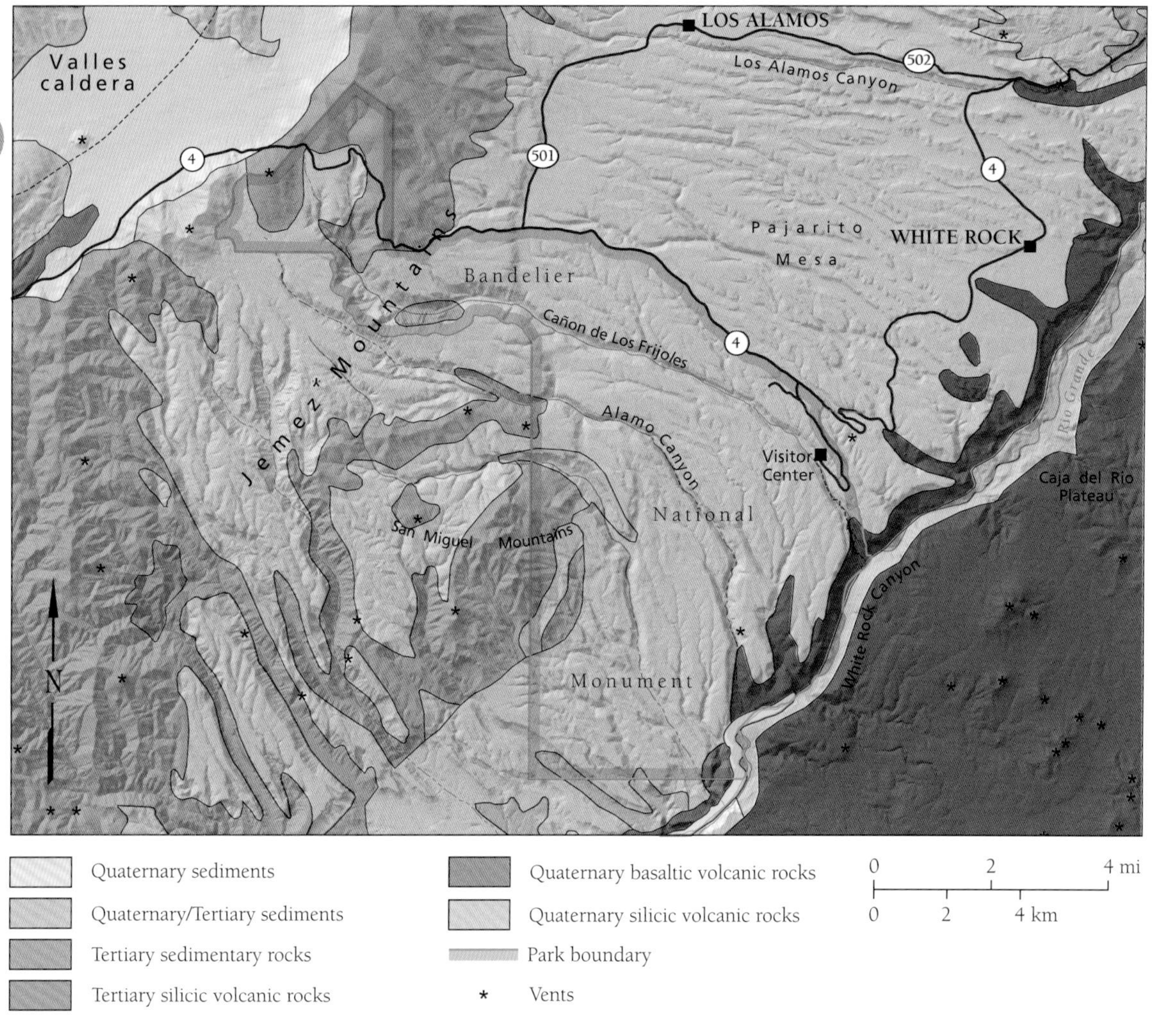

Generalized geologic map of Bandelier National Monument and vicinity.

sitions and eruptive types. These were followed by the two very large rhyolitic eruptions mentioned above.

The Rock Record

The oldest rocks exposed near the headquarters of Bandelier National Monument are the Cerro del Rio basalts, which are interbedded with minor occurrences of river gravels. These can be seen on the hike down Frijoles Canyon toward the Rio Grande. These basaltic rocks are 2–3 million years old and represent a number of different eruptive styles. The black cliffs in the walls of Frijoles Canyon are lava flows formed from passive outpouring of fluid basaltic lavas. Some of these lava flows display columnar joints, vertical fractures formed during cooling, that give the rock a columned appearance.

The lower part of Frijoles Canyon exhibits deposits from two other volcanic features: cinder cones and maar deposits. Both of these types of deposits are layered, or bedded and represent more explosive styles of volcanism. The cinder cones formed during a fire fountaining event, when cinders rained down around the eruptive vent, producing a cone-shaped deposit. A typical cinder cone may contain not only cinders but large volcanic bombs and thin lava flows. The bedding angle of cinder cones is typically steep, around 30°, and this bedding angle can be seen if the cinder cone is dissected by erosion.

The *maar* deposits, which can be seen further down Frijoles Canyon, closer to the river, were formed by hydromagmatic processes. Hydromagmatism occurs when hot magma rising through the earth's crust interacts with water, either ground water or surface water associated with a river, lake, or ocean. The interaction between the hot magma and the cold water leads to very violent explosions, forming a type of volcanic deposit called a maar. The deposits from maar eruptions are typically bedded, but the bedding is flatter-lying than those in cinder cone deposits. When observed closely, maar deposits may contain more glassy material, because of the quenching effect of the water on the magma. The particles in maar deposits may also contain fewer vesicles (gas bubbles), and maar deposits may exhibit non-planar, or wavy bedding. All of these features result from the difference in eruptive mechanism between explosive volcanic eruptions that involve water, and those that don't.

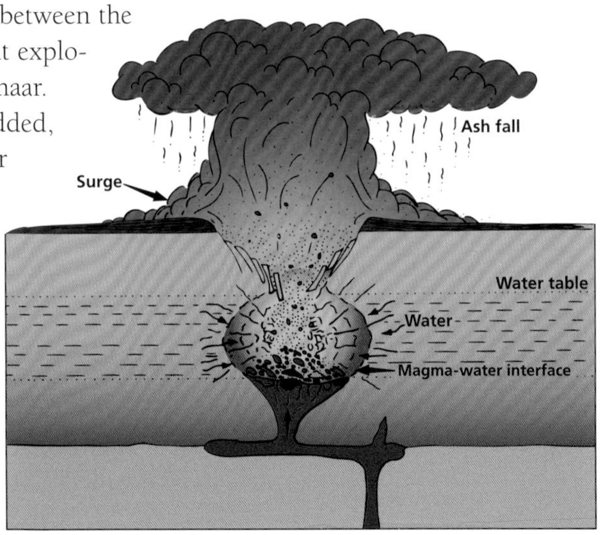

In a maar volcanic eruption, hot magma interacts with ground water to produce powerful explosive eruptions. The surge deposits from this kind of eruption form wavy beds that may be interbedded with ash deposits. Large rocks called "ballistic blocks" may also be ejected from the vent and fall back into the surrounding deposits, sometimes deforming the underlying layers.

The rock that dominates the landscape at Bandelier National Monument is the Bandelier Tuff. This rock forms the whitish cliffs on either side of most of Frijoles Canyon, and into which the cliff dwellings are excavated. This rock was formed during two large, highly explosive eruptions that occurred 1.6 and 1.2 million years ago. These eruptions were of a scale that has never been witnessed by humans, so what is known about the eruptive processes is deduced from studying the eruptive products, rather than drawing a direct analogy to described eruptive events. Based on investigations of the deposits, each of these large eruptions is thought to have begun with an ash fall event, producing relatively thin, bedded pumice deposits on the landscape. Following the ash fall phase of the eruption, collapse of the eruptive column would have resulted in deposition of a type of rock called an *ignimbrite* or *ash-flow tuff*. This type of rock is formed of a mixture of pumice, ash, and crystals and, once deposited, would have solidified to form the rock in which the cliff dwellings are found. These ignimbrites constitute a large part of the visible rock record at Bandelier National Monument.

Geologic History

The geological history at Bandelier National Monument involves several episodes of different types of volcanic activity, separated by periods of erosion and minor sediment deposition. One part of the geological history of the area, for which no deposits are visible near the headquarters of the national monument but which is nevertheless important, is the early evolution of the Jemez Mountains volcanic field. This phase consisted of many smaller eruptions of varied composition over the initial 12 million years of formation of the volcanic field. These eruptions formed the foundation of the Jemez Mountains.

Starting around 3 million years ago, eruption of the Cerro del Rio basalts began. Some of the early phases of these eruptions involved interaction between basaltic magma and ground water associated with the Rio Grande, to form maars and other hydromagmatic deposits. At times, the Rio Grande may have been dammed by volcanic activity, resulting in the formation of local, ephemeral lakes through which some basaltic lavas may have erupted. The association of the hydromagmatic deposits with the river channel, and the presence of interbedded river gravels in some of the deposits, suggests the close association between the presence of the river and hydromagmatism.

At the same time that the hydromagmatic volcanism was occurring near the river, more conventional basaltic volcanism was taking place elsewhere. This volcanic activity consisted of passive events, producing cinder cones and lava flows. The style of these eruptions would have been very similar to volcanism observed in Hawaii today. The thick lava flows and cinder deposits in Frijoles Canyon are the result of this activity.

Cerro del Rio basaltic volcanism appears to have been over by 2 million years ago. In the interval following this basaltic volcanism and prior to the large Bandelier Tuff eruptions there appears to have been an interval of deep erosion, at least in the area around Frijoles Canyon. Catastrophic erosion typically follows episodes of volcanism, because volcanic activity can fundamentally disrupt the landscape, onto which new drainage patterns must be established.

Cavate dwelling (above) in Bandelier Tuff in Frijoles Canyon. Obsidian (below) from the Valles caldera was used to make lithics and tools.

Approximately 1.6 million years ago the landscape around Bandelier National Monument underwent a profound change. At this time the first of the two catastrophic Bandelier Tuff eruptions took place. In the early stages of the eruption, pumice rained from the sky, stripping the leaves and branches off trees, and covering the landscape like a blanket of hot, dusty snow. Shortly afterwards, a hot, ashy cloud, possibly moving at close to the speed of sound, descended on the area, leaving behind a deposit that solidified into the lower member of the Bandelier Tuff. This depositional event would have obliterated and incinerated all living things in its path, leaving behind total desolation. The thickness of the lower member of the Bandelier Tuff in Bandelier National Monument isn't well known, because it mostly lies beneath ground level and is only present in part of the park. The Visitor Center is constructed approximately on the top of the Lower Bandelier deposit, but this deposit is absent in most of lower Frijoles Canyon.

Following a hiatus of 400,000 years, a second eruption of approximately the same size took place, forming the upper member of the Bandelier Tuff. This deposit is the light-colored rock that forms the walls of upper Frijoles Canyon in which the cliff dwellings are found. The upper member of the Bandelier Tuff, like the lower, consists of a bedded ash fall deposit (visible in some parts of the monument), as well as a local thickness of around 100 meters of ignimbrite.

In the 1.2 million years since the eruption of the upper member of the Bandelier Tuff, the main geological process that has occurred in the area around Bandelier National Monument is erosion of the deep canyons that dissect the flanks of the Jemez Mountains. Again, this deep erosion is a natural consequence of volcanic processes that cause instantaneous, fundamental

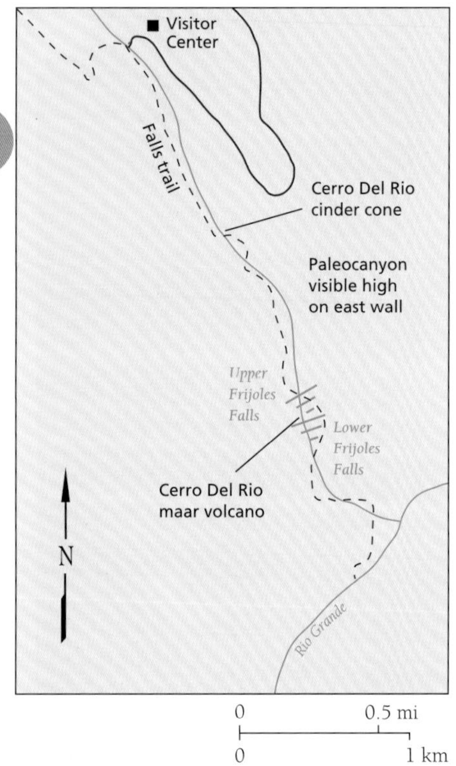

Upper Frijoles Falls trail

changes in local topography. Frijoles Canyon, a consequence of post-volcanic erosional processes, provided a hospitable environment for human habitation in the past, and a beautiful place to visit today.

Geologic Features

There are a number of geological features of note that can be observed in the Bandelier National Monument. These include the ash fall and ignimbrite phases of the upper member of the Bandelier Tuff; a location where the Bandelier Tuff fills in a paleotopographic valley in the underlying basalts; a dissected cinder cone; and a dissected tuff cone. All of these features can be observed on or near established trails.

BANDELIER TUFF—The ash fall and ignimbrite phases of the upper member of the Bandelier Tuff are well exposed in the west wall of a small arroyo just down canyon from the first dwelling site on the path to the Long House. At this location, the bedded, pumice-rich ash fall deposit can be seen, as well as the overlying ignimbrite deposit. Note the textural difference between the ash fall and the ignimbrite. The ash fall is formed by gravitational settling of pumice from an eruptive cloud; hence the pumice size is very uniform. The ignimbrite, deposited from a mixed cloud of pumice, dust, and crystals, shows all of these components mixed together. A bit further along the trail, near the dwellings, some pipe-like structures can be seen in the ignimbrite. These may represent places where gas escaped through the ignimbrite, carrying fine ash with it, but leaving coarser material behind.

This paleocanyon is visible high on the east wall along the Falls Trail to the Rio Grande (down canyon from the Visitor Center). The Bandelier Tuff fills a large channel in the underlying basalt.

PALEOCANYON FILLED WITH BANDELIER TUFF—Down canyon from the Visitor Center, near an area of tent rocks (arrived at after crossing 3 footbridges), a spectacular example of Bandelier Tuff infilling paleotopography can be seen on the northeast face of the canyon wall. This dramatic thickening of the whitish Bandelier Tuff occurred because there was a large canyon in the underlying basalt at the time that the upper member of the Bandelier Tuff erupted. The eruptive cloud of the Bandelier Tuff ignimbrite eruption filled this canyon just as fluid magma would fill a topographic depression. In addition to providing information about the paleotopography 1.2 million years ago, this infilling provides information about the physical processes of the Bandelier Tuff eruptive cloud.

CERRO DEL RIO CINDER CONE—Further down canyon, in the flat area above the Upper Frijoles Falls, a dissected basaltic cinder cone is present in the east side of the canyon. Note the tilted bedding, and the vesicular basaltic cinders that make up the deposit.

CERRO DEL RIO MAAR VOLCANO—Below Upper Frijoles Falls, the trail to the river passes through a well-exposed section of a maar volcano. Note the orange-red color of the beds formed by the interaction of the black basaltic material with river water, the relatively flat-lying beds, and the presence of wavy bedding, all typical of hydromagmatic deposits.

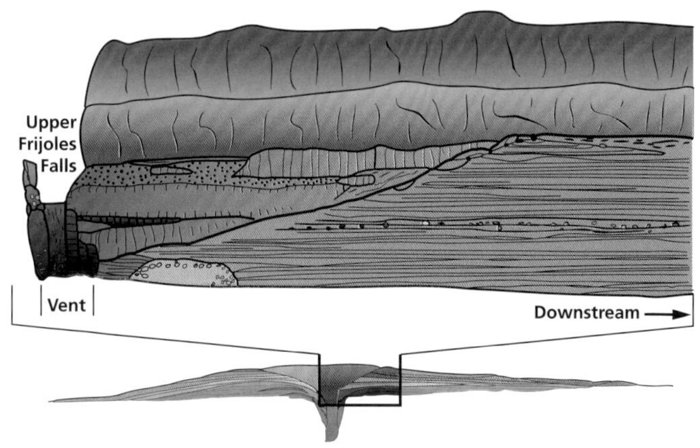

Remnants of the Cerro del Rio maar volcano can be seen on either side of Upper Frijoles Falls (above) as red bedded deposits. Schematic cross-section of Frijoles Canyon rocks near the upper Frijoles Falls (below). Orange bedded rocks represent maar deposits overlain by massive grey lava flows and river gravels (striped pattern).

PAJARITO FAULT ZONE—The Pajarito fault zone, which drops the younger 1.2-million-year-old tuff down 650 feet to the east, forms a prominent topographic scarp along the west side of Bandelier National Monument. This young (less than 1.2 million years old) fault is related to Rio Grande rift extension. The fault scarp can be viewed from overlook points on the way into the monument and can be accessed via backcountry trails.

—*Nelia W. Dunbar*

If You Plan to Visit

Bandelier National Monument is located between Los Alamos and Santa Fe on the southeast flank of the Valles caldera. From Santa Fe: Take NM–68 north to Pojoaque, turn west on NM–502 to NM–4. Go south on NM–4 past White Rock and look for signs for the park entrance on the left. NM–4 continues west along the rim of the Valles caldera and through a portion of the Valles Caldera National Preserve. For more information:

Bandelier National Monument
15 Entrance Road
Los Alamos, NM 87544
(505) 672-3861 x 517 (visitor center)
(505) 672-0343 (visitor information)
(505) 672-3861 x 534 (group reservations)
www.nps.gov/band/

Kasha-Katuwe Tent Rocks National Monument

BUREAU OF LAND MANAGEMENT

Kasha-Katuwe Tent Rocks National Monument, located on the southern flank of the Jemez Mountains in north-central New Mexico, preserves a visually striking and geologically fascinating landscape. The distinctive white color of the rocks, along with the conical tent-like landforms (*hoodoos*), make this a popular hiking destination, with many short, accessible hikes. The small winding canyons and scenic beauty have provided the background for a number of movie and television productions.

Regional Setting

The Kasha-Katuwe Tent Rocks are part of the Jemez Mountains volcanic field, which is situated at the intersection of the Rio Grande rift, a major zone of crustal weakness formed by stretching of the continental crust, and the Jemez lineament, which is a second, more poorly defined, crustal zone along which volcanism has occurred. The large and long-lived nature of the Jemez Mountains volcanic field may be related to its location at the intersection of these two major crustal anomalies. The Jemez Mountains volcanic field has been active for the past 15 million years. The volcanic rocks that form the tent rocks erupted approximately 7 million years ago.

The tent rocks at Kasha-Katuwe Tent Rocks National Monument are eroded from soft volcanic sediments of the 7-million-year-old Peralta Tuff.

Several different lithologies are represented within the Peralta Tuff. Ash-fall deposits (1), characterized by planar bedding, accumulated during pyroclastic fall events following an explosive volcanic eruption. Pyroclastic surge deposits (2) are typically cross-bedded and are the result of the reworking of volcanic material by currents of either wind or water. Such deposits are called volcaniclastic. Pyroclastic flows (3) are poorly sorted and massive, characterized by a lack of distinctive bedding. All three deposits may occur in rapid succession, as seen in the photo on the opposite page.

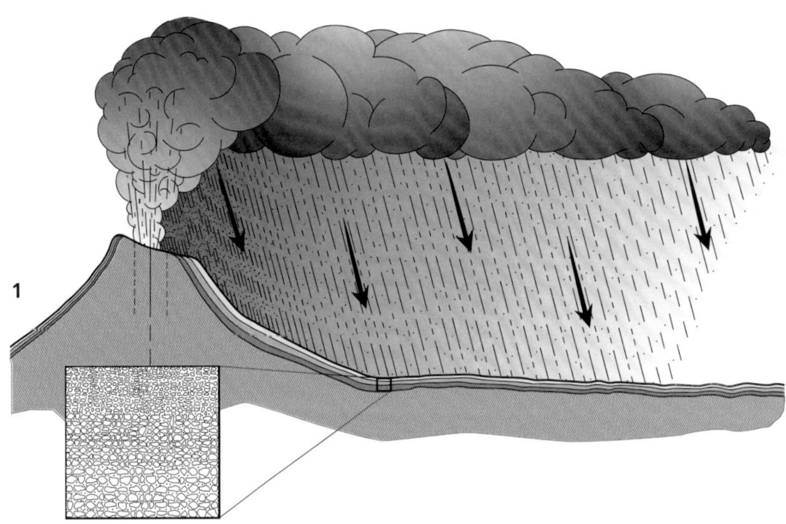

Ash fall

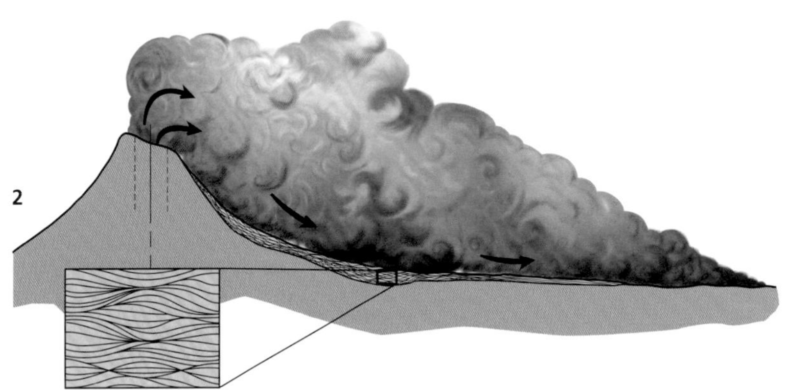

Pyroclastic surge

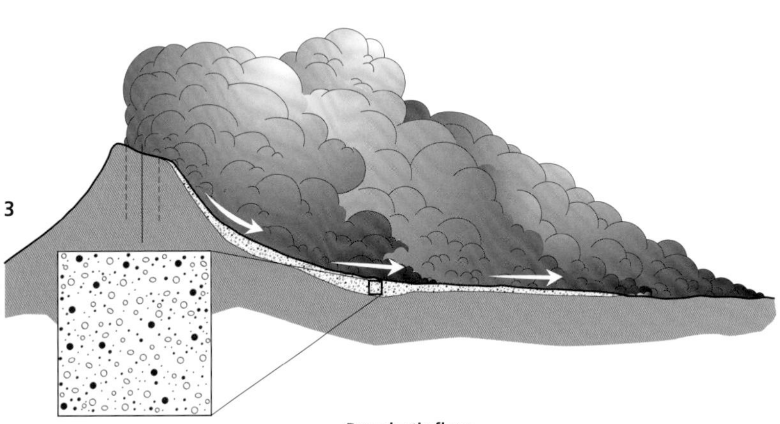

Pyroclastic flow

The Rock Record

The rocks found in Kasha-Katuwe Tent Rocks National Monument are the Peralta Tuff, which formed at a time of very active volcanism approximately 7 million years ago. At this time at least twenty small volcanoes in the area erupted repeatedly, producing large quantities of volcanic ash, pumice, and other material. The distinctive layering seen in the deposits at Tent Rocks clearly indicate that most of these layers were deposited either directly by a volcanic eruption, or were formed when loose volcanic material was reworked, either by wind or by water.

This type of sedimentary deposit, called volcaniclastic, is typical in areas of active volcanism where there is an abundant supply of loose volcanic debris that can then be easily transported and redeposited. Volcaniclastic layers can be difficult to tell from some true volcanic layers, because the material and sedimentary structures in both can be similar. Despite the superficial similarity in appearance between the Peralta Tuff and some of the younger volcanic deposits in the region—namely, the Bandelier Tuff—these are very different deposits.

Shown here are examples of the deposits that result from each of the events illustrated on the previous page: ash-fall deposits (1), surge deposits (2), and pyroclastic flows (3).

The Peralta Tuff is considerably older than the Bandelier Tuff and belongs to an entirely different episode of volcanism. The small volcanoes that produced the Tent Rocks are located within 5 miles of the site. Some of the volcanoes are in the area of nearby Bearhead Peak.

Several distinct types of volcanic deposits are present at Tent Rocks, each one appearing subtly different, and each related to a different style of volcanic eruption, including pyroclastic fall, pyroclastic surge, and pyroclastic flow. All three of these eruptive styles are formed from explosive volcanism, but subtle differences in the eruptive mechanism leads to differences in the characteristics of the deposits. Pyroclastic fall, or ash fall deposits, are similar to a bed of fallen snow, and show certain distinctive features: They mantle the topography, maintaining a constant thickness in a local area, and the particles in the deposit are all more or less the same size. Pyroclastic surge deposits form from a hot cloud of ash, pumice, and gas that travels across the landscape, producing a deposit that shows distinctive, wavy bedding. These deposits can be very difficult to tell from deposits produced when volcanic rocks are reworked by water. The third type of deposit, also formed when hot clouds of volcanic material travel over the landscape, is a pyroclastic flow. Like a surge, this deposit is composed of ash and pumice, but does not exhibit any bedding and contains a range of grain sizes. On a much larger scale, the Bandelier Tuff is also a pyroclastic flow deposit. A number of ash fall, pyroclastic surge, and pyroclastic flow beds can be observed from the hiking trails in the Tent Rocks area.

View to the northeast at Kasha-Katuwe Tent Rocks National Monument. The Sante Fe Range is visible on the horizon.

Geologic History

The layered rocks that form the tent rocks were all a result of an intense period of volcanism during the middle part of the history of the Jemez Mountains volcanic field. This volcanism peaked at around 7 million years ago and was the source of both the layers formed by actual volcanic events, as well as the volcanic material reworked to form the volcaniclastic sedimentary layers. In some parts of the layered rock sequence a type of layer called a *paleosol* is seen. Paleosols, some of which contain rodent burrows, represents the formation of soil, and indicates that the landscape was stable enough for soil formation to take place, suggesting a hiatus in volcanic activity.

Some time after deposition of the layered tent rock deposits, at least one major earthquake took place in the area. The evidence for this is visible in the 350-foot offset of the stratified beds in the area along a subsidiary fault associated with the large Pajarito fault, which passes just to the east of the tent rocks area. This type of offset requires at least one, and probably many more, episodes of earthquake activity. The Pajarito fault offsets the 1.2-million-year-old Bandelier Tuff, so we know that at least some motion on the fault must be younger than that.

Another important part of the geologic story is the formation of the actual tents, or hoodoos. These erosional features were formed after the volcanic and sedimentary layers had been slightly hardened. As erosion proceeds, large rocks in the deposit protect the underlying material from erosion, eventually resulting in the characteristic tented shapes (see sidebar). Most of this erosion was caused by water, but wind erosion probably played a role as well. Many of the tents, and the less common "pedestal rocks" (large rock supported by a column of sediment) have an obvious capstone, although the capstones eventually fall, leaving an uncapped tent. One interesting aspect of the presence of balanced capstones is that they indicate that there hasn't been major recent seismic activity in the local area, because even a small seismic event would cause many capstones to fall. The length of time that has passed since the last earthquake is hard to determine, because we don't know how long it takes for a tent or pedestal to form.

Following the deposition of thick layers of Peralta Tuff, erosion has shaped the receding cliff faces into "tents." Large rocks more resistant to erosion protect the softer material underneath, resulting in the conical shapes we see today.

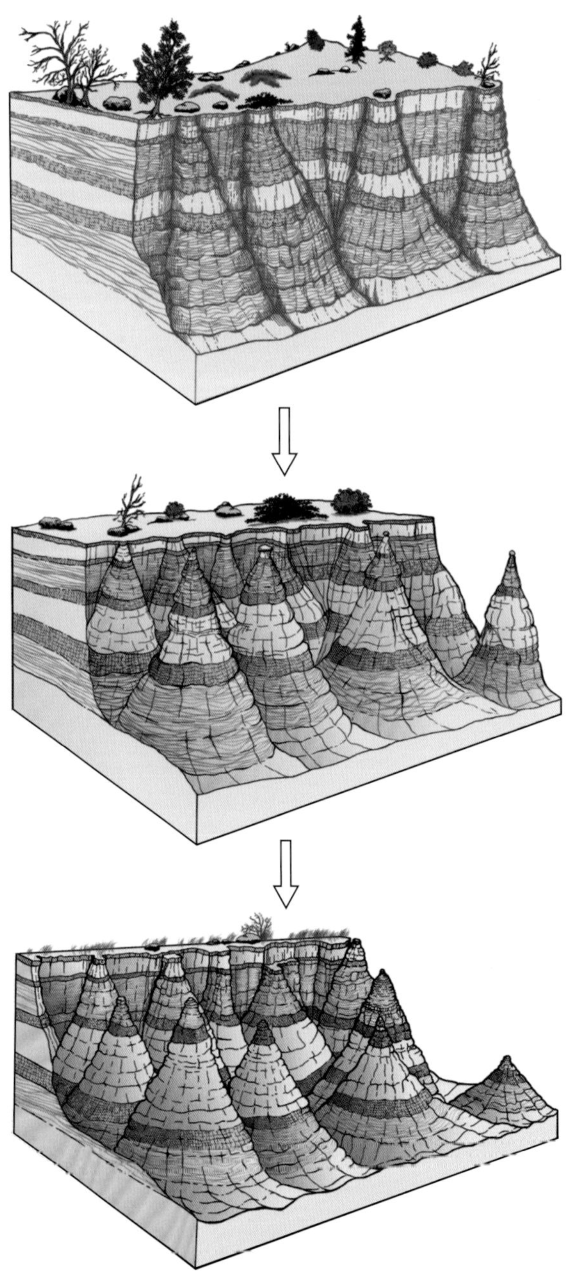

Geologic Features

There are several geological features worthy of note in the monument. The first is the rock itself, a thick interbedded sequence of volcanic and volcanic-rich sedimentary rocks. This type of rock sequence could only form in a time of very abundant, active volcanism, and is a good example of what occurs during the interplay of volcanic activity and water and wind acting on a landscape choked with loose volcanic debris. Look particularly for the ash fall deposits in the sequence, which would have formed by volcanic ash raining from the sky onto the surrounding terrain. A deposit from an ash fall event (pyroclastic fall) is illustrated on page 155, and deposits can be observed along the trail through the tents themselves. Deposits from pyroclastic surges and pyroclastic flows, also illustrated here, can be observed elsewhere in the monument.

Another unique feature is the tents themselves, and the presence of tents in many stages of evolution. These unusual landforms only form under a certain combination of rock properties and local climate, and their interesting beauty is one of the main reasons that Tent Rocks is a popular hiking destination. There are other parts of New Mexico where tent rocks can be seen, but few have the same scenic appeal as the Kasha-Katuwe site.

A final interesting geological aspect of the Tent Rocks area is the presence of abundant obsidian fragments called "Apache Tears" in some of the sedimentary rock layers. This obsidian is another indication of the volcanic activity that was taking place when these rocks were forming. One type of volcano called a volcanic dome, a number of which are present in the Valles Caldera National Preserve, can contain an outer shell, or carapace, of obsidian, a dark-colored volcanic glass. In some cases, the obsidian may be fractured and easily transported by water, leading to obsidian-rich sedimentary beds interlayered with pumice-rich volcanic deposits. The Apache Tears can be seen along the floor of the slot canyon accessible from the main trail through the tent rocks.

Apache Tears

—Nelia W. Dunbar

If You Plan to Visit

The monument is located on the Pajarito Plateau in north-central New Mexico, 40 miles southwest of Santa Fe and 55 miles northwest of Albuquerque. The most direct access is from I–25 via Exit 259 if you are coming from the south, or via Exit 264 if you are coming from the north. Day use only; hours vary seasonally. The monument is managed by the Bureau of Land Management, but access is across Pueblo de Cochiti tribal land. For more information:

Bureau of Land Management
Rio Puerco Field Office
435 Montano Road NE
Albuquerque, NM 87107
(505) 761-8700
(505) 761-8911 (Fax)
www.nm.blm.gov/aufo/aufo_home.html

Jemez State Monument

Jemez State Monument, located at the north end of the town of Jemez Springs, offers insights into both geology and historic human culture. The monument preserves the partially reconstructed ruin of the church of San José de los Jemez, which was built in 1621 by the Franciscans on the site of a pueblo occupied by the Jemez Indians. Jemez State Monument, Soda Dam, and Battleship Rock are all located in the scenically spectacular San Diego Canyon along the east fork of the Jemez River. San Diego Canyon is one of several radially oriented drainages that have eroded through the volcanic rocks of the Jemez volcanic field and cut deeply into older underlying sedimentary rocks. Jemez State Monument offers a close look at this older sedimentary sequence, impressive distant views of the overlying volcanic rocks, and insight into how the native Americans and the newly arrived Spanish used geologic materials in their architecture.

The mission church of San José de los Jemez, built in 1621.

Regional Setting

Jemez State Monument is located on the south flank of the Jemez Mountains, a long-lived volcanic field along the southwestern edge of the Colorado Plateau. The Jemez Mountains volcanic field lies at the intersection of the Rio Grande rift and the Jemez lineament, two linear zones of weakness in the crust of the earth. Volcanic activity in the Jemez Mountains spanned more than ten million years. Older sedimentary rocks beneath the Jemez volcanic rocks have been significantly uplifted. This gentle domical upwarping is probably related in part to the volcanism, and in part to tectonic uplift along the west flank of the Rio Grande rift.

The Rock Record

Rock outcrops within Jemez State Monument are gray-colored layers of limestone, sandstones, and shale of Pennsylvanian age, deposited beneath inland seas that once covered much of New Mexico. This sedimentary sequence, named the Madera Group, contains abundant fossils of more than 90 species of marine animals, including snails, clams, brachiopods, trilobites, corals, and fish. Just outside Jemez State

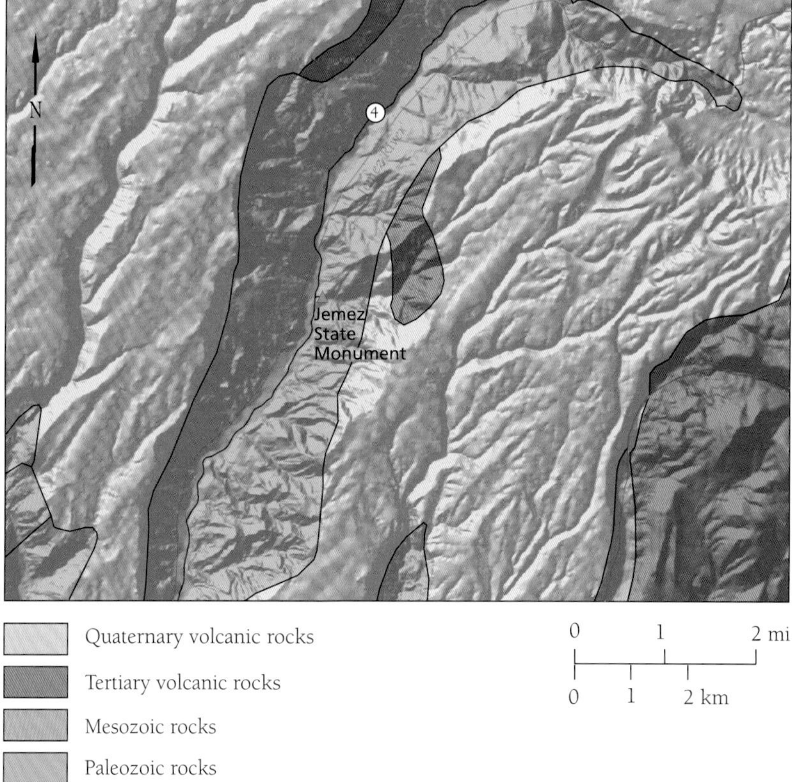

Generalized geologic map of the area surrounding Jemez State Monument.

Monument, the sequence of gray marine rocks is overlain by Permian red sandstones and siltstones of the Abo Formation, deposited by south-flowing rivers after the withdrawal of the inland sea. Similar brilliant red Abo sandstones form dramatic cliffs along San Diego Canyon. Overlying the red Abo sandstone is a sequence of much younger volcanic rocks erupted from the Jemez volcanic field. The view to the west from Jemez State Monument affords excellent distant views of this volcanic sequence, including dark basaltic lavas at the base overlain by brilliant white Bandelier Tuff. The base of the Bandelier Tuff west of Jemez State Monument is eroded into cone-shaped pillars known as hoodoos or tent rocks.

Geologic History

East Fork of the Jemez River. The unconformity between Permian red sandstones and the Pliocene volcanic rocks is visible in the far cliffs.

The rocks exposed along San Diego Canyon help tell the story of geologic events ranging from 325 million years ago to the present. About 325 million years ago, a vast, shallow inland sea covered much of what is now the central United States. The gray layers of limestone, sandstone, and shale exposed in Jemez State Monument were deposited near the western edge of this inland sea. Repeated alternating cycles of these three rock types were probably caused by sea level changes driven by ancient climate cycles. About 290 million years ago, the inland sea retreated, leaving gentle plains traversed by rivers that deposited the red sandstones of the Abo Formation. Much later, about ten million years ago, volcanic activity and associated tectonic uplift began in the Jemez Mountains.

After uplift and some erosion, dark-colored basaltic lavas erupted onto the eroded surface, then eruptions of lighter colored tuff followed, including the catastrophic eruption of the upper Bandelier Tuff from the Valles caldera 1.2 million years ago. Rapid erosion followed, cutting San Diego Canyon into the flank of the Jemez Mountains and revealing the cross section of rock now visible from Jemez State Monument.

Geologic Features

CYCLIC SEDIMENTARY ROCKS—Repeated sequences of different rock types are commonly the result of cyclic climate changes. The alternating layers of limestone, sandstone, and shale exposed in Jemez State Monument probably record worldwide sea-level changes caused by waxing and waning of ancient ice ages in the polar regions at that time.

UNCONFORMITY—The abrupt transition between red sandstones and volcanic rocks, visible in the cliffs surrounding Jemez State Monument, represents a time period from about 250 million to 10 million years ago for which no rocks are preserved. Time breaks of this nature are common in the geologic record and are termed unconformities.

TENT ROCKS—The conical pillars near the base of the prominent white tuff west of the Jemez State Monument are an erosional landform called hoodoos or tent rocks. These cylindrical to conical rock pillars are common in the very soft volcanic tuffs throughout the Jemez Mountains.

They formed when progressive erosion of the soft tuff by rain and running water encountered a harder rock fragment, which protected the tip of the pillar from eroding, while the sides and base of the pillar were slowly carved away. Cycles of wetting and drying can also harden the surface of the hoodoo, slowing further erosion.

HUMAN USE OF EARTH MATERIALS—The ruins at Jemez State Monument provide insight into how the Native Americans and newly arrived Spanish used geological materials. Rock walls of the pre-Spanish pueblo, as well as the church of San José de los Jemez and associated structures are constructed of local Madera limestone, Abo sandstone, and river cobbles from the nearby riverbed. Many of these cobbles are rugged fragments of basalt lava rounded by river transport. Although a small part of the church is constructed of adobe, the local builders clearly preferred the stronger, readily available rock cobbles quarried and delivered to the building site by the natural geological processes. Archeological excavations have revealed an additional example of the use of geological materials in the church. Fragments of selenite, a well crystallized form of gypsum, have been found buried in the ruins, suggesting that sheets of this locally available translucent mineral were used in early windows to bring light into the church.

—William C. McIntosh

If You Plan to Visit

Jemez State Monument is located 18 miles north of the intersection of NM–4 with US 550, and 1 mile north of the town of Jemez Springs on NM–4. The visitor center is open daily except Tuesday. Jemez State Monument is one of six sites administered by New Mexico State Monuments, a division of the New Mexico Department of Cultural Affairs. There is an admission charge. For more information:

Jemez State Monument
P.O. Box 143
Jemez Springs, NM 87025
(800) 426-7850 or (575) 829-3530
giusewa@sulphurcanyon.com

New Mexico State Monuments
P.O. Box 2087
Santa Fe, NM 87504
(505) 476-1150

Battleship Rock

SANTA FE NATIONAL FOREST

Battleship Rock is a spectacular prow of black volcanic rock located at the head of San Diego Canyon, near the southern margin of the Valles caldera. This prominent landmark formed when a young flow of volcanic ash filled an ancestral canyon of the Jemez River, then was exposed by subsequent stream erosion on both sides. This type of erosional landform, where formerly low areas are now topographic highs, is termed *inverted topography*. Inverted topography is common on the flanks of volcanoes, where rocks of varying hardness are rapidly eroding. In addition to its spectacular scenic value, a number of volcanic features are easily visible in the vicinity of Battleship Rock.

Regional Setting

Battleship Rock was formed by a young volcanic eruption in the Jemez Mountains. The Jemez Mountains have been the site of many volcanic eruptions over the last ten million years. The Rio Grande rift and the Jemez lineament, two linear zones of crustal weakness, intersect in this area. Their intersection provides pathways for volcanism to reach the surface. Gentle upwarping of older rocks preceded and accompanied volcanism in the Jemez Mountains. Volcanism in this area peaked 1.2 million years ago with the catastrophic eruption of the Bandelier Tuff and collapse of the Valles caldera. This huge eruption was followed by a serious of much smaller eruptions. One of the youngest of these eruptions produced the ash flow that later eroded to form Battleship Rock.

The Rock Record

The volcanic rocks at Battleship Rock overlie much older fossil-bearing limestones from the Pennsylvanian Madera Group, similar to those exposed at Jemez State Monument. Battleship Rock itself is composed of a type of volcanic rock termed *welded tuff*. It erupted as a red-hot mixture of pumice, ash, and volcanic gas, which flowed down a preexisting canyon as if it were a liquid. The canyon walls channeled this ash flow and helped to retain heat. When the flow eventually slowed and stopped, the ash and pumice fragments were still hot enough to compress and weld together to form the hard, solid black rock visible today. Outcrops along the base of Battleship Rock show the transition from soft, non-welded tuff to overlying, progressively more welded tuff, containing lenses of black obsidian produced by flattening of pumice fragments. The volcanic tuff, both welded and non-welded, contains angular fragments of other types of rock that were mixed into the tuff during eruption and flow.

Geologic History

The gray limestones of the Pennsylvanian Madera Group that underlie the black volcanic rocks at Battleship Rock were formed by an ancient inland sea that covered much of New Mexico about 300 million years ago. Long after retreat of these ancient seas, the limestones were gently uplifted by crustal upwarping during Jemez Mountain volcanism, which began about ten million years ago. Volcanism peaked with the catastrophic eruption of the Bandelier Tuff from the Valles caldera at 1.2 million years, and erosional cutting of San Diego Canyon by the ancestral Jemez River began soon thereafter. The huge Bandelier Tuff eruption was followed by several much smaller eruptions of lava domes and tuffs. One of the youngest eruptions, about 50,000 years ago, produced a hot ash flow that flowed down and filled an ancestral canyon of Jemez River, then welded to form a solid, black lava-like rock. Erosion of softer rock along the margins of this hard welded tuff eventually exposed the dramatic black prow of Battleship Rock.

Welded tuff from the upper cliffs of Battleship Rock. Note the flattened pieces of volcanic glass, known as *fiamme*.

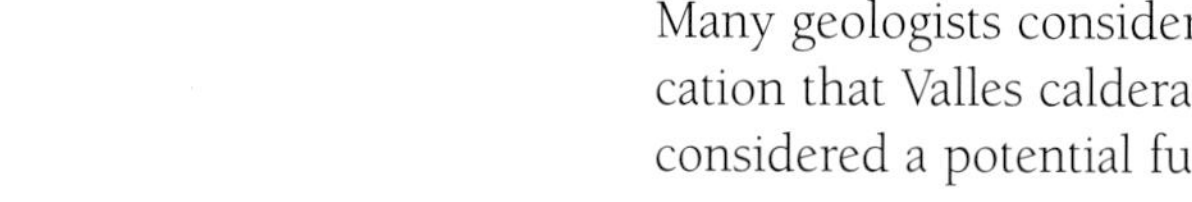

The Battleship Rock welded tuff erupted about 50,000 years ago. Many geologists consider this relatively young eruption age as an indication that Valles caldera volcanism is not yet extinct, and should be considered a potential future geologic hazard in this area.

Geologic Features

A number of specific volcanic features are clearly visible and easily identified in the vicinity of Battleship Rock. The black rock forming the steep cliffs at Battleship Rock originally erupted as a low-density mixture of pumice (frothy volcanic glass), ash, and volcanic gas. The glassy fragments within some of this mixture were hot enough to weld together after they came to rest, producing the hard, dense, lava-like rock seen today, which we call welded tuff. Gray-colored pumice fragments in the rock exposed in the lowest parts of the cliffs at Battleship Rock are still rounded and frothy, because the lowest parts of the tuff deposit cooled too quickly for welding to occur. These undeformed pumice fragments can also be seen in readily accessible boulders that have rolled down from the cliffs above. Higher outcrops at Battleship Rock are densely welded and contain excellent examples of flattened lenses of black volcanic glass (obsidian). These originally erupted as fragments of low-density frothy pumice and were later flattened by compression during the welding process.

In addition to pumice, the welded and non-welded tuff at Battleship Rock contains a variety of angular rock fragments that show no sign of flattening. These *lithic fragments* are a common feature of volcanic tuffs. They typically form during explosive eruptions when they are violently torn from the walls of the volcanic vent.

—*William C. McIntosh*

If You Plan to Visit

Battleship Rock is located 5.6 miles north of the Jemez Ranger Station on NM–4 (about 3 miles south of La Cueva). The best access is via the Battleship Picnic Area, a day-use fee area in the Santa Fe National Forest. The paved parking area provides access to picnic tables and grills; drinking water and chemical toilets are available. There is also an unnamed pullout just north of Battleship Picnic Area on NM–4 (on the east side of the road) that provides a spectacular view of Battleship Rock. For more information:

Santa Fe National Forest
1474 Rodeo Road
Santa Fe, NM 87505
(505) 438-7840
www.fs.fed.us/r3/sfe/

Soda Dam

SANTA FE NATIONAL FOREST

Soda Dam, showing the travertine build-up over an active stream. Left of center is The Grotto, a readily accessible cave that contains an active spring.

Soda Dam, a travertine hot spring deposit located about a mile north of the town of Jemez Springs, is a highly popular roadside stop for visitors to the area. Soda Dam, Jemez State Monument, and Battleship Rock are all located in scenic San Diego Canyon, one of several radially oriented canyons on the southern flank of the Jemez Mountains. Soda Dam and other adjacent hot springs deposits offer insights into current and past behavior of hot geothermal water flowing out of the Valles caldera, and its relationship to faults, hot springs, and human activity in the area. *Note: Use extreme caution if crossing the highway at Soda Dam.* Traffic is heavy in both directions, and there are blind curves at either end of the parking area.

Regional Setting

Soda Dam and San Diego Canyon are located on the south flank of the Jemez Mountains, a long-lived volcanic field along the southwestern edge of the Colorado Plateau. The Jemez volcanic field lies at the

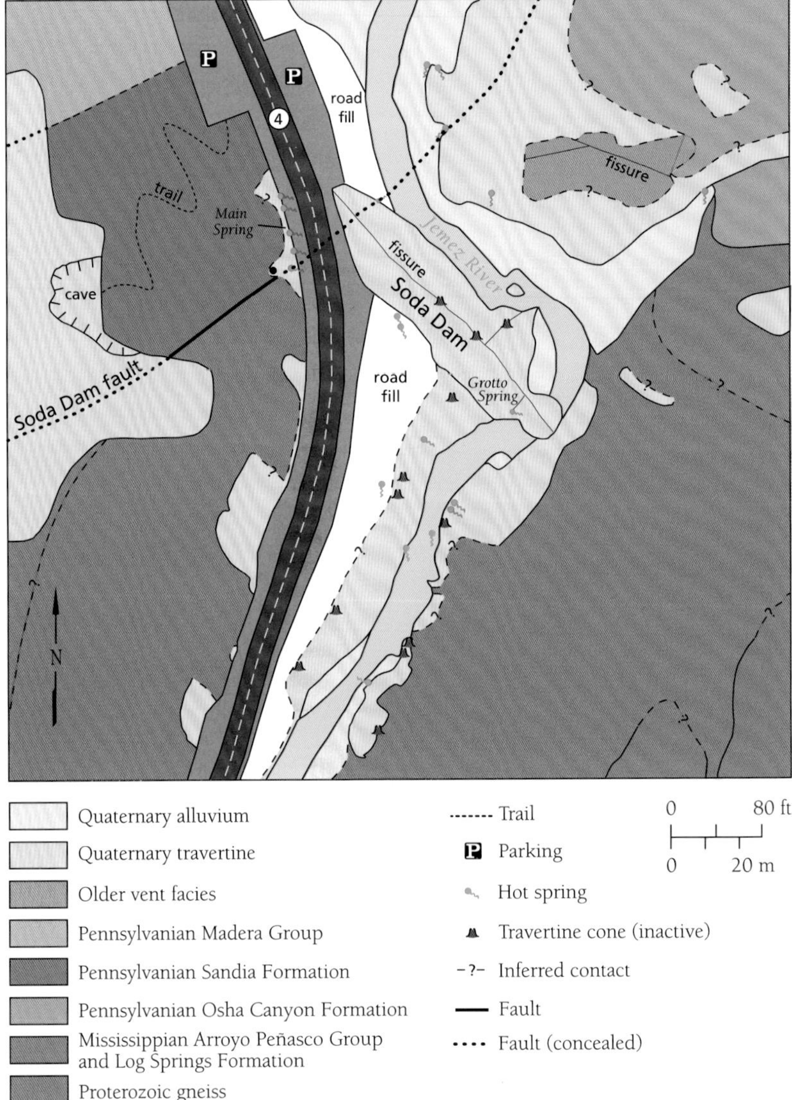

Generalized geologic map of the area in the immediate vicinity of Soda Dam. The trail to the cave on the west side of the highway is more of a steep scramble than a hike.

intersection of the Rio Grande rift and the Jemez lineament, two linear zones of weakness in the crust of the earth. Volcanic activity in the Jemez Mountains spanned more than 10 million years. Residual heat from this volcanism warms ground water within the Valles caldera. This hot ground water flows out of the Valles caldera beneath the ground surface along San Diego Canyon. Subsurface flow is largely guided by fractured rocks along faults caused by extension of the earth's crust along the Rio Grande rift. One of these faults intersects San Diego Canyon at Soda Dam, bringing mineral-rich geothermal waters to the surface and depositing the mound of travertine at Soda Dam.

The Rock Record

A wide variety of rock types are exposed at and near Soda Dam. Soda Dam itself is composed of *travertine*, a type of limestone formed where springs containing dissolved minerals discharge ground water to the surface where it interacts with the atmosphere. Before construction of the current highway, travertine was actively being formed all along the length of Soda Dam, by warm water flowing out of the central fissure along the crest of the dam. Travertine is still being deposited by an active hot spring immediately across the highway west of Soda Dam. The layered crusts, pools, and grottos at Soda Dam are common features of hot spring travertine deposits. In the area around Soda Dam, older travertine deposits mantle the slopes on both sides of the canyon.

The travertine deposits at Soda Dam were deposited onto older rocks exposed by erosion of San Diego Canyon. The oldest are Precambrian granitic rocks about 1.6 billion years old, which are exposed along a fault near Soda Dam. These are overlain by Mississippian through Permian sedimentary rocks, deposited in inland seas and rivers 400 to 250 million years ago. The sedimentary rocks are in turn overlain by volcanic lavas and tuffs erupted from the Jemez volcanic field over the last 10 million years. The abrupt transition from older red sedimentary rocks to younger black lavas and white tuffs is clearly visible high on the walls of San Diego Canyon.

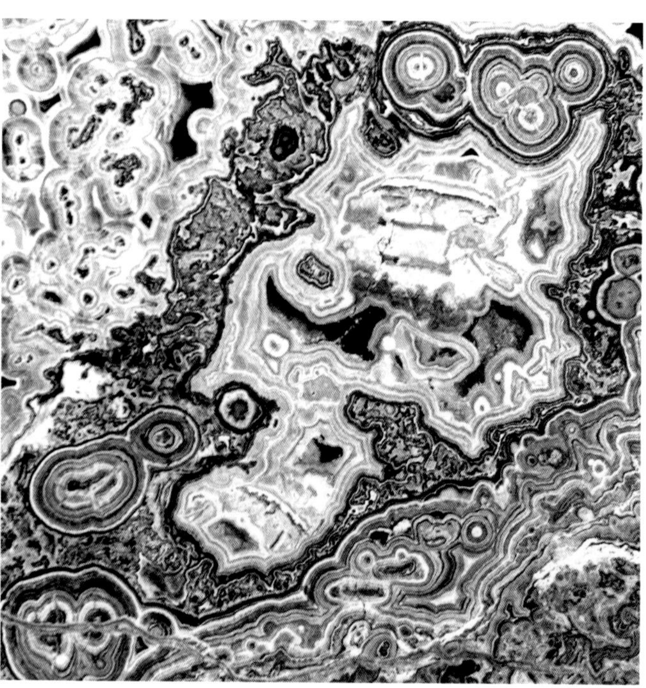

This polished slab of travertine provides a look at the structure and origin of such deposits. When surface or ground waters saturated with calcium carbonate flow over rocks or vegetation, successive, thin layers of calcium carbonate are deposited. The colors are due to impurities in the water.

Geologic History

The geological history of the Soda Dam area begins with the formation of the older rocks now exposed in the walls of San Diego Canyon. Cutting of the canyon and contemporaneous deposition of hot spring deposits occurred much later. Formation of the pre-canyon rocks now exposed in San Diego Canyon began with intrusion of the granite about 1.6 billion years ago, probably related to ancient volcanism along what was then the margin of the North American tectonic plate. Much later, between about 350 million and 250 million years ago, inland seas and rivers deposited fossil bearing sedimentary rocks. Volcanism in the Jemez Mountains began much later, about ten million years ago, culminating in the catastrophic eruption of the upper Bandelier Tuff and collapse of the Valles caldera 1.2 million years ago.

The travertine at and near Soda Dam reveals much about the history of the cutting of San Diego Canyon. Travertine from different elevations has been dated by isotopic methods. Travertine on the canyon walls is as much as one million years old, indicating that cutting of San Diego Canyon and discharge of geothermal waters began soon after formation of the Valles caldera. Travertine slightly higher than Soda Dam is as young as 60,000 years old, indicating that erosion of San Diego Canyon was nearly complete by that time. Dating of Soda Dam itself suggests that it formed within the last 7,000 years.

Geologic Features

HOT SPRINGS—The hot spring associated with Soda Dam (known as Main Spring) is one of fifteen springs and seeps that discharge along geologic faults in this area. The temperature of Soda Dam spring varies over time, reaching a maximum of 118° F (48° C). Warm water algae and actively depositing travertine can be seen in spring waters across the road from Soda Dam. Spring waters at Soda Dam contain a wide variety of dissolved elements, including elevated levels of arsenic and radium, derived from ground water passing thorugh volcanic rocks.

Polished fault surfaces like this one, known as slickensides, typically have lineations that indicate the direction of movement along the fault.

TRAVERTINE DAM—Soda Dam displays many features commonly seen in travertine deposits, including layered crusts and mounds, shallow pools, and grottos. One feature that is very unusual for a travertine deposit is that Soda Dam actually built over and across an actively flowing mountain stream.

Highway construction in the mid-1970s cut a notch at the west end of Soda Dam, changing the plumbing such that very little hot water now discharges along the crest of the dam. As a result, almost no travertine is actively being deposited, and Soda Dam is slowly disintegrating. Deposition of travertine is now largely restricted to a small area across the road from Soda Dam. Given sufficient time, this tiny travertine deposit might eventually rebuild a new Soda Dam.

POLISHED FAULT SURFACE—A polished surface along the Soda Dam fault is exposed in the road cut across the road from Soda Dam. Parallel scratches on this surface, termed *slickensides*, are the result of movement along this fault and show the orientation of movement.

UNCONFORMITIES—A short, steep, unimproved trail on the west side of NM–4 leads to a cave that formed at the contact between travertine-cemented ancestral Jemez River gravels and underlying Pennsylvanian Sandia sandstones that dip steeply to the north because they are caught in the Soda Dam fault zone. This is an excellent example of an unconformity. Just south of the cave, across the fault, Mississippian rocks sit on Precambrian rocks. Approximately 1.2 billion years of earth history is missing across the boundary between these two rock units.

—William C. McIntosh

If You Plan to Visit

Soda Dam is located .75 miles north of the town of Jemez Springs on NM–4 in the Santa Fe National Forest, just north of the Jemez Springs Ranger District. There are pull-offs on the east side of the road. Day use only; camping and campfires are prohibited. For more information, contact:

Santa Fe National Forest
1474 Rodeo Road
Santa Fe, NM 87505
(505) 438-7840
www.fs.fed.us/r3/sfe/

Fenton Lake State Park

NEW MEXICO STATE PARKS

Fenton Lake State Park lies in a broad, grass-covered valley on the west side of the Valles caldera. The lake is situated between imposing cliffs of Bandelier Tuff. Scattered along the lake, which is fed by the south-flowing Rio Cebolla, are a number of attractive lakeside campgrounds and picnic areas.

The park sits at an elevation of 7,900 feet and includes 700 acres of land. Before becoming a state park, Fenton Lake was purchased by New Mexico Game and Fish as a resting and nesting area for migratory waterfowl, and as a refuge for other wildlife. Now more of a fishing haven than a duck drop, it is still a great place to see wildlife. Waterfowl, turkey, deer, muskrat, elk, and bobcat can all be seen in the vicinity.

Regional Setting

Fenton Lake is in the Jemez Mountains volcanic field, on the western edge of the Valles caldera. Just to the west is the Sierra Nacimiento. NM–126 heading west from Fenton Lake traverses the lush, green forests and meadows on the western edge of the Jemez Mountains, crosses the scarp of the Nacimiento uplift, and descends to the town of Cuba, on the eastern edge of the San Juan Basin. The western edge of the Nacimiento uplift marks the location of the Nacimiento fault. Vertical displacement along this western edge of the Nacimiento uplift is on the order of 10,000 feet, which accounts for the remarkable west-facing scarp of the Sierra Nacimiento.

Rock Record

Three main rock units are exposed within the boundaries of the state park. The oldest unit is the Permian Abo Formation, a red-to-white sandstone interbedded with red siltstone (the basal part of the Abo is interbedded with limestone). It was deposited by an ancient river approximately 280 million years ago. This *arkosic* sandstone contains angular pebbles of quartz, potassium feldspar, and granite, indicating that the sediment has not traveled far from its granitic source. The pebbly sandstones were derived in part from the Peñasco uplift to the west of Fenton Lake, which roughly coincides with the present position of the Sierra Nacimiento. These Permian rocks are present at low elevation along both sides of the river and can be seen on the main road along the west side of the lake near the south end of the park.

Cliffs of Lower Bandelier Tuff.

The Permian red beds are overlain by the two members of the Bandelier Tuff. The lower of the two, the 1.6-million-year-old Otowi Member, sits directly on the Permian Abo Formation. Mesozoic rocks are preserved directly on the Abo Formation elsewhere in the Jemez Mountains, but here these Mesozoic rocks, which represent hundreds of millions of years of earth history, were eroded away before deposition of the tuff. This erosion probably occurred during the Laramide orogeny. The Otowi Member is composed of pumice, ash, crystals of quartz and sanidine, and dark-colored rock fragments that were violently erupted

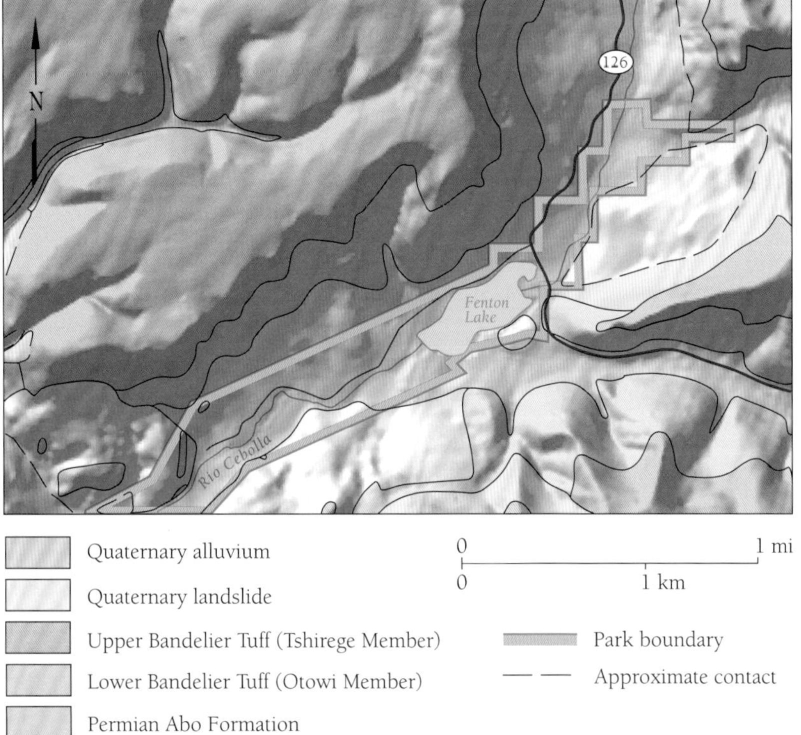

Generalized geologic map of Fenton Lake State Park and vicinity.

from the Valles caldera. The Otowi Member at Fenton Lake is unusually thick compared to other parts of the Jemez Mountains, and it exhibits welding, which is common in this unit along the western/northwestern quadrant of the caldera.

The upper (or Tshirege) member of the Bandelier Tuff overlies the Otowi Member. The upper member is similar in overall composition but contains fewer rock fragments. In this area the two members of the Bandelier Tuff are separated by 3 to 6 feet of Tsankawi pumice, deposited during beginning phase of the younger Tshirege eruption. Debris from the Tshirege eruption fills topographic lows in the rugged paleotopography that developed on the Otowi during the 350,000 years between eruptions of the upper and lower members of the Bandelier Tuff.

These rocks are overlain by much younger colluvium and landslide deposits, as well as terrace deposits and modern alluvium deposited by the Rio Cebolla. The hillsides here were denuded during a forest fire in August 2002. Debris flows resulting from erosion of these denuded slopes are periodically deposited on NM–126, temporarily blocking access to the lake. Some of this debris ended up in the lake shortly after the fire, forming a fan deposit on the eastern shore.

Geologic History

The uplift of the Ancestral Rocky Mountains, which occurred during late Pennsylvanian to early Permian time, is recorded in the erosional debris of the Abo Formation. The Peñasco uplift formed during the orogeny associated with the uplift of the Ancestral Rocky Mountains. Eventually the effects of the Laramide orogeny were felt in this part of New Mexico, about 55 million years ago. It was at this time that the Nacimiento uplift to the west was formed. Since then, of course, the entire region has been reshaped as a result of the complex evolution of the Jemez Mountain volcanic field and the Valles caldera. The Bandelier Tuff exposed at Fenton Lake records two of the more recent and widespread eruptive events, 1.6 and 1.2 million years ago. (For a complete discussion of the Bandelier Tuff, see the chapter on Bandelier National Monument.) Since those eruptions, 1.2 million years of erosion have further shaped this landscape.

—Shari A. Kelley and L. Greer Price

If You Plan to Visit

Fenton Lake is accessible from US 550 via NM–4 north from San Ysidro to La Cueva and NM–126 west from La Cueva, or from the west by way of NM–126 from Cuba. Fenton Lake is approximately 30 miles from Cuba; portions of the access roads from either direction are unpaved. A popular year-round retreat surrounded by beautiful ponderosa pine forests, Fenton Lake State Park features a cross-country ski and biathlon trail and wheelchair-accessible fishing platforms. Winter storms may temporarily close some of these roads. A number of the campsites may be reserved in advance. For more information, contact:

Fenton Lake State Park
455 Fenton Lake Rd.
Jemez Springs, NM 87025
(575) 829-3630
www.emnrd.state.nm.us/PDR/Fenton

Gilman Tunnels

SANTA FE NATIONAL FOREST

The Gilman Tunnels are on NM–485 along the Rio Guadalupe in the southwestern Jemez Mountains, approximately 5 miles northwest of the intersection of NM–4 and NM–485. Two narrow and unusually high tunnels were cut through Precambrian granite in the 1920s to facilitate passage of logging trains through this particularly rugged and constricted section of Guadalupe Canyon, known as the Guadalupe Box. Logs that were harvested in the western Jemez Mountains in the 1920s were taken by narrow-gauge railroad to a sawmill in Bernalillo. The tunnels were enlarged in the 1930s to accommodate logging trucks. Logs were hauled out of the mountains and then loaded on trains at Gilman logging camp, which was established in 1937 about two miles south of the tunnels. The railroad was shut down by flooding along the Jemez and Guadalupe Rivers in 1941. The highway now occupies the old railroad bed. Aside from providing access to the Guadalupe Box itself, NM–485 provides an unparalleled view of the stratigraphy of Guadelupe Canyon.

The Gilman Tunnels were carved out of 1.6-billion-year-old granitic gneiss in the 1920s.

Regional Setting

The Gilman Tunnels lie in the transition between the Jemez Mountains and the Sierra Nacimiento. The Jemez Mountains are part of a volcanic field that has been active for the past 16 million

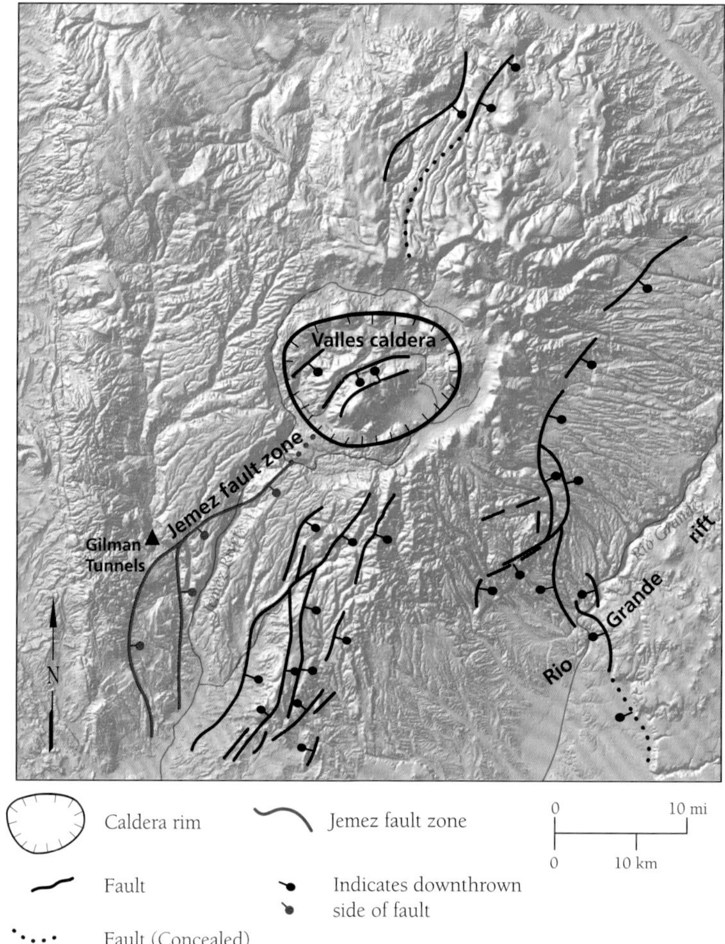

Displacement along the Jemez fault zone is responsible for bringing these Precambrian crystalline rocks to the surface. Older rocks on the west side of the fault have been upthrown, where they are now exposed at the surface.

years. The Sierra Nacimiento mountain range has a long, complex geologic history. The Sierra Nacimiento formed mainly during compressional Laramide deformation, starting about 75 million years ago, but has also been affected by extension along the Rio Grande rift. The Precambrian rock through which the tunnels are cut was brought to the surface along the Jemez fault, a major northeast-trending, rift-bounding fault, the same fault that formed Soda Dam to the northeast.

The Rock Record

Granitic rocks that formed in the roots of an ancient 1.6-billion-year-old mountain range are exposed up canyon of the tunnels, northwest of the Jemez fault. Also exposed in the vicinity is the most complete section of Mississippian to Pennsylvanian sedimentary rocks in the Jemez Mountains. Younger rocks, including brick-red sandstone and siltstone of the Permian Abo Formation, red-orange, cross-bedded sandstone of the Permian Yeso Group, white sandstone of the Permian Glorieta Formation, brick-red mudstone and sandstone of the Triassic Moenkopi Formation, and yellowish-tan, cross-bedded sandstone of the Shinarump (Agua Sarca) Formation in the Triassic Chinle Group, are exposed just downstream of the tunnels on the southeast side of the fault. Bandelier Tuff is preserved high on the cliffs.

Geologic History

The lower stretch of the Guadalupe River canyon exposes a thick section, including (from bottom to top) Permian redbeds of the Yeso Formation, Glorieta Sandstone, and Triassic Moenkopi and Chinle strata, capped by thick exposures of Bandelier Tuff.

The granitic gneiss at the Gilman Tunnels likely originated as granite that was intruded at great depth in a mountain range that formed the southwestern margin of the North American continent. The granite was subsequently deformed, causing platy micaceous minerals to become aligned or foliated, forming the gneissic texture we see today. Resting on the gneiss are gray Mississippian limestones that record the presence of a shallow ocean approximately 330 million years ago. A gap in the rock record of approximately 1.27 billion years, known as the Great Unconformity, occurs between the gneiss and the limestone. The shallow ocean persisted into Pennsylvanian time with the deposition of limestone, shale, and sandstone of the Osha Canyon Formation, Sandia Formation, and the Madera Group. All of these units are quite fossiliferous. Pieces of granitic gneiss in the upper beds of the Madera Group indicate that the Sierra Nacimiento was a mountain range even in Pennsylvanian time. The seas withdrew toward the south, to be replaced by the south-flowing river system preserved in the Abo Formation. The climate became increasingly dry during Permian time, which led to the deposition of the cross-bedded, eolian (wind-blown) sand dunes in the Yeso Group.

Sea level rose again during late Permian time, causing sedimentation of white sand beaches and offshore sand bars in the Glorieta Formation. Sea level dropped and the river systems established themselves in the area. These river systems are recorded in the Triassic Moenkopi Formation and the Shinarump (Agua Sarca) Formation of the Triassic Chinle Group. The yellow-tan, cross-bedded Shinarump Formation was

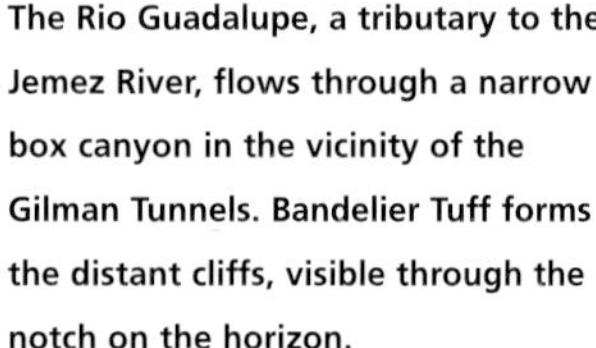

The Rio Guadalupe, a tributary to the Jemez River, flows through a narrow box canyon in the vicinity of the Gilman Tunnels. Bandelier Tuff forms the distant cliffs, visible through the notch on the horizon.

deposited by a river that flowed from Texas to Nevada and contains abundant petrified wood. No rocks that were deposited between 225 million years ago and 1.6 million years ago elsewhere in the Jemez Mountains are preserved in this part of the range; these rocks were either eroded away during Laramide deformation or were never deposited here. The region that includes the Gilman Tunnels was blanketed by the 1.6 million year old Bandelier Tuff when it erupted from the Valles caldera, about 13 miles to the northeast of this spot.

The hot ash, pumice, rock, and gas cloud rolled over a rugged landscape, filling in old river valleys. River gravels from those old valleys are now preserved under the tuff high on the canyon wall to the east of the tunnels, a classic example of inverted topography. A second large eruption covered the area with tuff 1.2 million years ago. In the 1.2 million years since that eruption, the Rio Guadalupe, which flows into the Jemez River about 5 miles downstream, has cut the beautiful canyon that we see today. The Jemez fault zone is responsible for bringing the ancient 1.6 billion year old rocks to the surface and has offset the 1.2-million-year-old Bandelier Tuff, dropping the tuff down about 50 feet to the southeast, indicating that this fault has been active in the relatively recent geologic past.

—Shari A. Kelley

If You Plan to Visit

The Gilman Tunnels are part of the Jemez National Recreation Area, on the Santa Fe National Forest. Access to the tunnels is by way of NM–485, a paved but narrow road that branches to the northwest off NM–4 just north of the Walatowa Visitor Center. From the north the tunnels can be reached via Forest Road 376 (unpaved), which heads south off of NM–126 several miles east of Fenton Lake. For more information:

Santa Fe National Forest
1474 Rodeo Road
Santa Fe, NM 87505
(505) 438-7840
www.fs.fed.us/r3/sfe/

Walatowa Visitor Center
P.O. Box 280
Jemez Pueblo, NM 87024
(575) 834-7235
www.jemezpueblo.com/

The Rio Grande Rift

The Rio Grande rift is the surface expression of a tear of the North American continent that is the result of regional stretching of the earth's crust. The rift extends north 600 miles from northern Mexico, through central New Mexico, and up into central Colorado with a diminishing width and degree of stretching to the north. Rifting began about 36 million years ago in the south and about 22 million years ago in the north. One consequence of this stretching is that the crust within the rift has become thinner (like pulled taffy), allowing higher heat flow from the earth's mantle and producing numerous volcanic features along the rift, including the chain of young volcanoes west of Albuquerque (at Petroglyph National Monument). Another consequence of this stretching or extension of the continent is that faults form along the margins of the rift and create *grabens*, much like keystones, that sink to create valleys as the rift pulls apart. There are several separate geologic basins where sediments have accumulated within the rift, which formed where faulting created depressions. In most geologic basins within the rift, there is a strong asymmetry to the faulting, so most basins form tilted half-grabens. Removal of material from the margins of the rift by the larger faults produces rift-flank uplifts as the earth's crust is unloaded.

High heat flow within the rift also modifies buoyancy; just as hot air is less dense and rises, hot rock is less dense and floats higher than it would otherwise. The lower density of the relatively hotter rocks beneath the rift also contributes to the uplift. Even though the rift is dominated by the Rio Grande valley, the average elevation of the rift and flanking uplifts is higher than the terrain outside the rift, especially compared to the High Plains to the east. This localized buoyancy is in addition to the striking high elevation of the entire western United States.

The rift begins as a series of eastward offsets between basins north of the Sandia Mountains. These offsets, called accommodation zones, are complex structures, because the deformation is being transferred from one set of faults to another. The northern end of the Sandia Mountains ramps down dramatically toward the town of Placitas, as displacement along the big faults bounding the east side of the mountains dies out and faults further east take up the slack. Some of the accommodation for this transfer of strain to the northeast, into the Santo Domingo sub-basin and the fault at the base of the hill at La Bajada, can be seen in the faulted blocks of the basalt-capped Santa Ana Mesa. From the Santo Domingo Basin, the rift steps to the east again at the La Bajada

OPPOSITE: View across the northern Albuquerque Basin of the Sandia Mountains looking southeast from above Rio Rancho. Vast quantities of sediment have accumulated within closed basins created by active faulting. Approximately 5 miles of displacement has occurred along the fault that forms the western escarpment of the Sandias. About 600,000 years ago the Rio Grande began cutting into these sediments, forming an inner valley and floodplain that today provide fertile agricultural land.

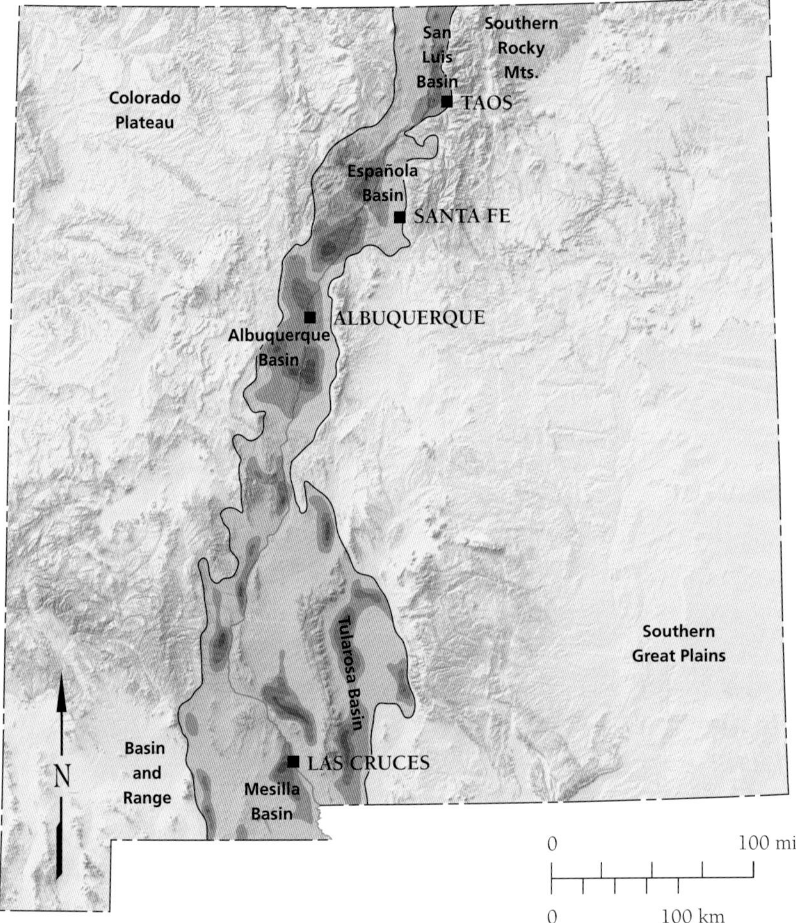

Basins of the Rio Grande rift (shown in pink) in New Mexico. Darker shading indicates deeper parts of the basin.

constriction, where strain on the west-side-down La Bajada fault transfers to the east-side-down Pajarito fault that bounds the west side of the west-tilted half-graben of the Española Basin. The Pajarito fault cuts across tuffs and lavas erupted from the Valles caldera and older volcanic centers in the Jemez Mountains. North of the town of Española, the Embudo fault accommodates another eastward offset of the rift into the San Luis Basin that extends from Taos into southern Colorado. The Embudo fault lies along the Jemez lineament, a northwest-trending zone of aligned volcanic features that is thought to be a zone of weakness related to how this part of North America was accreted to the continent 1.7 billion years ago. The San Luis Basin, extending from Taos into south-central Colorado, is the least dissected (or eroded) basin in the rift, largely because it is capped and filled with hard volcanic rocks. Nonetheless, the Rio Grande has carved a dramatic deep gorge into the basin west of Taos.

Geologic Evolution of the Rift

Rifting began as that period of mountain building called the Laramide orogeny started to wane about 30 million years ago. According to one tectonic model, the Laramide orogeny was caused by the low-angle subduction of a buoyant oceanic crust, the Farallon plate, beneath the North American continent. During Laramide deformation, traction between the shallowly dipping Farallon plate and the lithosphere (the rigid part of the earth's crust) beneath North America formed the Rocky Mountains. When the Farallon plate became less buoyant and began to sink into the earth's mantle at a higher angle, the contraction that formed the Rockies ended. Hot mantle material moved into the space above the descending slab, triggering melting and eruption of the volcanic centers to the northeast and east of the Sandia Mountains (the Ortiz Mountains, Cerrillos Hills, and South Mountain) and to the northeast of Taos (the Latir Wilderness).

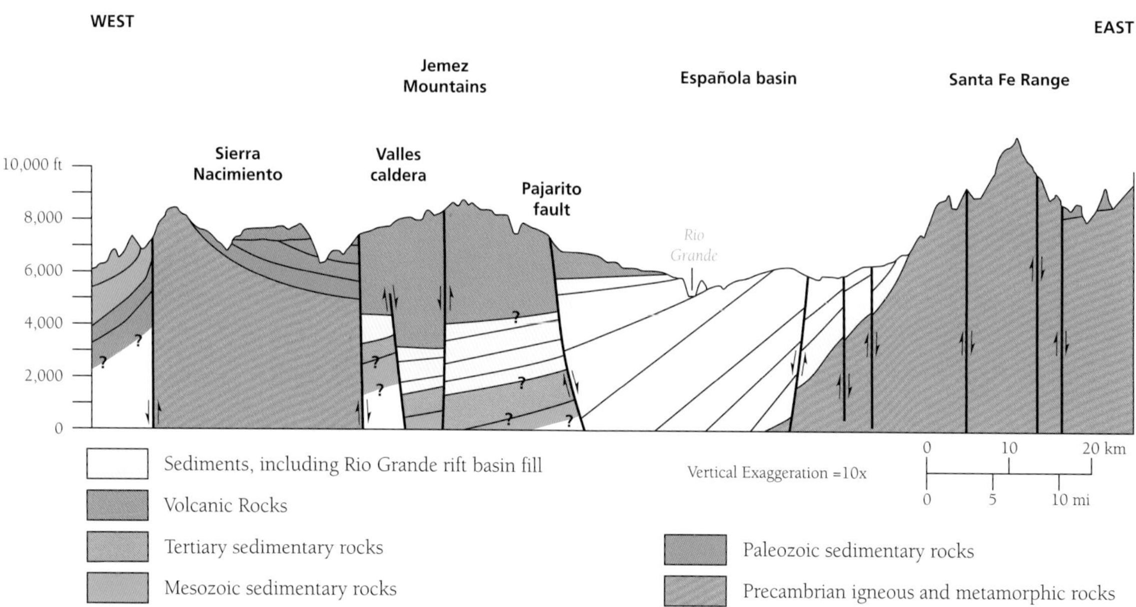

Generalized cross section through the Rio Grande rift in the vicinity of the Española Basin. The rift here extends beneath the Jemez Mountains.

High topography created by Laramide compression and by the buoyancy effects of high heat flow from the mantle could not support itself and began to collapse and extend under its own weight. Elevated regions are subject to greater collapse and extension, paradoxically often causing topography to be inverted: In many places, basins formed where mountains had been. The Colorado Plateau—an elevated region of anomalously undeformed crust—retreated under the weight of the collapsing high mountain ranges created to the north and east of it. Behind the southwest-retreating Colorado Plateau, a linear zone of extension—the Rio Grande rift—began to form. In southern New Mexico, extension has occurred over a broad and less distinctively linear zone. The rift here merges with the Basin and Range province, which wraps around the southern edge of the Colorado Plateau.

The basins of the Rio Grande rift deepened and filled with sediment as movement increased during repeated earthquake-producing ruptures along the faults bounding the rift. Initially the basins within the rift were internally drained, but as rifting slowed, the basins filled from north to south, and streams began to flow from one to the other. These streams gradually began to integrate, forming a through-flowing ancestral Rio Grande that reached the Gulf of Mexico about 600,000 years ago. The sediments that had accumulated in the depressions filled by the ancestral Rio Grande began to be eroded and carried into the sea, creating the inner valley of the modern Rio Grande.

Continued rifting may split a continent in two, or it may result in a failed rift (or *aulacogen*). Volcanism and faulting will continue to modify the landscape as rifting slowly proceeds. If rifting were to persist, eventually the ocean could once again cover central New Mexico, perhaps looking like the Red Sea. However, there is little danger of that happening, especially any time soon. Most of the sediments in the Rio Grande rift are 16 to 7 million years old. The peak of extension occurred in middle Miocene time, and the intensity of extension has waned significantly in the past 5 million years. Very few significant historic earthquakes have been recorded along rift-bounding faults. The presence of a magma body and related seismicity in the vicinity of Socorro, New Mexico, however, suggests that, while extension has slowed, the curtain hasn't entirely closed on activity in the Rio Grande rift. Although the risk is small now, it is certain that we can look forward to at least a few more volcanic eruptions and earthquakes along the rift in the geologic future.

—Adam S. Read and Shari A. Kelley

The Rio Grande Gorge

BUREAU OF LAND MANAGEMENT

OPPOSITE: **The Rio Grande gorge from the west side of the river looking northeast. This section of the river, just north (upstream) of the High Bridge and south of the Rio Hondo, is part of the stretch known as the Taos Box. The cliffs are Servilleta Basalt. Over 600 feet of basalt were deposited in 2 million years of episodic eruptions between 2.8 and 4.8 million years ago.**

The Rio Grande gorge is a spectacular, 75-mile-long, steep-sided canyon of the Rio Grande located in the San Luis Basin of southern Colorado and northern New Mexico. Due to its unspoiled beauty and diversity of recreational opportunities, a 68-mile stretch of this free-flowing river system was declared one of the nation's original national wild and scenic river systems in 1968. A variety of parklands along the river corridor provide access, interpretative sites, and environmental protection to this magnificent landscape.

For the last 30 million years, crustal forces have slowly torn the North American continent apart along the Rio Grande rift. The crust has been uplifted, stretched, thinned, broken, and intruded by magma. The resulting rift valley has cleaved New Mexico and half of Colorado for a distance of over 600 miles.

The 150-mile-long San Luis Basin is one of the major segments of the Rio Grande rift. It is bordered by the Sangre de Cristo Mountains on the east and the Tusas and San Juan Mountains on the west. The basin is roughly divided into two physiographic/geologic provinces: the narrow Taos Plateau of northern New Mexico, and the broad San Luis Valley of southern Colorado. The divide between the two consists of a prominent east-west zone of volcanoes between Questa and Tres Piedras. At the southern end of the basin, near Taos, the rift is about 20 miles wide and 3 miles deep.

Unlike the rift basins to the south, the San Luis Basin is relatively undissected. That is, the sedimentary material that fills the basin has not yet been extensively exposed by the action of rivers and streams. Instead, the Rio Grande and its three major tributaries have cut deep, narrow canyons through the volcanic rocks that cap most of the southern basin. The river canyons provide unparalleled exposures of a diversity of Tertiary volcanoes and their lava flows, and reveal an intriguing chronicle of the birth and adolescence of the mighty Rio Grande.

Regional Setting

The Rio Grande is the fifth longest river in North America, flowing 1,885 miles from the San Juan Mountains of southern Colorado to the Gulf of Mexico. The Rio Grande watershed is 336,000 square miles, equal to 11 percent of the continental U.S. The watershed encompasses parts of two countries (the U.S. and Mexico), eight states (Colorado, New Mexico, Texas, Chihuahua, Coahuila, Nuevo Leon, Tamaulipas, and Durango), and more than twenty Native American nations.

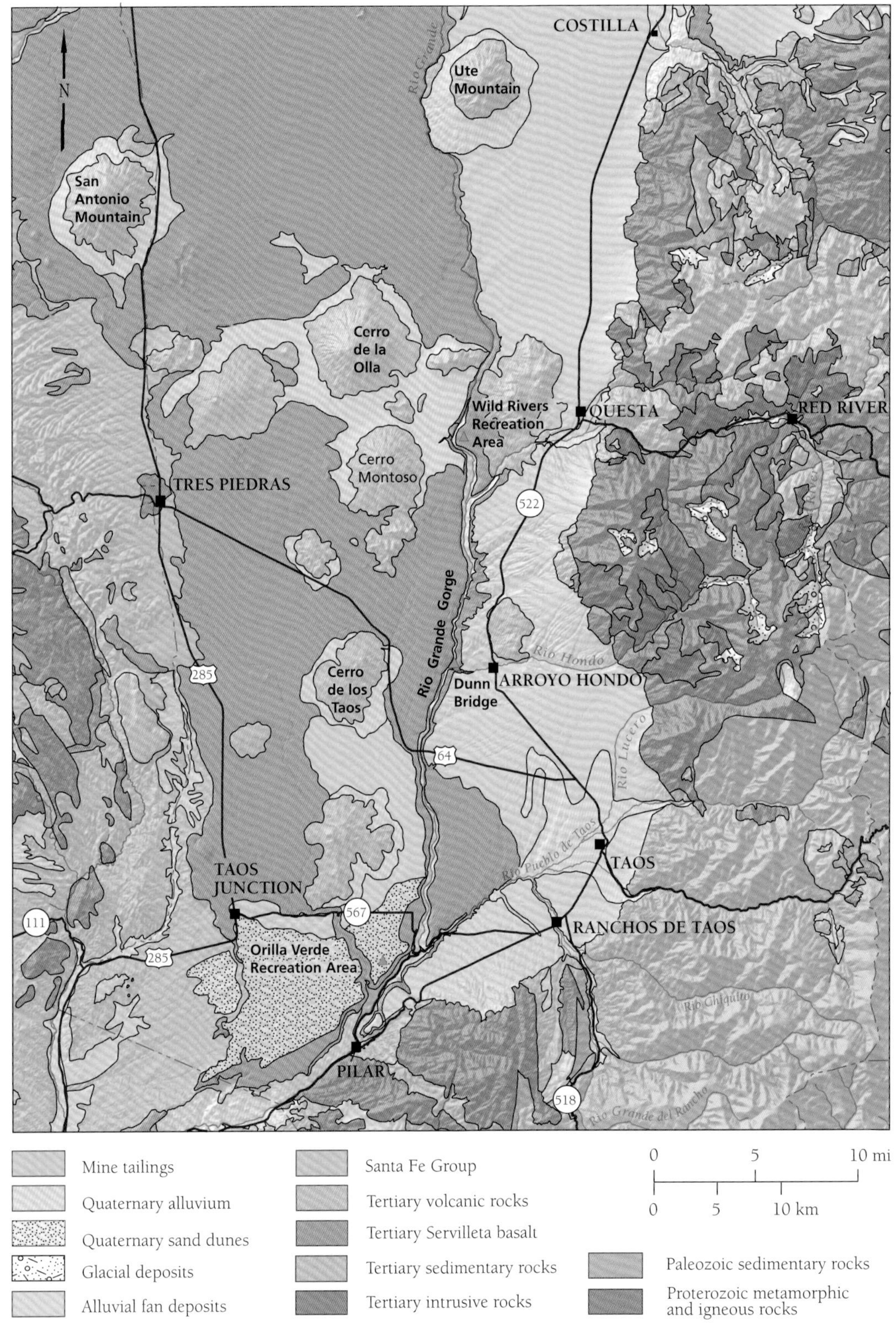
N
COSTILLA
Rio Grande
Ute Mountain
San Antonio Mountain
Cerro de la Olla
Wild Rivers Recreation Area
QUESTA
RED RIVER
Cerro Montoso
TRES PIEDRAS
522
Rio Grande Gorge
Rio Hondo
ARROYO HONDO
Dunn Bridge
Cerro de los Taos
285
64
Rio Lucero
Rio Pueblo de Taos
TAOS
TAOS JUNCTION
567
111
RANCHOS DE TAOS
Orilla Verde Recreation Area
285
Rio Chiquito
PILAR
518
Rio Grande del Rancho
Mine tailings
Quaternary alluvium
Quaternary sand dunes
Glacial deposits
Alluvial fan deposits
Santa Fe Group
Tertiary volcanic rocks
Tertiary Servilleta basalt
Tertiary sedimentary rocks
Tertiary intrusive rocks
Paleozoic sedimentary rocks
Proterozoic metamorphic and igneous rocks
0 5 10 mi
0 5 10 km

Upon exiting the San Juan Mountains, the Rio Grande turns southward, transects the San Luis Basin, and flows southward through successive rift basins. The river itself did not excavate the rift. Rather, the river follows the topographically lowest path within the rift. Beginning in southern Colorado, near the Lobatos Bridge, the Rio Grande has cut the steep-walled canyon we know as the Rio Grande gorge into the basalt caprock. The gorge deepens southward to a maximum of 850 feet at the Wild Rivers Recreation Area near Questa, and then gradually shallows as the Rio Grande flows through the southernmost San Luis Basin and into the Española Basin.

OPPOSITE: Generalized geology in the vicinity of the Taos volcanic field. Much of the Rio Grande gorge here is capped with Servilleta Basalt, which ranges in age from 4.8 to 2.8 million years.

The Rock Record

New Mexico has been called the "Volcano State" because of the hundreds of relatively young volcanoes that pepper the landscape, with a preponderance located in the Rio Grande rift. Nearly all of the isolated, rounded mountains scattered across the Taos Plateau are extinct volcanoes that erupted between 6 and 1 million years ago. At least thirty-five discrete volcanic vents have been identified on the plateau. The number of buried volcanoes is unknown but probably large.

The volcanoes of the Taos Plateau come in a variety of sizes and shapes. The shape of any volcano depends on several factors: chemical composition of the molten lava, conditions during eruption, and the amount of erosion since the eruption. The more silica (SiO_2) in a magma, the higher its viscosity, or resistance to flow. Silica percentages in magma range from about 50 to 75 percent. Viscosity controls the type of volcano that forms. Basalt has the lowest viscosity of any common magma.

Volcanoes are assigned to one of four types: cinder cones, composite volcanoes, shield volcanoes, and lava domes. Cinder cones are the simplest form. They are small, steep-sided, circular to oval cones that are constructed from pyroclastics (scoria, cinders, ash, blocks, and lava bombs) ejected from a central vent. These volcanoes can erupt for months to years. Cinder cones are found on the Taos Plateau.

Composite volcanoes (or stratovolcanoes) tend to be large, steep-sided, symmetrical cones that are built of combinations of pyroclastics and lava flows. No true composite volcanoes are seen along the Rio Grande, although Mount Taylor near Grants is a classic composite volcano. Famous composite volcanoes include Mount Fuji in Japan and Mount Rainier in Washington.

Shield volcanoes are gently sloping cones that are assembled entirely by successive, thin lava flows of basalt. Flows erupt from a central summit vent, or cluster of vents, and spread out in all directions, often flowing for miles before solidifying. The Hawaiian Islands are a chain of immense shield volcanoes. Most of the basalts exposed in the Rio Grande gorge were erupted from a series of shield volcanoes west of the river.

Lava domes (also known as lava cones or volcanic domes) are formed by eruptions of thick, viscous lava that are incapable of flowing very far. The lava piles over and around the vent, and commonly expands from within, forming steep-sided domes with lava rubble covering its surface. Lava domes are formed by dacite and rhyolite magmas, which have high silica content and are therefore more viscous and resistant to flow. Domes can be active from decades to centuries.

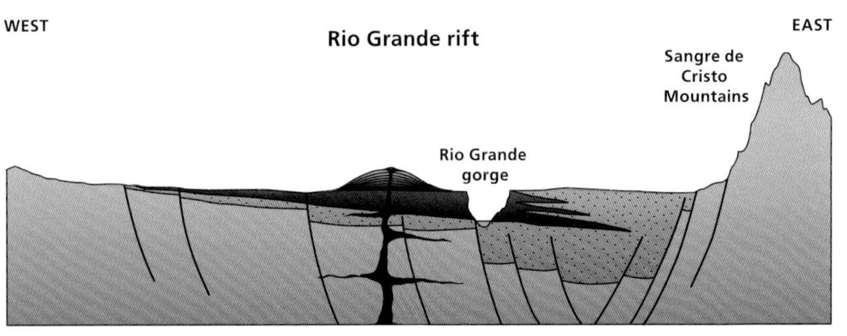

The Rio Grande gorge is a narrow, steep-sided canyon incised into the basin-fill sediments of the Rio Grande rift. At the south end of the basin, near Taos, the rift is 20 miles wide and 3 miles deep.

A single type of volcanic rock dominates the Taos Plateau landscape, the olivine-rich *tholeiite* basalts of the Servilleta Basalt. The gorge walls chiefly consist of thin, near-horizontal layers of this dark gray, vesicular lava. Most of the 50 cubic miles of basalt was erupted from a cluster of low-relief shield volcanoes near Tres Piedras, traveling as thin, molten sheets for tens of miles before solidifying. At the Rio Grande Gorge Bridge on US 64 west of Taos, over 600 feet of basalt were deposited in approximately 2 million years of episodic eruptions between 4.8 and 2.8 million years ago. These rocks can be seen from any location along the gorge, but they are especially well exposed near the Gorge Bridge. The Servilleta lavas are similar in composition to the modern basalts that periodically erupt in Hawaii, both having come from deep within Earth's mantle.

The volcanoes that flank the Rio Grande gorge span a wide variety of compositions. Although most are mafic (iron-rich) to intermediate in composition (basalts, andesites, dacites), rhyolites and rhyodacites are not uncommon. Cerro de la Olla (4.97 million years old), Cerro Montoso (5.88 million years old), and Cerro de los Taoses (4.84 million years old) are all andesite volcanoes. The topographically prominent Ute Mountain (2.7 million years old), San Antonio Mountain (3 million years old), and Guadalupe Mountain (5.3 million years old) volcanoes are all dacite domes. Cerro Chiflo volcano (5.3 million years old) is also composed of dacite but is quite distinct from other dacite volcanoes on the plateau. The principal rhyolite volcano, No Agua Peaks lava domes (4 million years old), is of special interest because of its valuable perlite deposits.

Interspersed with the volcanic deposits are a number of young sedimentary deposits. Although some of the sediment that fills the rift basin was deposited by the Rio Grande, most of the clay, sand, and gravel was eroded from the mountains during the past 25 million years. The San Luis Basin is surrounded by alluvial fans that have slowly advanced from the mountains into the basin. Over time, each alluvial fan has been buried under successively younger alluvium as the basin subsides. In the Rio Grande rift, the older rift-fill deposits are called the Santa Fe Group. Over most of the basin, we can see only the youngest basin fill at the surface. However, glimpses of Santa Fe Group sediments exist in the gorge, commonly as brick-red sandy layers sandwiched between basalts in the gorge walls. The youngest of these alluvial fans and Rio Grande river deposits sustain the many sand and gravel quarries in the Taos Valley.

Geologic History

A fascinating sequence of geologic events has conspired to create today's landscape. Although most of the rocks exposed in the gorge are no older than 5 million years, the history of events leading up to the development of the Rio Grande and its magnificent canyon date back hundreds of millions of years. This chapter emphasizes only the last 35 million years of history, a time span that encompasses the evolution of the headwaters of the Rio Grande in Colorado and the Rio Grande rift.

The Rio Grande rift is filled with sediments shed from the rift-flanking mountains. These sediments from the Taos area were deposited by debris flows in late Tertiary time.

A number of key geologic events took place before the Rio Grande began to carve the gorge. Around 35 million years ago, eruption of the San Juan volcanic field of southern Colorado created volcanic highlands that ultimately became the headwaters of the Rio Grande. For millions of years, vast aprons of sediment that were eroded from the volcanoes blanketed south-central Colorado and north-central New Mexico. The onset of rifting, and development of the Sangre de Cristo fault coincided with the earliest explosive eruptions of the Latir volcanic field near Questa 25 million years ago. For the next 10 million years, rift extension was slow, and sediment eroded from the San Juan and Latir volcanoes continued to fill the San Luis Basin. By 10 million years ago the rift had become much more active, with strong development of the Sangre de Cristo fault system and rapid subsidence of the basin. The character of the modern mountains was developed during this time. As the basin subsided, it was continuously filled with sediments shed from the adjacent mountains. By 5 million years ago the Taos Plateau volcanic field had begun to cover the southern San Luis Basin with volcanoes and their eruptive products, and by 3 million years ago the Servilleta Basalt had capped the sedimentary basin with a thick pile of resistant flows.

The origin of the gorge begins well before the river actually began to downcut. In early Pleistocene time the San Luis Basin was divided into three hydrologic basins separated by a pair of topographic highs near Questa and Alamosa. A large, shallow lake, now named Lake Alamosa, occupied the Alamosa Valley, and was dammed by the San Luis Hills. The Sunshine Valley area contained a smaller lake, now known as Sunshine Lake, that was fed principally by streams of the northern Sangre de Cristo Mountains. Sunshine Lake was dammed by the volcanic cones and fault scarps west of Questa. South of the volcanoes was a small ancestral Rio Grande, the headwaters of which were the modern Red River. This entirely New Mexican river system flowed southward over the basalt plateau along a wide, meandering floodplain, similar in form to the modern Rio Grande near Alamosa.

Some time after 2.8 million years ago, after the last Servilleta basalts had erupted, the ancestral Red River/Rio Grande began to carve a channel into the plateau. Although the river was limited by a modest watershed of only about 200 square miles, it easily sliced through the basalt-capped plateau.

About 440,000 years ago, during a wet climatic cycle, Lake Alamosa filled and flowed over its igneous dam. The lake rapidly eroded a canyon through the San Luis Hills. As the lake drained, it filled Sunshine Lake, which in turn overtopped its volcanic dam. As the water eroded a canyon between Guadalupe Mountain and Cerro Chiflo, the Rio Grande at long last became a fully integrated river system, and the Red River was demoted to tributary status through this brazen act of piracy. The river had by that time vastly increased its volume and erosive power, and it proceeded to carve a deep gorge north of the Red River confluence. This drama continues to unfold today, as the steep river gradient upstream of the Red River confluence struggles to catch up to the gentler gradient of the upper gorge. Over the next several hundreds of thousands of years, this fluvial nick point will slowly migrate upstream, until the wild rapids have migrated upstream to Colorado.

Geologic Features

THE WILD RIVERS RECREATION AREA—The Wild Rivers Recreation Area 35 miles north of Taos provides some of the most impressive views in

In the Wild Rivers Recreation Area, the Rio Grande has exposed a variety of Tertiary volcanic features. This upstream view, taken from the fault scarp of the Red River fault zone, shows Servilleta Basalt (layered rocks on both rims), dacite flows from the Guadalupe Mountain volcano (massive orange-brown outcrops in lower canyon walls), and Cerro Chiflo volcano (high ridge and cliff on left skyline). On the right distant skyline are the high peaks of the Sangre de Cristo Mountains of New Mexico and Colorado. Three of the rapids of the Class IV Razorblades section of the Rio Grande are visible in the river.

New Mexico. Here the deeply incised Rio Grande and Red River converge in a geomorphologically matched set of basalt-capped canyons that illustrate their shared history of river piracy. To the west are the conspicuous volcanoes of the Taos Plateau volcanic field, and to the east are the Sangre de Cristo Mountains. The canyon ecosystem, from rim to river, contains a unique diversity of plants and animals. Piñon and juniper forests are home to 500-year-old trees, mule deer, red-tailed hawks, mountain blue-birds, and prairie dogs.

The Wild Rivers Backcountry Byway winds along the rim of the gorge, offering access to spectacular overlooks and trailheads. Twenty-two miles of rim and river hiking trails exist in the park. Most trailheads are in campgrounds where day-use parking is available.

The confluence of the Red River and the Rio Grande at La Junta Point offers an unparalled three-dimensional view of the volcanic stratigraphy of the plateau. The west gorge wall at Chiflo Campground offers a fine view of the partially buried lava dome that formed when Chiflo volcano erupted. The west wall of the gorge at the BLM Pay Station parking area exposes a small cinder cone that erupted and was later entombed by Servilleta Basalt flows.

THE RIO GRANDE GORGE BRIDGE—Located on US 64 west of Taos, the "High Bridge" (as it is sometimes known), perched 650 feet above the river, provides impressive views of the gorge. The award-winning bridge was completed in 1965 at a cost of $2,153,000. Its 1,272-foot length makes it the second-longest truss bridge in the U.S. It provides fine views of the lower, middle, and upper Servilleta Basalt flows.

The "Racecourse" section on the Rio Grande provides a wet ride for white-water rafters. The rapids on this stretch of the river are due to rock falls and debris flows.

THE DUNN BRIDGE AT ARROYO HONDO—A drive into the gorge at Arroyo Hondo and across the John Dunn Bridge on County Road B–007 provides visitors with a close-up of the river, the basalts, and the sediments sandwiched between the basalt flows. The base of a basalt flow and its underlying brick-red baked sediments are visible just west of the bridge. This is the launch site for rafting trips through the famous Taos Box, a thrilling, 15-mile class IV whitewater trip. For many, rafting is an unsurpassed means of experiencing the Rio Grande gorge. The opportunities for rafting range from placid stretches suitable for canoes to extreme whitewater suitable only for the best kayakers. Commercial outfitters offer raft trips from April to October. A trip through the Taos Box provides an unforgettable combination of spine-tingling whitewater and an intimate geologic experience.

In the 1890s Long John Dunn of Taos bought the bridge at Manby Springs, 2 miles downstream of the Rio Hondo. After the bridge was destroyed by floods, Dunn rebuilt in Arroyo Hondo near the site of the modern bridge and operated a passenger and freight business for many years. John Dunn's toll bridge across the Rio Grande near Arroyo Hondo gave him a monopoly on road travel in and out of Taos.

Located in the gorge just downstream from the bridge, Black Rock Hot Spring is one of the most scenic outside the Jemez Mountains. The pool is located along the west bank. The water temperature remains at about 101 degrees except when the pool is flooded by high river flows. Manby Hot Springs is two miles downstream from the bridge on the east bank. Several sandy, 100-degree pools hold five or six soakers, but the lower pool tends to be cooler from river water seepage. From Manby Hot Springs, Dunn's old stagecoach trail switchbacks to the east rim.

Both of these hot springs are located on the Dunn fault, which runs beneath and parallels the course of the river at this point. The fault provides conduits for the ascent of deeply circulating thermal waters to the surface. These springs were once owned by Arthur Manby, an English

The Dunn Bridge on the Rio Grande, looking downstream (on the right), just upstream of the confluence with the Rio Hondo (entering on the left). The cliff-forming unit at river level is a unique alkali basalt whose source is unknown; note the columnar jointing. This is the start of the section known as the Taos Box, a class IV run. The river follows the Dunn fault at this point.

mining engineer who was at one time deemed the most hated man in Taos. In 1929 Manby's decapitated body and head were found in separate rooms of his Taos home. The cause of death was declared to be from natural causes.

THE ORILLA VERDE RECREATION AREA—The Orilla Verde Recreation Area is nestled along the banks of the Rio Grande between Taos and Española on NM–570. This park offers a wide variety of riverside recreational opportunities including boating, fishing, swimming, camping, and rock climbing. The elevation along the river is 6,100 feet, rising steeply to an elevation of 6,800 feet at the basalt-capped rim of the gorge. Because of the dramatic range of habitat, from riparian to mesa-top scrubland, the Orilla Verde draws many species of wildlife including eagles and hawks, songbirds, waterfowl, beaver, cougar, ringtail, and mule deer. It is also archeologically rich in petroglyphs and ancient habitation sites.

La Vista Verde Trail is located halfway up the switchback road of NM–567 west of the Taos Junction Bridge, in the Orilla Verde Recreation Area. From the parking area trailhead, a footpath runs atop an extinct landslide terrain with fine views of volcanic features such as pahoehoe flows, vesicles, and columnar joints. The easy, 2.5-mile trail has wonderful panoramic views of the basalts and landslides near the confluence of the Rio Grande and Rio Pueblo de Taos canyons.

THE TAOS VALLEY OVERLOOK—Just five miles north of the Rio Grande Gorge Visitor Center near Pilar is a pullout on the east side of NM–68, just a couple of miles beyond the roadside table. Informally known as the Horseshoe Bend Parking Area, it provides a superb vista of the Taos Plateau and Rio Grande gorge. To the north, isolated, rounded mountains are scattered across the Taos Plateau. Most are extinct volcanoes of the Taos Plateau volcanic field and range in age from 10 to 2 million years. Tres Orejas volcano is in the middle distance due north. Behind Tres Orejas in the far distance, the large round peak is San Antonio Mountain, a lava dome volcano located near the Colorado border. Just to the north of here is the widest section of the Rio Grande gorge, which turns out to have the same dimensions as Hadley Rille, the lunar landing site for Apollo 15. Because of this, the gorge and gorge rim were chosen by NASA for astronaut training in the 1960s.

Much of the land encompassed in this stunning view was recently protected through a unique, multi-partner agreement that saved the land from residential and commercial development. A consortium of partners formulated a plan that allowed the BLM to acquire the land from the Taos Valley Overlook to the Rio Grande. The parcel provides critical habitat for peregrine falcon and the endangered southwestern willow flycatcher.

—*Paul Bauer*

Additional Reading

Geology of the Taos Region, edited by Brian S. Brister, Paul W. Bauer, Adam S. Read, and Virgil W. Lueth. New Mexico Geological Society Guidebook No. 55, New Mexico Geological Society, 2004.

To Possess The Land: A Biography of Arthur Rochford Manby by Frank Waters. Swallow Press, 1993.

If You Plan to Visit

The Rio Grande has been designated a wild and scenic river from 6 miles north of the Colorado/New Mexico border at the Lobatos Bridge to Velarde, New Mexico, 16 miles north of Espanola. The Wild Rivers Recreation Area about 15 miles west of Questa provides spectacular views of the river and is open for day use and camping. Shelters and a visitor center are available on site. The Orilla Verde Recreation Area is about 15 miles southwest of Taos on NM–570. The Rio Grande Gorge

Visitor Center in Pilar at the intersection of NM–570 and NM–68 is also an excellent source of information. All of these are managed through the Taos Field Office.

Taos Field Office, Bureau of Land Management
226 Cruz Alta Road
Taos, NM 87571-5983
(575) 758-8851
River Information Recording: (888) 882-6188
Rio Grande Gorge Visitor Center: (575) 751-4899
www.blm.gov/nm/st/en/fo/Taos_Field_Office.html

Wild Rivers Visitor Center
1120 Cerro Road
Cerro, NM 87519
(575) 770-1600

The Sandia Mountains

CIBOLA NATIONAL FOREST

The Sandia Mountains viewed from the west, with Rincon Ridge in the foreground. I-25 is visible at the bottom of the photo.

The Sandia Mountains dominate the eastern skyline of Albuquerque. Although the Rio Grande made settlement of the region possible, it is the mountains that give the city much of its scenic character. When the massive cliffs of pink granite glow in the dusky red light of sunset, the Sandia Mountains resemble a slice of watermelon, their Spanish namesake. The arching range crest, capped by layered white limestone and dotted with green spruce forests, resembles the rind of this rocky melon. Viewed from the north or south, it is obvious that the range is a large block of the earth's crust that has been lifted and tilted to the east. Although the broadly curving and tilted geometry of the Sandia Mountains may appear simple, the rocks record a complicated interaction of geological forces operating over a vast amount of time.

Regional Setting

Most of the Sandia Mountains are protected wilderness. Given the proximity of Albuquerque, New Mexico's largest city, considerable wildness exists within the dramatic rugged canyons and ridges of the west face and on the densely forested eastern slopes. Bear, mountain lion, deer, and smaller creatures thrive on this sky island surrounded by a sea of piñon-juniper forest, grassland, and desert scrub.

The Sandia Mountains are bounded to the south by Tijeras Canyon, which formed along the Tijeras fault and separates this imposing range from the more diminutive, flat-topped Manzanita Mountains. The crest ascends northward to North Sandia Peak, the highest point in the range (10,447 feet), before descending toward the village of Placitas. The Sandias are the northernmost of a series of mountain ranges that bound the eastern side of the Albuquerque Basin, one of the largest basins of the Rio Grande rift, and are one of the finest examples of what is known as a rift-flank uplift. The Sandia Mountains are frequently confused with the Rocky Mountains; however, they are much younger and were formed by different processes. Instead of the compression that pushed up the Rockies, the Sandia Mountains owe their present stature to crustal stretching across the Rio Grande rift.

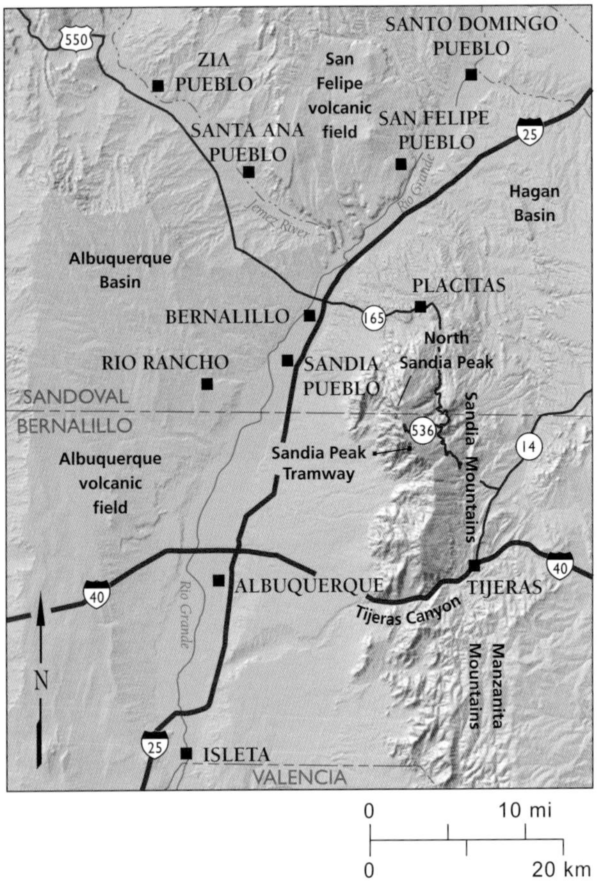

Rifting has stretched the Albuquerque Basin nearly one-fifth beyond its original width. As in most geologic basins within the Rio Grande rift, there is a strong asymmetry to the faulting here. Smaller rift-related faults bound the western margin of the basin and Colorado Plateau, but the larger faults lie on the east side, beneath Albuquerque. The scale of faulting along the mountain front is difficult to visualize but can be deduced from geologic mapping of rock units and from deep wells. The geologic contact separating the pink Sandia granite from the limestone cliffs of the Madera Group is nearly 6,000 feet above the city. This same contact lies about 25,000 feet beneath the Rio Grande. Over time, uplift across the range-bounding faults caused erosion that ultimately sculpted the overlying block of crust into the Sandia Mountains. This crustal block (like all continental crust) contains lighter rocks that essentially float on denser, partially molten rocks deep below the surface. Rift-related faults are not vertical but tilt 60°–70° from horizontal. This tilting has important consequences to the shape of the range. Movement along these tilted faults removed rock from the western flank of the Sandias, allowing one side to rise and creating the dramatic western escarpment and gently sloping eastern flank that characterize rift-flank uplifts.

The Rock Record

Granite is the dominant rock type exposed in the Sandia Mountains and forms the massive pink cliffs of its western face. The Sandia granite is pink because of the ubiquitous large, rectangular potassium feldspar crystals that also give the rock its rough texture. The Sandia granite is an igneous rock that crystallized about 6 miles deep in the crust from magma at a temperature of about 1,300°F. As it slowly cooled, potassium feldspar crystals grew up to two inches across. Fluids from the crystallizing granite formed quartz veins and pegmatite dikes that cross-cut the granite. The granite also contains blobs of the darker magma and older rocks that mixed with the granite during its emplacement. The Sandia granite intruded these older rocks (formerly lava, sandstone, and shale) that had metamorphosed into amphibolites, quartzites, and schists. The intense heat related to emplacement of granite created a metamorphic aureole in the surrounding rocks.

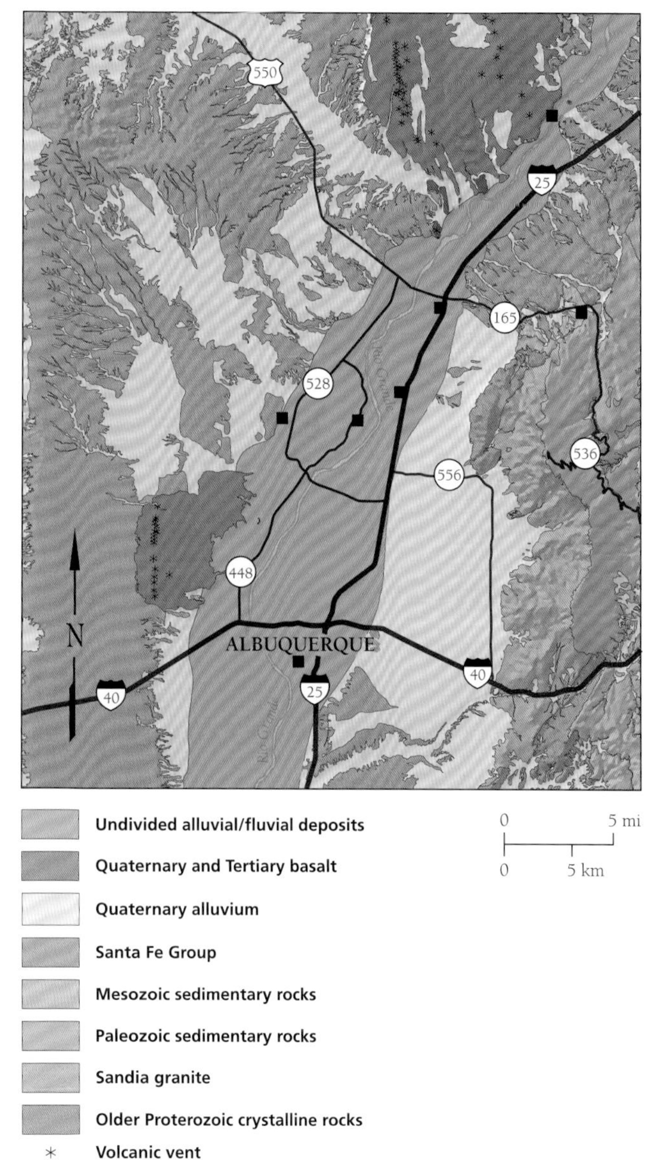

Generalized geologic map of the Albuquerque area.

One of the most remarkable facets of the geology of the Sandia Mountains is what is missing. The Sandia Mountains contain a spectacular gap in the rock record called the Great Unconformity. The Great Unconformity was first described by John Wesley Powell during his exploration of the Grand Canyon in 1869. It is recognized throughout much of the western United States as the boundary between crystalline basement rocks and overlying sedimentary and volcanic rocks. In the Sandia Mountains the Great Unconformity separates the Sandia granite from the overlying sedimentary rocks on the crest and eastern slope. The Great Unconformity represents a long period of erosion amounting to over 1.1 billion years of missing geologic record in the region.

The Great Unconformity is overlain by forested slopes of the Sandia Formation and cliffs of the Pennsylvanian Madera Group. The Madera Group is a series of thick fossil-bearing bluish-gray and white limestones, greenish-gray and tan shales, and coarse-grained sandstones that form the crest and eastern slope of the range. Red and orange sandstones and mudstones of the Permian Abo and Yeso Formations overlie the Madera Group. These red rocks were deposited by large east-flowing rivers. They have since been eroded from the crest but can be seen along the northern, southern, and eastern flanks of the range.

Geologic History

The oldest rocks in the Sandia Mountains once lay on the floor of a former ocean and along the shores of ancient volcanic islands. Between 1.67 and 1.65 billion years ago (during the Mazatzal orogeny) these islands collided with the ancient continent of Laurentia, which would later become North America. Mountain building thickened the continental crust, and granitic intrusions, like the Sandia granite, eventually sutured the crust of this newly formed edge of the continent.

These early rocks remained deeply buried for 200 million years, when another episode of mountain building, granitic intrusion, and metamorphism culminated with the emplacement of the Sandia granite, about 1.42 billion years ago. The Sandia granite is part of a large group of similarly aged igneous rocks that intruded a large swath of the earth's crust. The region became elevated by the increased buoyancy of the hotter and therefore less dense granite. Continental collisions and uplift continued through the Grenville orogeny, which created the ancient supercontinent of Rodinia by 1.3 billion years ago. About 1.25 billion years ago, this supercontinent began to rift apart, and uplift and erosion began bringing the Sandia granite closer to the earth's surface.

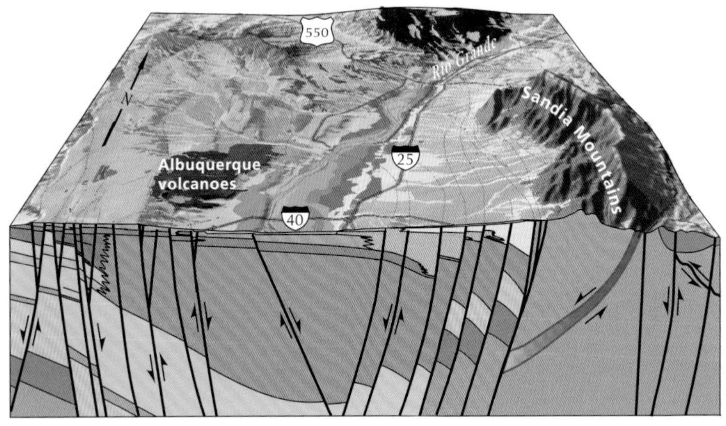

Oblique view of the Albuquerque metropolitan area, with the geologic map draped over a 3D digital elevation model. The 1.4-billion-year-old Sandia Granite is shown in pink on the east; the 156,000-year-old Albuquerque volcanoes are shown in red on the west.

This region remained part of a broad, persistent highland called the Transcontinental Arch until the region became inundated by seas that were teeming with tropical life about 350 million years ago (during the late Paleozoic Era). The late Paleozoic sedimentary rocks we see today accumulated in these seas. There almost certainly were other rocks deposited above the Sandia granite during the vast amount of time represented by the Great Unconformity, but none of these older rocks have been preserved here.

By late Pennsylvanian time, another continental collision resulted in the Ancestral Rocky Mountain orogeny. By Permian time the seas retreated south, followed by large southeast-flowing rivers that deposited the Abo and Yeso Formations. Over the next 200 million years, thick accumulations of terrestrial sediments were deposited in successive layers during a period of little tectonic activity.

Toward the end of the Cretaceous Period, the continental interior warped down and allowed the sea once again to invade from the southeast. The Western Interior Seaway reached its maximum area about 90 million years ago, extending from the Gulf of Mexico to the Arctic Ocean. In central New Mexico, these seas flooded and receded many times, leaving thick accumulations of sandstone, mudstone, and sparse limestone that are exposed east of Tijeras, in the Hagan Basin, and at Placitas. Regional uplift finally drove the seas away for good and culminated with another round of mountain building called the Laramide orogeny. This orogeny is enigmatic because the compressive forces responsible for it lay far to the west, in what would become California. The Laramide orogeny was responsible for thickening the continental crust and creating massive uplifts near Santa Fe and the Rocky Mountains to the north, but this deformation created little, if any, relief in the Sandia Mountains.

The Laramide orogeny ended about 35 million years ago, leaving New Mexico high above sea level. The region was then covered by extensive lava flows and volcanic debris until about 30 million years ago. As volcanic activity waned, the region began to stretch, as this high-elevation land began to collapse under its own weight. Crustal extension created the series of uplifted mountain blocks and down-dropped basins we now know as the Basin and Range province and the Rio Grande rift. The Albuquerque Basin began to sag and fill with sediments by the beginning of the Miocene, 23 million years ago. It is during this later phase of extension that the Sandia Mountains were born.

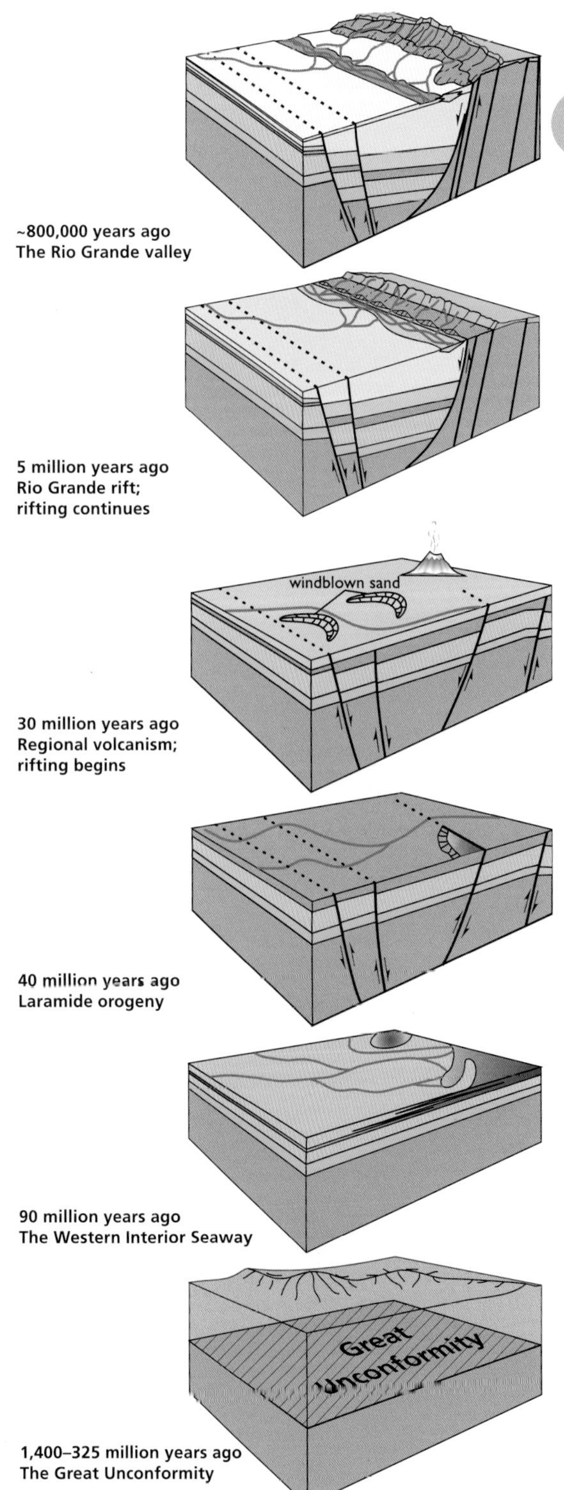

Geologic Features

The two most striking geologic features in the Sandia Mountains are the Great Unconformity, and differences between the steep western front and gentle (15°) eastern slope of the range. Both of these features are readily apparent when viewing the mountain from Albuquerque or from the crest.

THE VIEW FROM THE WEST SIDE OF THE SANDIAS—The Sandia granite itself and the large cliffs it forms are the most obvious geologic features of the Sandia Mountains. The texture of the Sandia granite affects how it weathers. The minerals in granite, because they formed at high temperature and pressures deep within the crust, are unstable at the earth's surface and are susceptible to chemical weathering and erosion. Water alters mica crystals and feldspars, causing them to expand and gradually turn to clay. The altered crystals begin to disaggregate, forming granite detritus or grus, a common type of sediment of the alluvial fans along the western flank of the range and Northeast Heights of Albuquerque. Core stones, the large, rounded granite boulders scattered on the hillsides, are a unique feature of granitic landscapes. These boulders form in place because of the abundant fractures that allow water to seep through granite and round the sharp corners through weathering.

Core stones in the Sandia Mountains.

Prominent triangular spurs mark the base of the Sandia Mountains. These are called facets and are particularly well developed flanking the deep V-shaped La Cueva Canyon, between the La Luz trailhead and the lower tramway terminal. They represent the exhumed faces of faults and are common along geologically young faults and define the base of the western range front.

THE VIEW FROM THE CREST—The view from Sandia Crest is spectacular and well worth the trip. Just one tenth of a mile before the Doc Long group picnic area (en route to the crest via NM–536), the Great Unconformity is exposed on the east side of the highway (but watch out for traffic on this stretch of road). Further up the mountain on Sandia Crest, you can see over 90 miles of the central New Mexican landscape. Looking west, you can see the edge of Albuquerque Basin. The prominent peak in the distance (60 miles west) is Mount Taylor, a large stratovolcano that was built 2–3 million years ago. The deepest part of the basin sits beneath the Albuquerque volcanoes, one of the youngest volcanic features (about 156,000 years old) in the

The Sandia Crest, north of the radio towers and the tramway and south of North Sandia Peak (the high point on the left). View is to the north; the east-dipping beds are Madera Limestone.

Albuquerque area. Looking to the east toward the Great Plains, there are no significant mountains until you reach the northern Appalachian Mountains, some 1,500 miles away. To the south, the Manzano Mountains and other ranges flank the eastern side of the rift. A hike north of the radio towers to North Sandia Peak provides a good view of the faulted 2–3 million-year-old basaltic lavas of Santa Ana Mesa and the 1–2 million-year-old volcanic features of the Jemez Mountains. Almost anywhere along the crest, you can see the fossil remains of ancient sea creatures preserved in the Madera limestone.

THE VIEW FROM PLACITAS—From the north side of the Sandias you can better appreciate the eastward tilt of the range. The white limestone bands along the crest descend towards Placitas along a ramp formed where two major rift-margin faults overlap. The many faults that cut the lavas on Santa Ana Mesa are also clearly visible from here. Because of the steeply sloping ramp of the range crest, younger (Permian and Mesozoic) rocks that have since eroded from the crest are preserved in the Placitas area.

—Adam S. Read and Sean D. Connell

Additional Reading

Towns of the Sandia Mountains by Mike Smith, Arcadia Publishing, 2006.

Albuquerque: A Guide to Its Geology and Culture by Paul W. Bauer, Richard P. Lozinsky, Carol J. Condie, and L. Greer Price. New Mexico Bureau of Geology and Mineral Resources, Scenic Trip 18, 2003.

Geology of the Sandia Mountains and Vicinity by V. C. Kelley and S. A. Northrop. New Mexico Bureau of Geology and Mineral Resources, Memoir 29, 1975.

Geologic map of the Albuquerque–Rio Rancho metropolitan area and vicinity by Sean Connell. New Mexico Bureau of Geology and Mineral Resources, Geologic Map 78, 2008.

Field Guide to the Sandia Mountains by Robert Julyan and Mary C. Stuever. University of New Mexico Press, 2005.

If You Plan to Visit

One of the best places to see the Sandias is from the crest. Depending on your fitness, interest, and time, you can choose how best to make the trip. You can drive to the crest via a well maintained paved road (NM–536), you can take a spectacular ride on the longest tramway in the world, or you can hike any of many trails. One popular option is to hike up the La Luz trail and then ride the tramway down. In good weather, if you choose to drive, you might consider taking the dirt road through Las Huertas canyon south of Placitas as part of a loop around the mountain. For more information:

Sandia Ranger District
Cibola National Forest
2113 Osuna Road, NE
Albuquerque, NM 87113
(505) 346-3900
(505) 281-3304 (Sandia Ranger District)
www.fs.fed.us/r3/cibola/districts/sandia.shtml

Petroglyph National Monument

NATIONAL PARK SERVICE

The images at Petroglyph National Monument are carved into the weathered faces of basalts that erupted between 210,000 and 155,000 years ago.

Petroglyph National Monument is best known for the 25,000 images carved into basalt that erupted from the Albuquerque volcanic field on Albuquerque's west side. These young volcanoes are only 7 miles from downtown Albuquerque. Using stone chisels and hammerstones, the ancestors of the Puebloan Indians cut most of the petroglyphs into the desert varnish between A.D. 1300 and 1680. A few of the markings are much older, dating back to perhaps 2000 B.C. Spaniards and later generations of Albuquerque inhabitants have produced younger petroglyphs with more modern themes. The monument, created in 1990, includes about 17 miles of petroglyph-covered basalt cliffs and five extinct volcanoes.

Regional Setting

The Albuquerque volcanic field is in the western Albuquerque Basin of the Rio Grande rift. The Albuquerque Basin is just one of a series of linked basins between central Colorado and west Texas that began forming about 30 million years ago when the earth's crust extended or stretched in an east-west direction. As extension was accommodated by normal faults, deep basins and prominent rift-flank uplifts formed. The monument offers spectacular views of the Sandia Mountains directly to the east and Manzanita and Manzano Mountains to the southeast. These east-tilted rift-flank ranges on the eastern margin of the Albuquerque Basin rise as much as 5,700 feet above the elevation of the Rio Grande, exposing Precambrian granitic and metamorphic rocks on the west side, with Pennsylvanian limestone and shale capping the mountain blocks.

The western margin of the Albuquerque Basin is a much more subtle topographic feature that lies about 12 miles to the west of the monument on the west side of the Rio Puerco, where Cretaceous marine sedimentary rocks are faulted against rift-fill sediments. The volcanoes formed along faults near the center of the basin, perhaps in a place where the crust is most thinned by extension.

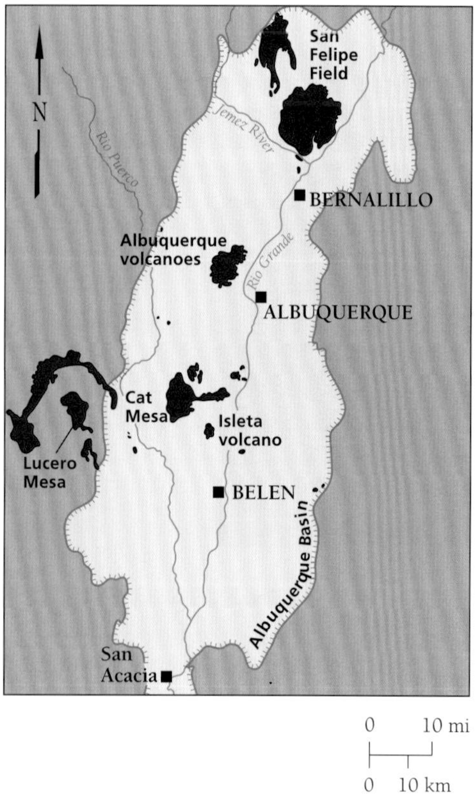

The Albuquerque volcanoes are only one of a series of volcanic fields in the Albuquerque Basin. All of these fields are young, and related to the crustal weakness and thinning associated with the Rio Grande rift.

The Rock Record

Three main rock units are visible within the monument. The oldest unit is the Ceja Formation of the Santa Fe Group, a light brown-to-yellow-brown sand and gravel deposit derived from areas to the northwest and west of the monument. The gravel includes well-rounded cobbles and pebbles of granite and quartzite derived from Precambrian rocks, chert and petrified wood eroded from Triassic sedimentary rocks, and rare volcanic rocks. One very distinctive clast in this gravel is Pedernal chert that is likely eroded from the northeastern part of the Sierra Nacimiento. The Llano de Albuquerque, a flat surface that developed on top of the Ceja Formation, represents the maximum elevation of basin fill of the Albuquerque Basin at the end of Santa Fe Group deposition. This surface is about 705 to 360 feet above the modern Rio Grande floodplain.

Younger terrace deposits and valley alluvium that are inset below the Llano de Albuquerque surface were laid down by an ancestral Rio Grande and tributaries feeding into the river. The tops of the terrace and valley alluvium deposits are at levels 140 feet to a few tens of feet above the modern elevation of the Rio Grande. The terrace deposit in the monument, the Los Duranes Formation, is made up of brown-to-reddish-brown sand, gravel, and clay. Inset into the Los Duranes Formation are two generations of valley alluvium.

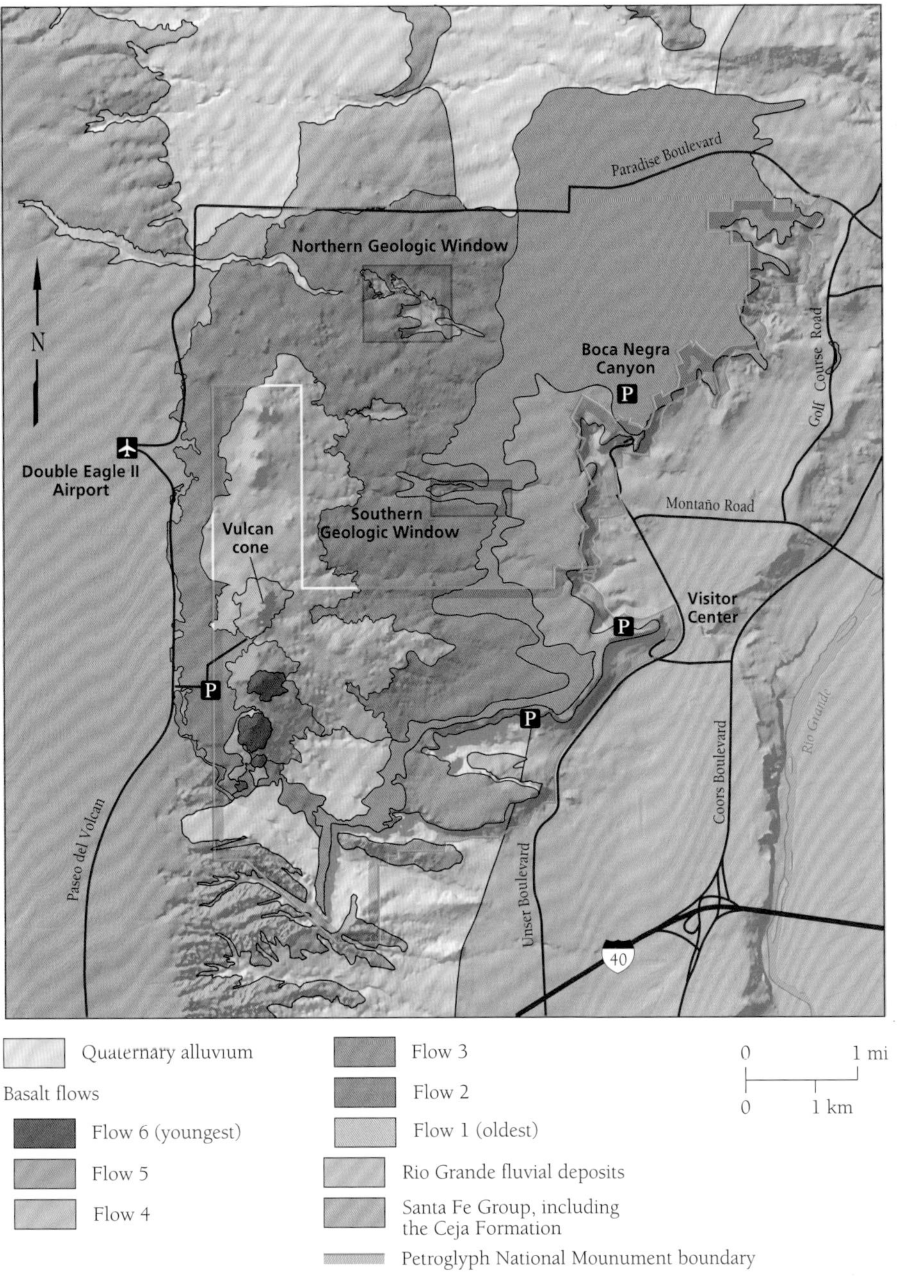

Generalized geologic map of the area around Petroglyph National Monument. Basalt flows from the Albuquerque volcanic field erupted largely onto the surface of the Llano de Albuquerque, an erosional surface that developed in this area on top of the Ceja Formation.

The youngest unit consists of a series of at least six basalt flows erupted from an aligned set of spatter cones and fissures that developed along a significant rift-related fault, named the County Dump fault for its fine exposures at an abandoned landfill. The weakened, fractured rocks around the fault acted as conduits, bringing molten rock to the surface. The fissures and cones erupted about 211,000 to 155,000 years

Erosion here has exposed the rock unit below the flows (the Ceja Formation). Photo below shows exposures of Ceja Formation pebbles in the Northern Geologic Window.

ago. Older middle to late Pleistocene soils have been offset by the fault, but the fault has not moved significantly in the last 20,000 years. A small earthquake (magnitude 4.4) was recorded along this fault in 1971.

Early in the eruptive cycle of the Albuquerque volcanic field, very fluid lava was extruded along fissures and the older flows covered a large area. The lava became more viscous as the eruptive cycle proceeded and later eruptions were focused around more centralized vents. The fissures and spatter cones shot fountains of ash, cinders, and lava about 30 feet into the air. The lava flows, which encompass an area of 23 square miles, erupted on the Llano de Albuquerque surface and flowed slowly (5–10 mph) downslope toward the Rio Grande, covering the younger terrace and valley alluvium deposits.

Five large cones and at least ten small volcanoes and spatter cones have been recognized in the Albuquerque volcanic field. Several of the basalt flows that erupted from the cones contain abundant white plagioclase crystals that are easily visible to the naked eye. Generally the tops and bottoms of the individual flows are full of holes called vesicles, which formed as gas bubbles escaping from the cooling lava were trapped and preserved in the rock. The tops of the flows variably have a ropy (pahoehoe) or a rubbly (aa) texture. Wind-blown spatter and cinder deposits, frozen lava lakes, and small lava tubes are among the well-preserved volcanic features that can be viewed in the monument.

This modern view of a fissure eruption in Hawaii provides some idea of what the eruptions in the Albuquerque volcanic field might have resembled. Note the cinder cones scattered along the trace of the fissure.

Modern wind-blown sand, stream, and playa lake deposits locally cover the basalt. These sediments hold an important paleoclimatic record through the last glacial-interglacial cycle in New Mexico.

Geologic History

Extension in this part of the Albuquerque Basin began about 26 million years ago, with sediments eroded from the surrounding developing highlands accumulating in the basin. These basin fill deposits, known as the Santa Fe Group, are over 16,000 feet thick below the Albuquerque volcanoes. The uppermost sand and gravel member of Pliocene to early Pleistocene Ceja Formation, the youngest unit of the Santa Fe Group in this part of the basin, was deposited by streams draining the area to the west and northwest of the monument. Filling of this part of the Albuquerque Basin ended 1.8 million years ago and the Llano de Albuquerque surface developed during a period of landscape stability. Beginning 1.2 to 0.7 million years ago, the Rio Grande started to cut down through the older Santa Fe Group deposits, in response to both climatic changes and integration of the river system. This downcutting was not a continuous process; there were several episodes of downcutting, aggradation, and renewed incision. This episodic development of the river system led to the formation of four terrace levels along the Rio Grande in the Albuquerque area. Tributaries to the main river later deposited valley alluvium along the margins of the Rio Grande floodplain.

About 210,000 to 155,000 years ago, basaltic magma from deep within the earth migrated up along the fractured rock in the vicinity of the County Dump fault, and fountaining lava erupted along two north-south striking fissures. The first eruption along the fissures sent lobes of highly fluid lava toward the east and southeast into the Rio Grande valley. The lava from the second eruption covered a larger area than the first flow, rolling toward the northeast, east, and southeast, again into the river valley. There followed a pause in activity, and thin sediments were deposited. When activity was renewed in the Albuquerque volcanic field, the style of eruption changed. The magma was slightly more sticky, so it flowed both east and west of the main fissure, but not very far. The final three eruptions were localized around central vents.

These steeply dipping lava flows on the north side of Vulcan cone are 150,000 years old. The view is to the north from the summit of the cone.

Geologic Features

THE ALBUQUERQUE VOLCANOES—The volcanoes on Ceja Mesa are aligned along two segments that trend in slightly different directions. The southern segment, which strikes 2° east of north, includes, from south to north, the JA, Black, and Vulcan cones. The trail system of the Volcano Day Use area meanders through this southern set of cones. One of the cones that was part of the southern segment, named Cinder, which was south of JA cone, has been mined out of existence. Cinder from the cones was mined for railroad bed material, cinder blocks, and landscaping material. The northern set of cones, including Butte and Bond cones, is offset to the west of the southern segment by about 650 feet and strikes 3° east of north. These cones are harder to visit because there are no trails.

The largest of the cones in the Albuquerque volcanic field is Vulcan, named after the Roman god of fire. From a vantage point on top of the cone 200 feet above mesa, the alignment of the 5-mile-long chain of vents is particularly noticeable. Vulcan is a spatter cone, formed primarily by fire fountains that were active in the central vent and in smaller vents on flanks of the cone. Spatter forms when blobs of lava are emitted from a vent. The blobs cool as they fly through the air, and the partially molten blobs then land on the side of the cone to weld together to form a hard crust. The volcanic deposits dip at angles as high as 55° away from the central vent on the eastern and southern side of the Vulcan. The spatter material is thickest on the southeastern side of Vulcan, indicating that it was blown by the wind toward the south and east during the fountaining events. A solidified lava pond that consists of a massive gray basalt with weakly-developed columnar jointing occupies the crater of Vulcan. Modern graffiti has been carved into this flow on the west side of the cone. Radial, sinuous lava tubes 8 to 20 inches across and 300 feet long are preserved on the northeast and northwest flanks of Vulcan.

INVERTED TOPOGRAPHY, DESERT VARNISH, AND THE PETROGLYPHS—A classic example of inverted topography is displayed on the east side of the monument. Basalt from the Albuquerque volcanoes filled in low spots along the edge of Rio Grande valley about 200,000 years ago. Subsequent downcutting by the Rio Grande has now formed a mesa capped by basalt. Erosion of the soft sediments under the hard basalt has caused large blocks of basalt from the two older flows to tumble down the eastern escarpment of the mesa.

Most of the petroglyphs are on these large basalt blocks. The petroglyphs are chiseled into a black, metallic-looking patina on the basalt called desert varnish. This coating forms in arid environments on protected surfaces that are resistant to weathering. Desert varnish is composed mainly of clay mixed with manganese and iron oxides. Its formation is enhanced by organic processes and the evaporation of dew, which causes the concentration of manganese oxide. The best petroglyphs can be seen from trails in Rinconada Canyon to the south of the Visitor Center and trails in Boca Negra Canyon and Piedras Marcadas Canyon to the north of the Visitor Center.

The images we refer to as petroglyphs are, in fact, carved or pecked into the desert varnish that forms on the weathered surfaces of the basalt flows. This exposes the lighter rock beneath the weathered surface, creating the two-tone images. Once created, the images themselves continue to weather, but these images are fairly young, most of them between 300 and 700 years old.

THE NORTH AND SOUTH GEOLOGIC WINDOWS—Two small erosional windows cut by streams through the basalt flows have been preserved as part of Petroglyph National Monument. There are no formal trails or parking areas to access these windows, but they can be reached by hiking along arroyos. The northern window can be accessed via dirt roads located south of Paseo del Norte NW or by walking up North Boca Negra Arroyo. The southern window can be reached by walking along South Boca Negra Arroyo. The basalt flows are thin in the vicinity of these windows compared to areas to the north and south, suggesting that there might have been small hills on top of the Ceja Formation prior to the eruption of the Albuquerque volcanoes. Basal flow features and flow breaks are well-exposed in these windows. Although the Ceja Formation is poorly-exposed in these drainages, pebbles and cobbles of granite, quartzite, and chert litter the slopes below the lava flows. A few petroglyphs were carved into the basalt flows of the geologic windows.

—Shari A. Kelley

Additional Reading

Albuquerque: A Guide to Its Geology and Culture by Paul W. Bauer, Richard P. Lozinsky, Carol J. Condie, and L. Greer Price. New Mexico Bureau of Geology and Mineral Resources Scenic Trip 18, 2003.

Geologic map of the Albuquerque–Rio Rancho metropolitan area and vicinity, Bernalillo and Sandoval Counties, New Mexico compiled by Sean Connell. New Mexico Bureau of Geology and Mineral Resources GM-78, 2008.

If You Plan to Visit

Petroglyph National Monument is located on West Mesa on the west side of Albuquerque. To get to the Las Imagines Visitor Center from Albuquerque, travel west on I–40, take Exit 154, and drive north on Unser Boulevard approximately 3.5 miles. The visitor center is located near the intersection of Unser Boulevard and Western Trail. Turn left at the light and drive up the road to the parking lot for the visitor center. The Volcanoes Day Use Area can be reached using Paseo del Volcan at Exit 149 going west from Albuquerque on I–40. The Volcanoes Day Use Area is 4.8 miles north of I–40. For more information, contact:

Petroglyph National Monument
6001 Unser Blvd. NW
Albuquerque, NM 87120
(505) 899-0205
www.nps.gov/petr/index.htm

PART 4

The Southern Rocky Mountains

The Sangre de Cristo Mountains recommend themselves for study because no other region in all of North America so richly combines both ecological and cultural diversity.

—William deBuys
Enchantment and Exploitation—
The Life and Hard Times of a New Mexico Mountain Range

OPPOSITE: **View of South Truchas Peak (13,102 feet) from lower Truchas Lake in the Pecos Wilderness.**

The Rocky Mountains are one of the foremost continental mountain ranges on the planet. Extending over 3,000 miles from New Mexico to Canada, the range is the physiographic backbone of North America. The Rockies are composed of many segments, the southernmost of which is the Sangre de Cristo Mountains, stretching 225 miles from Poncha Pass, Colorado to Glorieta Pass, New Mexico. Early Spanish texts referred to the Sangre de Cristo Mountains as *La Sierra Nevada* (the Snowy Range), *La Sierra Madre* (the Mother Mountains), or *La Sierra*. Early American explorers called them *the Snowies*. In 1965 they earned the official designation of Sangre de Cristo Mountains by the U.S. Board on Geographic Names.

The Sangre de Cristo Mountains include ten peaks over 14,000 feet in elevation and more than twenty peaks over 13,000 feet. Blanca Peak in Colorado, at 14,345 feet, is the highest peak in the range. The New Mexican section of the range, the southern Sangre de Cristo Mountains, represents the southern terminus of the Rockies and consists of the Santa Fe Range, the Rincon Mountains, the Cimarron Mountains, the Picuris Mountains, the Taos Range, and the Culebra Range at the Colorado state line. These ranges are indisputably New Mexico's premiere high country, containing the fifty highest peaks in the state, all of which are over 12,000 feet in elevation. Although the Truchas Peaks area of the Santa Fe Range contains several of the highest prominent peaks in the mountain belt, the Taos Range boasts the loftiest point of 13,161 feet on Wheeler Peak. The millions of acres of public land in the southern Sangre de Cristo Mountains contain a vast diversity of notable and photogenic geologic sites, and a large number of public lands, parks, trails, and streams. The area contains six ski areas and some of the best hiking, fly-fishing, rock climbing, mountain biking, birding, horseback riding, and hunting in the nation.

The dramatic topographic margin between the Southern Rocky Mountains and the Great Plains arguably represents the most profound physiographic/geologic boundary in the United States. To the east are the flat-lying sedimentary rocks of the tectonically quiescent continental

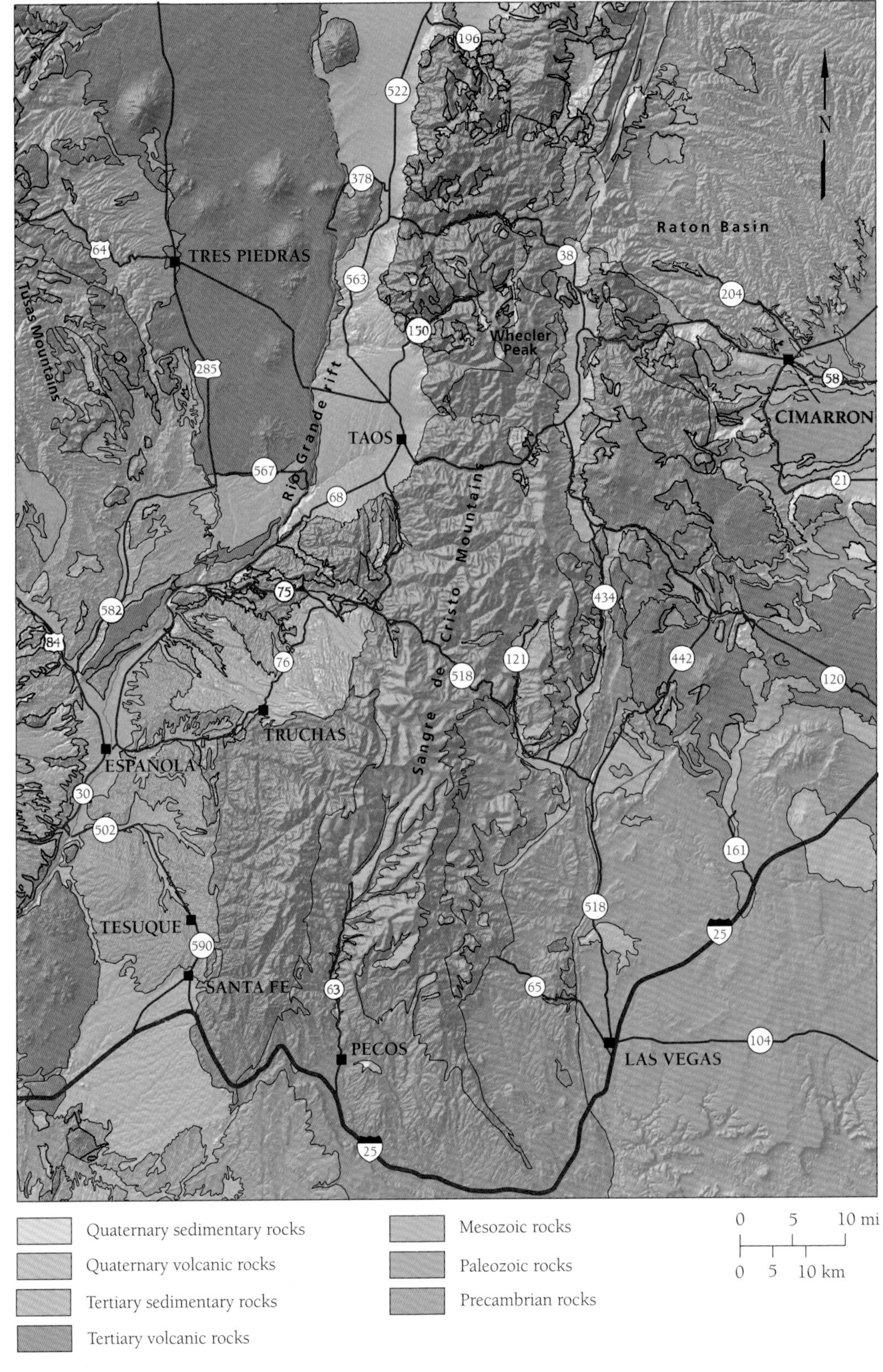

N
Raton Basin
TRES PIEDRAS
Tusas Mountains
Wheeler Peak
CIMARRON
TAOS
Rio Grande rift
Sangre de Cristo Mountains
TRUCHAS
ESPAÑOLA
TESUQUE
SANTA FE
PECOS
LAS VEGAS
196
522
378
64
563
38
204
150
58
285
567
68
21
75
582
84
434
76
518
121
442
120
30
502
161
518
590
25
63
65
104
25
Quaternary sedimentary rocks
Quaternary volcanic rocks
Tertiary sedimentary rocks
Tertiary volcanic rocks
Mesozoic rocks
Paleozoic rocks
Precambrian rocks
0 5 10 mi
0 5 10 km

platform. To the west are the broken and contorted crustal blocks of western North America, with youthful mountains, closed basins, young volcanoes, and vigorous earthquake-producing faults. The southern Sangre de Cristo Mountains are the easternmost outpost of this tectonic terrain, and their landscapes reveal the overprinting of local geologic processes such as volcanism, faulting, and erosion on multiple cycles of continent-scale mountain building.

The Sangre de Cristo Mountains have tremendous geological significance, as they provide a 225-mile-long window into the origin and evolution of the North American continent. The highest peaks near Taos are composed of Precambrian rocks that originated at the surface, were later buried and metamorphosed 7 miles deep at nearly 1,000° F, and are now exposed at 13,000 feet elevation. During the last 1.7 billion years a tectonic elevator has been at work, with the last trip transporting the rocks 10 miles upward through the crust to their present lofty location. South of Taos, the crest of the range is capped by Paleozoic sedimentary strata that formed beneath the sea about 300 million years ago. These strata are now 2 miles above sea level and hundreds of miles from the nearest ocean.

Lengthy and diverse geologic histories commonly generate a wealth of rock- and mineral-related materials that human civilization finds valuable. The southern Sangre de Cristo Mountains are no exception. Valuable commodities include the rich placer gold fields of the Elizabethtown–Baldy mining district, the world-class molybdenum deposit near Questa, the metal deposits of the Twining/Gold Hill and Red River regions, the vast Cretaceous coal beds and coalbed methane of the Raton Basin, the copper at Copper Hill near Peñasco, the "fairy cross" staurolites in the Picuris Mountains, and the micaceous clay prized by Picuris Pueblo potters.

The Sangre de Cristo Mountains have had a profound effect on patterns of human activities and habitation in the region. European merchants and settlers were funneled through the few manageable mountain passes that connect the Great Plains with points west. In New Mexico, the easiest passage is at Glorieta Pass at the southern tip of the range. The Santa Fe Trail traversed Glorieta Pass, channeling pioneers and trade into the Santa Fe area. Similarly, the construction of the railroad and interstate highway through Glorieta Pass influenced the dispersal of New Mexican settlements. The Battle of Glorieta Pass on March 28, 1862, was a turning point of the Civil War, when Union forces repelled the Confederate invasion of New Mexico Territory, effectively stopping the Confederate army from invading the Southwest. The mountains themselves are rugged, remote, and mostly inhospitable, factors that ultimately led to their designation as public lands of the national forest system, and as New Mexico's premiere outdoor recreational region.

OPPOSITE: This generalized geologic map of the southern Rocky Mountains in New Mexico illustrates the long and complex geologic history through the great diversity of rocks in the region.

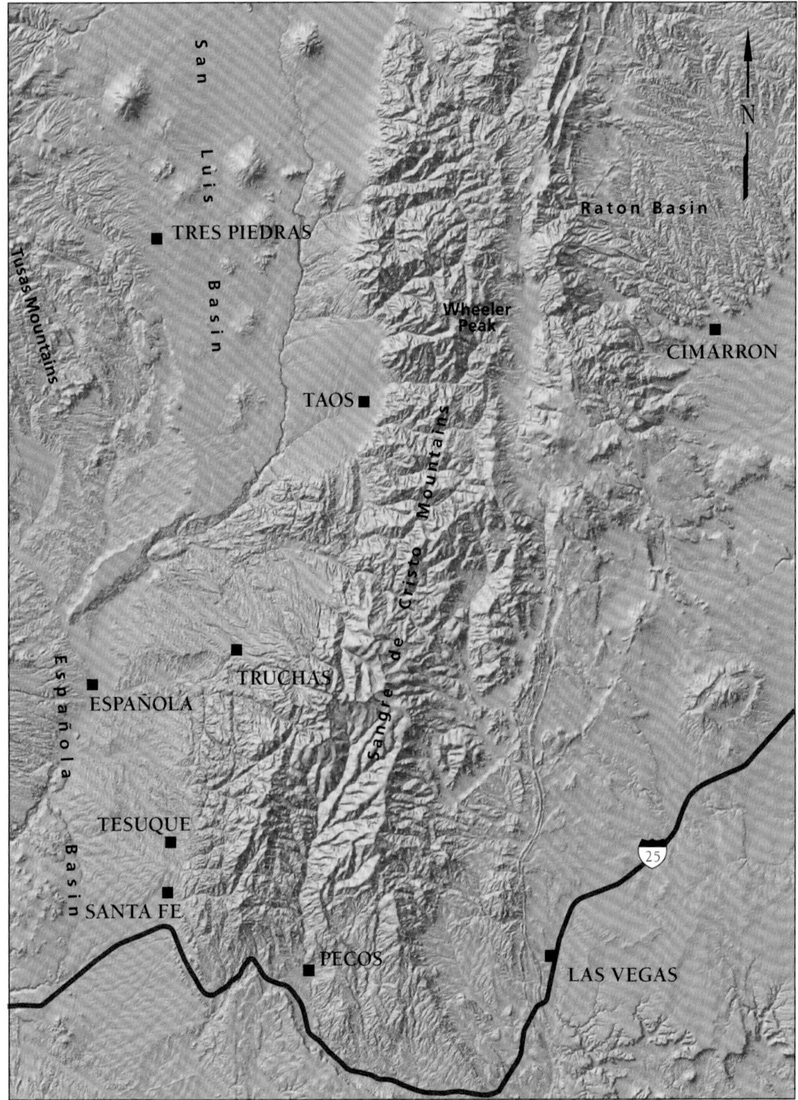

Regional Setting

The Sangre de Cristo Mountains are flanked by the Raton Basin to the east, and the San Luis and Española Basins of the Rio Grande rift to the west. The Raton Basin is a broad *syncline* that extends 150 miles from Huerfano Park, Colorado to Las Vegas, New Mexico. Cretaceous and Tertiary rocks on the western edge of the basin are folded and faulted along the edge of the Sangre de Cristo Mountains, where 13,000 feet of vertical offset exists between the basin and the mountains. The Rio Grande rift is a relatively recent development, having evolved only in the past 25 million years, but it is responsible for the impressive topographic relief along the western flank of the mountain range. The recently active Sangre de Cristo fault separates the mountains from the east-tilted San Luis rift basin. South of the Picuris Mountains a series of much smaller faults exists between the mountains and the west-tilted Española rift basin. The range also contains notable geologic and physiographic intramontane complexities, including small, late Tertiary-age, structural basins such as the Valle Vidal and the Moreno Valley.

Geologic History

Like all of the other great orogenic mountain chains on Earth, the geologic history of the Rocky Mountains covers vast spans of time and a myriad of geologic events. The current configuration of the Sangre de Cristo Mountains is a direct result of incidents that can be traced back in time nearly 2 billion years, when the ancient rocks that now make up the high Sangre de Cristo Mountains began to form. During that time of continental growth, immense tectonic forces caused the earth's crust to buckle and break, resulting in what most certainly was an immense mountain range, perhaps comparable in topographic form to the modern Himalayan Mountains. Those primordial peaks have long since eroded, and no direct evidence of their form remains today. The modern Sangre de Cristo Mountains are much younger than that Precambrian mountain range, and in fact, are only the latest in a series of mountains ranges in the location of the present-day Rocky Mountains. However, only a small fraction of the last 1.8 billion years of the geologic history is preserved in north-central New Mexico.

During the Precambrian, sediments that had accumulated at the surface were deeply buried and metamorphosed under conditions of great temperature and pressure. During times of orogeny, these metamorphosed sediments (the darker rock) were intruded by granites (the light-colored bands), resulting in the wild patterns of alternating dark and light bands of rock we see today.

PRECAMBRIAN TIME: THE CONTINENT IS FORMED—The Precambrian rocks of the southern Sangre de Cristo Mountains include a wide variety of rock types (granite, gneiss, quartzite, schist, and amphibolite) that range in age from 1,750 million years old (the oldest dated rock in New Mexico is near Wheeler Peak) to about 1,450 million years old. Although some of these rocks originally accumulated on the surface as lava flows, beach sands, and ocean muds, most are plutonic igneous rocks, and all were metamorphosed during deep burial and heating. While buried, the country rocks were intruded by great volumes of granitic magma that slowly solidified into *plutons*. The rocks that we now see at the surface show the effects of this turbulent history of metamorphism and plutonism. They form the crustal foundation for the younger fossil-bearing sedimentary rocks of Phanerozoic time.

In general, Precambrian rocks are dense and strong, and therefore highly resistant to erosion. Consequently, most of the highest and most rugged peaks in the Sangre de Cristo Mountains are composed of such rocks. These rocks are easily seen in many places: the towering cliffs near Pilar, at the Taos Ski Valley, at Ponce de Leon Hot Springs, at Red River Pass, and on top of Wheeler Peak.

Unfortunately, no rock record exists for the next billion years of earth history, from about 1,400 to 330 million years ago. This enormous time gap is represented by the Great Unconformity, the surface in the rock record that represents a period for which no rocks are preserved. Unconformities can represent times in which rocks were never deposited or times when rocks formed but later eroded. The Great

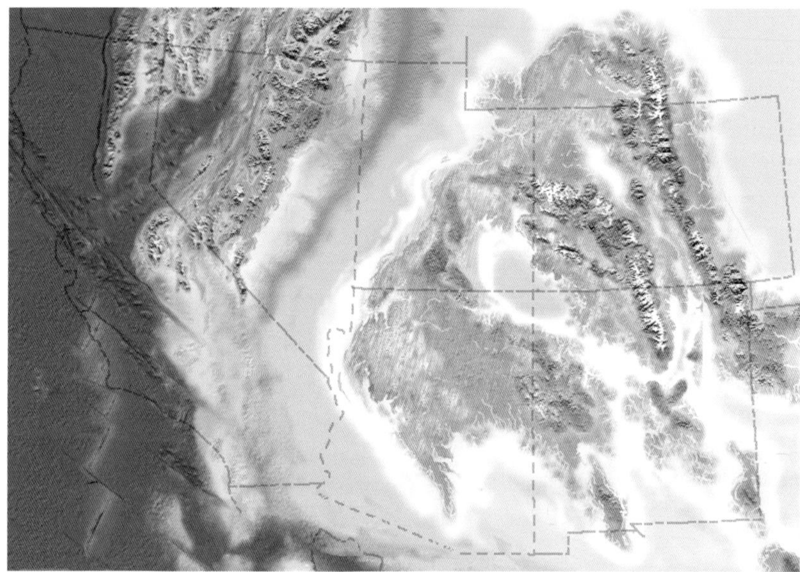

Paleogeographic map of the Southwest during Early Pennsylvanian time, 300 million years ago. Eighty percent of New Mexico at that time was submerged beneath warm, shallow equatorial seas.

Unconformity is found nearly everywhere on Earth (it is perhaps best known from the Grand Canyon in Arizona) and always divides rocks devoid of visible fossils from rocks containing animal and plant fossils. This same Great Unconformity is also exposed at the crest of the Sandia Mountains above Albuquerque, where strata of Pennsylvanian age rest directly upon Precambrian granite.

THE PALEOZOIC ERA: THE ANCESTRAL ROCKY MOUNTAINS RISE AND LIFE FLOURISHES—Early Paleozoic rocks are missing from the southern Sangre de Cristo Mountains. Only small patches of Mississippian rocks are found in the Sangre de Cristo Mountains, above the Great Unconformity, such as near Ponce de Leon Hot Springs, near Mora, and along the Pecos River. Pennsylvanian rocks, however, are plentiful.

During Pennsylvanian time the portion of North America that today includes New Mexico sat close to the equator. Eighty percent of New Mexico was submerged beneath warm, shallow, equatorial seas. Northern New Mexico probably resembled modern-day North Carolina, with a flat coastal plain, swampy forests, and high mountains to the west. Mud, silt, sand, and gravel were eroded from these highlands into a large sedimentary basin known as the Taos trough. Over time, as thousands of feet of sediments were buried, compacted, and cemented, they formed the sedimentary rocks that we now see from Taos to Glorieta Pass. Pennsylvanian limestones, siltstones, shales, sandstones, and conglomerates are exposed in the southern two thirds of the southern Sangre de Cristo Mountains, with excellent exposures along many of the highways in the southern part of the range.

A close examination of the Pennsylvanian rocks reveals evidence of their environments of deposition (rivers, deltas, shorelines, tidal flats, shallow seas), including features such as ripple marks, raindrop imprints, channels, and crossbeds. The warm Paleozoic seas teemed with ancient life, and paleontologists have identified the fossilized remains of hundreds of marine species, including many varieties of clams, snails, sea lilies, corals,and brachiopods.

During late Pennsylvanian time a major event known as the Ancestral Rocky Mountain orogeny caused widespread uplift, erosion, faulting, folding, and tilting. The eroding highlands furnished enormous volumes of rock detritus to the broad basins of northern New Mexico. Much of the Pennsylvanian rock is known as the Sangre de Cristo Formation, which is separated from overlying Mesozoic rocks by another major unconformity.

During the Ancestral Rocky Mountains orogeny, coarse sediments from the eroded highlands accumulated in the Taos trough about 300 million years ago. Today, these Pennsylvanian rocks are exposed in the southern Sangre de Cristo Mountains. This outcrop contains tarantula-sized cobbles of chert (black), quartzite (gray), and vein quartz (white).

THE MESOZOIC ERA: LIFE DIVERSIFIES—The Triassic and Jurassic periods were characterized by deposition of nonmarine sandstones and shales over much of northern New Mexico and the evolution of a vast diversity of life, including dinosaurs, birds, flowering plants, and mammals. The Triassic rocks are mostly sandstones and mudstones of floodplain origin, being derived from material shed from the Ancestral Rocky Mountains onto long, broad river valleys. At the close of Triassic time, the sediments were slightly warped and eroded before they were covered by sediments of Jurassic age. The Jurassic rocks begin with the Entrada Sandstone, a spectacular, cliff-forming sandstone composed of stacked sand dunes. The Entrada is overlain by Todilto Formation gypsum and limestone deposits of a shallow sea or brackish lake. The overlying Morrison Formation consists of the typical floodplain silts and muds of slow, sluggish streams.

During the Cretaceous, the sea again invaded northeastern New Mexico. This Western Interior Seaway stretched across the midcontinent from the Arctic to the Gulf of Mexico. Until the Late Cretaceous, the area was alternately land and sea, as the shoreline repeatedly advanced and retreated. Sand and gravel were deposited along streams on the flat coastal plain, and coal beds were formed in the abundant swamps. Great sequences of sandstone, shale, and limestone were deposited on the sea bottom, perhaps due to climatic cycles triggered by changes in Earth's orbit around the Sun. Mesozoic rocks

Paleogeographic map of the Southwest during the Middle Eocene, 50 million years ago. at that time the landscape of New Mexico was primarily terrestrial.

are exposed in the Moreno Valley, in the northeastern part of the southern Sangre de Cristo Mountains, and near the southern tip of the range. Cretaceous rocks are extensively exposed along the western edge of the Raton Basin.

Dinosaurs roamed the lush Mesozoic landscape of shorelines, river valleys, and swamps for over 100 million years, until 65 million years ago, when a large meteorite struck off the coast of Yucatan, Mexico. The resulting ecological catastrophe probably caused the great mass extinction that marked the disappearance of nearly half of Earth's life forms, including the dinosaurs. The impact blanketed the planet with a thin layer of chemically distinctive clay at the Cretaceous–Tertiary boundary, which is preserved in the northeastern Sangre de Cristo Mountains.

The Sangre de Cristo Mountains were reincarnated when the North American continent collided with a fast-moving plate of oceanic crust on the Pacific Ocean margin. That event initiated the widespread and long-lasting mountain-building event we refer to as the Laramide orogeny. About 70 million years ago, as the land began to rise, the interior seaway retreated to the northeast, never to return. Although the Laramide orogeny may have begun as a broad uplift, it progressed to a major cycle of folding and faulting, forming high-relief mountains and basins. By the end of the Eocene the general features of the eastern part of the Sangre de Cristo Mountains were formed. The modern mountains south of Taos contain abundant evidence of this orogeny, including tilted strata, extensive fault zones, and overturned folds.

THE CENOZOIC ERA: THE MODERN LANDSCAPE EVOLVES—The early Cenozoic was characterized by widespread erosion of the Laramide highlands, leading to a low-relief landscape that lasted until about 37 million years ago, when the San Juan volcanic field of southern Colorado began to erupt. Volcanism progressed southeastward through time, until the Latir volcanic field near Questa began to erupt about 25 million years ago, blanketing the hills with red-hot lava and welded ash. Coincident in time with the volcanism, the last major orogenic event began, dramatically changing the shape of the western slope of the Sangre de Cristo Mountains. With regional extension of the crust, the Rio Grande rift was born, and linear basins began to subside. The basins filled with coarse sediments, known as the Santa Fe Group, shed from the surrounding mountains. From late Miocene into the Pliocene, there was continued uplift, forming the modern chain of high peaks. Streams draining the eastern flank of the Sangre de Cristos deposited an extensive blanket of clay, silt, sand, and gravel into the eastern basins. This material, known as the Ogallala Formation, proceeded to fill valleys, and, as the valleys over-filled, bury the plains. Volcanic activity resumed late in the Miocene, 6 million years ago, and has continued almost to the present day.

The Truchas Peaks, which display many of the classic geomorphic features that are associated with glacially sculpted landscapes.

During the Pleistocene Epoch, alpine glaciers periodically covered the higher peaks, carving U-shaped valleys, and scouring out arcuate depressions called cirques high on the mountains around Wheeler Peak and the Truchas Peaks. Today, snow can be found in shady spots on the higher peaks late into the summer. If the average annual temperature were only slightly cooler, this snow would slowly accumulate, turn to ice, and form small glaciers, like those found in the Rocky Mountains of Colorado. Instead, the current warming climate probably marks the end of Colorado's permanent ice fields.

—*Paul Bauer*

The Wheeler Peak Wilderness

CARSON NATIONAL FOREST

OPPOSITE: Wheeler Peak high country.

The 1.5-million-acre Carson National Forest contains some of the finest mountain scenery and geologic sites in the Southwest. With elevations that range from 6,000 to over 13,000 feet, these forest lands contain a great diversity of ecological conditions, plants, and animals. With 330 miles of trails, 400 miles of mountain streams, and 86,193 acres of wilderness, recreational opportunities abound.

Designated as wilderness in 1964, the Wheeler Peak Wilderness is the headwaters for major streams that flow both east and west from the mountains. This relatively small alpine wilderness of 19,661 acres is in the central southern Sangre de Cristo Mountains and is bordered by Taos Ski Valley to the north. The focal point of the area is Wheeler Peak (13,161 feet), the highest point in New Mexico, accessible by well-marked trails to any energetic intermediate-level hiker.

With elevations from 7,650 to 13,161 feet, the wilderness contains a tremendous range of ecosystems, including rare above-timberline alpine tundra vegetation, unusual forests growing above 12,000 feet in elevation, and marmots and pikas. The alpine tundra vegetation consists of dwarf plants with small colorful flowers, such as Indian paintbrush, nailwort, moss-pink campion, blue bells, mouse ear, alpine willows, and sedum. At lower elevations are Englemann spruce, corkbark fir, bristlecone pine, and aspen. Common large animals are mule deer, elk, bear, Rocky Mountain bighorn sheep, mountain lion, blue grouse, and ptarmigan. Marmots, also known as whistling pigs, are the fat, furry creatures seen on talus slopes. Marmots hibernate eight months per year, spending their four-month summer foraging and feeding on grasses and forbs. The more circumspect pikas, which are members of the rabbit family, do not hibernate and spend the summer storing vegetation in caches.

Regional Setting

The southern Sangre de Cristo Mountains, which are the southernmost section of the Rocky Mountains, are sandwiched between the Raton Basin of the Great Plains to the east and the Rio Grande rift basins to the west. The Rio Grande rift, along which the crust has extended during the past 25 million years, is responsible for the impressive fault-related topographic relief along the western flank of the mountains.

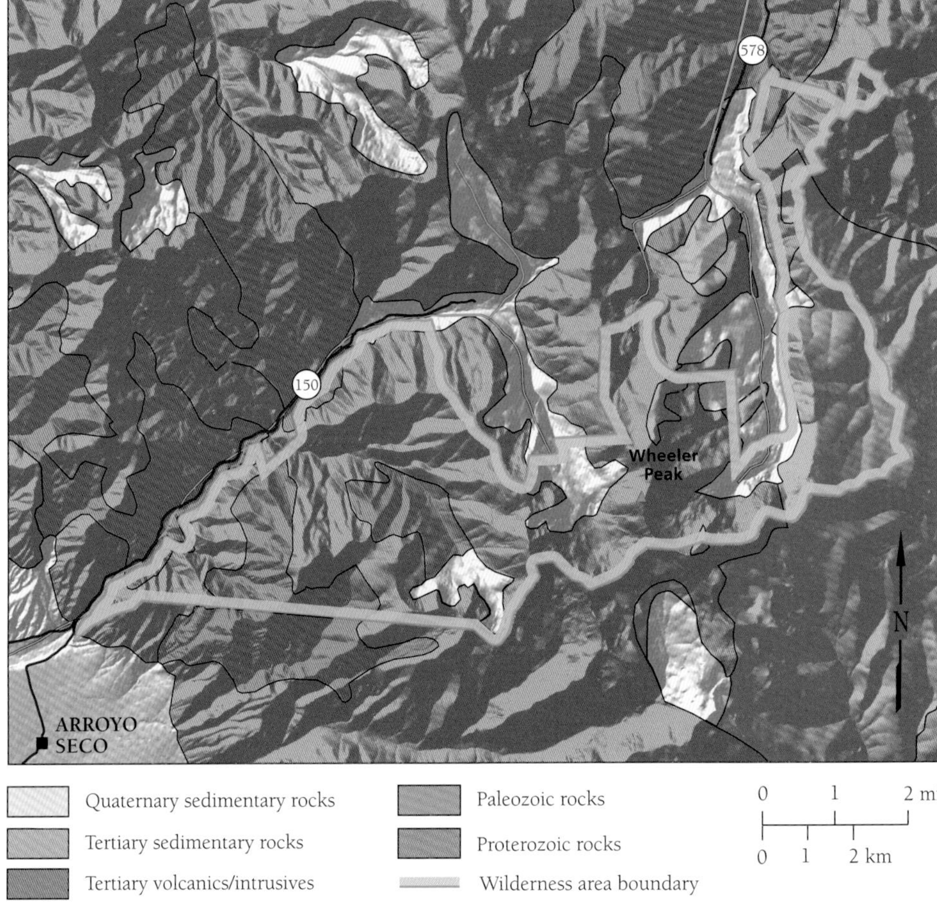

The Wheeler Peak area consists of Precambrian basement rocks that are overlain by Paleozoic sedimentary rocks and perforated by Tertiary igneous rocks.

The Rock Record

The geology of the Wheeler Peak Wilderness is exceedingly complex. Most of the high peaks in the Wheeler Peak area are composed of Precambrian metamorphic and igneous rocks. Wheeler Peak itself is composed of an especially distinctive and attractive layered gneiss that displays a range of compositional bandings and a well-developed foliation of minerals such as biotite, hornblende, feldspar, quartz, epidote, calcite, and magnetite. Although the gneiss has undergone extreme metamorphism and deformation while deeply buried in the crust, geologists have deduced that the original rocks were a thick sequence of volcanic and sedimentary rocks, which probably accumulated under water about 1.7 billion years ago.

Another common rock in the Wheeler Peak area is the Red River tonalite, a plutonic rock that is composed of an interlocking mosaic of crystals of quartz, feldspar, biotite, and hornblende. This rock crystallized from magma deep underground, approximately 1.75 billion years ago. West and north of Wheeler Peak are other Precambrian rock types and a bewildering assortment of Tertiary igneous rocks affiliated with the Questa magmatic system. The Tertiary rocks include both plutonic and volcanic rocks and display complex cross-cutting relationships, such as dikes intruding older intrusive rocks.

Rock glaciers like this one in the Pecos Wilderness are common in the Wheeler Peak Wilderness.

Most of the high valleys of the Wheeler Peak Wilderness are covered by a notable series of Quaternary deposits that reflect the impact of Pleistocene ice ages. In addition to scouring out deep valleys and cirques, the alpine glaciers deposited large amounts of rock debris (till) in unstratified landforms known as lateral moraines (along the sides of glaciers) and terminal moraines (at the front of glaciers). These deposits commonly also contain erratic boulders, large rocks that have been transported by the glaciers. The steep slopes of unvegetated bedrock have encouraged the post-glacial development of landslides and rock glaciers in the high country. The landslides are lobate accumulations of debris derived from both the bedrock and pre-existing glacial deposits. The rock glaciers may be composed of rock debris that has a core of ice, ice-cemented rock formed in talus that is subject to permafrost, or ice-cemented rock debris formed from avalanching snow and rock. Such Quaternary deposits cover at least half of the Wheeler Peak Wilderness area.

Geologic History

Even though Precambrian time represents most of Earth history (4.54 billion to 543 million years ago), our knowledge of that time is sketchy due to the difficulties inherent in peering back through all the subsequent geologic happenings. Much of what we have discovered of New Mexico's early history comes from the Sangre de Cristo Mountains, where rocks display signs of at least five major orogenies.

Tonalite is a coarse-grained intrusive igneous rock composed primarily of quartz and feldspar (the light-colored grains), biotite and hornblende (the dark-colored grains).

During much of the latter part of Precambrian time, the rocks now exposed at the surface in the Wheeler Peak area were miles down, and thus tell us little of what was happening at the surface. We do know that the crust of northern New Mexico was constructed from a continental nucleus that grew southward from Canada about 1.8 to 1.4 billion years ago. We also know that on occasion, tectonic plates collided and great mountain ranges emerged. Although those ancient peaks are long gone, the Precambrian rocks of the Wheeler Peak area represent the deeply eroded, metamorphic roots of those mountains. These so-called basement rocks reflect a turbulent history of deformation, metamorphism, and plutonism, and form the crustal underpinning upon which the younger Paleozoic fossil-bearing sedimentary rocks have accumulated.

The high Sangre de Cristo Mountains contain no rock record for the next billion years of Earth history, from about 1.4 billion to 330 million years ago. This enormous time gap is called "the Great Unconformity," a period in the record for which no rocks are preserved. During this time, the Precambrian rocks underwent cycles of orogeny that included miles of vertical uplift and massive erosion.

The dramatic landscapes of the Wheeler Peak region have resulted from the overprinting of local geologic processes such as volcanism, faulting, glaciation, and erosion on such cycles of continent-scale mountain building. The three most recent episodes of orogenic upheaval began at about 310 million years ago (Ancestral Rocky Mountains), 70 million years ago (Laramide), and 25 million years ago (Rio Grande rift).

By about 310 million years ago, during Pennsylvanian time, the Ancestral Rocky Mountains had emerged, leaving most of New Mexico submerged beneath tropical seas. Vast quantities of mud, silt, sand, and gravel were eroded from nearby island highlands into a large sedimentary basin known as the Taos trough. As thousands of feet of sediments were buried and compacted, they became the sedimentary rocks that we can see in the southwestern Sangre de Cristo Mountains.

About 70 million years ago, the Laramide orogeny rearranged the landscape, setting the stage for the modern Rocky Mountain landscape. The Laramide uplift evolved from a broad highland to a series of high-relief mountains and basins, such that, by the end of the Eocene Epoch (33.7 million years ago) the general features of the eastern part of the Sangre de Cristo Mountains had been fashioned. The rocks south of Taos contain abundant evidence of this mountain-building event, including wide fractured zones and complex contortions of sedimentary layers. The scene was then set for the final chapter in the geo-drama—development of the Rio Grande rift.

For the last 25 million years, plate tectonic forces have slowly torn apart the North American continent along the rift. The lithosphere has been uplifted, stretched, thinned, broken, and intruded by magma. The resultant rift valley has sliced New Mexico and half of Colorado in two for a distance of over 600 miles. As the San Luis Basin dropped and the mountains rose, many thousands of feet of rock were stripped from the mountains and transported into the valleys.

Periodically during the Pleistocene Epoch (the last 1.8 million years), great ice ages, separated by warmer interglacial periods, have chilled New Mexico. Recent ice ages include the Bull Lake Glaciation that began about 150,000 years ago and the Pinedale Glaciation that probably maintained full glaciation until about 15,000 years ago. Glaciers are effective sculptors of mountains, and the modern sharp peaks and rounded alpine valleys reflect this.

The top of New Mexico at 13,161 feet, Wheeler Peak is well above timberline, resulting in good exposures of its Precambrian core.

Geologic Features

WHEELER PEAK—At 13,161 feet, Wheeler Peak beats out the next tallest prominent peak, Truchas Peak of the Santa Fe Range, by only 59 feet. Wheeler Peak is named for Major George Montague Wheeler (1832–1909), a Massachusetts-born, West Point graduate who led the ambitious, congressionally authorized plan to map west of the 100th meridian at a scale of 8 miles to the inch. Wheeler and his team of surveyors and naturalists collected topographic, planimetric, geologic, and biologic data in seven southwest states. In 1879 the Wheeler Survey, along with the Powell and King Surveys, was folded into a new federal agency named the U.S. Geological Survey.

Wheeler believed that the Truchas Peaks were the highest summits in New Mexico, and not until Harold D. Walter's amateur survey of 1948 was Wheeler Peak confirmed as the high point. Just north of the Wheeler summit is Mount Walter (13,133 feet), named in honor of the surveyor after his death in 1958, and the second highest named peak in New Mexico. However, due to its lack of topographic prominence, Mount Walter is generally considered a sub-peak rather than an independent peak. Lake Fork Peak (12,881 feet) lies just across Williams

Wheeler Peak Wilderness

Lake to the west of Wheeler, and to the southeast is the third highest named summit in the state, Old Mike Peak (13,113 feet).

All of these peaks are composed of Precambrian metamorphic and plutonic rocks that constitute some of the oldest rocks in New Mexico. Wheeler Peak itself is composed of a layered gneiss that probably originated as a sedimentary rock 1.75 billion years ago that was later deeply buried, heated, and squeezed. Old Mike Peak is composed of quartz monzonite, a granite-like rock that intruded the nearby layered gneiss when it lay deeply buried, nearly 1.7 billion years ago.

CIRQUES AND TARNS—The Wheeler Peak area was covered by alpine glaciers repeatedly during Pleistocene time. The presence of these glaciers is recorded by a variety of erosional and depositional features that are especially visible above timberline. Alpine glaciers commonly scour out dome-shaped basins (cirques) in the bedrock at the heads of the glaciers. Cirques are partially surrounded by steep bedrock cliffs, the highest of which is called a headwall. In the northern hemisphere, cirques commonly face northeasterly, as shade and shelter from the wind favor the accumulation of snow and ice.

After the glacier melts, the cirque may fill with snowmelt water and form a cirque lake, or tarn. Many cirques contain tarns that are dammed by glacial till or moraines. The lakes are usually small, circular, and less than about 150 feet deep. Some tarns have stream outlets, others do not. The word tarn is derived from the Old Norse word *tjörn*, meaning pond.

Nestled within the rugged glacial highlands around Wheeler Peak are dozens of cirques and at least 20 lovely cirque lakes. Within the wilderness area are three large lakes, the most famous is Williams Lake, west of Wheeler Peak at 11,000 feet elevation. Williams Lake is a natural lake that does not have fish because it is often too shallow to maintain a fish population. Horseshoe Lake (11,950 feet) is at timberline and is ringed by ancient bristlecone pine shrubs. Horseshoe Lake is stocked by helicopter with native cutthroat trout. Nearby is Lost Lake (11,495 feet), also stocked with native cutthroat fry.

GOLD, SILVER, AND COPPER—In 1892 William Fraser, Al Helphenstine, and partners discovered rich gold and silver ore in the upper Rio Hondo drainage. When word got out, the rush was on, and the mining camp of Amizette was born. The camp grew and thrived through 1893, with promises of a mill and a railroad spur. New strikes nearby and on Gold Hill and Fraser Mountain stoked the excitement, and prospectors, retailers, and other mining camp workers poured into town. But by the end of the year, the boom had collapsed due to the spotty and low-grade nature of the ore, and Amizette was nearly a ghost town. William Fraser continued to prospect, eventually discovering rich copper and gold seams upstream near the mouth of the Lake Fork. In 1901 Albert C. Twining and a group of New Jersey capitalists partnered with Fraser to incorporate the Fraser Mountain Copper Company. Fraser was named mine superintendent and appointed postmaster of the thriving new town christened Twining in honor of the company president. Workers feverishly erected a four-story mill and smelter, a 2,000-foot cable tram for moving the ore, a sawmill, a hydroelectric plant, a blacksmith shop, bunkhouses, and the Twining Hotel. By the summer of 1903 the equipment was all in place, and smelting began. Inexplicably, the molten ore froze to the sides of the furnace, a fatal occurrence in

The "great hope" of Twining was the mill and smelter erected near the base of Fraser Mountain in 1902. This view is of the maintenance shop at the mill; hydroelectric power supplied the large motors shown here.

any mining operation. By the end of the summer, Twining was nearly deserted, the eastern investors had withdrawn, Mr. Twining was bankrupt, and the claims reverted to the near-penniless William Fraser. Although sporadic mining efforts continued, even after Fraser was shot between the eyes by his partner in 1914, the Amizette/Twining boom was finished. The buildings were razed in 1924, and the smelter burned in 1932. Although Taos Ski Area now occupies the Twining townsite, the north edge of the wilderness area is littered with the history of this promising mining district, and the area still contains some abandoned mines and the ruins of prospectors' cabins.

—*Paul Bauer*

If You Plan to Visit

The wilderness can be accessed from the west and north. From Arroyo Seco, NM–150 follows the Rio Hondo to the Taos Ski Area along the northern boundary of the wilderness. Campgrounds and a forest service district office are scattered along the route. From Twining Campground, Trail 90 follows Bull-of-the-Woods Fork about eight miles to the Wheeler Peak summit. From Taos Ski Valley, the steep Trail 62 follows Lake Fork of the Rio Hondo to Williams Lake. On the north side, from the town of Red River, NM–150 and then Forest Road 58 follow the Red River to the confluence of the Middle Fork and East Fork where a 10-mile trail climbs the East Fork valley into the high country near Horseshoe Lake. For more information, contact:

Carson National Forest
208 Cruz Alta Road
Taos, NM 87571
(575) 758-6200
www.fs.fed.us/r3/carson/

The Latir Peak Wilderness

CARSON NATIONAL FOREST

Williams Lake

This 20,506-acre wilderness area of the northernmost Carson National Forest is a relatively unknown treasure of emerald-green meadows, rare alpine tundra, small glacial lakes, spruce-fir forests, and spectacular peaks. This fifth-smallest New Mexico wilderness is easily overlooked by hikers, yet four of the state's 20 highest summits are here: Venado Peak (12,734 feet), Latir Peak (12,708 feet), Latir Mesa (12,692 feet), and Virsylvia Peak (12,594 feet).

Most of the area is drained by the Lake Fork of Cabresto Creek, which originates at Heart Lake (named for its anatomical shape) and joins the Red River near Questa. Many species of wildlife indigenous to the Hudsonian zone of the Southern Rocky Mountains, including elk, bear, mountain lion, mule deer, Rocky Mountain bighorn sheep, badger, beaver, bobcat, ferret, fox, marmot, pika, marten, muskrat, grouse, ptarmigan, and the uncommon boreal owl, can be found in this remote and dazzling setting.

Regional Setting

The Latir Peak Wilderness of north-central New Mexico is the northernmost public land in the southern Sangre de Cristos, as the mountains to the north are privately owned. The southern Sangre de Cristo Mountains represent the southern terminus of the Rocky Mountains,

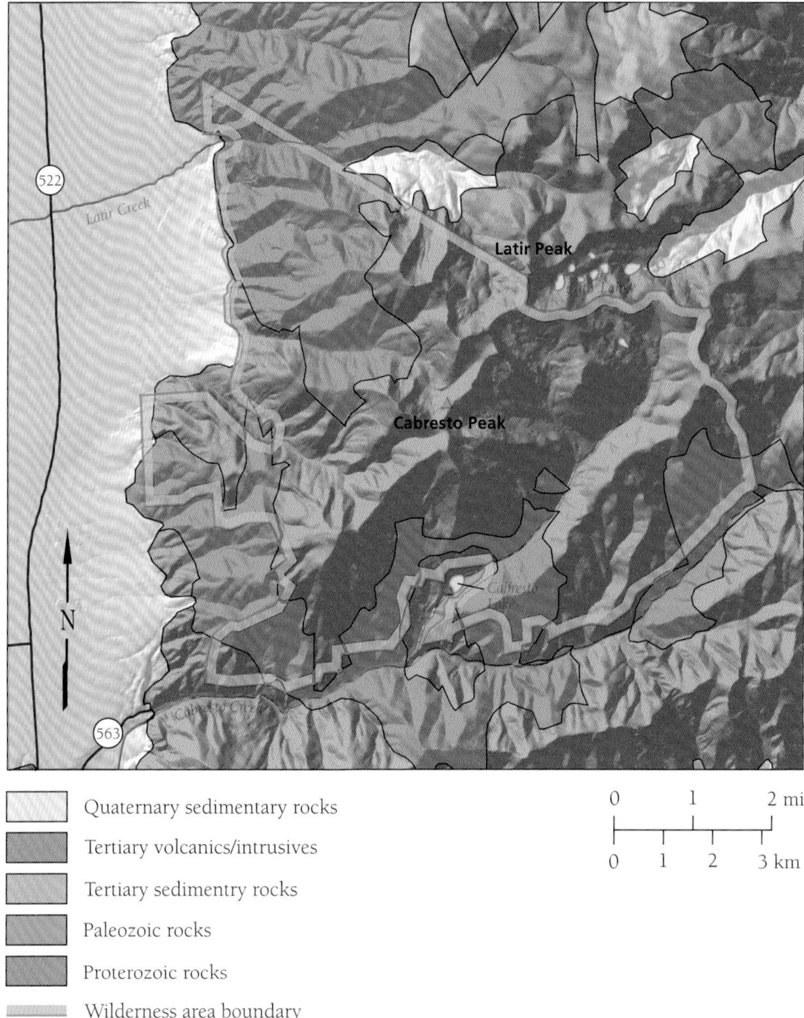

Generalized geologic map of the Latir Peak Wilderness and vicinity.

the preeminent American mountain chain. The mountains lie between the Raton Basin of the Great Plains to the east, and the San Luis and Española Basins of the Rio Grande rift to the west. The dramatic landscapes of the Latir Peak region have resulted from the overprinting of local geologic processes such as volcanism, faulting, glaciation, and erosion on multiple cycles of continent-scale mountain building.

The Rock Record

The Latir Peak area consists of a riotous mosaic of two varieties of rock, separated in time by 1.7 billion years. On the western slopes are ancient metamorphic sedimentary rocks and granitic plutons that are found throughout the Sangre de Cristo Mountains. These Precambrian rocks consist of quartzite, schist, and gneiss, which are intruded by a variety of plutons, such as the Quartz Monzonite of Costilla Creek and the Granodiorite of Jaracito Canyon.

The basement rocks are pervasively interlaced by a suite of Tertiary-aged volcanic rocks affiliated with the Questa magmatic system, especially in the eastern half of the wilderness area. The deep dissection of the Questa caldera by the Red River and Cabresto Creek has exposed the complex forms of the Tertiary igneous rocks that are intruded into, and erupted onto, the Precambrian basement. The high ridge between the two streams is composed of Amalia Tuff that accumulated within the caldera. Pinabete Peak is composed of remnants of the volcanic floor of the caldera that were later uplifted during post-caldera resurgence. The northern high peaks of the wilderness area, Latir Peak, Cabresto Peak, Venado Peak, and Virsylvia Peak are mostly capped by pre-caldera lava flows, domes, and tuffs. The northern border of the wilderness area approximately coincides with the northern edge of the caldera.

Much of the bedrock in the high country is covered by thin deposits of glacial origin. Extensive moraine deposits are found on the slopes and in the valleys surrounding the highest peaks. The oversteepened glaciated slopes have also generated some large landslides.

Geologic History

During middle Tertiary time, there existed a continuous chain of volcanoes from the San Juan Mountains of Colorado to the Latir volcanic field near Questa. Most of the volcanism predated the development of Rio Grande rift basins, and therefore much of the volcanic chain is now buried under the San Luis Valley. Prior to eruption of the Questa caldera, a variety of smaller volcanoes erupted between about 28 and 26.5 million years ago. The explosive eruption of the Questa caldera 25 million years ago was much larger, destroying some of the older volcanoes, and spreading ash-flow tuff over a vast area. Named the Amalia Tuff, remnants of this rhyolite tuff are now found as far afield as across the rift near Tres Piedras and near the crest of the Sangre de Cristo Mountains at the Colorado border.

As the crust extended during rifting, the western half of the Questa caldera dropped slowly into the San Luis Basin along the Sangre de Cristo fault, and is now deeply buried by sediments. Meanwhile, the eastern half has been faulted, uplifted, and eroded during the last 25 million years, resulting in an exceptionally well-exposed cross section through the plumbing system of the volcanoes of the Latir volcanic field, including the Questa caldera.

Heart Lake

Like the summits to the north and south, the high country of the Latir Wilderness was covered by alpine glaciers during parts of Pleistocene time. The presence of these glaciers is recorded by a variety of erosional and depositional features, such as cirques, arêtes, horns, moraines, and till.

Geologic Features

SUMMIT SCENERY—The above-timberline views from Pinabete Peak, Cabresto Peak, Venado Peak, and Virsylvia Peak are spectacular. On a clear day, this handful of summits provide stunning views north to Blanca Peak (14,345 feet) the highest peak of the Sangre de Cristo Mountains, northwest to the San Juan Mountains, west into the San Luis rift valley and across the Tusas Mountains to the Colorado Plateau, southwest to the Jemez Mountains, and south to the Wheeler Peak country.

Relatively few hikers investigate the Latir Peak Wilderness, but those that make the effort are rewarded by a genuine Rocky Mountain wilderness treasure. Most hikers are drawn to the summits, all of which are well above timberline. The walk from Cabresto Lake Campground to the peaks makes for a long day. Instead, many backpackers set up a base camp at Heart Lake, thus making several of the 12,000 foot summits very reasonable day hikes.

PATERNOSTER LAKES—In and around the wilderness area are over a dozen beautiful glacial lakes set high in the alpine valleys. The lakes, known to geologists as tarns, are situated in depressions excavated by Pleistocene glaciers. Just north of the wilderness boundary, east of Latir Peak, is a linked set of seven tarns, known as the Latir Lakes. Each small round lake lies within a separate glacial basin at a different elevation, but all are connected by streams and waterfalls. In some cases, the tarns are separated by glacial moraines rather than bedrock, and were dammed by the advance and retreat of the glacier.

Such a series of glacial lakes, connected by streams, rapids, or waterfalls, are given the unusual name of paternoster lakes. The name is derived from the words Pater Noster (Latin for "Our Father"), an alternate name for the Lord's Prayer. The lakes were named for their resemblance to rosary beads. Paternoster lakes are alternatively given the more secular names of beaded lakes, rock-basin lakes, and step lakes.

—Paul Bauer

If You Plan to Visit

Access to the wilderness is from Cabresto Campground, reached via Forest Roads 134 and 134A from Questa. The Latir Peak Wilderness has few maintained trails. Trail 82 from Cabresto Lake to Heart Lake and Latir Mesa follows Lake Fork of Cabresto Creek. Latir Peak, at the northern edge of the wilderness, is actually private land, as is the string of glacial lakes east of Latir Peak. Forest Service Trails 167 and 85 link many of the high peaks that are on public land. For more information:

Carson National Forest
208 Cruz Alta Road
Taos, NM 87571
(575) 758-6200
www.fs.fed.us/r3/carson/

The Enchanted Circle Scenic Byway

CARSON NATIONAL FOREST

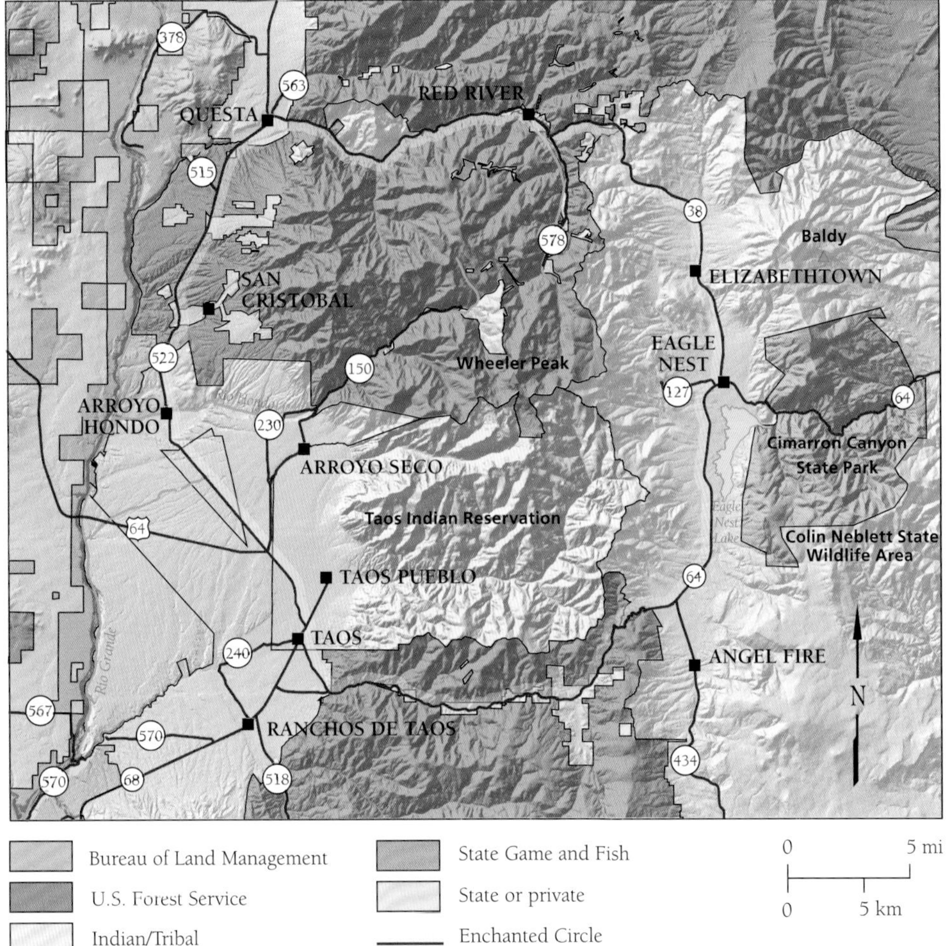

The 83-mile loop drive through northern New Mexico known as the Enchanted Circle crosses federal, state, and tribal lands and provides a look at some of the state's most spectacular scenery.

Roads with special scenic, cultural, or scientific value may be designated as scenic byways by government agencies such as states, the National Park Service, the U.S. Forest Service, and the Bureau of Land Management. The roughly circular set of highways that surround Wheeler Peak has been designated the "Enchanted Circle Scenic Byway" by both the U.S. Forest Service and the state of New Mexico. It was designated a U.S. Forest Service Scenic Byway in 1989. It was designated a New Mexico Scenic & Historic Byway by the New Mexico State Highway & Transportation Department in 1994.

The 83-mile Enchanted Circle loop drive is surely the finest overall day trip in the state. In addition to the stunning, continuously shifting scenery, the drive traverses a region of rich and diverse geology,

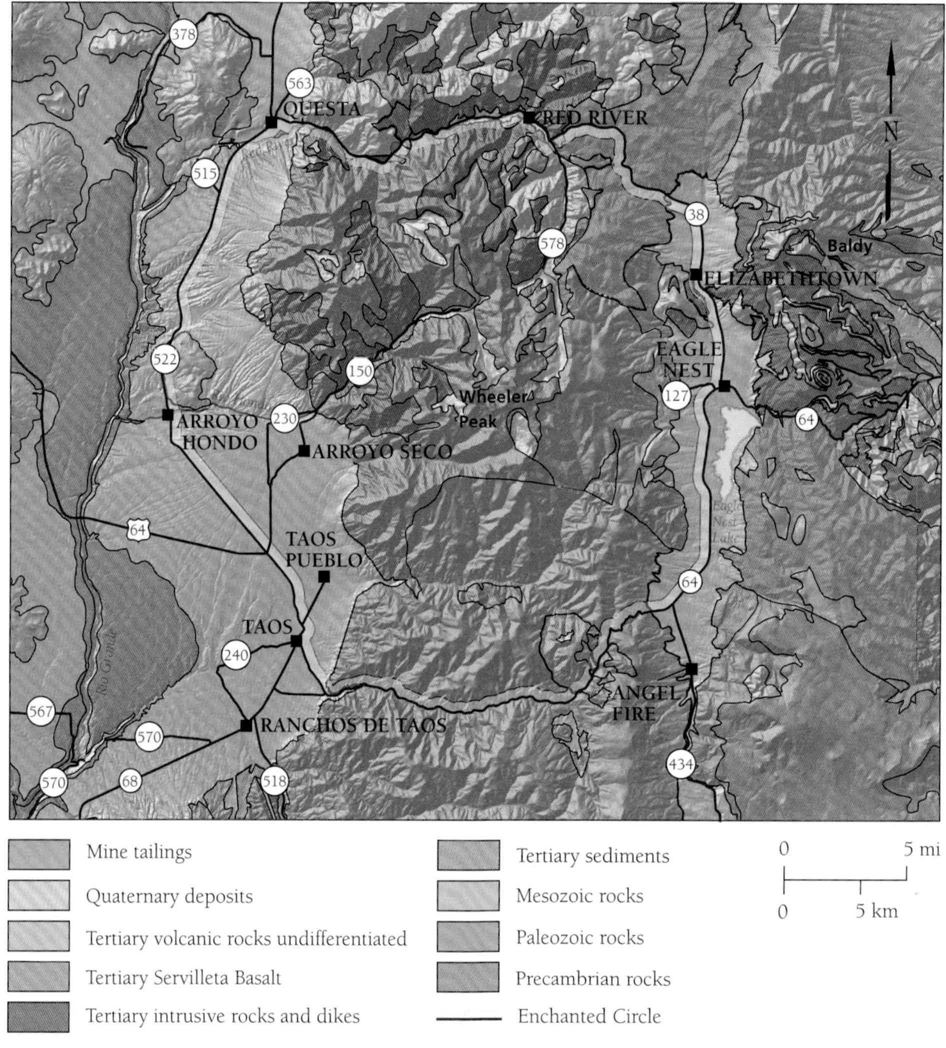

Generalized geologic map for the Enchanted Circle Scenic Byway and vicinity.

topography, human history, and culture. Highlights include Taos Pueblo (a World Heritage site and the oldest continuously occupied residence in New Mexico), the Questa molybdenum mine, the old mining town of Red River, magnificent views from Red River Pass, the rich gold fields of the Moreno Valley, the ghost town of Elizabethtown, Eagle Nest Lake and Dam, Vietnam Veterans Memorial State Park, and the fossils of Palo Flechado. A handful of short side trips take in the Rio Grande Gorge Bridge, the D. H. Lawrence Ranch, the Wild Rivers Recreation Area, the former ghost town of Twining (now Taos Ski Valley), Wheeler Peak, and Angel Fire Ski Area. Along much of the loop are campgrounds, trailheads, and recreational opportunities in the Carson National Forest.

Regional Setting

The southern Sangre de Cristo Mountains lie between the Raton Basin of the Great Plains and the San Luis Basin of the Rio Grande rift. At the latitude of Taos, the mountains consist of the Taos Range to the west and the Cimarron Mountains to the east. Nestled between the two ranges is a high intramontane valley, called the Moreno Valley. The Enchanted Circle encircles the Taos Range, and connects the Rio Grande rift, the Taos Range, and the Moreno Valley. The Sangre de Cristo fault system, which separates the mountains from the rift basin, has developed in the past 25 million years, and is responsible for the impressive fault-related topographic relief along the western flank of the mountains.

The Rock Record

The Enchanted Circle crosses four distinct geologic landscapes, each of which is underlain by a distinctive package of rocks. The Rio Grande rift is filled with Cenozoic volcanic rocks and sedimentary deposits. Tertiary volcanoes of the Taos Plateau volcanic field dot the western horizon. Near Taos, the rift basin is filled with many thousands of feet of sand, gravel, and clay of the Tertiary and Quaternary Santa Fe Group.

The Red River Valley exposes both Precambrian rocks and Tertiary plutonic and volcanic rocks of the Questa magmatic system. In Tertiary time, the igneous rocks intruded into, and erupted upon, the Precambrian basement. Superimposed by faulting and erosion, the result is a dizzying collage of gneiss, granite, monzonite, amphibolite, tuff, andesite, latite, and more. The high ridge between the Red River and Cabresto Creek is composed of densely welded Amalia Tuff, which was explosively ejected from the Questa caldera 25 million years ago. Well exposed along NM–38 between Questa and Red River is the Bear Canyon pluton, one of many Tertiary plutonic bodies in the canyon. The pluton was emplaced at depth as a hot mushy mass about 24 million years ago. This Tertiary magmatism is responsible for much of the mineral wealth along the Enchanted Circle, including the gold and copper at Taos Ski Valley, molybdenum along the Red River Valley, and the rich placer gold deposits at Elizabethtown.

The Moreno Valley contains rocks that range in age from Precambrian to Quaternary. Although the entire valley is underlain by Precambrian rocks, much of the valley is covered by thick sections of Paleozoic strata, thin sections of Mesozoic rocks, Tertiary igneous rocks, and Quaternary alluvial deposits. One of the Tertiary units, a quartz-diorite porphyry, is especially significant, as it was the host rock for the Elizabethtown gold rush of the 1870s.

The climb from Angel Fire over Palo Flechado Pass to Taos on US 64 crosses through a remarkable thickness of Pennsylvanian sedimentary rocks, many of which are fossil-rich. Most of the section belongs to the Porvenir Formation and the overlying Alamitos Formation. The Porvenir Formation consists of interbedded sandstones, conglomerates, siltstones, mudstones, and limestones. The Alamitos Formation consists of similar rock types, but with less limestone. The thickness of the sedimentary pile exceeds 3,000 feet.

Geologic History

Nearly 1.8 billion years of Earth history are represented within the Enchanted Circle, from the oldest known rock in New Mexico to modern alluvium. The modern landscape, however, was established in the Cenozoic as a result of a complex cycle of orogeny that involved uplift, faulting, sedimentation, volcanism, plutonism, and erosion.

Nicely symmetrical Ute Mountain is a complex dacite lava dome that erupted approximately 2.7 million years ago.

The early Cenozoic was characterized by widespread erosion of the Laramide highlands, resulting in a low-relief landscape that lasted until about 37 million years ago when the San Juan volcanic field of southern Colorado began to erupt. Vast aprons of sediment that were eroded from the volcanoes blanketed south-central Colorado and north-central New Mexico for millions of years. Volcanism progressed southeastward through time, until the Latir volcanic field near Questa began to erupt about 25 million years ago, blanketing the region with red-hot lava and welded ash now known as the Amalia Tuff.

The late Cenozoic was dominated by faulting and erosion related to the Rio Grande rift. As the San Luis Basin subsided, streams eroded deeply into the Rocky Mountains, forming canyons and youthful mountain ranges. Coarse sediments accumulated in the rift basin to the west and the Great Plains to the east. In Pleistocene time, a cool wet climate brought alpine glaciers to the high country. Glacial sculpting of the bedrock peaks created the rugged mountains that we see today from the Enchanted Circle.

Geologic Features

TAOS PLATEAU VOLCANIC FIELD—The drive north from Taos on the Enchanted Circle provides a fine view of the Pliocene to Pleistocene Taos Plateau volcanic field, one of the largest and most diverse volcanic fields of the Rio Grande rift. Volcanic rocks exposed on the Taos Plateau cover approximately 60 square miles and erupted over a five million year period from approximately 6 to 1 million years ago. Nearly 40 discrete vent areas have been identified and there are probably many more vents buried beneath the youngest lava flows. The most common rocks are the black to dark gray lava flows of the Servilleta Basalt, consisting of more than 50 cubic miles extruded onto the Taos Plateau. The rest of the volcanoes display a great range of compositional diversity, as the lava flows and associated pyroclastic rocks of the volcanic field span a compositional range from basalts to andesites, dacites, and even rhyolites. The geomorphic form of the volcanic edifices is broadly correlative with composition—the dacites typically formed steeper-sided lava domes like Ute Mountain, whereas the basalts formed broad, low-relief shield volcanoes.

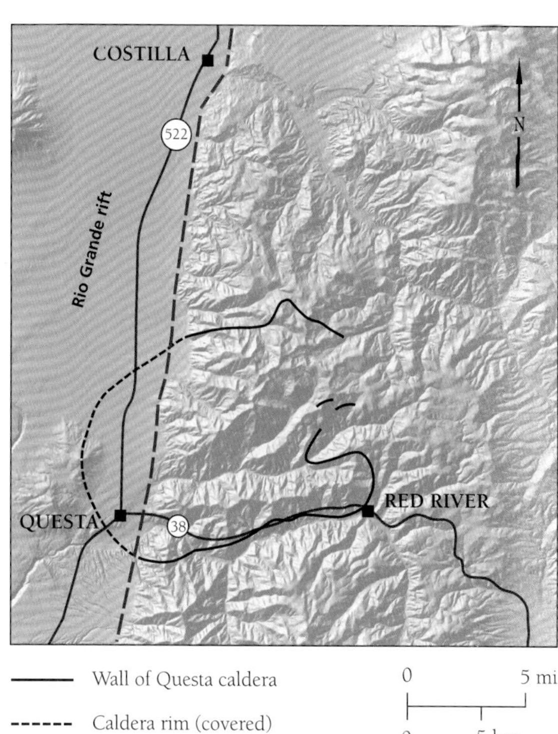

Traces of the 9-mile-wide Questa caldera have been obscured in the 25 million years since its eruption through erosion on the east side of the Sangre de Cristo fault. Much of the west side has been buried beneath sediments that have accumulated in the Rio Grande rift.

THE QUESTA CALDERA—In Tertiary time, volcanism moved progressively southeastward from the San Juan volcanic field, reaching the Latir volcanic field at the time the Rio Grande rift began to form 26 million years ago. About 25 million years ago, a major explosive eruption occurred in the Questa area, covering the region with red-hot lava and welded ash now known as the Amalia Tuff. The Amalia Tuff was the only regional ash-flow tuff erupted in the Latir volcanic field and remnants are preserved as far north as the Colorado border near the crest of the Sangre de Cristo Mountains and 25 miles southwest near the town of Tres Piedras.

Such a large amount of material was explosively ejected that the volcano collapsed along a great circular crack, called a ring fracture, forming a huge topographic depression, or caldera. The 14-mile-wide Valles caldera of the Jemez Mountains is one of the worlds finest young calderas. The Questa caldera was about 9 miles wide. After the caldera collapse, molten rock continued to intrude along the ring fractures. As the magmas solidified, hot fluids percolated through the rock, depositing minerals such as molybdenite, quartz, and pyrite in small fractures within the granites. These fracture-fillings, or veins, are the targets of mineral exploration at the Questa molybdenum mine.

Unlike the much younger Valles caldera, the Questa caldera lacks the distinctive circular topographic depression of the volcano. During the last 25 million years, the caldera has been cut in half by the Sangre de Cristo fault. The eastern half has been deeply eroded, exposing the complex volcanic plumbing system that is seen along Red River Canyon. The western half is buried under rift sediments.

Amalia Tuff

QUESTA MOLYBDENUM MINE—The workings of the Questa mine are obvious on the drive through Red River Canyon. The mineral molybdenite (molybdenum sulfide, MoS_2) is an ore of the metal molybdenum (from the Greek, "molybdos" for "lead" or "lead like") and is found in unusually high concentrations in the area. Molybdenum is used primarily in the steel industry for high-temper alloys and stainless steels. Very pure molybdenum is a key ingredient in industrial lubricants. The soft, shiny, black, greasy-feeling molybdenite is in veins and thin cracks along the edge of an igneous intrusion of the same type of granite as the Bear Canyon pluton, which intruded below the Questa caldera 24 million years ago.

The molybdenum operation spanned three phases of mining: the original underground mine of the 1920s in Sulphur Gulch; the large open pit of the 1960s that mined down into the same area of mineralization as the underground mine; and the modern underground mine, started in the 1980s, which is situated below Goat Hill. The Goat Hill ore body originally contained about 125 million tons of ore. Mining is done 2,000 feet below the surface by "gravity block caving," where networks of permanent tunnels are excavated beneath the ore body, and blocks of ore are shattered by explosives and lowered into railroad cars. The cars deliver ore to a 7,000-foot-long underground conveyor belt that rapidly transports the ore up an inclined tunnel to the mill site. By this method, 18,000 tons of ore per day can be extracted, producing 90,000 pounds of molybdenite. The large concrete tower near Goat Hill is the main service shaft to the modern underground mine.

The ore is processed in the mill. The large chunks of ore are crushed, milled to a fine powder, and mixed with chemicals and oils and then fed into flotation machines that separate the molybdenite from the waste materials. The molybdenite mixture then passes through

Only from the air can one appreciate the scope of the Questa molybdenum mine. The large hole is the now-inactive open pit mine that was excavated in the 1960s and 1970s.

thickeners, filters, and dryers where the remaining water is removed. This dry concentrate, containing more than 90 percent molybdenite, is shipped to a processor where it is roasted to remove the sulfur. The tailings are suspended in water and moved 9 miles down the canyon in 14-inch, rubber-lined pipes that parallel the highway to large tailings ponds near Questa. Some of the 360 million tons of waste rock from the Molycorp molybdenum mine are visible in steep piles along NM–38. Responding to concerns about the safety of the piles, the company has re-engineered some of the piles so that the threat of a catastrophic landslide is reduced. The mine has generated a number of serious environmental problems, including acid drainage pollution of the Red River and air and water quality issues related to the waste slurry.

HYDROTHERMAL ALTERATION SCARS—Between the mine and the Red River are barren, yellow-stained areas high along the canyon walls, known as alteration scars. The rock in these barren areas has been highly fractured, and hot water carrying pyrite (iron sulfide) has percolated upward to the surface through these zones. When exposed to oxygen and water, pyrite decomposes to iron oxides. It is these iron oxides (not sulfur) that stain the rocks yellow and brown. Sulphur Gulch was named for the yellow color of its walls in the mistaken belief that the coloring agent was sulfur. The scars are notorious for their contribution to debris flows that sometimes occur following heavy rains. These acidic debris flows run down drainages into nearby creeks and (ultimately) the Red River.

Elizabethtown began as a tent city in the 1860s when gold prospectors converged on Baldy Mountain. Founded by the commander of Fort Union, Captain William H. Moore, it was named for his daughter, Elizabeth Catherine Moore. It became New Mexico's first incorporated town and the county seat of Colfax County, with over 7,000 residents in 1870. By 1871 mining operations had all but ceased, and a fire in 1903 destroyed most of what was left of the town.

BALDY MOUNTAIN AND THE DEEP TUNNEL MINE—Baldy Mountain (12,441 feet) of the Cimarron Mountains was the scene of several gold booms in the late 1800s. In 1897 the town of Baldy, high on the mountainside at 10,000 feet elevation, had 200 residents, two boarding houses, a school, church services, twelve operating mines, four stamp mills, a blacksmith, tailor, barber, launderer, justice of the peace, livery stable, general stores, and more than one saloon. In October 1900 the Gold and Copper Deep Tunnel Mining and Milling Company was formed to drive a prospect tunnel completely through Baldy Mountain. Slightly inclined shafts were driven into the east and west sides of the mountain. Incredibly, the two tunnels met within a few inches of one another, 36 years later, in 1936. The tunnel failed to intersect any high-grade ore deposits, but certainly was a remarkable feat of engineering and persistence. Although the town of Baldy was razed in 1941, scattered slag piles, foundations, and mine dumps remain. Philmont Boy Scout Ranch now owns much of the land on the east side of Baldy Mountain.

ELIZABETHTOWN—Elizabethtown is now a ghost town, but it was once a thriving mining town with over 5,000 inhabitants. In 1866 soldiers found placer gold in the area. The next spring, during a rush to the discovery, gold was also discovered along all of the creeks and in veins on the west side of Baldy Mountain. Prospectors quickly staked claims, and by 1868 Elizabethtown had seven saloons, five general mercantiles, two hotels, and three dance halls. In 1870 Elizabethtown became the first incorporated town in New Mexico, and the county seat of newly formed Colfax County. The town's fortunes began to decline by 1870, and in 1872 Cimarron replaced Elizabethtown as the county seat. When a fire roared through town in 1903, the community never recovered.

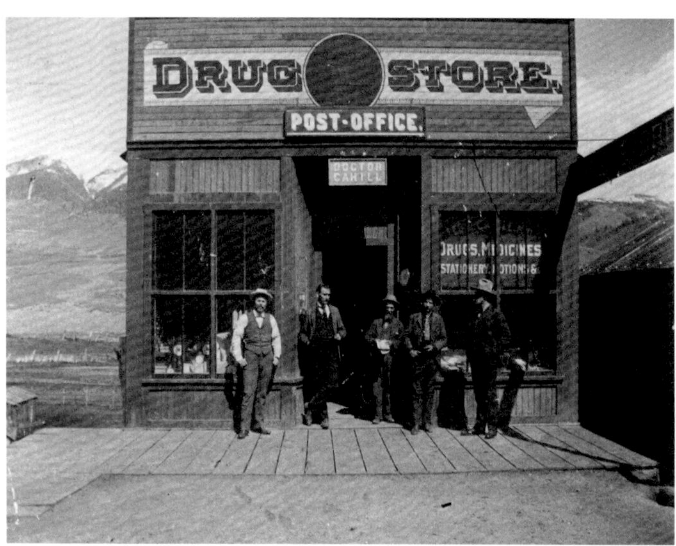

Dr. Leo L. Cahill's drug store in 1899 Elizabethtown.

Placer gold deposits are formed when gold, eroded from veins, is concentrated in streambeds. Where the channel of a rapidly flowing stream widens or where the gradient decreases, stream velocity drops. Heavy materials, such as gold, settle out and can be concentrated in the stream gravels. If enough gold accumulates, the gravels are considered placer gold deposits. Near the turn of the century a large dredge named Eleanor successfully worked Moreno Creek downstream from Elizabethtown. Although the dredge operated for only four seasons, it recovered approximately $200,000 worth of gold. Eleanor was abandoned near Elizabethtown, and by the 1940s had sunk completely from sight beneath the sandy gravels of Moreno Creek.

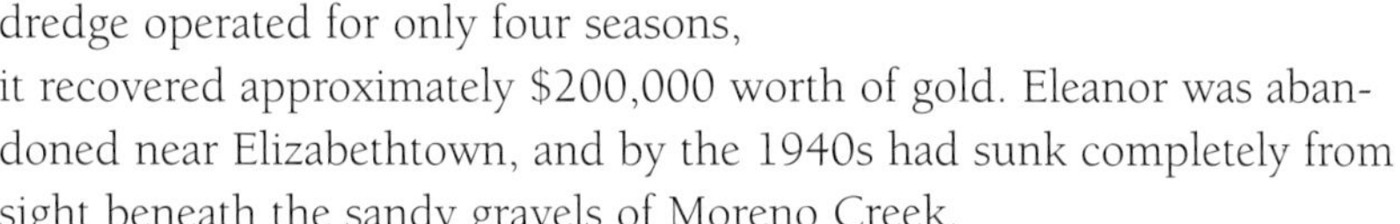

Hydraulic mining, which used powerful jets of water from giant nozzles to wash down high banks of gravel, was a method successfully used at Elizabethtown. The piles of gravel along the highway mark the sites of past placer mining operations. To supply the large amounts of water needed to recover gold, an aqueduct was constructed to bring water from the headwaters of the Red River, across Red River Pass, and along the flanks of Baldy Mountain to the goldfields near Elizabethtown. This engineering marvel, known as The Big Ditch, was 41 miles long, even though its ends were only 11 miles apart. The aqueduct was constructed between May 1868 and July 1869 by a force of 420 men, at a cost of about $230,000. The aqueduct leaked so badly that less than 20 percent of the water reached the placers. In places, remains of the old wooden flumes can still be seen. The flush production was over by about 1881. In a conservative estimate, the Elizabethtown mining district produced about $3 million worth of gold.

The Vietnam Veterans Memorial, built in 1968, became New Mexico's thirty-third state park in 2005.

The 2006 value of this gold is nearly $100 million.

VIETNAM VETERANS MEMORIAL STATE PARK—At an elevation of 8,500 feet on the western slope of the Moreno Valley, this small but significant park provides a stunning view of the valley, the Cimarron Mountains, Angel Fire Ski Area, and volcanoes to the east. This new, 30-acre park was transferred by the David Westphall Veteran Foundation to the state on Veterans Day, November 11, 2005. The chapel was erected in 1968 by Dr. Victor Westphall in memory of his son and all other U.S. personnel killed in Vietnam. It was first dedicated as the Vietnam Veterans Peace and Brotherhood Chapel, and then on May 30, 1983 it was rededicated as the DAV Vietnam Veterans National Memorial. The chapel was designed by Ted Luna, a young Santa Fe architect.

The park is an excellent place to scan the southern end of the Moreno Valley. The four rounded peaks to the left of the Angel Fire chair lift make up Cieneguilla Mountain. The area at the top of the chair lift and Cieneguilla Mountain are composed of Tertiary ash-flow tuff. The slopes below are underlain by steeply dipping river delta and marine strata of Pennsylvanian age. The dark red slopes to the south are composed of Pennsylvanian/ Permian Sangre de Cristo Formation.

The high mountain to the southeast of the ski area is Agua Fria Peak (11,086 feet), a major volcanic center in the northern part of the Ocate volcanic field. Agua Fria Peak is a shield volcano; the largest of several vents in the area. Most of the vents are topographic highs marked by abundant scoria, basalt, and some tuff and tuff breccia. Flows from these vents, that are between 5 and 4 million years old, consist mainly of basalt and minor andesite and dacite. The flows can be traced more than 20 miles to the southeast and cap many of the high mesas that surround the village of Ocate.

PALO FLECHADO PASS—The drive over Palo Flechado Pass (9,101 feet) crosses through the Flechado Formation, a Middle Pennsylvanian sequence of shales, sandstones, and limestones that contains one of the most diverse and well-preserved, fossil-bearing assemblages of marine animals in North America. Approximately 320 million years ago, this area was characterized by deltas and bays that were located between highlands to the west and a shallow sea to the east. A great number of animals and plants thrived in this setting, and after death, their remains were entombed in the sediments, ultimately becoming the fossils that now weather out of the rocks. Paleontologists have deduced that the Pennsylvanian sedimentary environment contained plenty of organic material to support a dense population of grazing, sediment-feeding, and suspension-feeding creatures. The invertebrate fossils include molluscs (especially snails and clams), brachiopods, bryozoans, corals, fusulinids, echinoderms, sponges, conularids, crinoids, echinoids, ostracods, foraminifers, and rare trilobites. Rare vertebrate fossils, such as sharks teeth and an early reptile, have also been found. Excellent exposures of the Flechado Formation also exist along NM–518 south of Talpa.

—*Paul Bauer*

If You Plan to Visit

The Enchanted Circle Scenic Byway begins in Taos, although you can start at any point. The entire loop is 85 miles long. Although much of the trip is through or adjacent to U.S. Forest Service lands, the trip also takes you across or skirts the Taos Pueblo Indian Reservation, New Mexico State Park lands, and private land. For more information, contact the Carson National Forest.

Carson National Forest
208 Cruz Alta Road
Taos, NM 87571
(575) 758-6200
www.fs.fed.us/r3/carson/
www.enchantedcircle.org

New Mexico State Parks
P.O. Box 1147
Santa Fe, NM 87504
(505) 476-3355
(888) 667-2757
www.emnrd.state.nm.us/PRD/index.htm

These Pennsylvanian invertebrate fossils are typical of those found in limestones of the Flechado Formation. The sandstones exposed at the summit of Palo Flechado Pass are not fossiliferous. Pictured here are three brachiopods and (third from top) a mollusc.

The Valle Vidal

CARSON NATIONAL FOREST

OPPOSITE: The Valle Vidal, in the Sangre de Cristo Mountains.

Ranging in elevation from 7,700 to 12,584 feet, the 100,000-acre Valle Vidal Unit of the Carson National Forest is home to a splendid assortment of mammals, birds, reptiles, amphibians, and fish—including rare native Rio Grande cutthroat trout, mountain lion, Merriam's turkey, bison, black bear, mule deer, and one of the largest elk herds in New Mexico. Valle Vidal is translated from Spanish as "valley of abundant life," which seems a suitable name indeed. Originally part of the nearly two million-acre Maxwell Land Grant, and later a private playground for the rich and famous, the land was donated to the federal government by Pennzoil Company in 1982 and is now managed by the U.S. Forest Service.

Regional Setting

The Valle Vidal Unit straddles the boundary between the Sangre de Cristo Mountains and the Raton Basin, giving the park two distinct geologic/topographic personalities. The western half contains high peaks and steep-sided valleys, whereas the eastern half is a broad plateau cut by small canyons. The western edge of the geologic Raton Basin and the Raton coal field are defined by the appearance of the Cretaceous Trinidad Sandstone at the surface. As much as 10,000 feet of sedimentary rocks fill the Raton Basin. The Taos/Colfax boundary, which crosses Little Costilla Peak, follows the topographic divide between creeks that drain west to the Rio Grande with those that flow east to the Canadian River.

The Rock Record

The western Valle Vidal Unit consists of Precambrian metamorphic rocks such as gneiss, schist, quartzite, amphibolite, and pegmatite, all of which have been metamorphosed, folded, and faulted during a lengthy orogenic history. From near the Taos/Colfax County line eastward are sedimentary strata that range from the Pennsylvanian–Permian Sangre de Cristo Formation, to the familiar Triassic and Jurassic units of the Chinle, Entrada, and Morrison Formations. These are overlain by a thick section of Cretaceous sedimentary formations that includes the Dakota Sandstone, the Graneros, Carlile, Greenhorn, Niobrara, Pierre Shales, the Trinidad Sandstone, and the Vermejo Formation. Overlying this section are the Poison Canyon and Raton Formations, which span the Cretaceous/Tertiary boundary. All of these rocks have been affected by Tertiary igneous activity, principally the intrusion of sheet-like

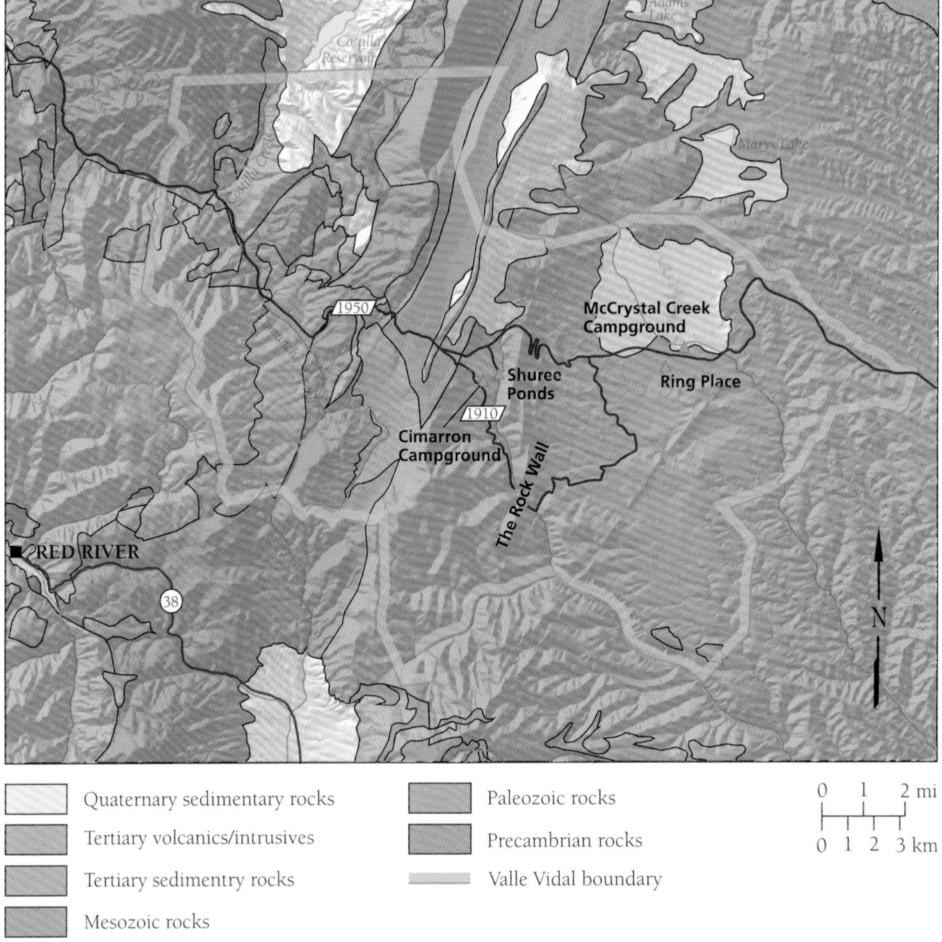

Generalized geologic map of the Valle Vidal Unit, Carson National Forest, and vicinity.

igneous bodies such as sills (Costilla Reservoir sill), dikes (the Rock Wall and Ash Mountain), and laccoliths (Comanche Point). The hot fluids that accompanied these intrusions carried the precious metals that were later mined at La Belle, Bitter Creek, and elsewhere in the area.

Geologic History

The Precambrian rocks of the western Valle Vidal Unit formed at the surface as sedimentary and volcanic rocks nearly 1.7 billion years ago. As an ancient orogeny buried them several miles down, heat and pressure increased until the very minerals of the rocks changed form, resulting in the metamorphic schist, gneiss, quartzite, and amphibolite that are now exposed at the surface.

During late Pennsylvanian time the Ancestral Rocky Mountain orogeny caused uplift, deformation, and erosion of the Valle Vidal area.

The eroding mountains sent great amounts of clastic sediments of the Sangre de Cristo Formation into the broad basins of northern New Mexico. During Triassic and Jurassic time, terrestrial sandstones and shales accumulated over much of the region. The Triassic rocks are mostly sandstones and mudstones of floodplain origin, derived from material shed from the Ancestral Rocky Mountains onto long, broad river valleys. At the close of Triassic time, the sediments were slightly warped and eroded before they were covered by Jurassic sediments of the eolian Entrada Sandstone and alluvial silts and muds of the Morrison Formation.

As the Cretaceous Western Interior Seaway covered northeastern New Mexico, sediments accumulated along the advancing and retreating shoreline, and coal beds formed in the abundant swamps. Thick sequences of sandstone, shale, and limestone accumulated on the sea bottom until late Cretaceous time, when the sea retreated. Life flourished until about 65 million years ago when a large meteorite struck off the coast of Yucatan, Mexico. The prevailing theory connects this event with the great Cretaceous/Tertiary mass extinction that marked the disappearance of nearly half of Earth's life forms, including the dinosaurs.

The Laramide orogeny, which began in latest Cretaceous time, ultimately forged the fundamental architecture of the modern Rocky Mountains. Mountain ranges were uplifted and tilted along thrust and reverse faults. In the eastern Valle Vidal, Precambrian rocks were thrust over Paleozoic and younger strata. Uplift culminated in the Eocene. Adjacent basins, such as the Raton Basin, subsided and filled with great thicknesses of clastic sediment—over 3,000 feet of Tertiary sediment in some areas.

In mid-Tertiary time, the tectonic setting changed from crustal compression to crustal extension, as the Rio Grande rift system began to open west of the Sangre de Cristo Mountains. Widespread volcanic eruptions and magma intrusions occurred in the rift, in the mountains, and in the Raton Basin. Tectonic activity slowed during the late Tertiary and Quaternary, although volcanoes continued to erupt. As wide-spread uplift of the southern Rocky Mountains again occurred in the late Tertiary, streams excavated deep canyons in the highlands and transported enormous quantities of sediment into the adjacent basins.

Geologic Features

COMANCHE POINT—Visitors entering the Valle Vidal from the west are greeted by Comanche Point, a prominent rock sentinel at the junction of Comanche and Costilla Creeks (FR 1950 and FR 1900). The point is composed of a 25-million-year-old shallow rhyolite intrusion that is

Comanche Point is the erosional remnant of an igneous intrusion that solidified underground about 25 million years ago. Shown is the confluence of Costilla Creek (on the left) and Comanche Creek.

part of a laccolith complex that was emplaced along a fault that separates volcanic rocks to the south from Precambrian rocks to the north. The rhyolite is columnar jointed in "cordwood" style on the north face of the point. This outcrop, along with other nearby exposures of the Costilla Reservoir sill, have been studied by geologists who are interested in understanding the processes and characteristics of magma bodies that cool and crystallize underground.

Columnar rhyolite on the north face of Comanche Point.

VALLE VIDAL—Originally called the Valle de Vidal, now shortened to Valle Vidal, the broad valley drained by Vidal Creek and Comanche Creek is the centerpiece of the Valle Vidal Unit. As you drive east from Comanche Point you will reach a parking area and overlook with a wooden corral on the right. The view south is along the axis of the Valle Vidal itself. On the far horizon to the southwest is the Wheeler Peak Wilderness, about 30 miles distant.

The Valle Vidal proper is part of the north-south linear *graben* system that includes the Mora and Moreno Valleys to the south and Costilla Valley to the north. The broad openness of the valley results from erosion of the relatively soft quartz monzonite that constitutes the upper plate of a major thrust fault. Although the thrust fault is poorly exposed, a line of springs and vegetation along the eastern edge of the valley mimics the fault.

COALBED METHANE—Methane (CH_4) is the most abundant hydrocarbon of natural gas produced from oil and gas fields. Coalbed methane is natural gas produced from coal. The methane can be released by drilling into the coal seams and pumping out water that naturally exists in fractures in the coal. The Raton Basin became New Mexico's newest natural gas-producing region in 1999, when a pipeline was completed to transport natural gas to an interstate pipeline at Trinidad, Colorado. Since then, most of the flurry of drilling has been within Ted Turner's Vermejo Park Ranch.

Clayton corrals, in the Valle Vidal. The Valle Vidal is a broad valley that was formed by erosion of a fault zone. Wheeler Peak area is on the skyline.

In June 2002 El Paso Corporation of Houston applied to drill for coalbed methane on about 40,000 acres of the Valle Vidal Unit. The process of extracting the gas produces surface disturbances, such as well pads, roads, pipeline corridors, compressor stations, and dehydration units. Other environmental issues associated with the development of coalbed methane resources include the injection of hazardous chemicals into the drill holes, contamination from toxic waste pits, the depletion of ground water from coal seams, ground subsidence, methane leaks, and the potential for pipeline explosions. Local opposition to the proposal was phenomenal, and a grueling three-year battle led to the unanimous congressional support of the Valle Vidal Protection Act of 2005. The new law permanently protects the Valle Vidal Unit by withdrawing it from all forms of mineral activities.

THE WATERS—The Valle Vidal contains the headwaters of two of New Mexico's most important watersheds: Costilla Creek, which empties into the Rio Grande, and the Canadian River, which ultimately flows to the Mississippi River. The headwaters of the Valle Vidal are so significant that 15 stream segments have been deemed eligible for inclusion in the national Wild and Scenic Rivers system, including Comanche, McCrystal, and Costilla Creeks. Several of these creeks are home to New Mexico's state fish, the Rio Grande cutthroat trout. In 2006 the State of New Mexico designated all waters within the Valle Vidal Unit as Outstanding National Resource Waters—the highest level of protection offered under the federal Clean Water Act. The designation allows the state to impose stringent restrictions and requirements on land uses that affect surface water quality. The designation does not affect existing uses of the land, which include hunting, fishing, other recreational activities and livestock grazing. Visitors can easily reach most of these splendid streams from Forest Road 1950.

Costilla Creek

LA BELLE TOWNSITE—The ghost town of La Belle is on private land up La Belle Creek in the western Valle Vidal. The first European prospectors to reach La Belle arrived in 1866. By 1895 the gold boom had attracted over 600 people to a town that could brag of a newspaper, five general stores, four liveries, six saloons, two barber shops, three hotels, two laundries, and a jail that was reportedly never occupied. Speculators were so optimistic that the 80 rooms of the four-storied Southern Hotel were painstakingly moved 50 miles from Catskill to La Belle. Because of its remote location, the town was a favored hangout for bandits and rogues, including the notorious Black Jack Ketchum.

Ultimately, the gold ore was of insufficient grade to maintain the mines, and by 1900 La Belle was nearly deserted. The Southern Hotel was sold at auction for $50. Prospecting and exploration occurred from time to time through the 1970s. Visitors can still see a landscape peppered with old prospects, mine adits, and mineralized rocks. The gold, along with elevated levels of mercury, molybdenum, lead, and zinc, is in hydrothermally altered Tertiary volcanic rocks associated with the Questa magmatic system.

The town of La Belle in 1897.

THE CRETACEOUS/TERTIARY BOUNDARY—Near the eastern boundary of the Valle Vidal is one of the most studied, debated, and significant stratigraphic contacts in the world, the boundary between the Cretaceous and Tertiary Periods—often referred to as the "K/T boundary." Although the boundary zone has not been thoroughly studied here, and the iridium-rich boundary claystone layer has not been found, the rocks appear to preserve a continuous section across the boundary. In this location the K/T boundary is found within a single unit, the Raton Formation. The Raton Formation consists of three zones: a lower coal zone of sandstone, mudstone, conglomerate, and thin coal beds; a middle zone of sandstone that lacks coal; and an upper coal zone that contains the thick coal beds that were mined commercially in the Raton coal field. The formation represents a river/delta sedimentary environment that existed along the west coast of a vast interior seaway. The coal accumulated in a poorly drained back swamp on a broad, low gradient, alluvial

The feature known as the Rock Wall is a Tertiary dike, one of a number of similar intrusive volcanic features that radiate from the vicinity of Baldy Mountain.

plain. The thickness of the coal beds indicates that large peat bogs were stable for a long time. The K/T boundary lies somewhere near the top of the lower coal zone.

Just to the east of here, near Raton and Sugarite, are K/T boundary sites that have been extensively studied. The Raton (or Goat Hill) site was the first outcrop discovery of the iridium anomaly in the Raton Basin. Both studies used palynology (the branch of science concerned with the study of pollen, spores, and similar palynomorphs, living and fossil) to locate the boundary—specifically, the disappearance of the fossil pollen *Proteacidites*, which became extinct abruptly at the boundary. The Sugarite site also showed a spike of fern spores just above the extinction horizon, a trend interpreted as opportunistic fern species replacing the normal plant community that was devastated by the extinction event.

THE ROCK WALL—Just east of Shuree Ponds is a high, linear ridge known as The Rock Wall. Forest Service Road 1950 crosses the ridge through Windy Gap, and switchbacks down the eastern side into the Park Plateau of the Raton Basin. The overlook on the uppermost switchback provides a spectacular view of the eastern Valle Vidal, Ted Turner's Vermejo Park Ranch, and out into the Great Plains. The dark mountain on the northeast horizon is near Trinidad, Colorado.

This ridge is held up by one of many parallel, Tertiary-age intrusive dikes that permeate the region. The Rock Wall dike is composed of dacite that intrudes the Tertiary-age Poison Canyon Formation sandstone and conglomerate. This dike and several others nearby were intruded radially from Baldy Mountain, about 10 miles south of Windy Gap in the Moreno Valley. The higher ridge to the west, Ash Mountain (10,972 feet), is composed of a thick rhyolite dike that is probably affiliated with the Latir volcanic field. The dike rocks are much more resistant to erosion than the surrounding sedimentary strata, resulting in their spectacular topographic demarcation.

—*Paul Bauer*

If You Plan to Visit

Access to the Valle Vidal is via Forest Road 1950, which connects Amalia to the west with Cimarron to the east. Both routes involve long drives on light-duty gravel roads that are very rough in places. Motorized travel in the unit is restricted to a few forest service roads; these roads are not plowed in winter. Carry drinking water. Also carry a good spare tire and the tools to replace or fix a flat tire, as the roads are rough and remote and have a reputation for producing flat tires. The unit is closed to the public in the winter and spring for wildlife protection. Sections of the park are closed from January 1 to March 31 for elk winter range, and from May 1 to June 30 for elk calving.

Contact the Carson National Forest about road conditions, camping, hunting, fishing, wood-gathering and other permits, water availability, and general information about the areas you intend to visit. The U.S. Forest Service has an excellent map of the Valle Vidal Unit.

Carson National Forest
208 Cruz Alta Road
Taos, NM 87571
(575) 758-6200
www.fs.fed.us/r3/carson/

The Pecos Wilderness

SANTA FE & CARSON NATIONAL FORESTS

The popular Pecos Wilderness contains some of the most exceptional alpine landscapes in the Southwest. It is renowned for combining bountiful wildlife, rugged alpine peaks, pristine forests, cool cirque lakes, wildflower-filled meadows, waterfalls, 150 miles of clear streams, and dozens of trails and trailheads. The 223,667-acre wilderness ranges in elevation from 8,400 to over 13,000 feet, and contains Truchas Peak, the southernmost 13,000-foot peak in the United States. Lake Katherine (11,700 feet), near Santa Fe Baldy, is considered to be the most beautiful high mountain lake in the region, and one of the largest glacial lakes in the state. The Pecos Wilderness is unique in the Americas, as it contains up to ten ecological zones, from the semi-arid plains of the Rio Grande valley to the alpine zone above timberline, where the combination of cold, wind, storms, drought, and solar radiation creates an extraordinarily inhospitable environment.

Regional Setting

The Pecos Wilderness Area lies in the southernmost Sangre de Cristo Mountains, the end of the line for the Rocky Mountains. To the south, near Glorieta Pass, the Precambrian core of the Sangre de Cristo Mountains plunges under the flat-lying Mesozoic rocks of Rowe Mesa.

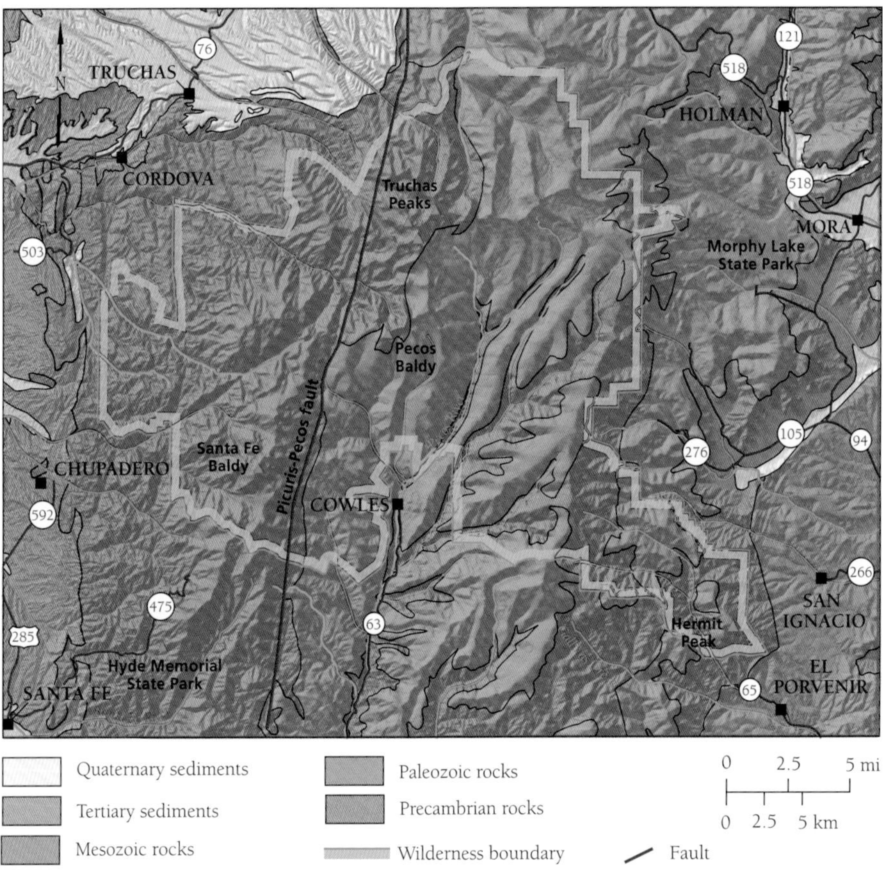

Generalized geologic map of the Pecos Wilderness and vicinity.

East of the wilderness area is the Raton Basin, a relatively young geologic basin filled with thousands of feet of Cretaceous and Tertiary sedimentary rock. To the west is the Española Basin, a 25-million-year-old extensional basin of the Rio Grande rift that is responsible for the impressive topographic relief of the Santa Fe Range and Truchas Peaks. Although the wilderness contains only old rocks of Precambrian and Paleozoic age, the landscapes are young, representing the multiple orogenic events and erosional activities of Cenozoic time.

The Rock Record

Although the Pecos Wilderness area has experienced an exceedingly long and complex geologic history, only three general geologic units exist in the area. The entire region is underlain by Precambrian rock that is conveniently separated into two terrains by a large fault known as the Picuris-Pecos fault. West of the fault is a veritable sea of granites (Embudo Granite) that are part of a global event in which Earth's crust was pervasively intruded by magma 1.45 billion years ago. East of the fault is a remarkable sequence of quartzite and schist that represents the metamorphosed and folded remains of a mile-thick pile of quartz-rich sediments that filled an ocean basin nearly 1.7 billion years ago. The most notable part of the rock sequence is the Ortega Quartzite, a layer of nearly pure quartz sandstone that is well over 3,000 feet thick, and probably represents one of the thickest sequences of pure beach sand ever accumulated on Earth. Although the sandstone is now a quartzite that was heated to over 900°F (500°C) while deeply buried, original sedimentary forms such as crossbeds and ripple marks are still preserved in the rocks.

Deep in the crust, metamorphic rocks can partially melt, or be intruded by granitic magma. The result is called migmatite, a rock exhibiting the characteristics of both igneous and metamorphic rocks, commonly characterized by contorted bands of light and dark rock. This migmatite is from south of Santa Fe Baldy.

East of the Picuris-Pecos fault, a thin veneer of Paleozoic rock unconformably overlies the Precambrian terrane. Just above the Great Unconformity is a very thin zone of gray Mississippian limestone, then a sequence of Pennsylvanian sedimentary rocks consisting mostly of tan to gray sandstone, dark shale, and gray limestone. Precambrian rocks are exposed in stream valleys where the streams have cut down below the sedimentary blanket. In the southernmost wilderness, along the Pecos River and Rio Mora, are outcrops of *mafic* and *ultramafic* metamorphic rock, known as the Pecos Complex, that represent some of the earliest continental crust in New Mexico.

More recently, Pleistocene glaciers are responsible for a variety of sedimentary deposits in the alpine valleys. Glacial moraines and rock glaciers are common in the highest valleys, and glacial till covers many of the lower valley bottomlands.

Geologic History

The modern Rocky Mountains did not exist until about 70 million years ago, a mere juvenile range by geologic standards. Careful study of rocks in the Pecos wilderness has helped geologists piece together parts of the geologic history of New Mexico, beginning with the original formation and evolution of the continent.

The continental crust of northern New Mexico was constructed from a continental nucleus that grew southward from Canada about 1.8 to 1.4 billion years ago, mostly by accreting fragments of exotic crust and intruding great volumes of magma. During much of Precambrian time, the rocks now exposed at the surface were miles down, and thus tell us little of what was happening at the surface. As the continent matured, tectonic forces caused the crust to buckle and break, and great mountain ranges evolved. Although those primordial peaks have long since eroded, their metamorphic roots are now exposed in the Pecos Wilderness area due to a succession of uplift and erosion during the last 300 million years.

Sometime around 300 million years ago, the Pecos region landscape had been eroded down to a flat plain punctuated by small hills and valleys, and a sea slowly advanced over the landscape, leaving Precambrian-hilled islands in its wake. After some preliminary advances and retreats, in early Pennsylvanian time, the sea deepened and sediments began to accumulate on the sea bottom. Over time, many thousands of feet of limestone, shale, sandstone, and conglomerate had blanketed the entire region. As it thickened, the sediment pile was compacted and cemented as it turned to rock. During late Pennsylvanian time, sea coverage was only part time, with sedimentation alternating between marine and nonmarine conditions. By Permian time, the sea had retreated. Following uplift of the Rocky Mountains at the end of Mesozoic time, during the Laramide orogeny, the wilderness area was never again covered by seas.

Although the Laramide orogeny began as a broad uplift of the Rocky Mountain region, it progressed to a major orogeny as high-relief mountains and basins developed in late Cretaceous time. By early Tertiary time, the mountains were enthusiastically eroding and the general features of the southern Sangre de Cristo Mountains had formed. With Rio Grande rifting, about 25 million years ago, the erosional profile of the western slope of the mountains began to develop. During Pleistocene time, the actions of alpine glaciers chiseled the craggy peaks that we see today.

Geologic Features

THE TRUCHAS PEAKS—The Truchas Peaks include four of the tallest ten peaks in the state. At 13,102 feet, Truchas Peak is the second-highest mountain in New Mexico, with Middle Truchas Peak (13,066 feet) and North Truchas Peak (13,024 feet) close behind. The line of high peaks, from Jicarilla Peak to Pecos Baldy represents one of the most impressive range crests in the Southwest. It is possible to walk the entire crest without ever dropping below about 11,500 feet. Approximately 30 percent of the Truchas Peaks area lies above timberline, including twenty summits above 11,500 feet. It is closer to a vertical landscape than horizontal, with 1,500 foot cliffs commonplace. The Truchas Lakes (11,900 feet) provide a fine view of all three Truchas Peaks, whose steep sides of Precambrian quartzite tower 1,000 feet over the lakes.

This view of the Truchas Peaks is derived from a color enchanced digital orthophoto draped over a 10-meter digital elevation model. The image was manipulated to provide an oblique view to the south over the Truchas Peaks, which show many classic glacial features. The illustration below shows the same area as it might have looked in the late Pleistocene, with valley glaciers receding in the face of an increasingly warm climate.

The high peaks of the Pecos Wilderness owe their dramatic appearance to the relatively recent actions of Pleistocene glaciers. Ice ages have occurred periodically during the last 2 million years, separated by warmer interglacial periods. During the last great ice age, about 18,000 years ago, approximately 30 percent of the planet's land surface was covered by glaciers. At high altitudes, glaciers begin to form when temperatures are low and snowfall is heavy. A glacier is a body of ice that forms on land by the compaction and recrystallization of snow, and moves outward under its own weight. Alpine glaciers have sculpted some of the most spectacular scenery on Earth, including the Cascades, the Swiss Alps, and the Rockies. There are three types of alpine glaciers. *Cirque* glaciers create semicircular basins on the sides of mountains usually near the heads of valleys. Valley glaciers occupy preexisting stream valleys. Ice caps form at the tops of mountains.

Mountains are dramatically changed by alpine valley glaciers due to the enormously erosive activities of the moving glacial ice, and the contribution of frost wedging. In highland areas, the most obvious glacial features are those created by erosion, not deposition. Glaciated mountains tend to be angular, with jagged peaks and ridges, and oversteepened slopes. Glaciers shape the landscape through two processes, abrasion and quarrying (or plucking). Abrasion occurs when rock fragments embedded in the ice scrape along the underlying bedrock as the glacier moves. Quarrying occurs when the glacier lifts fragments of bedrock from its bed. These processes create a variety of distinctive landforms that are beautifully developed in the Truchas Peaks area.

Alpine valley glaciers widen, deepen, and straighten stream valleys into U-shaped troughs, leaving tributary hanging valleys above the steep truncated spurs of the valley walls. The waterfall west of North Truchas Peak is glacially formed. Just below the headwalls of high mountain valleys, are glacially carved, bowl-shaped depressions called cirques. At least twenty cirques have been carved into the high Truchas Peaks area. Cirques commonly contain glacial lakes called *tarns*, such as Jose Vigil Lake and Trampas Lakes. A string of lakes in a glacial valley are called *paternoster* lakes, such as the Truchas Lakes (11,900 feet). When three or more cirques form around a mountain peak they create a sharp peak called a horn. The Matterhorn in Switzerland is the classic shape, and although the Truchas Peaks are not as grand, they are all horned peaks. When two glaciers on opposite sides of a mountain erode upslope, they form a sharp, jagged, steep-sided ridge of rock called an arête, another common feature of the Truchas Peaks area.

Hermit Peak

HERMIT PEAK—Hermit Peak (10,260 feet), formerly known as Cerro del Tecolote (Owl Peak) lies in the extreme southeast corner of the wilderness. The broad summit lies atop an enormous granite *massif* with a massive eastern escarpment. The precipitous cliffs give the mountain a distinctive appearance that is clearly visible from the Great Plains. From the popular Porvenir Campground, a trail leads 4 miles to the summit where Precambrian granites and gneisses of the mountain are capped by a thin layer of Mississippian and Pennsylvanian limestone.

The peak traces its name to an intensely pious Italian named Juan Maria de Agostini. Born to a noble family, he rejected his privileges, and left home to walk through Europe, Mexico, South America, and Cuba.

At the age of 62 he walked the 600-mile Santa Fe Trail, arriving in Las Vegas in 1863. He later took up a hermits residence in a cave 250 feet below the rim of Hermit Peak. The *Penitentes* believed in the hermit's holiness, and made pilgrimages to his cave. He traded carved crucifixes and religious items for food. In 1867 he left the cave, wandering southward through Texas, Mexico, and southern New Mexico where he was mysteriously murdered.

PECOS BALDY LAKE AND THE PICURIS-PECOS FAULT—Pecos Baldy Lake occupies a cirque below Pecos Baldy. The cirque is naturally dammed by a low glacial moraine on its southeast side. Until the 1930s there was only a small pond in the cirque, and water drained out through a fracture in the limestone. The New Mexico Department of Game & Fish plugged the fracture to create a lake suitable for trout. Later, the Forest Service raised the dam a few feet to create the modern picturesque lake. Visitors to the lake are also provided with a fine view of one of the largest faults in the state.

Pecos Baldy Lake

In a state famous for the quantity and variety of its geologic faults, the Picuris-Pecos fault stands out as a showpiece. The fault has been traced for 40 miles, from the northern Picuris Mountains south of Taos, to I–25 near the village of Cañoncito. From Cañoncito, the fault can be traced southward for an additional 35 miles. A length of at least 75 miles arguably makes the Picuris-Pecos fault the largest exposed strike-slip fault in the state.

The Picuris-Pecos fault was originally described as a *geofracture*, an antiquated term for a major, long-lived fault zone that has periodically reactivated. Some geologists believe that the fault has been active several times during the last 1.5 billion years, and that rocks exposed in the Truchas Peaks are equivalent to the rocks of the Picuris Mountains, offset laterally along the fault by a distance of about 16 miles.

The Pecos Wilderness contains some of the best exposures of the Picuris-Pecos fault, including one on the steep slope between Pecos Baldy Lake and Pecos Baldy. The fault juxtaposes dense, gray-white

Precambrian rocks of Pecos Baldy against the Pennsylvanian limestone, shale, and sandstone that underlie the lake. Fossils of invertebrates that inhabited shallow seas 300 million years ago can be found in the sedimentary rocks.

—*Paul Bauer*

Additional Reading

Trail Guide to Geology of the Upper Pecos by P. K. Sutherland and A. Montgomery. Scenic Trip 6, New Mexico Bureau of Geology and Mineral Resources, 1975.

Beatty's Cabin: Adventures in the Pecos High Country by Elliott Speer Barker. University of New Mexico Press, 1953. Now out of print, this story of the Pecos Wilderness from territorial times to the 1950s has become a classic.

If You Plan to Visit

Dozens of trailhead entry points are scattered around the wilderness area. From Santa Fe Ski Area, the Winsor Trail heads into the heart of the wilderness, with access to Nambe Lake (a small cirque lake) and to Santa Fe Baldy, the highest summit in the Santa Fe area. From Las Vegas, NM–263 runs east to El Porvenir, and U.S. Forest Service campgrounds and trailheads.

The Pecos Wilderness extends through two ranger districts in the Santa Fe National Forest and into the Carson National Forest to the north. Like all Wilderness areas, the Pecos Wilderness has restrictions on access. For more information:

Santa Fe National Forest
1474 Rodeo Road
Santa Fe, NM 87505
(505) 438-7840
www.fs.fed.us/r3/sfe/recreation/wilderness.htm#pecos

Carson National Forest
208 Cruz Alta Road
Taos, NM 87571
(575) 758-6200
www.fs.fed.us/r3/carson/

Hyde Memorial State Park

Just 8 miles from the Santa Fe Plaza in the southwestern Sangre de Cristo Mountains, this 350-acre park is a local favorite for day-use and easy access to the surrounding Santa Fe National Forest. At about 8,500 feet elevation, the park is vegetated with dense stands of evergreens and aspen. The Precambrian rocks at Hyde Memorial State Park near Santa Fe date back to the formative years of the southwestern U.S.

The lodge at Hyde Memorial State Park, which was constructed in 1938 by the Civilian Conservation Corps. It was extensively remodeled in 1998.

Regional Setting

Hyde Memorial State Park is in the southwestern Santa Fe Range, not far from the boundary between the Sangre de Cristo Mountains and the Española Basin of the Rio Grande rift. Although the boundary is topographically impressive, it lacks the large, active, rift-bounding fault zone that is found to the north along the western flank of the Taos Range.

The Rock Record

Hyde Memorial State Park is almost entirely underlain by a single, lithologically diverse, pink-to-red Precambrian granite that contains conspicuous crystals of the dark-colored mica, biotite. This granite is quartz-rich: in places it is up to 40 percent quartz crystals. The remainder of the rock is feldspar, with minor amounts of the minerals chlorite, magnetite, zircon, apatite, and allanite. Much of the rock is strongly foliated, indicative of a history of tectonic deformation after the granitic magma had solidified. To the west of the state park, and well exposed along NM–475 in Little Tesuque Creek, are a variety of layered metamorphic rocks that have been intruded by such granites. Precambrian rocks in the vicinity of Hyde Memorial State Park are overlain in places by Paleozoic sedimentary rocks, thought to be sandstones and limestones of the Mississippian Arroyo Peñasco Group.

Paleozoic sedimentary rocks overlying Precambrian granites along the road from Santa Fe to Hyde Memorial State Park. This is a classic exposure of the Great Unconformity.

Geologic History

The crust of northern New Mexico was constructed from a continental nucleus that grew southward from about 1.8 to 1.4 billion years ago, partly by emplacement of great volumes of granitic magma into an ever-evolving lithosphere. Much later, during late Precambrian and Phanerozoic time, pieces of the middle crust were uplifted and exposed in many of the fault-block mountains of northern New Mexico. The Santa Fe Range contains a remarkably broad diversity of the plutons that built the continent, some of which can be seen in Hyde Memorial State Park. The granites in the park region were emplaced around 1.65 billion years ago, although some may be as young as 1.45 billion years. Geologic studies of these rocks have added to our knowledge of the tectonic conditions that contributed to the growth and evolution of the North American continent.

Geologic Features

From Santa Fe to Hyde Memorial State Park NM–475 follows Little Tesuque Creek, which makes a dramatic bend to the north at the south end of the state park boundary. Where the creek flows north-south, it follows a major fault known as the Borrego fault, which bisects the western Sangre de Cristo Mountains from I–25 east of Santa Fe to Mesa Borrego south of Truchas. Although the Borrego fault juxtaposes very different types of Precambrian rocks to the north and south of the park, in the state park area there are only minor differences between the granites to the east and west of the fault. However, extensive zones of fault breccia indicate that the Borrego fault is nearby. Although the history of the Borrego fault is not completely understood, like the nearby better-known Picuris-Pecos fault, it certainly has a long history of reactivation, including during the Ancestral Rocky Mountain and the Laramide orogenies.

Fault breccia along the Borrego fault.

In 2005, in Precambrian rocks not far from Hyde Memorial State Park, geologists discovered features that appear to be shatter cones. These features are thought to be the remnants of a deeply eroded impact structure in the Sangre de Cristo Mountains. The structures have been mapped over a large area of more than a square mile and may indicate the impact site of a meteorite of unknown diameter. The impact structure is at least as old as 320 million years, and may be much older. Geologists continue to search for additional clues to the exact age and origin of these features.

—Paul Bauer

If You Plan to Visit

Hyde Memorial State Park is eight miles northeast of Santa Fe Plaza via Hyde Park Road. Gate hours are 8 a.m. to 11 p.m. Facilities include a visitor center, shelter, picnic areas, campsites, and a lodge, which may be reserved (for a fee) for group events. For more information, call (505) 983-7175 or visit the Web site listed below.

From just past the park on NM–475, is the popular Borrego Trail, a major north-south route within the Pecos Wilderness, and historically used by early Spanish settlers to move sheep from rural villages to market in Santa Fe. The Borrego Trail also connects with the Winsor and Bear Wallow Trails, which permit a variety of loops and hiking experiences.

New Mexico State Parks
1220 South St. Francis Drive
Santa Fe, NM 87505
P.O. Box 1147
Santa Fe, NM 87504
(505) 476-3355
1-888-NMPARKS
www.emnrd.state.nm.us/PRD/Hyde.htm

Coyote Creek State Park

Coyote Creek is nestled in a small valley in the Sangre de Cristo Mountains, 17 miles north of Mora. These waters, which are stocked by the New Mexico Department of Game and Fish, provide some of the best trout fishing in the state.

Coyote Creek State Park is nestled within a small valley on the eastern flank of the Sangre de Cristo Mountains, 17 miles north of Mora. The park is at the bottom of Guadalupita Canyon, elevation 7,700 feet, where Coyote Creek flows through meadows surrounded by mountain forest before joining the Rio Mora of the Canadian River drainage. Private campsites are scattered along the creek, which is sheltered by cottonwoods and willows. The park offers 1.5 miles of hiking trails through a ponderosa pine forest. Coyote Creek State Park is fortuitously situated in an area that is key to deciphering the Cenozoic geologic history of the southern Sangre de Cristo Mountains and the Great Plains.

Regional Setting

The transition from the southern Sangre de Cristo Mountains to the Great Plains is a structural zone that represents the easternmost expression of the Laramide orogeny. Along the transition zone, rocks that range in age from Precambrian to Cretaceous are tilted, folded, and faulted. In places, such as near Coyote Creek State Park, the older rocks and structures are covered by Cenozoic basalt flows from the Ocaté volcanic field. To further complicate matters, south of the Moreno Valley are a series of linked structural basins controlled by Laramide reverse faults and Basin and Range-style normal faults. Coyote Creek State Park lies within this geologically complex zone, and the Tertiary rocks provide essential clues to the timing of development of the Sangre de Cristo Mountains and the Great Plains.

The Rock Record

Coyote Creek State Park is on a sliver of Paleozoic/Mesozoic sedimentary rock that is sandwiched between Precambrian rocks to the west and Cenozoic basalts to the east. The rugged mountain ridge to the west of the park, the Rincon Range, consists of Precambrian metamorphic rocks (gneiss, amphibolite, schist, and quartzite) of the Vadito and Hondo Groups. Outcrops of these rocks are locally exposed along NM–434. Eroded boulders and pebbles of multicolored white to gray to brown gneiss, schist, and quartzite are found along Coyote Creek and throughout the park.

The oldest outcrops in the park are Pennsylvanian to Permian sedimentary rocks, poorly exposed along the forested slopes of La Mesa, the ridge to the east. They consist of gray sandstone, gray to brown siltstone, and gray to black shale of the Sandia Formation, Madera Group, and Sangre de Cristo Formation. These sediments accumulated in an Ancestral Rocky Mountains basin, beginning about 300 million years ago.

Precambrian rocks of the Vadito and Hondo Groups are exposed outside the park along NM–434.

Geologic History

The rugged form of the Sangre de Cristo Mountains is the result of a series of relatively recent geologic actions. Starting about 70 million years ago during Late Cretaceous–early Tertiary time, the region experienced uplifting, faulting, folding, and tilting during the Laramide

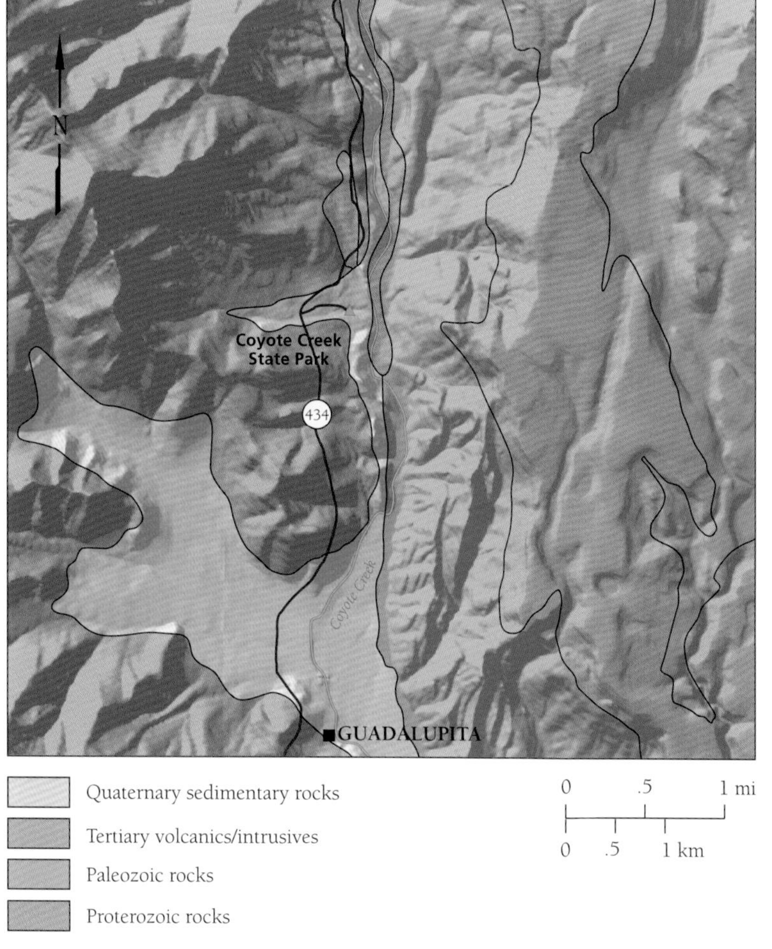

Generalized geologic map of the area surrounding Coyote Creek State Park.

orogeny. Evidence of this mountain-building event is evident to the south of the park, where the Rocky Mountains meet the Great Plains along a dramatic zone of linear ridges.

Uplift of the Rockies culminated in Eocene time, whereupon erosion of the lofty peaks and subsidence of the flanking basins proceeded until Oligocene time when the crust began to extend and fracture as rifting began to the west. It was during the time of Eocene tectonic quiescence, under a subtropical climate, that vast amounts of the rapidly eroding mountains were transported onto the Great Plains by streams that fed rivers that flowed into the Gulf of Mexico. The result was a low-relief plain that was covered by an extensive, thin blanket of sediment. This late Miocene erosion surface bore little resemblance to the modern, rugged Rocky Mountains.

Major periods of erosion followed, carving deep canyons and building alluvial fans along the eastern foothills. The fan deposits have been

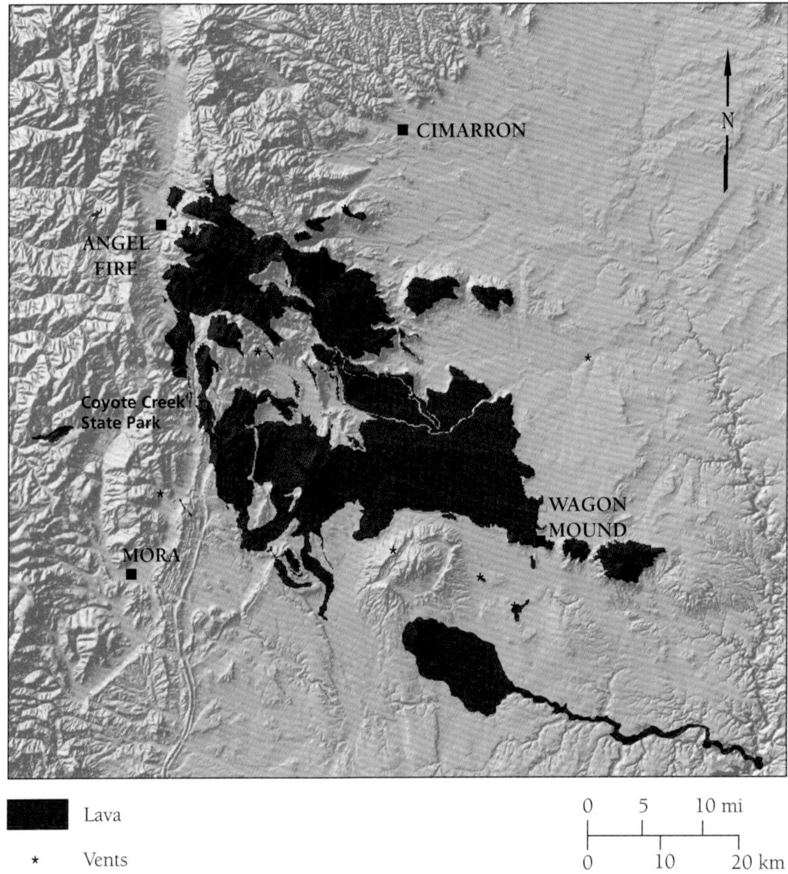

The Ocaté volcanic field straddles the southern Rocky Mountains and the Great Plains. The oldest flows (more than 8 million years old) cap the high mesas; the youngest flows (less than one million years old) roughly follow the modern drainage patterns. The basalts that cap the mesas in the vicinity of Coyote Creek State Park are about 4 to 5 million years old.

eroded away in the Coyote Creek area, but are preserved in the Great Plains. The area was geologically quiet until about 8 million years ago when volcanoes of the Ocaté volcanic field erupted east of Coyote Creek. The Ocaté volcanic field is the only volcanic field that straddles the boundary between the Southern Rocky Mountains and the Great Plains, and it is therefore useful in bracketing the timing of late Tertiary sedimentary and tectonic events. Eruptions continued until about 4 million years ago in the park area. Basalt flows cap La Mesa, and are visible from the park. Similar basalts are found in the canyon in the northern part of the park and northward along NM–434. Basalt boulders are common in the park, and were used to build the group shelter. The basalts are black, fine grained, vesicular, and porphyritic, contain crystals of olivine, clinopyroxene, augite, plagioclase, magnetite, and rare biotite and quartz.

Coyote Creek was part of a complex river system that started high in the Sangre de Cristo Mountains to the west and north, including the Moreno Valley. However, about 4.5 million years ago, basalt flows from the Ocaté volcanic field dammed the Coyote Creek drainage near Black Lake, effectively isolating the Moreno Valley watershed. Outcrops of these basalts can be seen along NM–434 at the head of Guadalupita Canyon, south of Black Lake. Although Coyote Creek was deprived of much of its watershed, and flowed from diminished highlands, it continued to downcut, ultimately forming the modern Guadalupita Canyon.

Geologic Features

The hills surrounding the park are distinctive landforms known as mesas (Spanish for "tables"). Mesas are landforms characteristic of arid environments, particularly in the Southwest. Grand Mesa, of western Colorado, is considered to be the world's largest mesa. Most mesas are formed when an uplifted area, which is capped by a hard, flat-lying rock layer, known as "caprock," is subjected to the forces of erosion. The caprock protects the areas between stream valleys, resulting in a landscape of flat-topped, steep-sided tablelands (also known as fortress hills). Although basalt flows are common caprocks, resistant sandstone over easily eroded shale also works, such as throughout the Colorado Plateau.

The mesas that surround Coyote Creek State Park are formed from a basalt caprock over soft, easily eroded Paleozoic sandstone and shale. As the underlying rock is removed by stream action, the slopes become oversteepened, and slabs of basalt caprock break away and roll down the slopes. Such slope debris covers many of the Pennsylvanian and Permian sedimentary rocks in the park area. Eventually, over geologic time, the mesas will erode into small, isolated, flat-topped hills known as buttes, before being completely consumed by erosion.

—Paul Bauer

If You Plan to Visit

Coyote Creek State Park is 17 miles north of Mora via NM–434. For more information:

New Mexico State Parks
1220 South St. Francis Drive
Santa Fe, NM 87505
P.O. Box 1147
Santa Fe, NM 87504
(505) 476-3355
1-888-NMPARKS
www.emnrd.state.nm.us/PRD/CoyoteCreek.htm

Pecos National Historical Park

NATIONAL PARK SERVICE

OPPOSITE: **Aerial view of Pecos National Historical Park, showing the mission complex and the trail through the pueblo. The circular structures along the trail are kivas. Glorieta Mesa is visible on the horizon.**

Pecos National Historical Park lies in the extreme western portion of San Miguel County, in the broad valley of the Pecos River where the river leaves its deep canyon in the Sangre de Cristo Mountains. The timeless cycles of geologic history are on display in the ancient and modern river deposits in the park. The spectacular cliffs of sedimentary rocks on Glorieta Mesa to the south and the rugged mountains to the north provide a beautiful geologic setting for the ruins and contain rocks that record shifting shorelines and the birth and erosion of mountains.

The site is of enormous cultural and historical significance. The pueblo here was occupied at least as early as 1450. The Coronado Expedition passed through here in 1541 en route to the Great Plains. Spanish missionaries followed soon thereafter. In 1621 the Franciscans built the adobe church whose ruins tower over the park today. In 1680 the Pueblo Revolt put an end to the efforts of the church throughout northern New Mexico; the priest at Pecos was killed and the church laid waste. The site was occupied by the Pecos Indians until 1838.

Regional Setting

The park is located in the Pecos River valley in the foothills of the Sangre de Cristo Mountains, part of the Southern Rocky Mountains geologic province. The forested plateau on the southern skyline is Glorieta Mesa. From an elevation of 8,000 feet at its northern rim, the smoothly rolling surface of the mesa slopes gently downhill to the south and east, merging into the plains of southwestern San Miguel County. The gently tilted sedimentary rocks of the mesa are characteristic of the Great Plains geologic province, whereas east, north, and west of the park the sedimentary rocks are folded and faulted against upthrust crystalline rocks that form the mountain summits.

Ruins of the mission church at Pecos in 1846, by which time both the settlement and the church had been abandoned.

The Rock Record

The pueblo and mission are built on a low ridge of bright red, maroon, and purple mudstones and tan-to-red sandstones and

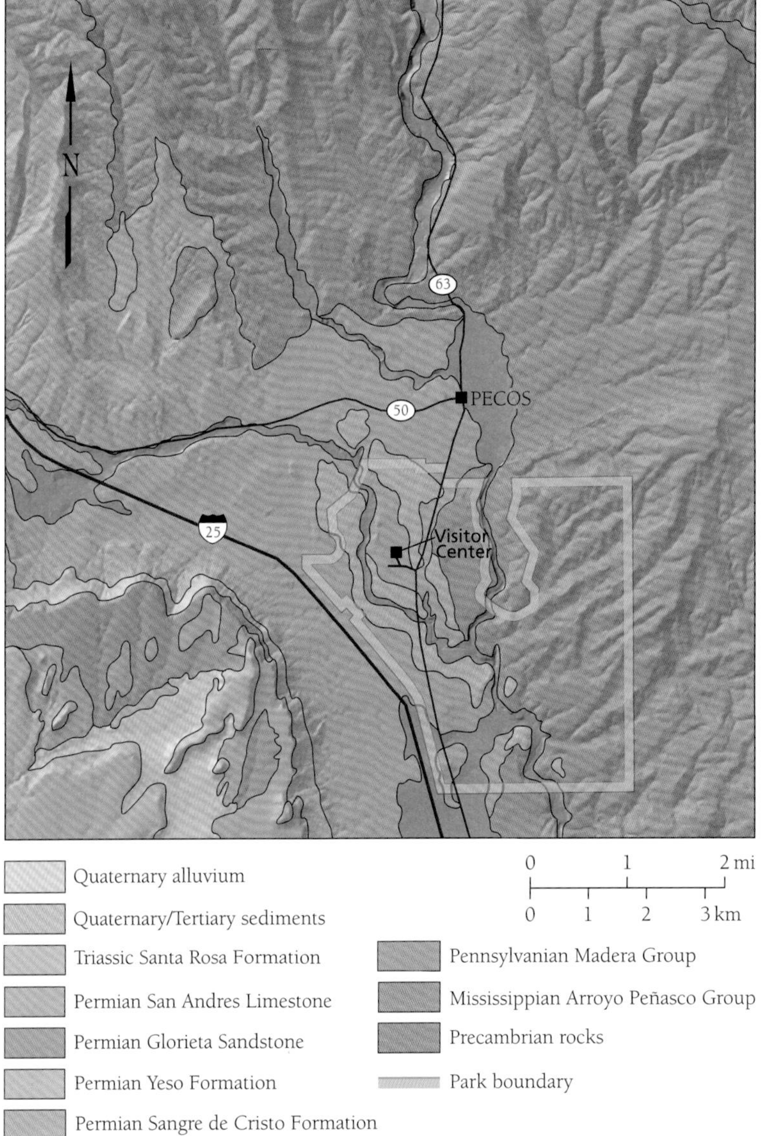

Generalized geologic map of Pecos National Historical Park and vicinity.

conglomerates of the Sangre de Cristo Formation. These rocks floor the valley here and were deposited by rivers and on muddy floodplains about 290 million years ago, during the late Pennsylvanian and early Permian Periods. The formation is approximately 2,600 feet thick. The sandstones and conglomerates are composed of sand and pebbles of clear-to-tan quartz and pink feldspar grains and have gently tilted cross-beds. These rocks were deposited in meandering river channels and form narrow deposits enclosed in the surrounding mudstones that were floodplains.

Around the ruins and covering much of the valley floor are much younger Pleistocene sand and gravel deposits, deposited 150,000 to 300,000 years ago by the Pecos River as it carved the broad valley here. These deposits as much as 30 feet thick and are composed of rounded cobbles of crystalline and sedimentary rocks.

AGE	UNIT	ROCK TYPE	ENVIRONMENT OF DEPOSITION	BEST SEEN
Pleistocene	Pecos River sands and gravels	Sand and gravel	River deposits	Terraces of the Pecos River
Tertiary/ Quaternary		Older river gravels	River deposits	
Triassic	Santa Rosa Formation	Sandstones and conglomerates	River deposits, with abundant fossil wood	Top of Glorieta Mesa
	Moenkopi Formation	Purplish-red sandstones, conglomerates, mudstones, and siltstones	Rivers/terrestrial environments. Vertebrate bones/footprints.	
	Artesia Formation	Orange-to-brick red sandstones and siltstones	Broad, shallow margin of a sea	
Permian	San Andreas Limestone	Limestone	Warm, shallow marine waters	Glorieta Mesa
	Glorieta Sandstone	Clean quartz sand	Beach deposit	
	Yeso Formation	Reddish-orange mudstones, siltstones, and sandstones	Coastal tidal flats	
	Sangre de Cristo Formation	White-to-tan sandstones and red and maroon mudstones	River and floodplain deposits, from the Ancestral Rockies	Base of Glorieta Mesa
Pennsylvanian	Madera Group	Sandy limestone	Warm, shallow marine waters	Sangre de Cristo Mountains
Mississippian	Arroyo Peñasco Group	Sandy limestone	Warm, shallow marine waters	Cow Creek
Precambrian	Igneous and metamorphic rocks	Granite, gneiss, quartzite, schist		High peaks of the Sangre de Cristo Mountains

The geologic record in the vicinity of Pecos National Historical Park (not to scale).

The most striking geologic feature here is the colorful cliff of Glorieta Mesa. The 1,200-foot-high escarpment is composed of Pennsylvanian, Permian, and Triassic sedimentary rocks that record roughly 70 million years of geologic time. At the base are white-to-tan sandstones and red and maroon mudstones of the Pennsylvanian to Permian Sangre de Cristo Formation. These river and floodplain deposits form the base of the escarpment and extend across the valley floor. Above these are reddish-orange mudstones, siltstones, and sandstones of the Permian Yeso Formation. These rocks were deposited in coastal tidal flats called *sabkhas*, much like those surrounding the modern Persian Gulf.

The prominent white cliff above the Yeso Formation is the Glorieta Sandstone. This rock is composed of clean quartz sand that was deposited in a beach environment, complete with dunes and meandering streams emptying into the sea. The Glorieta Sandstone is a major oil producer in the subsurface of southeastern New Mexico. Hidden in the trees above the Glorieta Sandstone is the San Andres Formation. Composed mostly of limestone, the San Andres Formation was deposited in warm shallow waters. Only 15 to 45 feet thick here, this rock unit thickens to more than 1,000 feet in southern New Mexico, where it is an important aquifer and reservoir for oil and natural gas. The isolated

The mission church at Pecos was built south of the pueblo in the early 1600s. It was destroyed in the Pueblo Revolt of 1680 and subsequently rebuilt on the same site during the Spanish Reconquest.

hills on the mesa top are composed of rocks of the Permian Artesia Formation and the Triassic Moenkopi and Santa Rosa Formations, but they are generally tree-covered and not easily distinguishable from the park.

To the north, northeast, and northwest of the park are the heavily wooded Sangre de Cristo Mountains. Much of the area is underlain by Pennsylvanian Madera Group limestones and sandy limestones. These rocks extend beneath the Sangre de Cristo Formation in the park. Their presence on the high ground to the north indicates that the sedimentary strata are dipping to the south, so that from north to south progressively younger strata are exposed. In fact, the oldest rocks in the region are exposed on the bare summits of Glorieta Baldy, Thompson Peak, and Santa Fe Baldy to the northwest. These igneous and metamorphic rocks are more than 1 billion years old and have been uplifted along faults.

Geologic History

The Sangre de Cristo Formation was deposited in river channels and intervening floodplains in a broad coastal plain. The rivers drained from northern highlands of the Ancestral Rocky Mountains, an ancient mountain range that was similar to the present day Rocky Mountains. The earliest evidence of the Ancestral Rockies is preserved in the sandy limestones beneath the Sangre de Cristo Formation. From bottom to top, these rocks become increasingly dominated by coarse sand and gravel, recording the greater influx of eroded debris into the shallow seas. With increasing erosion at the onset of the Permian Period, the river system of the Sangre de Cristo Formation delivered enough sediment to move the shoreline south and bury the Madera Group rocks with channel sandstones and floodplain mudstones.

As the Ancestral Rockies eroded down to mere hills, the shoreline migrated north and south, resulting in alternating marine and terrestrial rocks. The Sangre de Cristo Formation itself was buried by the coastal tidal flat or *sabkha* deposits of the Yeso Formation. In central New Mexico, the Yeso Formation contains abundant gypsum, which forms by evaporation of sea water. This suggests that the sabkha environment at this time contained shallow closed basins that were periodically disconnected from the sea, in which water could evaporate.

The shoreline migrated once again in the middle Permian. The area that is now the park was a beach of clean quartz sand that was to become the distinctive Glorieta Sandstone. This was once again inundated by the sea, resulting in the thin deposits of San Andres Limestone and overlying Artesia Formation. Both of these rock units were deposited in a shallow sea on a broad shelf. The Triassic rocks capping Glorieta Mesa record another retreat of the sea and deposition in river floodplain environments. However, in this case the rivers flowed to the north and northwest, from highlands to the south and southeast.

Between the Triassic and Pleistocene, these sedimentary rocks were buried, lithified, and uplifted to the surface and eroded. The modern canyon of the Pecos River was cut in the late Tertiary, as the river carried sand and gravel from melting glaciers out of the mountains. The river alternately meandered from side to side and cut downward, leaving behind abundant gravel deposits on bedrock surfaces, called terraces, as the channel migrated.

Geologic Features

Much of the fascinating geologic story of Pecos National Historic Park can be seen while walking the self-guided tour on the loop trail through the ruins. The stops below correspond to the numbered stops on this loop trail (a brochure is available at the visitor center).

Arkosic sandstone blocks of the Sangre de Cristo Formation are visible in the retaining wall at Stop 3.

Cross-bedded sandstone is visible along the trail just beyond Stop 4.

Micaceous sandstone slabs in the floor of the pueblo at Stop 10.

STOP 1—Looking north from here, one can see the end of the low mesa on which the ruins sit. It is composed of a tan channel sandstone deposit overlying a floodplain deposit of red mudstone. The coarse sandstones and conglomerates break into large blocks and collapse as the mudstone erodes from beneath them—the characteristic weathering pattern of the plateau country of the American West.

STOPS 3 AND 4—The low wall and scattered outcrops along the left side of the trail in this area nicely display channel sandstones and conglomerates of the Sangre de Cristo Formation. Look for coarse pieces of pink feldspar in the conglomerates. These are derived from Precambrian granite in the mountains to the north. These rocks often contain crossbedding, the dipping planes formed in migrating bars in river and stream channels.

STOP 6—Follow the steps up the small knob here for a panoramic view of the valley and Glorieta Mesa. See if you can identify the rocks units in the mesa from the unit descriptions.

STOP 10—Take a close look at the sandstone slabs making up the floor of the ruin here. The mineral sparkling in the sun is mica, which eroded from the granite and metamorphic rocks in the mountains to the north. Sedimentary rocks with abundant mica and feldspar, such as the sandstones and conglomerates within the park, are said to be arkosic. These minerals weather easily when transported in streams, and their presence in the rocks indicates that the source area for the sediments was relatively close by.

STOP 15—The rounded cobbles forming the floor here are typical of the terrace gravels of the Pecos River. They are composed of Precambrian granite and metamorphic rocks eroded from the mountains to the north.

—*Geoffrey C. Rawling*

View of Glorieta Mesa looking to the southwest. From bottom to top: dark red and white "ledgy" Sangre de Cristo Formation, orange-red sloping Yeso Formation, cliffs of white-tan Glorieta Sandstone, thin San Andres Limestone hidden in the trees, and Santa Rosa Sandstone making up the elongate pyramidal hill on the mesa top.

Additional Reading

Geology of the Santa Fe Region, New Mexico, Paul W. Bauer et al., editors. Forty-sixth Annual Field Conference Guidebook of the New Mexico Geological Society, 1995.

If You Plan to Visit

The park is 25 miles southeast of Santa Fe, about 2 miles south of the town of Pecos, and north of I–25. It can be reached from I–25 via Exit 299 (coming from the south) or Exit 307 (coming from the north). It is managed by the National Park Service. For more information, contact:

National Park Service
Pecos National Historical Park
P.O. Box 418
Pecos, NM 87552-0418
(505) 757-6414 (Press 1 for Visitor Center)
www.nps.gov/peco/

This small, secluded park stands at an elevation of 8,000 feet at the end of a steep road, 7 miles southwest of Mora. Located within a thick forest of pines, just east of the Pecos Wilderness, the park provides a near-wilderness experience. The 15-acre lake was enlarged in the 1930s by an earthen dam. Morphy Lake State Park is covered by rocks deposited in vast Paleozoic seas, when much of the continent was submerged.

Regional Setting

Morphy Lake State Park is in the southernmost Rincon Mountains, a southeastern spur of the Southern Rocky Mountains. The Rincon Mountains are composed of an intricate mix of Precambrian rocks and Paleozoic sedimentary rocks that are typical of the region. The park lies just west of the geologically complex eastern boundary of the Rockies, where the rocks of the mountains tower over the younger rocks of the Raton Basin.

The Rock Record

From Morphy Lake State Park, the highest point on the western skyline is Cebolla Peak (11,879 feet), composed of Precambrian metamorphic rocks of the Vadito and Hondo Groups. Boulders of gneiss, schist, and quartzite can be seen throughout the park. Similar rocks, plus granites, form El Oro Mountains east of Morphy Lake State Park. Above the Precambrian rocks, across the Great Unconformity, is the Pennsylvanian Sandia Formation, deposited 320 to 315 million years ago in the Rowe-Mora basin. This is the rock unit exposed along the lake shore. The Sandia Formation here is composed of brown arkosic sandstone and conglomerate and interlayers of gray shale. The sandstone contains grains of quartz, feldspar, and mica, and rock fragments derived from the nearby Precambrian rocks. Brachiopod fossils (marine shelled animals) are found in thin limestone and shale beds south of the dam. In this region, most of the Pennsylvanian sediments were derived from the Uncompahgre uplift to the west.

Geologic History

By late Paleozoic time, the supercontinent of Pangea had formed, and much of the western continental U.S. was covered by shallow, equatorial seas. By about 310 million years ago, during Pennsylvanian time, the Ancestral Rocky Mountains of New Mexico and Colorado had emerged, shedding sediments into the surrounding ocean basins, and blanketing the Precambrian basement rocks across the Great Unconformity. The earliest of those Pennsylvanian sedimentary rocks are now exposed along the flanks of the southern Sangre de Cristo Mountains, including the Morphy Lake State Park area. After these rocks were buried by Mesozoic sedimentation, Laramide orogenic uplift exposed the Pennsylvanian strata to erosion.

Much later, during the Pleistocene ice ages, small alpine glaciers formed on the high Sangre de Cristo Mountains to the west of the park. As the glaciers advanced downward, they carved characteristic bowl-shaped cirques at the heads of steep-sided, U-shaped valleys. The retreating ice left three large cirque lakes (tarns), at 10,800 feet elevation, now named Pacheco, Santiago, and Enchanted Lakes. These lakes mark the terminus of the Pleistocene glaciers. Downstream from the glaciers, in the state park area, Rito Morphy transported glacial outwash into the valley, and on to the Mora River.

Geologic Features

Morphy Lake (also known as Murphy Lake) is a natural depression that was modified by local farmers to supply irrigation ditches for the residents of nearby Ledoux. The lake and grounds are leased to the state by the Ledoux Water Association for use as a state park. A small dam at the southwest corner of the lake contains an intake canal and an outflow works that charges the acequias. The 400 acre-feet of water storage in the 15-acre lake is recharged by stream flow and precipitation.

The geologic origin of the depression that contains the lake is uncertain. The lake is on a ridge, rather than in a valley. On the same ridge, a mile to the northwest, is Laguna de Agua, another remarkably round lake of about the same size. Nearby are two smaller round lakes, also set high onto the ridge. Among the possibilities for the origin of these peculiar round depressions are collapse due to karst processes and wind blowouts.

—*Paul Bauer*

If You Plan to Visit

Morphy Lake State Park is seven miles south of Mora on NM–94 and four miles west on a newly paved access road.

New Mexico State Parks
1220 South St. Francis Drive
Santa Fe, NM 87505
P.O. Box 1147
Santa Fe, NM 87504
(505) 476-3355
1-888-NMPARKS
www.emnrd.state.nm.us/PRD/MorphyLake.htm

Cimarron Canyon State Park

Cimarron Canyon State Park, 3 miles east of Eagle Nest State Park on US 64, is part of the 33,116-acre Colin Neblett Wildlife Area, the largest wildlife area in the state. In 1949 the New Mexico Game and Fish Department purchased these lands for $374,532. Originally named the Cimarron Canyon Wildlife Area, the name was changed to honor Colin Neblett, a Santa Fe judge, sportsman, and conservationist who helped establish the New Mexico State Game and Fish Commission. In 1979 the land was transferred to the State Park and Recreation Division and designated Cimarron Canyon State Park. The park is nearly surrounded by lands of the Philmont Scout Ranch, a 137,493-acre national camping area that was created by Oklahoma oilman Waite Phillips in 1938.

Cimarron Canyon has been a mountain-to-plain throughway for thousands of years. Nomadic Indians hunted mammoth and bison on the plains and elk in the mountains. European explorers later built roads along the Cimarron River. In 1867 miners from Elizabethtown improved the road and a stagecoach route connected Cimarron and Elizabethtown. In 1907 a railroad spur was built from Cimarron to Ute Park, but was never completed to Eagle Nest. The road was paved in the 1940s and designated US 64.

The Cimarron pluton is exposed along the banks of the Cimarron River along US 64 in the feature known as the Palisades.

Regional Setting

The Southern Rocky Mountain physiographic province consists of a linked network of major mountain ranges, each of which contains high peaks and complex geology. The easternmost range of the southern Sangre de Cristo Mountains is the Cimarron Mountains, a lengthy range that is topographically separated from the western ranges by a series of geologic valleys from the Valle Vidal in the north to the Mora Valley in the south. Baldy Mountain (12,441 feet), north of the park, is the highest point in the range. Elevations in the park range from 7,400 feet in the canyon to 12,045 feet at Touch-Me-Not Mountain. The Cimarron Mountains are sliced by the canyon of the Cimarron River, which links the Moreno Valley to the Great Plains physiographic province. Rocks exposed in the river valley provide a rare glimpse of the shallow plumbing system that supplied the Tertiary volcanoes of the Ocaté volcanic field.

The Rock Record

This part of the Cimarron Mountains contains rocks that range in age from Precambrian to Tertiary. Most of the Precambrian rocks have been metamorphosed, and a great variety of them are exposed along NM–64 and in the mountains to the south. Among the principal rock types are mafic and *felsic* schists and a mixture of gneisses, metagabbro, metadiorite, granodiorite, quartzite, and pegmatite. Above the Precambrian rocks is an angular unconformity overlain by Paleozoic and Mesozoic sedimentary rocks. All of these rocks have been extensively intruded by the middle Tertiary Cimarron pluton and its associated sills and dikes. The southern end of the pluton is exposed in the famous "Tooth of Time" ridge on the Philmont Scout Ranch.

Geologic History

Toward the end of Cretaceous time (approximately 65 million years ago) dramatic changes reshaped western North America. The great Western Interior Seaway had withdrawn, and plate tectonic interactions along the western continental margin triggered the Laramide orogeny and the resulting volcanism and uplift of the Rocky Mountains. As the Laramide compression changed to rift extension in mid-Tertiary time, widespread magma intrusions and volcanic eruptions occurred in southern Colorado (such as the Spanish Peaks) and northern New Mexico (such as the Taos Plateau and Ocate volcanic fields). Among the New Mexican activity was magmatic invasion of the rocks of the Cimarron Mountains, creating extraordinary, three-dimensional intrusive networks of laccoliths, sills, dikes, and necks—some of which are visible today in the Cimarron Canyon State Park area.

Geologic Features

The geological highlight in Cimarron Canyon State Park is the Palisades of Cimarron Canyon, a spectacular, vertically jointed rock

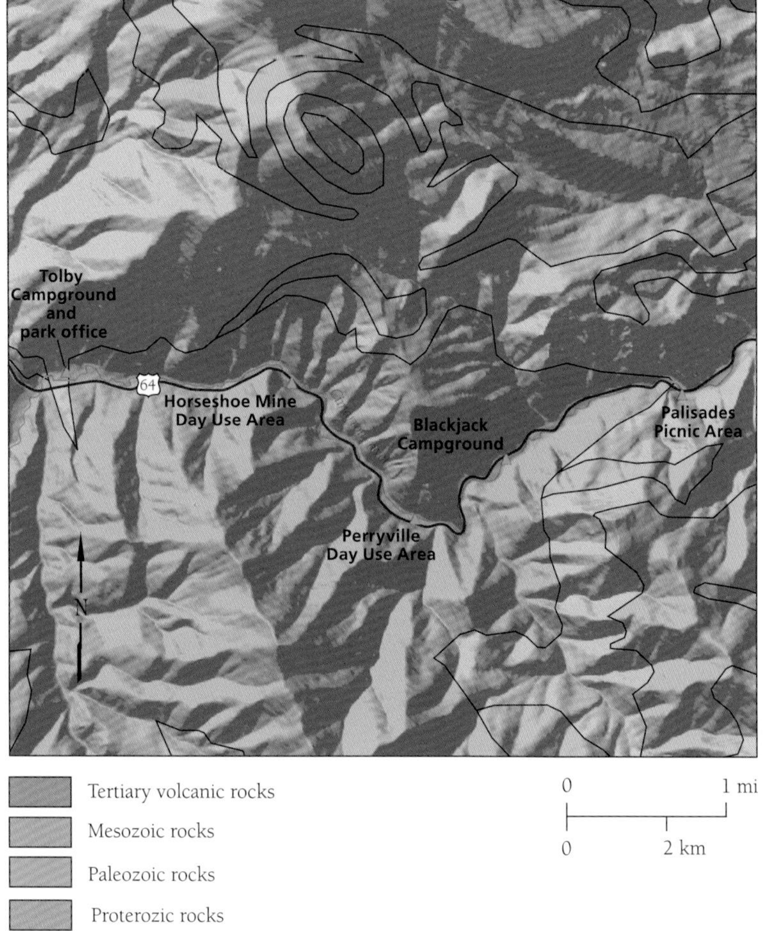

Generalized geologic map for the area surrounding Cimarron Canyon. The park boundary follows the Cimarron River through Cimarron Canyon. The entire region shown on this map is included in the Colin Neblett Wildlife Area.

face. Before Cimarron Canyon existed, a body of magma forcibly intruded along the Great Unconformity at a shallow level—perhaps less than 3,000 feet below the surface. Because of its shallow depth, the magma cooled rapidly, forming the fine grained igneous rocks of the Cimarron pluton. In the Palisades area, the base of the pluton rests on Precambrian gneiss. As it cooled and crystallized, it contracted, forming the pervasive, vertical columnar joints (fractures). Because the intrusion is a hard, dense rock (technically known as trachydacite), selective erosion by the Cimarron River has carved precipitous cliffs along Cimarron Canyon. Elsewhere in the park, the pluton is intruded into the overlying Paleozoic, Mesozoic, and Tertiary sedimentary rocks. The pluton is not a single body, but rather a composite of many small, stacked intrusive sheets known as laccoliths. Originally described by pioneering field geologist G. K. Gilbert in 1877, laccolith is Greek for "stone cistern" due to its distinctive three-dimensional shape. The pluton, which is approximately age-equivalent to the 25-million-year-old Questa caldera, is part of the Jemez lineament, a linear zone of Tertiary igneous rocks that cuts northeasterly across northern New Mexico.

—Paul Bauer

If You Plan to Visit

Cimarron Canyon State Park is three miles east of Eagle Nest along US 64. The park is managed jointly by the New Mexico State Park and Recreation Division and the New Mexico Game and Fish Department. For more information:

New Mexico State Parks
1220 South St. Francis Drive
Santa Fe, NM 87505
P.O. Box 1147
Santa Fe, NM 87504
(505) 476-3355
1-888-NMPARKS
www.emnrd.state.nm.us/PRD/CimarronCanyon.htm

Eagle Nest Lake State Park

The Moreno Valley is a magnificent alpine basin surrounded by the highest peaks of the Taos and Cimarron Mountains. At 8,300 feet in elevation, the valley offers a cool retreat from the summer heat and a frosty wonderland for winter recreationists. The valley abounds with eagles, elk, bear, mule deer, beaver, cougar, and wild turkeys. The 2,400-acre lake is known for its kokanee salmon, rainbow trout, and cutthroat trout fishing. The geomorphology of Eagle Nest Lake State Park highlights the dynamic interplay between tectonics, volcanism, and erosion in the creation of the modern landscape.

Regional Setting

The eastern prong of the Southern Rocky Mountains in New Mexico is called the southern Sangre de Cristo Mountains. The northern half of the southern Sangre de Cristo Mountains are divided into a western set of subranges (Culebra Range and Taos Range) and an eastern range

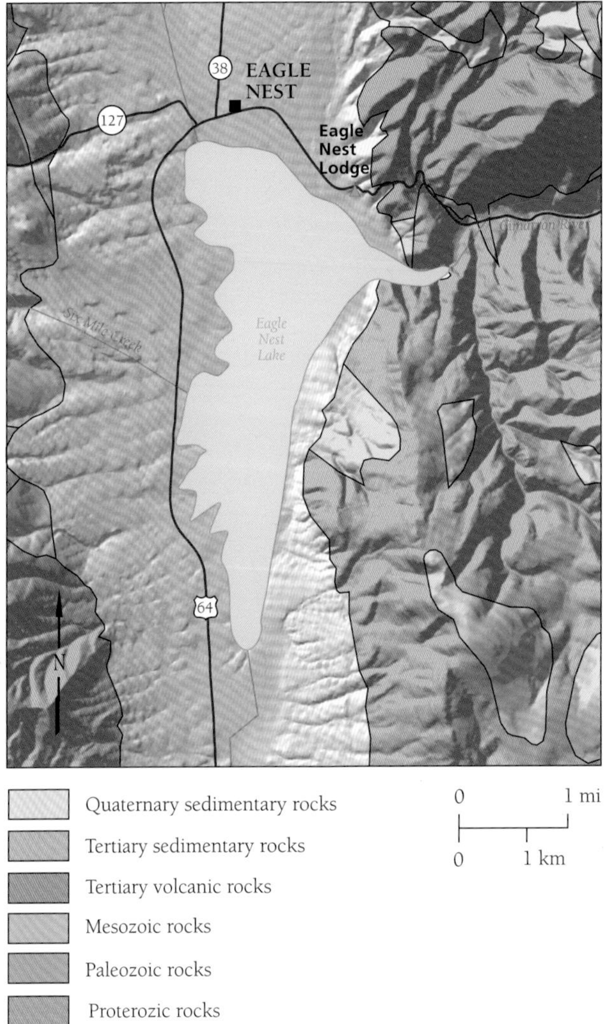

Geologic map of Eagle Nest Lake

(Cimarron Mountains). The two sets of ranges are separated by a linked chain of north-south topographic/geologic valleys—the Costilla Valley, the Valle Vidal, the Moreno Valley, and the Mora Valley. Eagle Nest Lake State Park is in the Moreno Valley at the headwaters of the Cimarron River, which drains eastward into the Great Plains. The Moreno Valley is a complex asymmetric graben whose east side is downdropped along Tertiary normal faults that are related to the Rio Grande rift.

The Rock Record

Few rocks are exposed at Eagle Nest Lake State Park. The reservoir occupies a broad alluvial valley that is bracketed by the Mesozoic and Precambrian rocks of the Sangre de Cristo Mountains and the Precambrian granites of the Cimarron Mountains.

The valley is partially filled by Cenozoic sedimentary deposits that are underlain by a Laramide-age syncline that is sandwiched between the Sangre de Cristo uplift to the west and the Precambrian rocks of the Cimarron Mountains to the east. On the east side of the Moreno Valley, as far south as Eagle Nest Lake, the Eagle Nest fault and its branches displace Cretaceous and Tertiary rocks down-to-the-west. To the west, the tree-covered lower slopes are underlain by Pennsylvanian to Cretaceous sedimentary rocks that have been cut by thrust faults that are older than the normal faults. Two thrust faults have been recognized. The upper one is named the Sixmile Creek thrust, and displaces Pennsylvanian, Permian, and Precambrian rocks in the Sixmile thrust sheet eastward over Permian through Tertiary sedimentary rocks. Below the Sixmile Creek thrust lies the Cimarron thrust sheet, which has moved eastward over Precambrian rocks along the Cimarron thrust. In the Cimarron Mountains to the east, Triassic strata have been mapped directly on Precambrian rocks.

Geologic History

Following the tumultuous times of the mid-Tertiary, tectonic activity gradually diminished. A few volcanic centers continued to erupt, but the Rio Grande rift had mostly stabilized. Beginning in the Pliocene, the crust of the entire Southern Rocky Mountains and Colorado Plateau regions was vertically uplifted as much as a mile. Massive erosion followed, and rivers eroded deep canyons, creating the modern landscape of peaks, ridges, plateaus, mesas, and buttes.

Prior to about 4.5 million years ago the Moreno Valley drained southward into Coyote Creek rather than eastward to Cimarron. However, after a basalt flow dammed the creek near Black Lake, the Moreno Valley became a closed basin, slowly filling with sediments eroded from the surrounding highlands. A lake and bordering swamps occupied the valley, growing and shrinking with the changing climate. The canyon of the Cimarron River was a modest stream that slowly eroded headwards into the Cimarron Mountains. Eventually, the river breached the eastern topographic divide to the Moreno Valley, capturing most of the drainage of that large region. Supplied by such a productive watershed, the now-perennial Cimarron River rapidly carved its modern, well-graded canyon.

Geologic Features

Eagle Nest Lake is actually a reservoir, made possible by a remarkable engineering project known as the Eagle Nest Dam. Until the state purchased the park in 2002 from the CS Cattle Company, this dam was probably the largest privately owned dam in the country. Built between 1916 and 1918, unhindered by government regulations, the dam is a concrete arch 140 feet tall, 400 feet long across the crest, 45 feet thick at the base, and 9.5 feet thick at the crest. Brothers Frank and Charles Springer of Cimarron conceived and constructed the dam for flood control and to provide dependable water supplies downstream. In addition to the modern-day recreational opportunities, the reservoir provides water for agriculture and the municipalities of Springer and Raton.

The dam abutments are constructed in Precambrian gneiss, at the eastern topographic boundary of the Moreno Valley, and have remained well sealed since 1918. Water is released through engineered outlets near the right abutment. Near the left abutment, a 40-foot-wide spillway is carved in bedrock 7 feet below the dam crest.

—Paul Bauer

If You Plan to Visit

Eagle Nest Lake State Park is 32 miles east of Taos and 65 miles southwest of Raton off of US 64. The park is open for day use only. For more information:

New Mexico State Parks
1220 South St. Francis Drive
Santa Fe, NM 87505
P.O. Box 1147
Santa Fe, NM 87504
(505) 476-3355
1-888-NMPARKS
www.emnrd.state.nm.us/PRD/EaglesNest.htm

Villanueva State Park

NEW MEXICO STATE PARKS

Villanueva State Park lies in the western portion of San Miguel County and straddles the Pecos River where it enters a narrow canyon one mile south of the village of Villanueva. At the park, reddish-yellow and tan cliffs of sandstone tower up to 300 feet above the park and the river. The rocks in these cliffs tell a geologic story of ancient landscapes and seas. Younger gravels on benches along the river and the topography of canyon itself carry this narrative to the present day.

Regional Setting

The park is located at the transition between the Great Plains and the Rocky Mountains geologic provinces. The high forested plateau forming the rim of the Pecos River canyon is Glorieta Mesa. From an elevation of 7,000 to 8,000 feet at its northern rim, the smoothly rolling surface of the mesa slopes gently downhill to the south and east, merging into the plains of southwestern San Miguel County. The gently tilted sedimentary rocks are characteristic of the Great Plains province. North

Villanueva State Park, on the Pecos River.

Cliff of Glorieta Sandstone at the park entrance.

of Glorieta Mesa they give way to the folds, faults, and ancient crystalline rocks of the high country of the Sangre de Cristo Mountains.

The Rock Record

The rocks forming the cliffs are sandstones and minor siltstones of the Glorieta Sandstone. These rocks were deposited by streams and windblown dunes on the margin of a sea in the Permian period, between 268 and 245 million years ago. It is up to 350 feet thick and forms most of the land surface on Glorieta Mesa. It is light reddish-yellow to tan colored when weathered, and is composed almost entirely of well-rounded grains of the colorless, translucent mineral quartz. The color is from minute particles of iron oxide staining the grains. The strata are layered in beds that range from less than one to two meters thick and weather as ledges in the cliffs. Crossbeds are common, dipping at 5–15° between the prominent horizontal beds, as are ripple marks undulating across horizontal bedding surfaces.

Just outside the park entrance and beneath the Glorieta Sandstone are reddish-orange sandstones and siltstones and minor gray limestones of the Permian Yeso Formation. The contact between these rocks is gradational and some siltstone beds similar to those of the Yeso are present at the base of the cliffs. Bright red mudstones and white sandstones of the Sangre de Cristo Formation are exposed around I–25 to the north. These rocks underlie the Yeso Formation and were deposited by rivers and on muddy floodplains. This pattern of older rocks exposed to the north indicates that the sedimentary strata around the Pecos River valley are gently tilted to the south. Scattered exposures of limestones of the Permian San Andres Formation overlie the Glorieta Sandstone on the mesa top.

The Glorieta Sandstone displays two near-vertical joint sets which cause the rock to break into angular fragments. Joints are fracture patterns caused by tectonic forces within the earths crust. They are common in brittle sedimentary rocks like the Glorieta Sandstone, and probably form in response to compression from distant mountain-building events.

Much younger than the Permian rocks are the terrace gravels and stream sediments of the Pecos River. The sediments and gravels in the valley bottom are less than 500 years old. The older terrace gravels are 80 to 90 feet above the river and are present on bedrock ledges beneath the town of Villanueva and the El Cerro Campground within the park. The partly eroded gravel deposits are 6 to 10 feet thick and are composed of cobbles of crystalline and sedimentary rocks. They are 10,000 to 50,000 years old and were deposited by the Pecos River before it cut the canyon to its present depth.

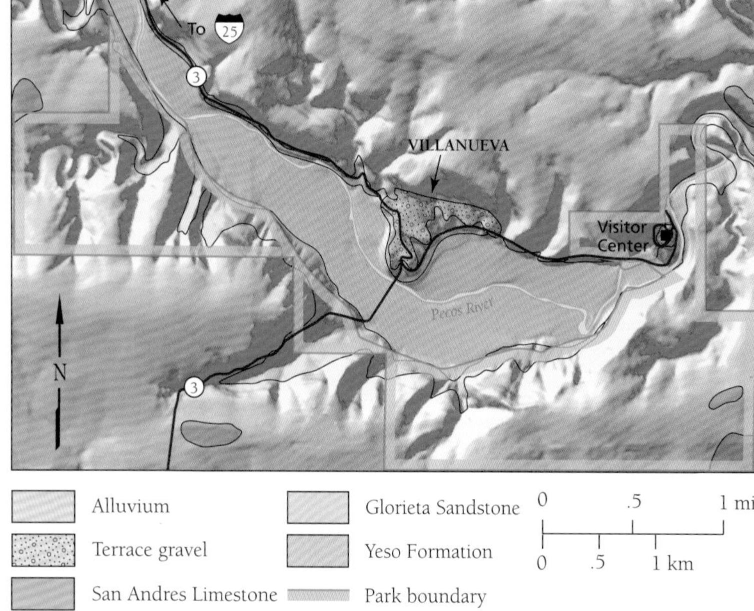

Generalized geologic map of Villanueva State Park and vicinity.

Geologic History

When the Glorieta Sandstone was deposited, north central New Mexico was a beach of clean quartz sand, crossed by meandering streams flowing towards the ocean to the south. Windblown sand and dunes were common. Millions of years before the Permian beach, this area was a broad coastal tidal flat (or sabkha) and fine sandstones, siltstones, and thin limestones of the Yeso Formation were being deposited. Slow migration of the shoreline resulted in the gradational contact between the Yeso Formation and the Glorieta Sandstone. Eventually the Permian Glorieta beach was flooded by the sea, and limestones of the San Andres Formation covered the sand.

Fast forward some 260 million years to the Pleistocene Epoch. The Permian sediments have been buried, lithified into rocks, and uplifted to the surface again, with thousands of feet of overlying rocks having been eroded. The Pecos River, swollen with water and sediment from melting glaciers on the high peaks of the Sangre de Cristo Mountains, is cutting its canyon through Glorieta Mesa. As the glaciers repeatedly advance and melt throughout the Pleistocene, the river alternatively flows placidly and cuts its canyon deeper, occasionally leaving isolated remnants of the old canyon bottom as cobble-covered ledges.

Cliff of Glorieta Sandstone between park entrance gate and pay station.

Crossbeds in Glorieta Sandstone.

Perpendicular joint sets along trail to El Cerro Campground.

Geologic Features

There are numerous easily accessible and geologically interesting outcrops in the park.

BETWEEN THE PARK ENTRANCE gate and the pay station is an outcrop on the left (north) side of the road. Here you can see the base of the Glorieta Sandstone. Note the angular, protruding sandstone beds and the rounded, recessive siltstone beds, which are similar to those of the underlying Yeso Formation. Joints are prominent in the sandstone beds but die out in the less brittle siltstone layers.

AT THE PARKING AREA CUL-DE-SAC at the end of the paved park road is a recent rockfall on the left (west). The joints in the rock cause it to break into angular fragments, and growing tree roots and freezing and thawing of water loosen the rock and help speed erosion. Just beyond the cul-de-sac is another outcrop on the left (west) which exhibits lovely cross-bedding in the sandstone.

EL CERRO CAMPGROUND sits on a river terrace covered with cobbles of crystalline rocks washed down from the mountains. Look for red and pink granite, gray "sparkly" schist, gray, red, and tan quartzite, bright pink pegmatite, and black and white amphibolite.

THE EL CERRO TRAIL to the canyon overlook provides an opportunity to see the abundant colluvium composed of loose boulders and sand that has weathered from the hillside. Look for crossbeds and ripple marks in rocks along the trail. The two joint sets are well exposed at the overlook.

—*Geoffrey C. Rawling*

If You Plan to Visit

Villanueva State Park is located on the Pecos River just off NM–3, ten miles south of I–25 (Exit 323) and 23 miles southwest of Las Vegas, New Mexico. The park entrance road is just south of the village of Villanueva. There are adobe picnic shelters, trails, and a small campground. For more information:

Villanueva State Park
P.O. Box 40
Villanueva, NM 87583
(575) 421-2957
www.emnrd.state.nm.us/emnrd/PRD/Villanueva.htm

PART 5

The Great Plains

The vast, low relief, mid-continent region of the United States between the Appalachians to the east, the Ouachita Mountains to the south, and the Rocky Mountains to the west is the physiographic province known as the Interior Plains. The Great Plains, a subdivision of the Interior Plains province, is an east-to-southeast-sloping plain bounded on the west by the abrupt, sharp topography of the Rocky Mountains and on east by glacial till deposits in North Dakota and South Dakota, by a prominent east-facing erosional escarpment in Nebraska, Kansas, Oklahoma, and the Texas Panhandle, and by the Balcones fault zone in central Texas.

The semi-arid Great Plains of northeastern New Mexico tilt gently southeastward from the foothills of the Sangre de Cristo Mountains. Rolling hills covered with grass, intervening low spots punctuated by small ponds, high mesas and escarpments capped by resistant lava flows, sandstones, or *pedogenic* carbonate (caliche) layers, and steep-sided canyons along the major rivers are common elements in the landscape of the plains. Eroded volcanoes and a few young cinder cones dot the countryside. The east-flowing Dry Cimarron River, the south-to-east-flowing Canadian River, and the south-flowing Pecos River, all with headwaters the Sangre de Cristo Mountains, have locally dissected the Great Plains.

The Great Plains of Northeastern New Mexico

The Great Plains province in New Mexico consists of three distinctive subdivisions defined by the underlying geology and regional drainage patterns. The Raton section straddles the New Mexico–Colorado state line and is characterized by high-elevation mesas capped by lava flows of the Raton–Clayton and Ocaté volcanic fields. Elevations vary from 8,000 feet on Raton Mesa to 4,800 feet on mesa tops near the New Mexico–Oklahoma line. Raton Mesa, which is capped by 9 million year old basalt, forms a pronounced drainage divide between the Canadian River and Dry Cimarron River drainage to the south and the Arkansas River drainage in Colorado to the north. The south-facing Canadian escarpment north of the Canadian River is considered to be the southern boundary of the Raton section. Cretaceous and Early Tertiary rocks preserved in the Raton Basin, a structural depression that formed during Laramide deformation, have been protected from erosion by the resistant lavas.

The Southern High Plains section of the Great Plains, otherwise known as the Llano Estacado, is capped by a geomorphic surface of enormous aerial extent that developed about 5 million years ago on top of a rock unit called the Ogallala Formation. The Ogallala Formation is composed of sand and gravel eroded from the Rocky Mountains to the west. As deposition began about 12 million years ago in northeastern New Mexico, the Ogallala Formation was confined to valleys cut into older bedrock. Through time, as the valleys filled and the climate became more arid, thus enhancing deposition of windblown deposits and reducing stream erosion, the Ogallala Formation overtopped the ridges between the valleys. Consequently, a relatively flat surface developed on top of the Ogallala Formation. The semi-arid climate 5 million years ago led to the formation of thick pedogenic carbonate soil horizons (caliche) that created a resistant layer atop the Llano Estacado. Near Cheyenne, Wyoming, the Ogallala surface actually laps across the Rocky Mountain front, but in New Mexico, erosion along the mountain front related to the development of the Pecos River has dissected this old surface. The west-facing Mescalero escarpment on the east side of the Pecos River and the north-facing Caprock escarpment south of the Canadian River mark the boundaries of the Llano Estacado in eastern New Mexico. Elevations on the caprock range from 5,300 feet on the northwest edge of the Llano Estacado to 4,200 feet near the New Mexico–Texas state line. Many small ponds and depressions, formed through dissolution of the carbonate cap by rainwater and wind erosion, cover the flat top of the Llano Estacado. During the cooler, wetter glacial periods in the Pleistocene, large mammals including mammoths, horses, and camels were attracted to these ponds. Some of the earliest hunters in North America were attracted to these ponds, as well.

The Pecos Valley section of the Great Plains includes the broad valley cut by the Pecos River southward from it headwaters in the Sangre de Cristo Mountains to the Rio Grande in Texas. The eastern border is the Mescalero escarpment and the western boundary is the eastern dip-slope of rift-flank uplifts of central New Mexico. The Pecos River near the southern edge of the area considered in this book changes character as it passes southward from continental Mesozoic sandstones and mudstones into marine limestone and evaporite in the Permian section. Karst topography has a profound affect on the flow of the Pecos River south of this point.

Geologic History

The oldest rocks exposed on the Great Plains of northeastern New Mexico are in the Pecos River valley; these sediments were deposited along the shoreline of a Permian ocean that once covered southeastern New Mexico and west Texas. The sea retreated to the south and the overlying Triassic Chinle Group was deposited by a westerly-to-northwesterly flowing river system. Triassic rocks are broadly exposed in east-central New Mexico and can be viewed at the state parks associated with the artificial lakes on the Canadian and Pecos Rivers (Ute, Conchas, and Santa Rosa Lakes). Jurassic sediments include the Entrada Sandstone, a dune field deposit; the Summerville Formation, a coastal flat deposit; and the Morrison Formation, a fluvial deposit. These strata are particularly well exposed in Mills Canyon along the Canadian River in the Kiowa National Grasslands. During Cretaceous time, the ocean returned to this part of New Mexico. The northwest-trending western shoreline of the Western Interior Seaway migrated generally southwestward across this area, leaving shallow marine and nearshore deposits. The tracks of dinosaurs walking near the shore of the seaway about 100 million years ago are preserved at Clayton Lake State Park. Subsequently the water depths increased significantly, and thick shale (Pierre Shale) was deposited. Later, the shoreline migrated northeastward across the area as the sea retreated. Cretaceous rocks are nicely exposed at Clayton Lake State Park, Fort Union National Monument, Storrie Lake State Park, and Sugarite Canyon State Park.

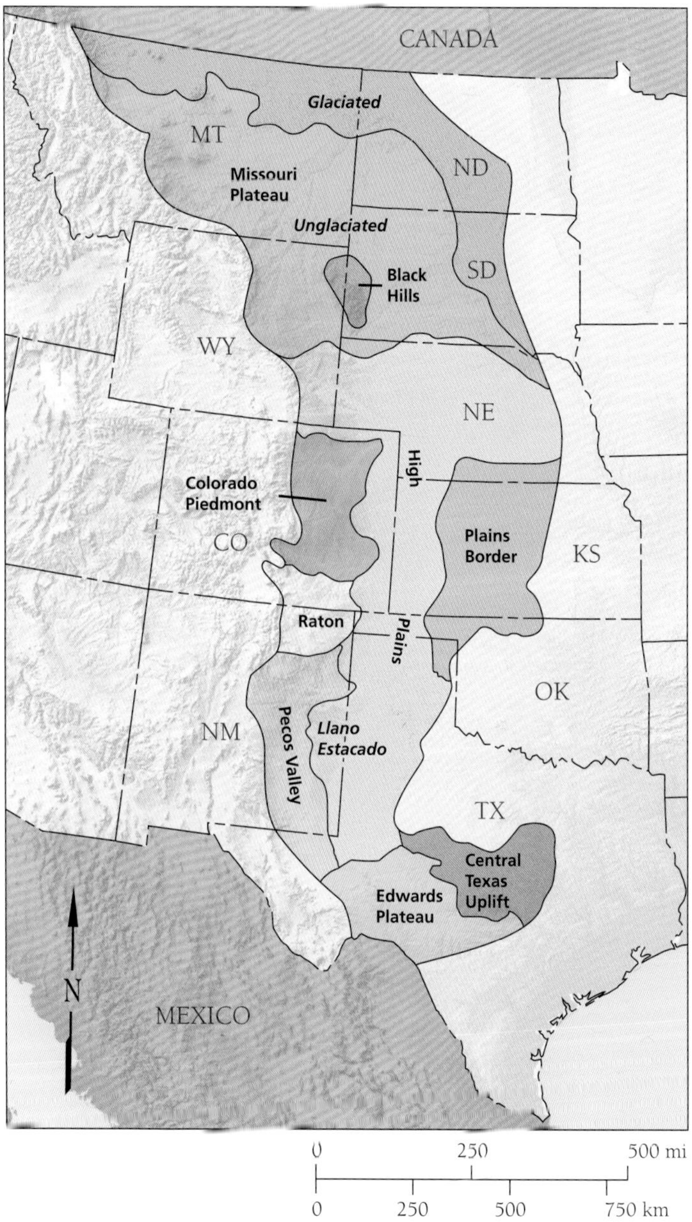

Beginning 75 million years ago, northeastern New Mexico was affected by compressional deformation associated with the Laramide orogeny, causing the Sangre de Cristo Mountains to rise and the Raton Basin and the smaller Las Vegas sub-basin to form. Sediments shed from the

The Great Plains province extends far north of the Canadian border and is bounded on the west for much of its length by the Rocky Mountains. In New Mexico it is subdivided into the Raton section, the Pecos Valley section, and the Llano Estacado.

mountains accumulated in the basins along the shore of the retreating seaway. Vegetation along the shoreline eventually died, decayed, was buried, and became coal. The coal beds in the Raton basin are generally too thin to mine economically, but coal in the subsurface has been buried to sufficient depths to produce coalbed methane. The few economic coal beds in the basin, such as those at Sugarite Canyon State Park, were mined out long ago. Rocks that record the mass extinction of many species including the dinosaurs at the end of Cretaceous time are particularly well exposed in the Raton basin. Laramide deformation and sedimentation in the Raton basin continued into Eocene time about 40 million years ago

A few sills and dikes were intruded into the older sedimentary rocks on the High Plains about 25 to 30 million years ago. The plains may have begun the rise to their current elevation in this same time frame. Erosion during middle Cenozoic time removed some of the Mesozoic rocks. Starting about 12 million years ago, sand and gravel of the Ogallala Formation began to accumulate in the valleys that were incised into older rocks during middle Cenozoic erosion. Ogallala Formation sedimentation ended about 5 million years ago as the climate became more arid. Pedogenic carbonate accumulated at the top of the Ogallala Formation, forming a resistant caprock. The coarse-grained sediments of the Ogallala Formation are an important aquifer on the High Plains.

As the Ogallala Formation was being deposited, significant volcanism occurred on the High Plains along a feature known as the Jemez lineament, starting about 9 million years ago. The youngest volcanic activity at 13,000 years is associated with the 56,000-year-old Capulin volcano. The Raton-Clayton and Ocaté volcanic fields formed during this episode of volcanism. The oldest lava flows cap the highest mesas, while the youngest flows are at elevations near modern drainage levels. This pattern indicates that uplift and erosion of the High Plains was active during volcanism. The oldest flows filled in low spots in the landscape and the flows were gradually uplifted. Erosion into the old flows created new valleys with bottoms at a lower elevation; these valleys were subsequently filled by younger flows inset below the older flows. Three phases of volcanism and incision have been recognized in northeastern New Mexico. The oldest phase was between 3.6 and 9 million years ago and is associated with eruptive centers near Raton. The voluminous eruptions near Clayton occurred 2.3 to 2.7 million years ago. The youngest volcanic activity, which began 1.4 million years ago, is centered in the Capulin Volcano National Monument area.

—Shari A. Kelley

Capulin Volcano National Monument

NATIONAL PARK SERVICE

This small park, established in 1916 by presidential proclamation, offers a close-up view of one of the most perfectly preserved cinder cones in North America. The road to the summit provides access to the summit crater, and if you have ever wanted to walk into a volcano, Capulin Mountain is one of the few places you can do so. A 0.2-mile-long trail from the summit parking lot descends to the vent at the bottom of the crater. The view from the crater rim encompasses all of northeastern New Mexico as well as parts of Texas, Oklahoma, and Colorado.

Capulin Mountain, which erupted approximately 56,000 years ago. A 2-mile-long paved road provides access to the crater rim.

Regional Setting

The park is on the western edge of the Great Plains. The Sangre de Cristo Mountains (the southernmost of the Southern Rocky Mountains) are barely visible on the far western horizon. Capulin Mountain is part of the Raton–Clayton volcanic field, which covers over 8,000 square miles. Much of northeastern New Mexico is covered by vast sheets of lava that flowed from more than a hundred now extinct volcanoes found in this region. The volcanic eruptions started about 9 million years ago and continued intermittently until about 13,000 years ago. The volcanic rocks here are mostly basaltic in composition and consist of lava flows and cinder cones, piles of cinders and volcanic centers from which many of these eruptions issued forth. Capulin Mountain, which erupted about 56,000 years ago, is one of the youngest and most perfectly preserved of these cinder cones.

The Rock Record

The oldest rocks known in northeastern New Mexico are the Precambrian granites, gneisses, and schists exposed in the Sangre de Cristo Mountains, west of Raton. The park itself is entirely composed of Capulin-age basalts, which in general range in age from 1.4 million years old to only 13,000 years old. Capulin itself is 56,000 years old, though there are younger features nearby, including Baby Capulin (whose exact age has not been determined). Nearby, in the valley of the Dry Cimarron River, there are impressive exposures of Mesozoic rocks, including the brightly colored shales of the Triassic Chinle Group, dune deposits of the Jurassic Entrada Sandstone, and Cretaceous sandstones of the Dakota Group. It is in Dakota Group sandstones that the dinosaur footprints at Clayton Lake State Park are found. Just outside the city of Raton on Goat Hill, the Cretaceous–Tertiary boundary is visible in exposures of the Raton Formation. The (by now) famous iridium-enriched clay layer, which marks the Cretaceous–Tertiary boundary worldwide, is exposed here, and at a few other places in northwestern New Mexico. The Tertiary Ogallala Formation, which holds up the High Plains, is exposed throughout much of this corner of the state.

Geologic History

Recent isotopic age determinations on the volcanic rocks of this region have allowed us to unravel the eruptive history of the Raton–Clayton volcanic field, which consisted of three major phases of eruption. The first major phase of volcanic activity (the Raton-age basalts) began about 9 million years ago, when basalts flooded down broad stream valleys that today are high mesas: Fisher's Peak, Horse Mesa, Johnson Mesa, and Oak Canyon (Kelleher) Mesa, forming the platform for the younger Emery Peak volcano. These early major eruptions ended about 8 million years ago.

As part of this same phase of volcanic activity, outpourings of basalt 7.3 million years ago produced the linear Larga Mesa and Kiowa Mesa

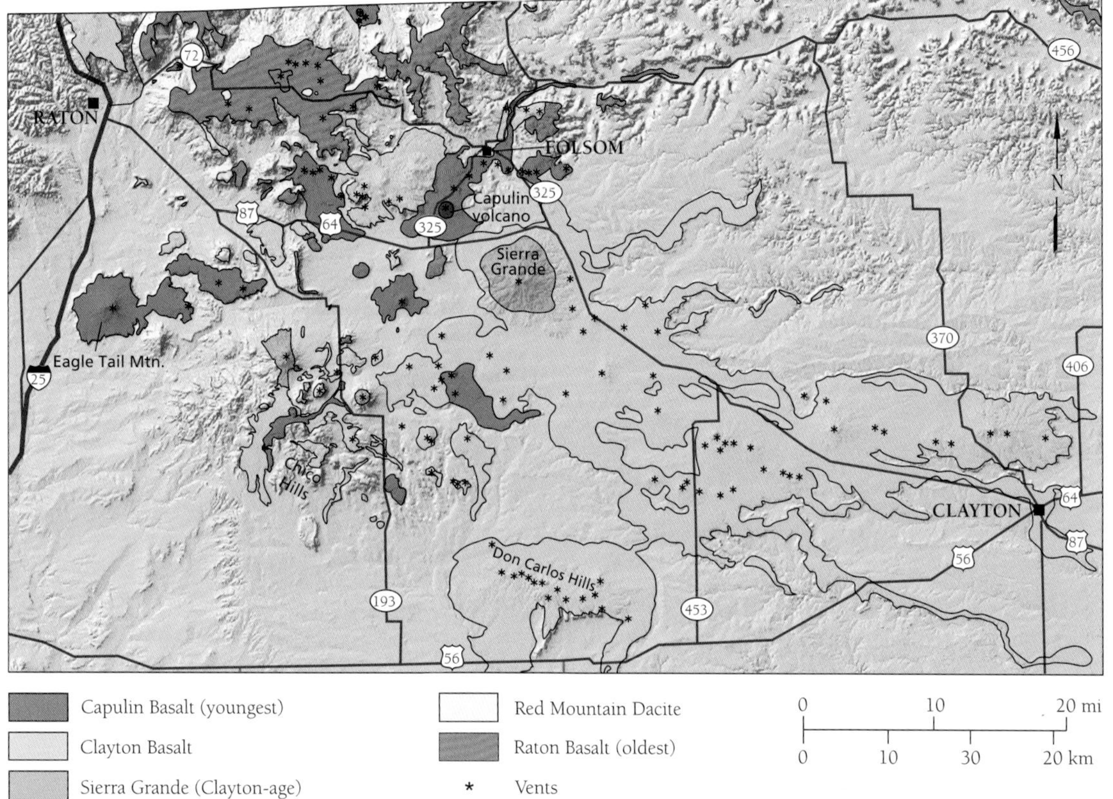

Generalized geologic map showing the major volcanic units in the Raton–Clayton volcanic field. The Capulin basalts (including Capulin Mountain) are the youngest of these.

flows, which are tiny in comparison with the earlier eruptions. This was followed 6.5 million years ago by small volume rhyolitic eruptions in a band from Red Mountain and Towndrow Mountain on Johnson Mesa south to Laughlin Peak and Palo Blanco Mountain. These rhyolitic eruptions were followed by more massive floods of basalt that produced Mesa de Maya, mostly in southeastern Colorado, and the Yates flows at the southernmost part of this volcanic field. Both flows erupted about 5.0 million years ago and are included in the Raton basalts. Colorado's Mesa de Maya flow extends across the northeast corner of New Mexico into the northwest corner of Oklahoma.

This was followed by the eruption of two very different and distinct types of magma. At 4.03 million years ago, Bellisle Mountain (Dale Mountain on some recent maps) erupted lava that flowed off Johnson Mesa and down the Dry Cimarron River to a few miles past Folsom. Other vents of this composition are found near Capulin Mountain and, although not dated, are presumed to be about the same age. The last of the Raton-age basalts erupted 3.6 million years ago and cap Bartlett Mesa above the city of Raton.

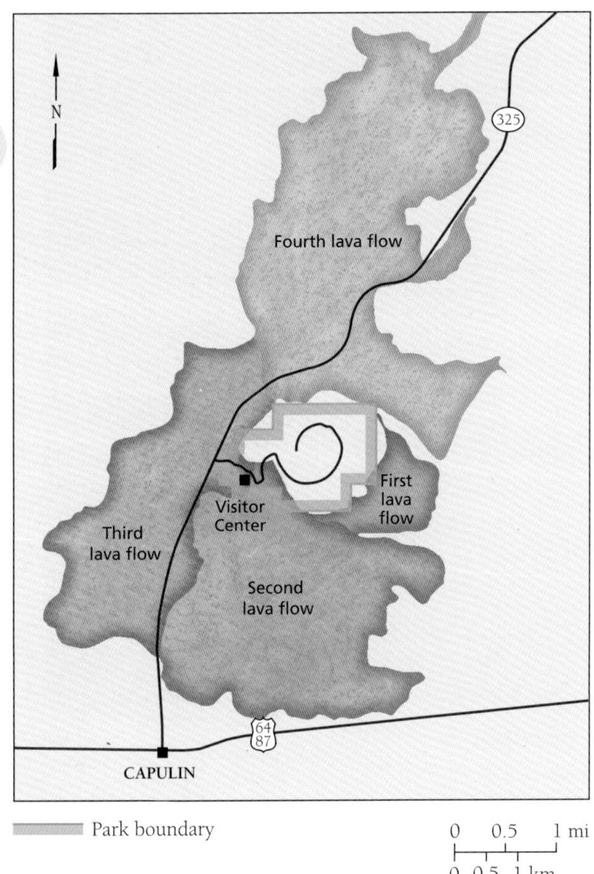

Detailed map of the four major lava flows associated with Capulin Mountain.

Then the largest eruptions of the region began. The Clayton-age basalts constitute the second of three major periods of eruption. The first eruption of this Clayton-age sequence was of Sierra Grande, which covers 43 square miles and rises 2,100 feet above the surrounding plain. Dates from four different locations on the mountain (including the summit crater) average 2.67 million years. The huge Clayton Basalt flows then poured forth; today they extend eastward from Sierra Grande for 40 miles. They cover 295 square miles and occupy many ancient drainages that reflect the trends of the earlier Ogallala drainages. The Clayton basalts range in age from 2.3 to 2.4 million years. Rabbit Ear Peak, west of the city of Clayton, is one of a line of east-southeast-trending vents for this episode of eruption.

The Capulin basalts represent the third and final phase of volcanism in this region; they range in age from 1.44 million years old to only 13,000 years old—practically yesterday, geologically speaking. Gaylord (Carr) Mountain and Yankee Volcano basalts erupted 1.7 and 1.1 million years ago, respectively. Capulin Mountain, the most prominent cinder cone from this phase of volcanism, erupted 56,000 years ago.

Geologic Features

ROAD TO THE SUMMIT—The road to the summit of Capulin includes several pullouts where one can stop and examine the inclined layers of cinders that make up the volcano. The view from the summit is quite spectacular, offering a glimpse of portions of four states, and of the many volcanic features surrounding Capulin Mountain. Below the parking area, near the base of Capulin Mountain, is the vent out of which the basaltic lava flowed. The tree-covered rim that surrounds the vent is part of the wall that formerly enclosed the lava pool. Turning around, one can look into the crater from which the gases escaped and blew the molten lava into the air, where it cooled and fell back to earth, forming the present cone.

Layers of volcanic cinders and bombs are exposed on the road to the summit. Thin layers of ash separate the layers of cinders.

CRATER RIMS—An interesting feature of many of the cinder cones in the area is the asymmetry of the crater rims, which tend to be lower on the southwest or west sides. This breaching of the craters suggests that when the volcanoes were active, the prevailing winds from the southwest to west caused the cinders to accumulate on the opposite downwind flank of the cone. The rim of Capulin is higher on the far side because that was the downwind side at the time of eruption. A trail around the rim of the crater gives spectacular views in all directions, as well as an opportunity to see birds and other wildlife. Another trail leads to the floor of the crater, about 415 feet below the highest point on the rim. Both trails are fairly short and well worth the walk.

PRESSURE RIDGES—The lava flow southwest of the base of Capulin Mountain has prominent pressure ridges, which formed at the time of eruption. These features formed when the upper surface of the flows cooled, becoming rigid while the liquid lava below the surface continued to flow, creating folds or ridges in the upper surface.

Stratified pyroclastic material (bombs, cinders, and ash) visible from NM-325 on the north flank of Mud Hill.

SIERRA GRANDE—The large mountain to the south is Sierra Grande, by far the largest and most imposing volcano in this region. It is 8 miles in diameter and rises nearly 2,100 feet above the plains. Volcanic breccias are present around the crest, but no true crater remains from its eruption about 2.5 million years ago. At an altitude of 8,720 feet above sea level, Sierra Grande is high enough to intercept the summer rain clouds, so that the grass on it is wet and green, even when the surrounding plains are dry and brown.

MUD HILL AND BABY CAPULIN—The big volcano about one mile to the north (with trees on far side) is Mud Hill. Behind it another mile is Baby Capulin Mountain (bare cone into whose crater we can see). Baby Capulin is the youngest volcano in this region.

—*William R. Muehlberger, Sally J. Muehlberger, and L. Greer Price*

Additional Reading

High Plains of Northeastern New Mexico: A Guide to Geology and Culture by William R. Muehlberger, Sally J. Muehlberger, and L. Greer Price. Scenic Trip # 19, New Mexico Bureau of Geology and Mineral Resources, 2005.

If You Plan to Visit

Capulin Volcano National Monument is located on NM–325 about 3 miles north of US 64/87, between the villages of Capulin and Folsom. It is administered by the National Park Service. There is a fee for admission, but the drive to the summit is well worth it. A small visitor center and campground are maintained near the park entrance. For more information:

Capulin Volcano National Monument
P.O. Box 40
Capulin, NM 88414
(575) 278-2201
www.nps.gov/cavo

Clayton Lake State Park

The far northeastern corner of New Mexico (Union County) is generally flat terrain punctuated by long-dead volcanoes. Just north of the town of Clayton is Clayton Lake State Park, which is a window into the more primeval world of dinosaurs. The 100-million-year-old rocks at Clayton Lake preserve multitudes of footprints of dinosaurs, who lived, hunted, and died on the shores of an ancient sea.

Regional Setting

Clayton Lake is on the High Plains of New Mexico, at the far western edge of the Great Plains. As the name suggests, this part of the state is generally flat, but at a fairly high elevation. The northeastern corner of the state is more hilly than the plains to the south (in southern Union County or Curry County) because of the many volcanoes that are scattered in this area. These volcanoes and lava flows are part of the Raton–Clayton volcanic field, which extends between those two cities. The volcanic field includes Capulin Volcano National Monument. The sedimentary rocks that underlie this portion of the state are mainly from the Cretaceous or the end of the age of dinosaurs. These rocks are generally visible only in ravines and road cuts.

Aerial view of Clayton Lake from the southeast. Seneca Creek extends into the distance, at the northern edge of an old lava flow.

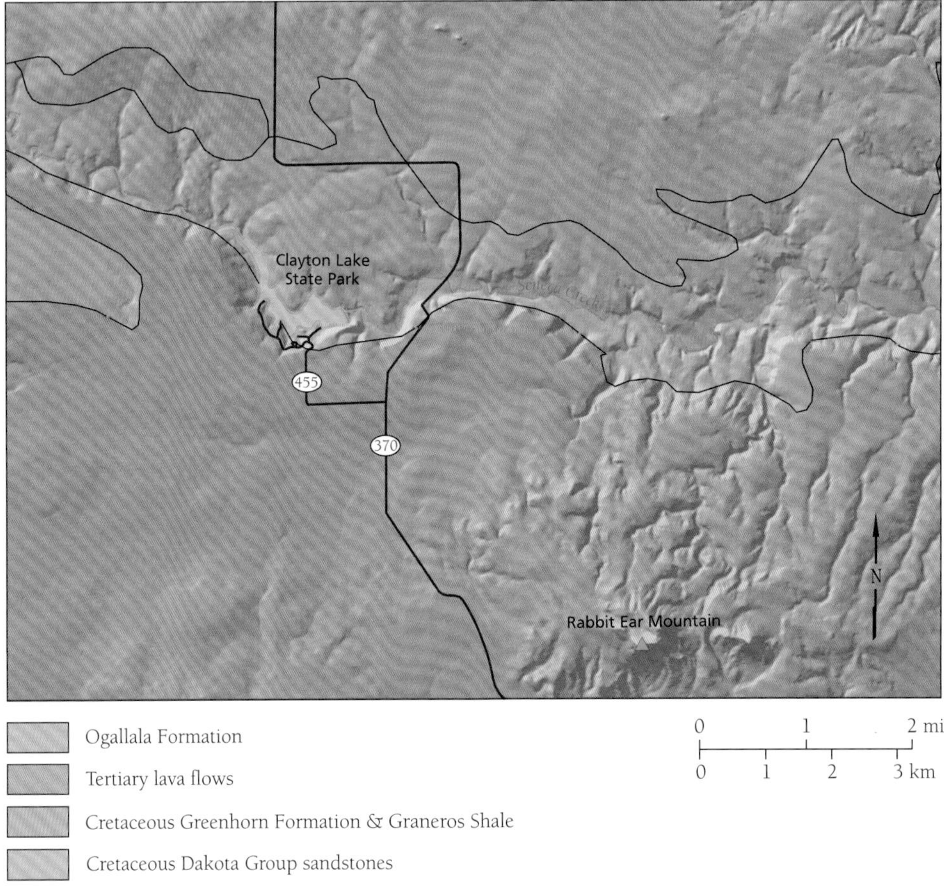

Geologic map of Clayton Lake State Park and vicinity. The Dakota Group includes the Mesa Rica, the Pajarito, and the Romeroville Formations.

The Rock Record

The majority of the formations at Clayton Lake State Park are from the Cretaceous Period, at the end of the age of dinosaurs. However, the first rocks that you see as you drive down into the park are black basaltic lavas that form the small cliff at the top of the valley. These rocks are Clayton Basalt and come from one of the many volcanoes that dot northeastern New Mexico. This particular lava flow is 2.0–2.5 million years old.

The rest of the rocks that form Clayton Lake State Park are Cretaceous. The oldest rocks in the park are located down Seneca Creek, which drains the valley to the east. These rocks can be viewed from the track site overlook. As you look down the valley you will see a brown sandstone below the level of most of the footprints. This is the Mesa Rica Formation, which formed on the shoreline of a 100-million-year old ocean. Just below the Mesa Rica, but not clearly visible, is the Glencairn Formation, which formed in the shallow sea offshore from

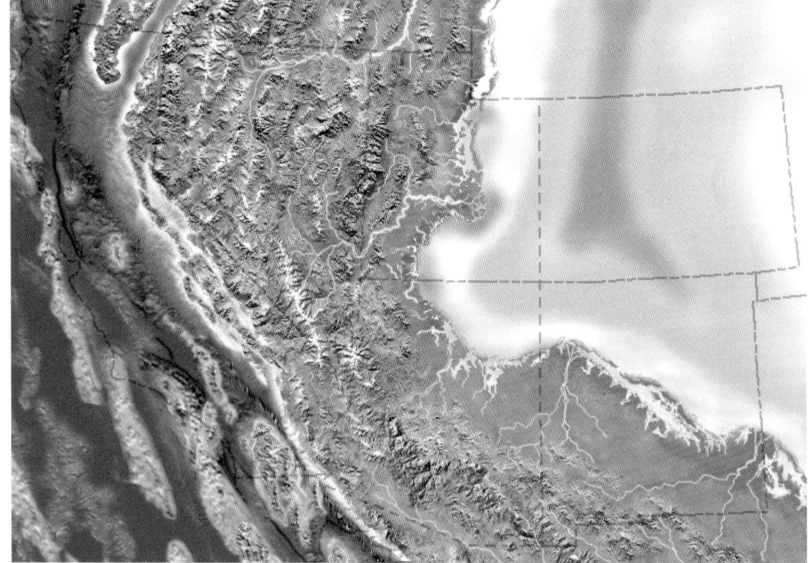

Paleogeographic map of the Southwest during the Middle Cretaceous, approximately 90 million years ago. The Western Interior Seaway, one of the largest continental seas of all time, stretched from central Utah to the western Appalachians and from the Arctic to the Gulf of Mexico.

the Mesa Rica and contains microscopic marine fossils. The bluish-gray layers that contain the majority of the dinosaur footprints are sandstones of the Pajarito Formation, part of the Dakota Group. The Pajarito formed in the swampy lands inland from the Mesa Rica shoreline.

The younger Cretaceous rocks are best seen on the opposite side of the lake from the dam and the footprints. On this western shore of the lake there are more brown sandstones that superficially look like the Mesa Rica Formation, but they are actually slightly younger. These rocks represent the Romeroville Formation, which is above the Pajarito. It is hard to see any rocks between the Romeroville on the lake shore and the Clayton Basalt at the lip of the valley. However, if you look carefully in gullies you will find soft, gray mud rocks of the Graneros Shale. This shale contains microscopic marine plankton that indicate it formed in a shallow sea. If you look carefully just below the basalt you will see a soft sandstone of the Ogallala Formation that represents rivers that flowed across the area just before the lava flows erupted onto the landscape, probably about 2.5 million years ago.

Geologic History

There are three geological stories represented at Clayton Lake State Park: the Cretaceous dinosaur-aged rocks, the younger lava flows, and the formation of the valley that now holds the lake.

The Cretaceous rocks are all approximately 100 million years old, and they tell the story of an ancient sea. In the middle of the Cretaceous a shallow interior sea divided North America into a western and eastern landmass. Northeast New Mexico was close to the shoreline about 100 million years ago. The Cretaceous rocks record the retreat of the sea to the east and then its return. The succession of rocks (from oldest to youngest) are shallow marine (Glencairn Formation), coastline/beach (Mesa Rica Formation), coastal river plain (Pajarito Formation), then back to coastline/beach (Romeroville Formation), and finally shallow marine again (Graneros Shale).

There is then a gap in the record of about 98 million years. About 2.5 million years ago northeastern New Mexico was a flat plain crisscrossed by sandy rivers and punctuated by many volcanoes. This is the landscape that produced the Clayton Basalt and the sandstone below it. Finally, Seneca Creek cut a valley down through the basalt, probably during the Pleistocene.

Geologic Features

The most impressive geologic feature visible at Clayton Lake State Park is the track site itself, the accumulation of hundreds of dinosaur footprints. The tracks were exposed during construction of the dam in 1955 and are visible in the spillway to the dam. Follow the road down towards the lake past the visitor center and turn right at the sign for dinosaur tracks. Drive to the locked gate at the end of the parking lot. From here you can follow a good trail along the edge of the lake and over the dam to a wooden overlook structure above the spillway (the trail is wheelchair accessible). Wooden steps lead down to the track level, and there is a walkway just above the footprints. There are informational signs in the overlook structure and along the walkway.

Artist's reconstruction of the large herbivorous dinosaurs responsible for the tracks at Clayton Lake, heading southeast along the shores of the Cretaceous Western Interior Seaway.

The Clayton tracks are among the largest assemblages of dinosaur footprints available to the public. They are also significant because, unlike most dinosaur footprints, the Clayton tracks were made in very wet conditions, so many are unusually deformed. The majority of tracks were made by large herbivorous dinosaurs similar to *Iguanodon* or *Tentontosaurus*. Smaller individuals walked on all fours but larger forms walked on their hind limbs. These two kinds of tracks probably represent different species of dinosaurs although it is conceivable that they represent juveniles and adults. The hind footprints have three blunt toe prints whereas the hand print is a round blob. Several trackways show evidence of tails dragging through the mud. This is unusual since dinosaurs on firm ground held their tails high off the ground to act as counterbalances.

A small number of tracks represent theropod or meat-eating dinosaurs. The larger form was bipedal and had three long narrow toes with sharp claws. It represents a dinosaur like *Acrocanthosaurus*. A second kind of track is visible near the northeast corner of the walkway. This long-legged meat-eater was smaller with tracks like a large bird.

The best preserved of the dinosaur tracks in the Pajarito Sandstone at Clayton Lake are of large, three-toed ornithopod dinosaurs, such as *Iguanodon*.

Footprints are rarely preserved. Think of how many footprints that you have made in your lifetime and how many survived even a day or two. The ideal conditions for the preservation of tracks are areas that are intermittently wet and dry, and areas that are regularly flooded. In these conditions the following sequence of events can occur: (1) tracks are made in wet sediment; (2) the sediment dries and the tracks are temporarily preserved; and (3) the track-bearing layer is quickly covered by another layer of sediment and the tracks are permanently preserved. These conditions are most common on shorelines of lakes and seas. Such ideal conditions existed along the north-south trending shoreline during Pajarito time. Tracks similar to those at Clayton Lake have been found as far north as Boulder, Colorado. In fact, there are many sites between these two areas and as far south as Mosquero, New Mexico. Collectively these sites are referred to as a "megatracksite" which is defined as a narrow time interval which preserves footprints over a wide geographic area.

The Pajarito Formation contains not only dinosaur footprints but also other features, including worm burrows, ripple marks and ancient mudcracks, easily recognized by the polygonal patterns, which are dessication cracks that formed as the muds dried. Virtually all the dinosaur tracks are preserved in the Pajarito Formation, but a few (visible to the east of the walkway) are in the upper Mesa Rica. The Mesa Rica also contains a few scrape marks made by crocodiles swimming in shallow water and "touching bottom."

—Adrian P Hunt

Additional Reading

Dinosaur Tracks of Western North America by Martin Lockley, Adrian Hunt, and Paul Koroshetz. Columbia University Press, 1999.

If You Plan to Visit

Clayton Lake State Park is 12 miles northwest of Clayton via NM–370 to NM–455, in the northeast corner of New Mexico. The route is well marked. For more information:

Clayton Lake State Park
Rural Route, Box 20
Seneca, NM 88437
(575) 374-8808
www.emnrd.state.nm.us/emnrd/PRD/Clayton.htm

Fort Union National Monument

NATIONAL PARK SERVICE

Fort Union was established in 1851 to provide a much-needed military presence to travelers on the Santa Fe Trail. The trail had been active since 1821. When much of what is now New Mexico became U.S. territory in 1848, at the end of the Mexican War. Fort Union's spectacular location on the western edge of the Great Plains was a strategic one, sited as it was near the junction of the Mountain Branch of the Santa Fe Trail with the Cimarron Cutoff. Between 1851 and 1891 Fort Union contained the largest American military presence in the Southwest; over 1,600 troops were stationed there in 1861. In 1878 the railroad came to New Mexico over Raton Pass, and by 1891 Fort Union had been abandoned. Visitors to the national monument can see some impressive historic ruins, including the foundations and adobe walls of many of the original buildings, and remnants of the Santa Fe Trail, whose deep ruts remain visible today.

Regional Setting

Fort Union National Monument sits at the western edge of the Great Plains, in the shadow of the southern Rocky Mountains. Technically, it is in the Pecos Valley section of the Great Plains province; the mountains to the west are the Sangre de Cristos. The Pecos River, which originates in the Sangre de Cristo Mountains, is not far to the west/southwest. This high, arid portion of the Great Plains west of the hundredth meridian is often referred to as the High Plains.

Fort Union also lies near the southern edge of the Ocaté volcanic field, which covers portions of the southern Rocky Mountains and the Great Plains. The cinder cones and lavas associated with this field are a prominent part of the landscape in the vicinity of Fort Union. The eruptions associated with the Ocaté volcanic field began a little over 8 million years ago and continued for more than 7 million years. The youngest flows are approximately 800,000 years old.

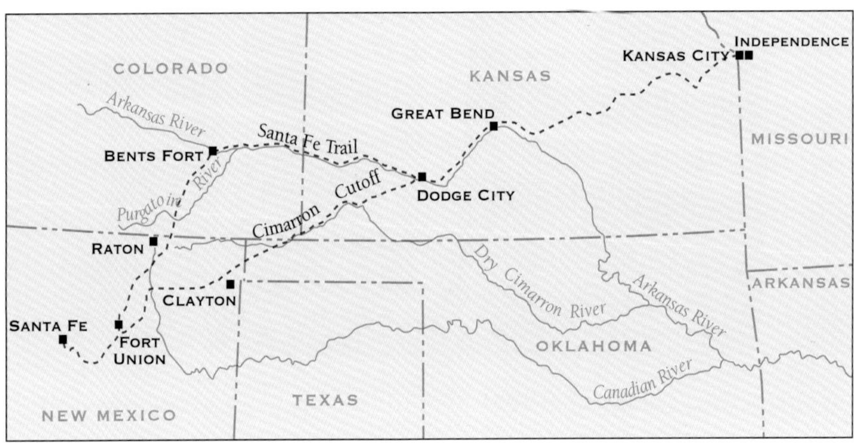

The Santa Fe Trail ran from Independence, Missouri, to Santa Fe, New Mexico. Fort Union was situated near the junction of the main trail, which went over Raton Pass, with the Cimarron Cutoff, which offered a shorter (but drier) route.

The Rock Record

To the north, the High Plains are mantled with thick accumulations of Tertiary sedimentary rocks. However, in this part of the High Plains, erosion has removed most of that, exposing Cretaceous marine sedimentary rocks. In many places these marine sediments are covered with late Tertiary volcanic rocks. The monument itself sits on Upper Cretaceous Graneros Shale. The cliff at the turnoff from Exit 366 on I–25 to the monument (via NM–161) exposes outcrops of Cretaceous Dakota Sandstone (or, more precisely, sandstones of the Dakota Group). Dakota Group sandstones are exposed on the west side of NM–161 between I–25 and the monument. Black Mesa, to the northwest, is capped with over a hundred feet of basalt from the Ocaté volcanic field.

Geologic History

During the late Cretaceous, much of the North American interior was occupied by a vast, shallow, inland sea that stretched from what is now northern Canada to Mexico. The Western Interior Seaway, as it has

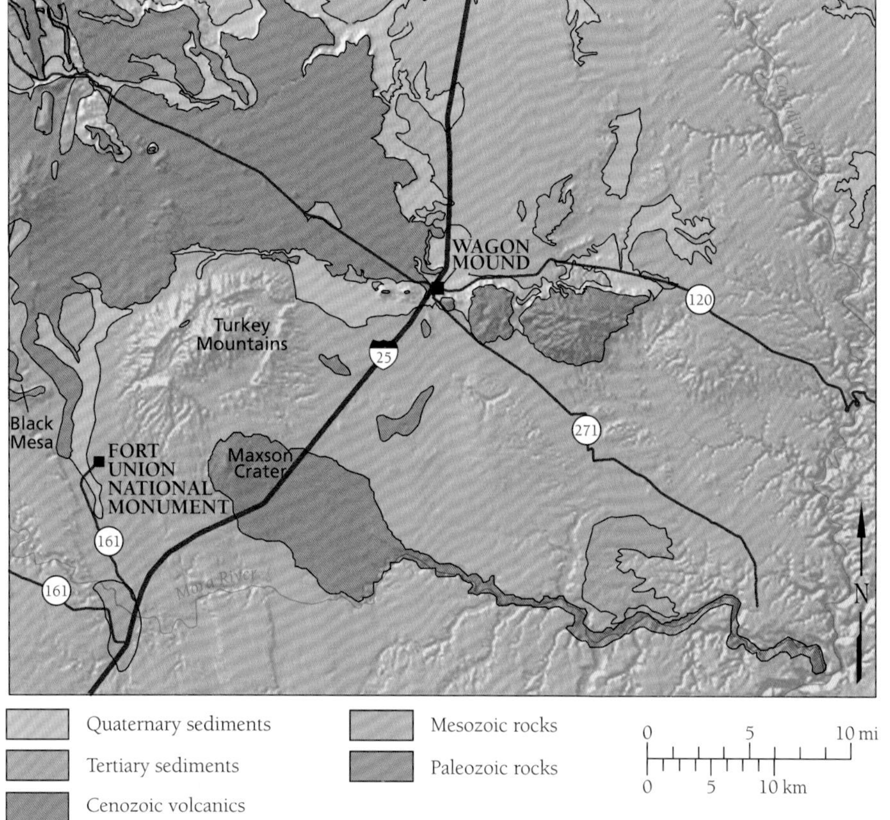

Generalized geologic map of the region surrounding Fort Union National Monument. This portion of the High Plains has been largely stripped of younger, Tertiary sediments. Cretaceous bedrock is exposed at the surface in much of the region.

come to be known, prevailed for 30 million years, reaching its maximum extent about 90 million years ago. The Dakota Sandstone was deposited as these seas first advanced from the north/northwest in the Late Cretaceous, in response (at least partly) to a worldwide rise in sea level 100 million years ago. The slightly younger Graneros Shale (here the basal unit of the Mancos Group) represents muds that were deposited in slightly deeper waters as the strand line migrated south/southwest. The precise age of such deposits obviously varies somewhat from place to place, and although we speak of regional transgressions as if they were single events, they in fact consisted of shorelines that likely migrated back and forth through time, as least locally, giving us complex, interbedded lithologies that are sometimes difficult to unravel.

The Laramide orogeny 70 million years ago marked the birth of the Rocky Mountains (including the Sangre de Cristos) and the end of the Western Interior Seaway toward the end of the Cretaceous. The Laramide orogeny, which lasted some 40 million years, was responsible for much of the structure and shape of this part of North America, including some of the broad, regional uplift associated with the High

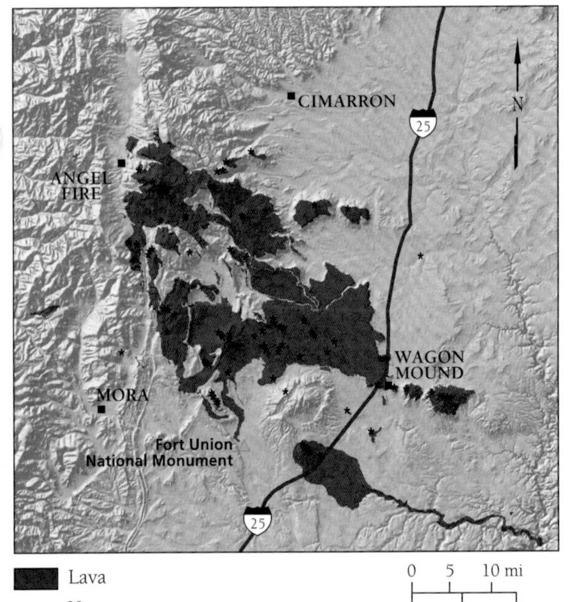

Fort Union sits near the southern edge of the Ocaté volcanic field, shown here in red. The field was active from 8 million years ago until less than a million years ago. Note the lava flow that follows the course of the Mora River, in the southeast corner of the map.

Plains. For the remainder of the Tertiary, this part of the continent was above sea level.

With the onset of the Laramide orogeny, enormous quantities of sediment were shed eastward from the rising Rocky Mountains and accumulated to great thickness on what is now the High Plains. For much of the Cenozoic, the plains saw alternating episodes of deposition and erosion, with streams from the mountains to the west shedding debris onto the plains in the east. In the late Cenozoic, streams draining the eastern flank of the Sangre de Cristos deposited an extensive deposit of sediment that includes the Ogallala Formation, the High Plains aquifer that today provides an enormous amount of water to the region, primarily for irrigation. This deposition was followed by another episode of uplift, and much of the elevation we now associate with the High Plains is the result of regional uplift that has occurred only in the past 5–10 million years. It is this most recent rejuvenation of regional uplift that has caused the streams in this area, including the Pecos and the Canadian Rivers, to incise their channels into this thick sedimentary cover.

The Ocaté volcanic field is one of a series of volcanic fields in northern New Mexico that appear to be part of a regional trend of Late Cenozoic volcanic activity that occurred in New Mexico over the past 10 million years. That regional trend known as the Jemez lineament, stretches from the Raton/Clayton volcanic field on the east, through the Valles caldera, Mount Taylor, and on into the Zuni–Bandera volcanic field on the west, extending ultimately into Arizona. The volcanic features in the immediate vicinity of Fort Union are all part of the Ocaté volcanic field, which was active from 8 million years ago until just under a million years ago.

Geologic Features

VOLCANIC FEATURES—The lava-capped mesa to the northwest is Black Mesa. The volcanic deposits on top of the mesa are Pliocene basalts from the Ocaté volcanic field. Maxson Crater, due east of the monument, is the source of the lava flow that follows the course of the Mora River to its confluence with the Canadian River (see map). The flows associated with Maxson Crater are young (about 1.6 million years old).

THE TURKEY MOUNTAINS—Visible on the horizon to the north are the Turkey Mountains. The uplift associated with the Turkey Mountains is the result of a laccolith, a relatively shallow igneous intrusion. The laccolith is not exposed, although drilling has confirmed its presence. The precise age of the intrusion is unknown, though it must be younger than the Cretaceous strata that were deformed when it was emplaced. Today the Turkey Mountains are surrounded by younger lavas of the Ocaté volcanic field.

—*L. Greer Price*

If You Plan to Visit

Fort Union is just a few miles north of Watrous, New Mexico. From I–25, take Exit 366 and follow NM–161 8 miles north to the monument. For more information:

Fort Union National Monument
P.O. Box 127
Watrous, NM 87753
(505) 425-8025
www.nps.gov/foun

Storrie Lake State Park

Storrie Lake with the Sangre de Cristo Mountains in the background. The unusual color is due to the extremely shallow water, and to the winds that stir up sediment from the lake bottom.

Robert C. Storrie built the earthen dam at Storrie Lake from 1916 to 1921 to provide water for irrigation. The lake impounds water from the Gallinas River (also known as Rio de las Gallinas), which begins in the Sangre de Cristo Mountains near Elk Mountain and flows southeastward to join the Pecos River. *Gallina*, Spanish for chicken or hen, typically refers to the wild turkey found throughout the mountains of New Mexico. The earthen dam is 1,400 feet long, has a concrete core, and is covered with Proterozoic gneiss, quartzite, and Cretaceous sandstone, probably derived from the hills to the west. A canal diverts water from the Gallinas River into Storrie Lake. In 1944 the Storrie Lake Water Users Association acquired management of the facilities, but the project was never a financial success. Over the years, the farms became unprofitable, and the water was used for cattle and for growing cattle feed. In 1960 Storrie Lake became a state park.

Regional Setting

Storrie Lake State Park lies in the northern Pecos Valley section of the Great Plains near the physiographic boundary with the Southern Rocky Mountains. The foothills of the Sangre de Cristo Mountains form the western skyline. The landforms in the east are primarily erosional landforms of sedimentary rocks. The Canadian River, north of the park, flows eastward from the Sangre de Cristo Mountains and has cut a deep canyon with sandstones of the Cretaceous Dakota Group forming the rim. The Pecos River, south of the park, flows southeastward from the mountains and has cut a deep canyon with Paleozoic limestones forming the rim of the canyon. Storrie Lake is the place where these streams first leave the mountains and begin their downcutting.

The Rock Record

Most of the bedrock at Storrie Lake State Park belongs to the Carlile Shale (Cretaceous), which was deposited when this area was covered by an interior seaway 70–80 million years ago. Fossil shark teeth, coiled ammonites, gastropods, cephalopods, and brachiopods are common in the dark gray-to-black shale and limestone from this unit at the park; they can be found weathered out along the lake shore. Shark Tooth Mesa, the ridge east of the park, was named for fossil shark teeth found there. Limestone concretions weather out of the shale and lie on the surface, resembling discarded wagon wheels.

Geologic History

Throughout the Paleozoic Era the area was invaded numerous times by marine seas, followed by subsequent erosion and the deposition of terrestrial deposits as the seas retreated. During the Cretaceous Period shallow seas covered much of New Mexico, including this region. After uplift of the Rocky Mountains during the Laramide orogeny, erosion of the mountains resulted in streams and rivers carrying sediment to the Great Plains. These streams and rivers from the Rocky Mountains have deposited sediment along their courses for 60 million years, since the final retreat of the Cretaceous seas. However, 10 million years ago the interior continent began uplifting again, and the streams and rivers were forced to cut into the older sediments, producing deep-sided river canyons.

Geologic Features

Two olive green-to-black *lamprophyre* dikes, probably of Tertiary age, testify to the volcanic activity that has affected much of northeastern New Mexico, especially near Raton and Wagon Mound. The 3-to-5-foot-wide dikes strike northwest and crop out along the northeast side of the lake, near the dam.

—*Virginia T. McLemore*

If You Plan to Visit

Storrie Lake State Park is north of Las Vegas, New Mexico, on NM–518. Fishing, sailing, windsurfing, water-skiing, picnicking, camping, hiking, and swimming are popular activities at the park. The park includes developed campsites (some with hookups), restrooms, showers, drinking water, boat ramps, hiking trails, a playground, a baseball diamond, a group shelter, and visitor center. The New Mexico Game and Fish Department stocks the lake with rainbow trout, German brown trout, and crappie. Storrie Lake attracts waterfowl, especially in the winter when Canadian geese, ducks, bald eagles, and crane stop for water. Other animals seen occasionally in the park include owls, blackbirds, falcons, doves, coyotes, antelope, and deer. For more information:

Storrie Lake State Park
HC33, Box 109 #2
Las Vegas, NM 87701
(505) 425-7278
www.emnrd.state.nm.us/PRD/StorrieLake.htm

Kiowa and Rita Blanca National Grasslands

CIBOLA NATIONAL FOREST

Kiowa National Grasslands

The Kiowa and Rita Blanca National Grasslands are located on the High Plains of northeastern New Mexico. They encompass two very different rock records—a geologically young (3 million years to present) history of volcanoes, rivers, and ponds during the ice ages, and a geologically older (210 to 90 million years ago) history of the many changing environments during the age of dinosaurs. Most of the grasslands are flat prairies with some low rolling hills. However, the Kiowa National Grasslands also cross the canyon of the Canadian River west of Mills, New Mexico, where the canyon is 2 miles wide and up to 800 feet deep.

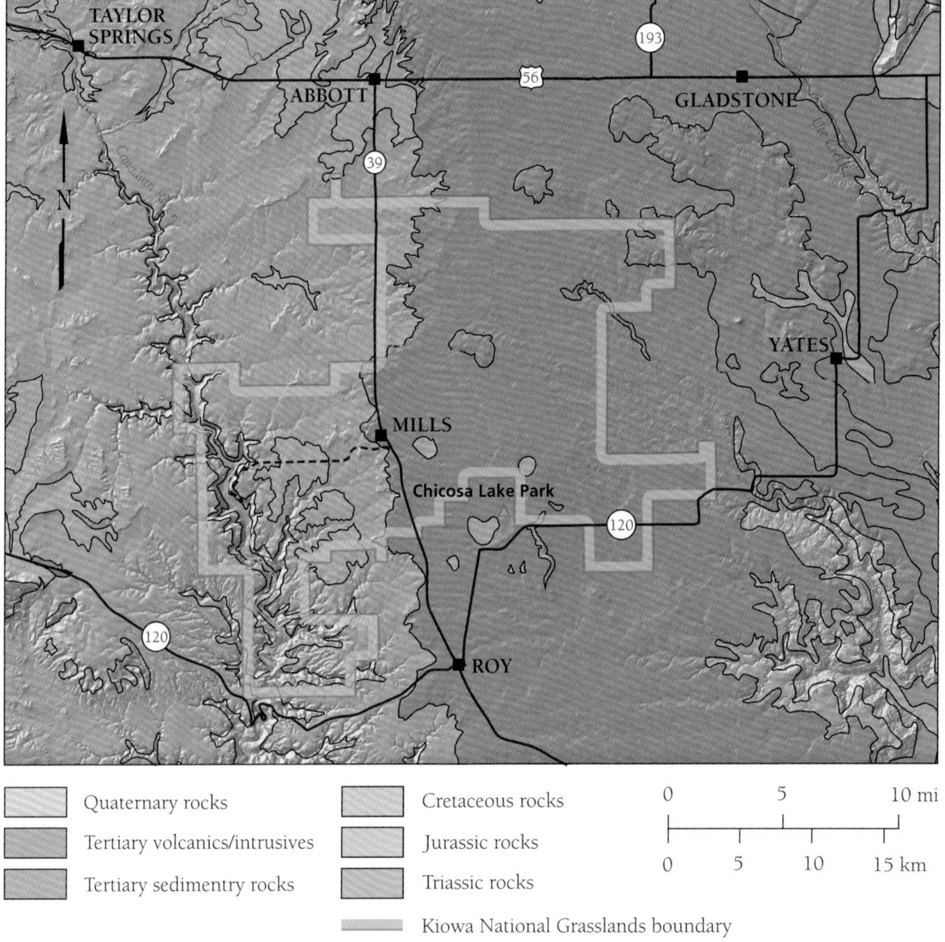

Generalized geologic map of the area surrounding the Kiowa National Grasslands in New Mexico. Included within the Kiowa National Grasslands are 14 miles of the Canadian River. The Kiowa and Rita Blanca National Grasslands encompass 230,000 acres in New Mexico, Texas, and Oklahoma.

Regional Setting

The Kiowa and Rita Blanca National Grasslands are in the Great Plains physiographic province. The Rita Blanca National Grasslands are in the Raton and Llano Estacado sections of that province, whereas the Kiowa National Grasslands are in the Raton and Pecos Valley sections.

The escarpments of the High Plains and adjoining river valleys of northeastern New Mexico expose nearly flat-lying layers of Mesozoic sedimentary rock. These are some of the most extensive exposures of these rocks in New Mexico; only the San Juan Basin in northwestern New Mexico has equally extensive outcrops of Mesozoic rocks. In northeastern New Mexico, Mesozoic rocks record a complex and long history of changing environments and yield a great variety of fossils, from petrified logs to clam shells to dinosaur bones.

The Rock Record

The Rita Blanca National Grasslands mostly expose geologically young, unconsolidated sediments. There are windblown sands and silts and water-laid sands and gravels of Pliocene and Pleistocene age (younger than 4 million years old). These sediments contain fossils of extinct peccary, camel, horse, and mammoth as well as fossils of land snails that lived around permanent water sources. The older bedrock exposed along some stream courses consists of sandstones and shales of

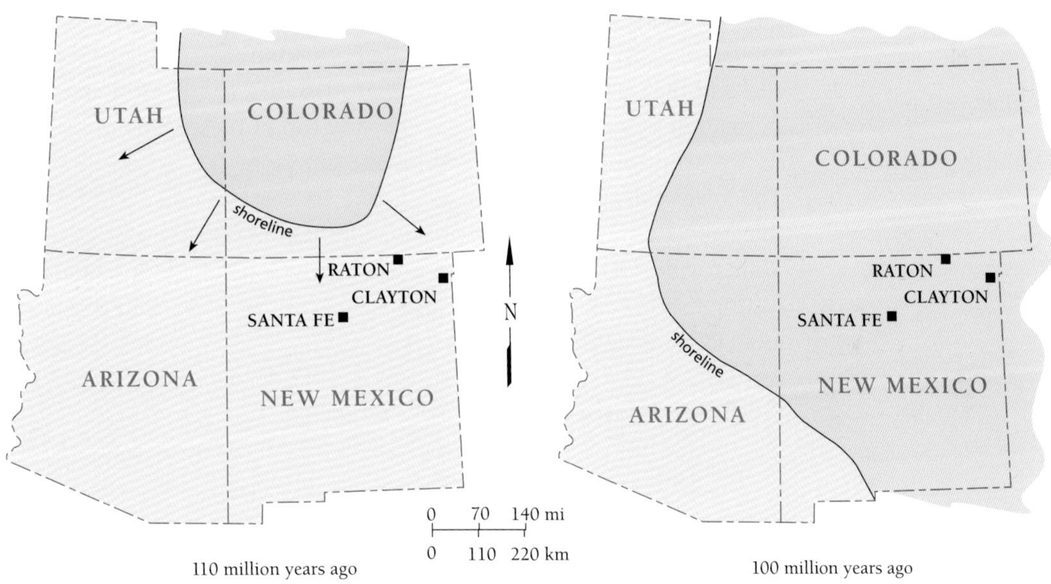

Sandstones of the Dakota Group were deposited as seas advanced from the north/northwest, in response to world-wide changes in sea level. This was the first advance of the Western Interior Seaway, in the Late Cretaceous.

the Early Cretaceous Dakota Group. These rocks represent ancient seashore and marine environments of the Early Cretaceous seaway that covered much of the United States about 100 million years ago.

In the Rita Blanca National Grasslands, basaltic lava flows and small volcanoes at the eastern edge of the Clayton volcanic field are some of the most striking geologic features. These volcanic rocks are about 3 million years old and are at the eastern edge of the Raton–Clayton volcanic field, a large volcanic field that erupted between 3.6 and 2.0 million years ago. The Raton–Clayton volcanic field extends from Clayton westward some 50 miles toward Raton.

Most of the geology of the Kiowa National Grasslands is similar to that of the Rita Blanca National Grasslands—geologically young, unconsolidated sediments on top of the High Plains. However, at Mills Canyon, the Canadian River has cut through some of the older sedmentary rocks beneath the High Plains like a knife cutting a piece out of a layer cake to reveal its interior. The rocks revealed are sedimentary rocks of the Cretaceous at the top of the canyon walls (sandstones, shales, and limestones) above an 800-foot-thick succession of Jurassic sandstones, siltstones, and mudstones. In some places on the canyon floor, red mudstones and sandstones are visible at the top of the Upper Triassic Chinle Group.

Thus, the cliffs of tan, brown, and gray sandstone visible all along the canyon walls as well as the slopes covered with soil, vegetation, and landslide debris are mostly Jurassic rocks. At the base, a single cliff of tan sandstone, the Entrada Sandstone, is overlain by a ribbed cliff (thin sandstone ledges) of the Summerville Formation. Most of the Jurassic rocks in the Canadian River Canyon are assigned to the Morrison Formation by geologists. Only at the very top of these walls can you see brown sandstone, gray shale, and white limestone of Cretaceous age. The lower cliffs of Cretaceous sandstone are the Mesa Rica Sandstone of the Dakota Group, and overlying rock formations (Pajarito, Romeroville, Graneros, and Greenhorn formations) are more difficult to distinguish from a distance because they are covered by soil, vegetation, and landslide debris.

Geologic History

The geologic history of the Kiowa and Rita Blanca National Grasslands can be divided into two distinct intervals, one during the Pleistocene and the other during the age of dinosaurs (the Mesozoic). During the ice ages (the last 3 million years or so), the High Plains of northeastern New Mexico were not icebound (the glaciers were to the north), but they were much wetter and cooler than today. Rivers flowed across the prairies, and ponds and lakes dotted the landscape. Mammoth, horses, and camels grazed on the lush prairies. Peccaries and other small mammals foraged in the brush, and water sources supported a rich fauna of land snails.

The much older world of the Mesozoic tells a longer and more complex story. This story begins in the Late Triassic, about 210 million years ago, when large rivers flowed to the northwest across northeastern New Mexico. Some of the earliest dinosaurs lived on the forested floodplains around these rivers.

By Jurassic time, the climate had changed considerably in what is now northeastern New Mexico, largely as a result of the northward drift of the North American continent. During the first 40 million years of Jurassic time, northeastern New Mexico had moved from about 10° north of the ancient equator to more than 20° north, and into the global belt of deserts. A vast desert (sand sea) covered the Southwest during the Middle Jurassic, about 160 million years ago. The oldest Jurassic sandstones in the Canadian River canyon, the Entrada Sandstone, are ancient sand dune deposits of that desert.

A Jurassic sea then advanced across the western United States, into Idaho and Utah, and its arid coastal plain, tidal flats, and beaches extended all the way across New Mexico into western Oklahoma. Thin beds of sandstone, siltstone, and gypsum formed on this coastal plain and are now the Summerville Formation.

By Late Jurassic time, however, uplifted areas in central Utah and Arizona drove out the sea, and rivers began to flow from west to east. These rivers and their vast, muddy floodplains deposited the famous Morrison Formation, which yields the fossils of the well known Late Jurassic dinosaurs *Apatosaurus* (also known as *Brontosaurus*), *Allosaurus*, and *Stegosaurus*. Most of the Jurassic rock layers exposed in the Kiowa and Rita Blanca National Grasslands belong to the Morrison Formation, though no dinosaur bones have yet been discovered in these grasslands.

By Cretaceous time, a dramatic change again took place in the landscape of northeastern New Mexico. Sea level rose, and a seaway covered most of the central United States. Initially, the western shoreline of the interior seaway was located in northeastern New Mexico. Sandstones at the base of the Cretaceous rock column (Dakota Group) in the Kiowa and Rita Blanca National Grasslands were deposited on beaches and at river mouths along that shoreline. At Clayton Lake State Park, these sandstones have preserved hundreds of dinosaur tracks, but no dinosaur tracks have yet been discovered in Cretaceous rocks exposed in the grasslands. By 90 million years ago, the seaway had enlarged so that the shoreline was in western New Mexico. Gray shale and white limestone layers accumulated on the sea bottom where the Kiowa and Rita Blanca National Grasslands are today. Fossils of clams, ammonites, and sharks teeth are found in these marine rocks.

Geologic Features

In the Rita Blanca National Grasslands, two geologic features of interest are the volcanoes north of Clayton, Rabbit Ear Mountain and Bible Top Butte. They were originally conical hills of volcanic cinders or cinder cones, but their original shapes have been much altered by erosion since they erupted. Rabbit Ear Mountain erupted between 2.2 and 2.3 million years ago. Bible Top Butte is of similar age.

Mills Canyon on the Canadian River is the outstanding geologic feature of the Kiowa Grasslands. It exposes 800 feet of rocks from the age of dinosaurs, discussed above. Cretaceous sandstones of the Dakota

Mills Canyon, on the Canadian River. Cretaceous Dakota Group sandstones are exposed at the rim; the Triassic Chinle Group is exposed at river level.

group are exposed at the canyon rim. The road to the canyon floor descends through Upper and Middle Jurassic strata to exposures of the Triassic Chinle Group at the river.

—Spencer G. Lucas

If You Plan to Visit

The Kiowa and Rita Blanca National Grasslands, managed as part of the Cibola National Forest, encompass about 230,000 acres in six counties in Texas, New Mexico, and Oklahoma. The New Mexico portion of the Rita Blanca National Grasslands is in Union County north and south of Clayton. The Kiowa National Grasslands is 136,417 acres located to the west, in Harding County and a small portion of southeastern Colfax County. These administrative units are not solid blocks of government-owned land; rather, they consist of many small government parcels, intermingled with privately owned tracts. Mills Canyon is accessible by way of a dirt road (impassable when wet) that heads west from NM–39 near the town of Mills. There is a small, primitive campground at the edge of the Canadian River here. For more information, contact:

Kiowa and Rita Blanca National Grasslands
714 Main Street
Clayton, NM 88415
(575) 374-9652
www.fs.fed.us/r3/cibola/districts/kiowa.shtml

Sugarite Canyon State Park

Sugarite Canyon State Park, once the site of a thriving coal-mining camp, was established as a state park in 1985, but the canyon has been a recreational attraction in northeastern New Mexico for decades. This heavily wooded mountain park has something for everyone year round. It is one of the few state parks in New Mexico that allows seasonal bow hunting. Trails are maintained through the ruins of the settlement and past coal waste rock piles and mines.

Lake Maloya

The Santa Fe Railroad built the first waterworks on Bartlett Mesa west of Sugarite Canyon and piped water into Raton. By 1891 additional water was required by both the town and the railroad, so Sugarite Canyon was selected for water development. Lake Alice, Lake Maloya, and Lake Dorothy were added as reservoirs for Raton's water supply. The lakes also supplied the town with ice in the winter. The Raton waterworks project was one of the first systems built in the territory of New Mexico and is still in operation today, supplying much of Raton's water.

The City of Raton established a municipal park in Sugarite Canyon, including 5,400 acres in Colorado, in order to protect the watershed. The state park today includes only the 3,600-acre tract in New Mexico; the Colorado tract, including Lake Dorothy, is currently part of the Lake Dorothy State Wildlife Area, administered by the State of Colorado.

Regional Setting

Sugarite Canyon State Park is in the northern Pecos Valley section of the Great Plains province and is part of the Raton Basin, a structural basin that extends from Cimarron, New Mexico, northeastward to Huerfano Park, Colorado. The basin formed during the Laramide orogeny as the San Luis highland rose to the west. Erosion of the highlands during and after uplift provided sediment that filled the basin. The park is on the western edge of the Raton–Clayton volcanic field, which extends from Fishers Peak Mesa, northeast of Raton to Rabbit Ear Mountain, near Clayton. Volcanic features associated with this field include Capulin Mountain volcano east of the park. The Raton–Clayton field was active from 9.5 million years ago until as recently as 56,000 years ago.

The Rock Record/Geologic History

The oldest rocks exposed in Sugarite Canyon formed from mud deposited in the Cretaceous sea and belong to the Late Cretaceous Pierre Shale. The Pierre Shale is overlain by the white sandstones of the Trinidad Sandstone that were deposited in delta-front and barrier environments along the coast of the Cretaceous sea.

As the Cretaceous seas receded eastward away from New Mexico, the coastal margin also migrated eastward. Meandering rivers and streams deposited sand, which later solidified into sandstone, whereas mud, which became shale, was deposited in the adjacent floodplains. Peat, which became coal, was deposited in poorly drained swamps. The floodplain and alluvial-plain deposits, known as the Raton Formation, were deposited unconformably on top of the Trinidad Sandstone. The Raton Formation is Late Cretaceous to Paleocene in age and consists of 1,100 feet of sandstone, siltstone, mudstone, coal, conglomerate, and carbonaceous shale. Ferns, leaf imprints, and other plant material can be found in this unit.

The Raton Formation is divided into three zones: the lower coal zone, the barren series, and the upper coal zone. The Sugarite coal bed is at the top of the 100-foot-thick lower coal zone. This unit consists of a basal conglomerate (not present in the park) and sandstone overlain by interfingering sandstone, shale, mudstone, and coal. The Sugarite coal is the lowest economic grade of coal in the Raton Formation. In other areas of the Raton Basin the coals in the lower zone are not of economic thickness or quality. The lower coal zone includes the Cretaceous–Tertiary boundary at or near the top of the zone.

Most of the barren series and upper coal zone in Sugarite Canyon are covered by vegetation, landslide debris, and debris from the basaltic mesa caprocks. The barren series consists of 500 feet of cliff-forming channel sandstone with minor slope-forming siltstone, shale, mudstone, and a few very thin coal seams. These rocks were deposited by meandering streams and in adjacent floodplain and alluvial-plain environments.

The upper coal zone, above the barren series, consists of 500 feet of floodplain sandstone, mudstone, siltstone, and shale interbedded with coal and carbonaceous shale that were deposited in swamps. Exposures of the upper coal zone can be seen near the dam at Lake Maloya.

Tertiary basalt flows in the park are part of the extensive Raton–Clayton volcanic field; they have been dated at 7–9 million years old. After eruption of the basalt, the Sugarite– Raton area continued to be uplifted. Streams and rivers cut around the basalt-capped mesas and slowly eroded valleys in the softer sedimentary rocks, such as Sugarite Canyon, leaving the basalt capped mesas as elevated plateaus. Even today, this erosion continues.

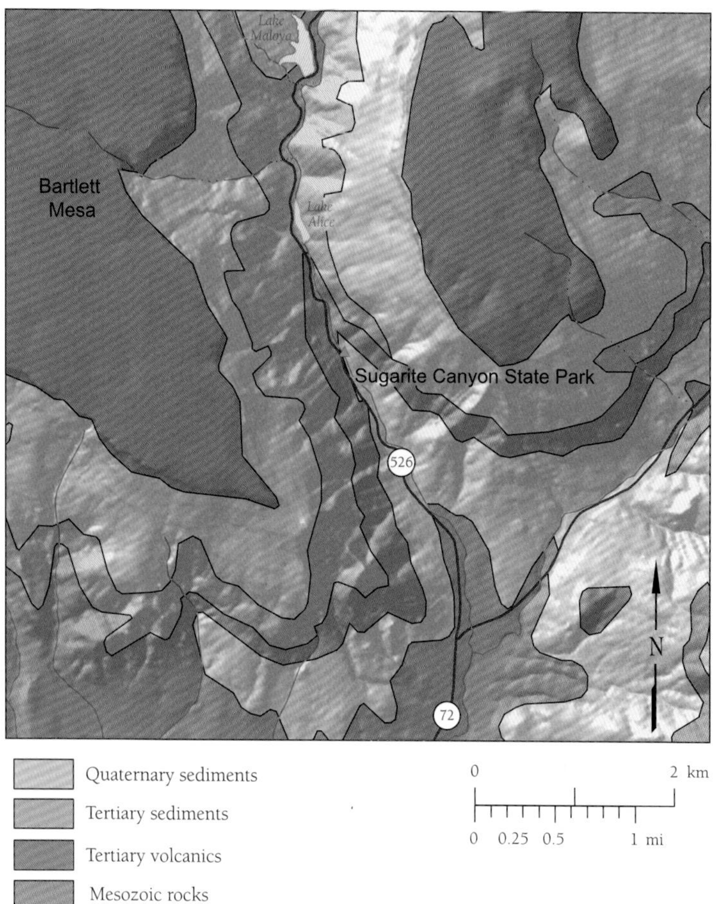

Generalized geologic map of the area surrounding Sugarite Canyon State Park

Geologic Features

THE CRETACEOUS/TERTIARY BOUNDARY—The lower coal zone of the Raton Formation includes the Cretaceous–Tertiary boundary at or near the top of the zone. At Sugarite the boundary is indicated by 1-to-2-inch-thick kaolinite-rich clay near the top of the Sugarite coal, approximately half way up the slope overlying the visitor center. This clay bed is characterized by anomalously high concentrations of iridium and other platinum-group metals, along with the absence of certain pollen species and the presence of shock-metamorphosed quartz and feldspar. Iridium is found in very low concentrations in rocks of the earth's crust, but is more concentrated in meteorites and rocks from deeper in the crust. This clay bed has been found throughout the Raton Basin and in a narrow belt that extends from New Mexico to Alberta, Canada. The Cretaceous–Tertiary boundary is known throughout the world for the mass extinction of numerous animal and plant species, including dinosaurs.

Interpretations of the Cretaceous–Tertiary boundary are controversial. Many scientists believe the mass extinctions at that time were the result of a catastrophic event, such as the impact of a large meteor or asteroid that produced the shock-metamorphosed mineral grains. Other scientists believe the mass extinctions were a result of a series of intense volcanic eruptions. Both of these theories suggest that a large amount of dust was ejected into the atmosphere, blocking sunlight and resulting in the decline of both plant and animal life. This material settled and formed the boundary layer we now see in both marine and nonmarine sedimentary rocks of this age throughout the world. Other scientists believe the mass extinction event has been exaggerated and suggest the extinction occurred over a period of several million years. Sedimentary rocks deposited at this time may have been eroded, so the problem may be simply missing rocks, rather than a sudden mass extinction. Dinosaur bones are found in rocks stratigraphically above the Cretaceous–Tertiary boundary; but these bones may have been eroded from older, late Cretaceous rocks. Dinosaur footprints are found only in the late Cretaceous rocks beneath the Tertiary–Cretaceous boundary. The Cretaceous-Tertiary boundary is not easily seen in the park. However, it is well exposed on Goat Hill, just outside Raton.

COAL MINES—One of the main reasons for the presence of the railroad in the Raton area was the discovery of vast quantities of coal. The Sugarite mines were adits or tunnels that were driven into the hillside along the coal seams. Mules were used in the mines to move coal cars to the surface where a tram was built to haul the coal down the steep slopes to the bottom of the canyon. Railway cars transported the coal to Raton where it was used as domestic fuel and as fuel to power the locomotives.

The Sugarite coal camp, ca. 1910.

THE SUGARITE COAL CAMP—The Sugarite coal camp was established in 1908 and was one of the last areas in the Raton coal field to be developed. Immigrants from Europe and Japan settled in Sugarite, which became known as one of the more pleasant coal camps in the area, with its mountain setting and running stream. However, the population never exceeded 1,000 people. The camp included a mercantile store, schoolhouse, post office, and community center. Only the post office and the mule barn still remain intact. After the coal mines closed in 1942, most of the buildings were abandoned or moved to Raton. The railroad was abandoned in 1944, marking the end of another mining town in northern New Mexico.

BASALT CAPROCK—Tertiary basalt flows overlie sedimentary rocks and cap the mesas bordering Sugarite Canyon State Park. They are part of the extensive Raton–Clayton volcanic field. The flows in Sugarite State Park erupted as broad flow sheets ranging in thickness from 10 to 100 feet. The basalt is fine-to-coarse grained and includes olivine and plagioclase phenocrysts; it has been dated in places at 7–9 million years old. Hiking trails at Little Horse Mesa and Horse Mesa allow the visitor to examine the basalt up close. Landslides and talus slopes are common along the base of the basalt flows. This material was displaced after Sugarite Canyon was formed. Rain and snow melt seep into cracks or cooling joints of the exposed rock surfaces. When the water freezes, it expands the cracks and eventually causes the rock to break into angular boulders, which slowly move downhill forming a talus slope of broken rubble. Rock falls and mud slides still occur today.

—*Virginia T. McLemore*

If You Plan to Visit

The park entrance is 2 miles north of NM–72 on NM–526 (NM–72 is accessed from I–25 via Exit 452). The Visitor Center, just outside the park entrance, is in the building that once housed the post office for the Sugarite coal camp. Facilities in the park include hiking trails, the Coal Camp Interpretative Trail through the ruins of the Sugarite coal camp, two campgrounds with restrooms and RV hookups, and a group shelter. Many of the visitors to Sugarite Canyon State Park are fishermen. The New Mexico Game and Fish Department periodically stock two lakes in the state park, Lake Alice and Lake Maloya, with cutthroat and rainbow trout. A third lake across the border in Colorado, Lake Dorothy, is open for fishing as well. Boats are allowed on Lake Maloya, the largest of the lakes (gasoline-powered boats are prohibited). In the winter, many of the trails are open for cross-country skiing. Other winter activities include tubing, ice skating, and ice fishing. For more information:

Sugarite Canyon State Park
HCR 63, Box 386
Raton, NM 87740
(575) 445-5607
(575) 445-8828 (Fax)
www.emnrd.state.nm.us/PRD/Sugarite.htm

Conchas Lake and Ute Lake State Parks

NEW MEXICO STATE PARKS

Here at the lower end of Ute Lake just above the dam, Triassic Trujillo sandstone (Chinle Group) is exposed along the shore.

Conchas Lake and Ute Lake State Parks are both centered around lakes created by dams along the Canadian River in east-central New Mexico. Sandstones exposed at both parks provide important clues to the vast Late Triassic river system that covered the western United States 200 to 225 million years ago.

The U.S. Army Corps of Engineers completed Conchas Dam in 1939. The dam is 235 feet high and 1,250 feet long and creates one of New Mexico's largest lakes, covering 9,600 acres with 60 miles of shoreline at an elevation of 4,200 feet. The lake extends upstream from the dam for 14 miles along the Canadian River and 11 miles along the Conchas River.

Ute Dam was built by the U.S. Bureau of Reclamation in 1963. In 1983–84 they enlarged it to its current size of 148 feet high and 2,050 feet long. At 13 miles in length, Ute Lake is one of the longest lakes in New Mexico. Its width never exceeds a mile.

Regional Setting

Both Conchas Lake and Ute Lake are in the Pecos Valley section of the Great Plains province, at the northern edge of the Llano Estacado (the "staked plains"). The Llano Estacado, a vast and flat upland, extends from the Pecos River on the west to Palo Duro Canyon, Texas, on the east, and to Hobbs, New Mexico, on the south, an area of about

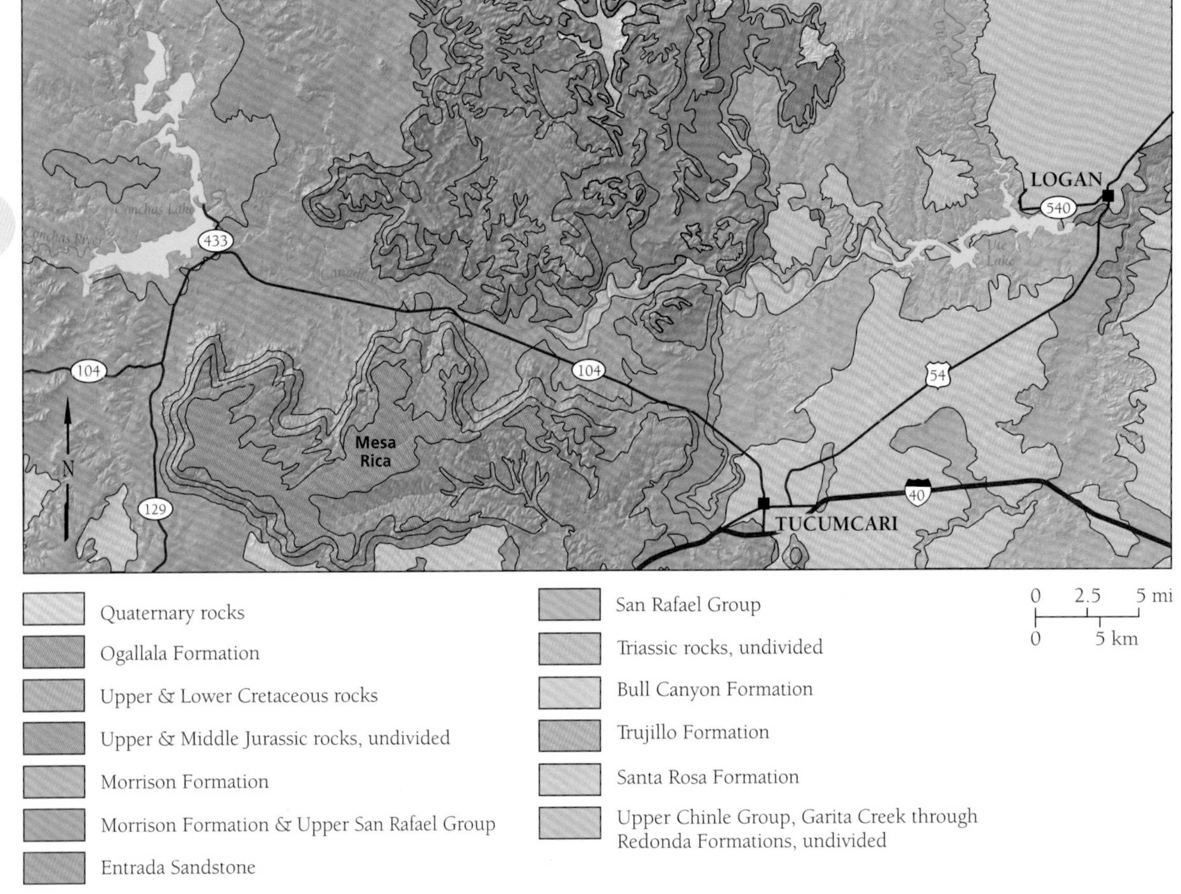

Generalized geologic map of the portion of northeastern New Mexico that includes both Conchas and Ute Lakes. The bedrock at both lakes is primarily Triassic sandstones of the Chinle Group. Mesa Rica (in orange) is an erosional remnant of the Llano Estacado.

32,000 square miles. Both Conchas Lake and Ute Lake are on the Canadian River, which forms the northern boundary of the Llano Estacado, separating it from the remainder of the High Plains to the north. The Canadian River and its tributaries have carved canyons and dissected badlands north of the Llano Estacado and south of the Canadian Escarpment, leaving only a few islands (such as Mesa Rica, southeast of Conchas Lake) of the once-continuous High Plains surface.

The Rock Record

The bedrock at both Conchas Lake and Ute Lake is primarily sandstones of the Chinle Group of Late Triassic age. At Conchas Lake, just below the dam, these Late Triassic rocks overlie a thin succession (less than 100 feet) of red sandstones of Permian and Middle Triassic age—the Artesia Group and Moenkopi Formation, respectively.

The Chinle Group rocks at Conchas Lake are about 400 feet thick and consist mostly of brown, gray, and yellow sandstone, with some pebbly layers and a few slopes of red mudstone. These are rocks of the 225-million-year-old Santa Rosa Formation. A few feet of red mudstone and sandstone of the Garita Creek Formation above the Santa Rosa Formation at Conchas Lake are the youngest Triassic rocks preserved in the park. Some younger, unconsolidated gravels and sands overlie the Triassic rocks, and they are Pleistocene (less than 1.6 million years old) river deposits of the ancestral Canadian River.

Sandstones of the Garita Creek Formation at Conchas Lake Dam.

The Triassic rocks at Ute Lake belong primarily to the 215-million-year-old Trujillo Formation of the Chinle Group. About 200 feet thick, the Trujillo sandstones are seen all along the shores of the lake and in the adjoining river canyons. They are gray, yellow, and brown, and contain some pebbly layers. Along the Canadian River below the dam, red mudstones and sandstones of the Garita Creek Formation are exposed beneath the cliffs and ledges of Trujillo Formation sandstones. Thus, the Triassic bedrock exposed at Ute Lake State Park is just a bit higher in the rock column (and, therefore, slightly younger) than the bedrock exposed at Conchas Lake State Park. In Ute Lake State Park, unconsolidated sands and gravels overlying the Triassic sandstones and mudstones are Pleistocene deposits of the Canadian River. Along Ute Creek, terrace gravels of Pleistocene age are as much as 20 feet thick. These gravels accumulated on flat surfaces (terraces) at different times during the downcutting of Ute Creek.

Geologic History

During the Late Triassic the western United States from Texas to Idaho was a vast, lowland river basin located less than 10 degrees north of the ancient equator. Mountain ranges in what are now Texas and Oklahoma were the headlands of rivers, some as large as the modern Mississsippi, that flowed to the west and northwest across much of New Mexico. These rivers piled up thick and extensive sheets of sand and gravel in their channels and along their margins. The Triassic rocks exposed at Conchas Dam are the products of a 225-million-year-old river

Red mudstones and sandstones of the Garita Creek Formation are exposed in the canyon of the Canadian River just below the dam at Ute Lake.

system, whereas those at Ute Lake were produced by a somewhat younger, 215-million-year-old river system.

These Triassic river systems teemed with fish, primitive amphibians, and the crocodile-like reptiles called phytosaurs. They were shrouded by forests of conifers, and the forest floors were home to some of the earliest dinosaurs and other extinct reptiles.

After the Triassic, many more rocks layers formed at the sites of Conchas and Ute Lakes, but erosion, most of it during the last few million years, has stripped away these rocks. The primary agent of this erosion was the Canadian River.

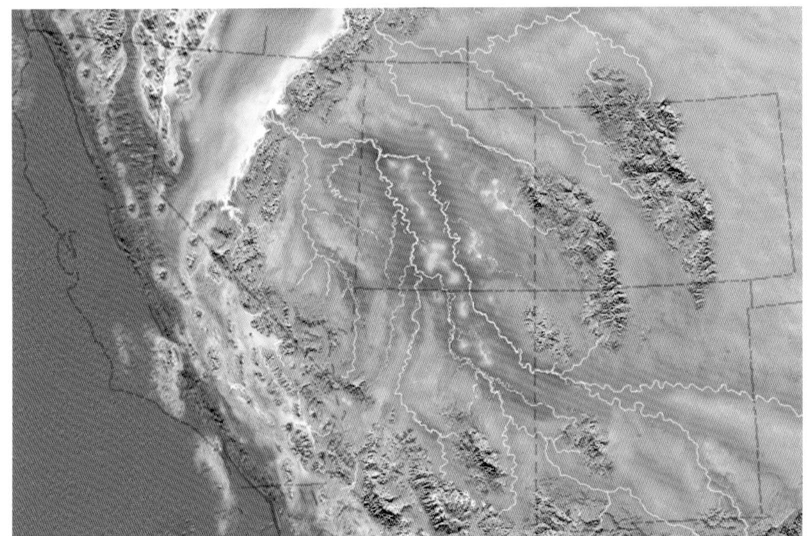

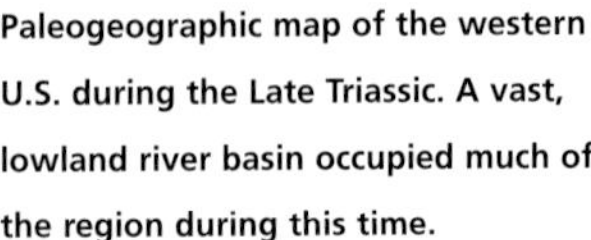

Paleogeographic map of the western U.S. during the Late Triassic. A vast, lowland river basin occupied much of the region during this time.

The geological history of the Canadian River extends back nearly 4 million years, when the ancestral Canadian River first flowed. At that time a nearly continuous, flat (it actually sloped slightly to the east) High Plains surface covered east-central New Mexico. The Canadian River cut into this surface, and by about 600,000 years ago the river had essentially created the modern topography between the Llano Estacado and the Canadian Escarpment.

Geologic Features

At Conchas Lake, the river canyon below the dam gives the best view of the cliffs and ledges of Triassic sandstone. In some places, pieces and logs of petrified wood can be found weathering from gravelly beds in the sandstone. A few fragments of Triassic reptile bone may also be encountered, and footprints of the ancient reptiles are sometimes found on the top surfaces of sandstone layers.

The view southeast from Conchas Lake State Park is of the western end of Mesa Rica, which extends nearly 25 miles from west to east, making it one of the largest mesas in New Mexico. The slopes of Mesa Rica are made up of Triassic sedimentary rocks and overlying Jurassic rocks. The cap of the mesa is Cretaceous and Miocene rocks. Mesa Rica is an erosional remnant of the Llano Estacado. During the last 4 million years, tributaries of the Canadian River carved canyons out of the northern edge of the upland surface, leaving Mesa Rica as a northerly island separated from the main portion of the Llano Estacado to the south by about 10 to 20 miles of canyons and lowlands.

Mesa Rica, visible on the southern horizon from Conchas Lake, is an extensive erosional remnant of the Llano Estacado.

At Ute Lake State Park, the best view of the Triassic sandstones is in the canyon of the Canadian River down-stream from the dam. These sandstones also contain some petrified wood and bone fragments. Access to the dam is on the south side of Logan, via NM–552.

Looking to the northwest from Ute Lake State Park, the Canadian Escarpment is visible in the distance. It is the southern edge of the High Plains north of the Canadian River drainage. Like Mesa Rica, the slopes of the Canadian Escarpment are made up of Triassic sedimentary rocks and overlying Jurassic rocks, and the cap is Cretaceous and Miocene rocks.

—*Spencer G. Lucas*

If You Plan to Visit

Conchas Lake State Park is 34 miles northwest of Tucumcari via NM–104, and 24 miles north of Newkirk via NM–129. Ute Lake is 3 miles west of Logan via NM–540 and 25 miles northeast of Tucumcari via US 54 and NM–39 and NM–540. For more information:

Conchas Lake State Park
P.O. Box 976
Conchas Dam, NM 88416
(575) 868-2270
www.emnrd.state.nm.us/emnrd/PRD/Conchas.htm

Ute Lake State Park
P.O. Box 52
Logan, NM 88426
(575) 487-2284
www.emnrd.state.nm.us/emnrd/PRD/UteLake.htm

Santa Rosa Lake State Park

NEW MEXICO STATE PARKS

Santa Rosa, "the city of natural lakes," lies in the semiarid, upper Pecos River Valley in Guadalupe County, where numerous natural artesian-spring lakes abound. But the largest lake in the area is not a natural lake; it is Santa Rosa Lake, a reservoir 7 miles north of the city on the Pecos River. The dam was completed by the U.S. Army Corps of Engineers in 1981 at a cost of $43 million for irrigation and flood control.

The dam is a rock-fill structure formed in layers. Pumping concrete slurry into holes in the ground to form a grout curtain sealed the foundation of the dam. The center of the dam consists of very fine-grained, impervious material, which prevents water seepage. The outer layer of the dam is constructed of coarse gravel including boulders as large as 48 inches in diameter. A control tower east of the dam within the reservoir, connects to a series of gates that regulate the water flow from the reservoir into the Pecos River. The spillway is 1,000 feet east of the dam and is 1,050 feet wide.

Santa Rosa Lake. The Pecos River is visible in the foreground, below the dam.

Regional Setting

Santa Rosa Lake State Park lies in the northern portion of the Pecos Valley section of the Great Plains province. The Pecos Valley is in the foothills of the Rocky Mountains. The landforms in the Pecos Valley are erosional landforms of sedimentary strata. Throughout the Paleozoic era, the area was occupied off and on by marine seas, with periods of erosion and deposition of continental deposits as the seas retreated. After uplift of the Rocky Mountains during the Laramide orogeny, erosion of the mountains resulted in streams and rivers that carried sediment to the Great Plains.

The Rock Record/Geologic History

Rocks exposed in Santa Rosa Lake State Park range in age from Triassic to Quaternary. The Triassic rocks were deposited during the erosion of the Ancestral Rocky Mountains. The oldest unit in the park is the Triassic Anton Chico Formation. The Anton Chico Formation is as much as 80 feet thick and consists of reddish-brown and grayish-red sandstone and conglomerate that formed in stream channels. The reddish color is a result of oxidation of iron to hematite. Although fossils are rare in the Anton Chico Formation, an amphibian skull was found in the sandstone near Dilia in Guadalupe County.

The Triassic Santa Rosa Formation (basal unit of the Chinle Group) overlies the Anton Chico Formation. The unit consists of 300 feet of maroon, reddish-brown, or tan sandstone, siltstone, and mudstone. Locally, the sandstone and siltstone are crossbedded and contain ripple marks, indicating the rocks were deposited in stream channels and on floodplains as overbank deposits in alluvial and deltaic environments. Tree branches, fossil leaves, and other plant remains have been found locally in these sandstones and mudstones. The Santa Rosa Formation was deposited in a semiarid continental environment, probably wetter than the present climate. Excellent exposures crop out in the dam spillway.

Deposits from the remaining units of the Triassic Chinle Group conformably overlie the Santa Rosa Formation. This unit consists of 800 to 1,200 feet of maroon-to-reddish-brown mudstone, siltstone, sandstone, and thin layers of conglomerate and limestone. These rocks were deposited in lacustrine (lake) and fluvial (river) environments.

Surficial deposits of soil, gravel, silt, and clay of late Tertiary and Quaternary age cover the Triassic rocks in places. Most of these materials were deposited during the past two million years as the Pecos River cut into its present valley. Along some valleys in the area, the alluvial fill may be up to 60 feet thick.

Geologic Features

Steep-sided mesas capped by flat-lying sandstone form much of the skyline surrounding Santa Rosa Lake. The sandstone is more resistant to erosion than the underlying softer shale, which erodes more quickly, forming steep slopes or cliffs. Once the sandstone loses underlying support, sandstone blocks begin to fall, covering the hill slope. With time, these isolated landforms are created.

The Pecos River changes character at Santa Rosa Lake. The Pecos River has its headwaters in the Sangre de Cristo and flows through steep walled canyons and over near flat alluvial valleys upstream of Santa Rosa Lake. South of Santa Rosa Lake, the Pecos River is not as steep in gradient and begins to form meanders and oxbow lakes. Part of this change is a result of the development of karst in the Santa Rosa area.

Most of the natural lakes in the vicinity of the town of Santa Rosa are the result of solution phenomena that began during the Triassic and continue today. The town itself lies in a huge sinkhole approximately six miles in diameter and 400 feet deep. Many of these karst depressions are nearly circular and are flanked by steep-sided cliffs of the Santa Rosa Formation. These features were formed by dissolution of underlying Permian limestone, gypsum, and evaporites of the San Andres Limestone and Artesia Group. Similar features are found at Bottomless Lakes State Park and Brantley Lake State Park. Ground water dissolves these rocks, creating subsurface cavities. The overlying rocks, including the Santa Rosa Formation, collapse into the voids, creating surface depressions. The resulting fractures and faults bounding the sinkholes provide conduits along which water can migrate. Ground water and surface drainage fills the surface depressions, forming lakes. In Santa Rosa Lake State Park, these circular solution features are not well developed. However, some outcrops within the park, such as part of the east wall of the spillway, are complexly faulted and deformed, probably as a result of these solution processes. The channel of the Pecos River in this area may have been influenced in part by the dissolution of underlying rocks.

The Anton Chico and Santa Rosa Formations have been utilized for crushed and dimension stone. Much of the rock material used to build the dam came from these units. The New Mexico Construction Company produced approximately 153,000 tons of asphalt or bituminous sandstone from 1930 to 1939 for road-surfacing material. The abandoned quarries are usually inundated by the lake, but are exposed occasionally when the water level is low.

—*Virginia T. McLemore*

If You Plan to Visit

Santa Rosa Lake State Park is seven miles north of Santa Rosa via NM–91. Facilities include campgrounds, picnic areas, and a visitor center. For more information:

Santa Rosa State Park
P.O. Box 384
Santa Rosa, NM 88433
(575) 472-3110
(575) 472-5956 (Fax)
www.emnrd.state.nm.us/PRD/santarosa.htm

Glossary

aa—Term for lava flows characterized by a blocky, rubbly surface.

agate—A translucent variety of quartz which has a waxy luster and in which the different colors are in bands, clouds, or distinct groups.

aggrade—To build up sediments within the channel of a stream in order to maintain its grade.

alluvial fan—A fan-shaped mass of sediment deposited by a stream at the mouth of a canyon in arid or semiarid regions.

alluvium—Unconsolidated mud, sand, and gravel deposited by rivers, streams, or sheetwash.

andesite—A dark, fine-grained volcanic rock composed principally of plagioclase feldspar and one or more mafic constituents.

anticline—An arch-like fold in which strata dip in opposite directions from a common ridge or axis; the core of an anticline contains the older strata.

aquifer—A body of rock or sediment capable of storing and transmitting water.

arkose—A coarse-grained, feldspar-rich sandstone composed of poorly sorted angular grains, usually derived from the disintegration of granitic rocks.

artesian water—Ground water that is under sufficient pressure to rise above the level at which it is encountered in a well.

ash (volcanic)—Fine-grained uncemented pyroclastic material.

ash flow—A superheated mixture of volcanic ash and gas that forms typically as a result of the explosive eruption of viscous lava and flows across the surface of the ground.

augite—A pyroxene mineral.

aulocogen—the failed arm of a rift system.

basalt—A dark-colored volcanic rock, rich in iron and magnesium, which typically erupts from fissures and low-relief volcanoes.

basin—A large depression or area of subsidence in which strata dip inward.

bombs—Volcanic fragments, from the size of an apple upward, blown from a volcano

brachiopod—A bivalved marine invertebrate, commonly found as fossils in Paleozoic rocks.

breccia—A coarse-grained clastic rock formed of angular fragments of broken rock.

bryozoan—A small, colonial aquatic invertebrate, usually secreting calcareous skeletons that as fossils resemble either twigs or moss-like patterns.

butte—An isolated flat-topped hill, a classic erosional landform found in areas of flat-lying (generally sedimentary) rock.

calcite—A mineral whose composition is calcium carbonate ($CaCO_3$).

calcium carbonate—The mineral calcite ($CaCO_3$), the primary constituent of limestone.

caldera—A large volcanic crater, often 10–20 miles in diameter, that forms when a gas-charged viscous magma body erupts explosively. Following the eruption, the shallow roof of the chamber collapses, forming a large, circular depression.

caliche—Gravel, sand, silt, etc., cemented by calcium carbonate. Forms at the sur face or near the base of the upper soil layers.

cephalopod—A marine mollusk; most fossil forms consist of a calcareous shell divided into numerous chambers. Modern cephalopods include squid, octopus, and cuttlefish.

chalcedony—A translucent variety of quartz having a waxy luster. May be white, blue, brown, gray, or black.

cinders—Nut-sized fragments blown from a volcano during eruption.

cirque—A steep, crescent-shaped wall at the head of a glacial valley, formed by the erosive activity of a mountain glacier.

clastic—The general term used for rock or sediment composed of broken fragments of pre-existing rocks that have been transported some distance.

colluvium—An accumulation of loose fragments of rock and soil at the base of a slope.

concretion—A rounded body found in sedimentary rocks; usually caused by chemical deposition of concentric layers of calcite or silica around a central nucleus.

conglomerate—A coarse-grained, poorly sorted clastic rock formed principally of rounded fragments of rock larger than 2 mm in size.

correlative—Belonging to the same age or stratigraphic position.

crater—A steep-walled depression on top of a volcanic cone above the pipe or vent that feeds the volcano.

crinoid An echinoderm with numerous radiating arms, typically attached to the sea floor. The segmented stems of Paleozoic crinoids are especially abun dant as fossils in Mississippian and Pennsylvanian rocks.

crossbedding—A type of bedding, typically found in sand dunes and stream-laid deposits, in which inclined internal layers are deposited at an angle to the predominant bedding orientation, indicating currents of moving water (or air).

cuesta—A hill or ridge with a gentle slope on one side and a steep slope on the other.

dacite—A volcanic rock consisting of plagioclase and orthoclase feldspars, quartz, and mafic minerals such as pyroxene.

detritus—A collective term for loose rock or mineral material that is mechanically eroded from pre-existing rocks and transported some distance.

diatreme—A breccia-filled volcanic pipe formed by a gaseous explosion.

dike—A tabular intrusive body of rock that cuts across adjacent rocks. eolian deposited by wind.

extrusive—Referring to igneous rocks that erupt and cool relatively quickly at the earth's surface—i.e., volcanic rocks like basalt, andesite, or rhyolite.

fanglomerate—A sedimentary rock that is composed of rock fragments that were deposited in an alluvial fan.

fault—A fracture along which movement has occurred.

felsic—The term applied to igneous rocks with an abundance of light-colored minerals, typically quartz, feldspar, and muscovite.

fiamme—Small, dark, elongate glassy inclusions in welded tuffs, thought to have formed from the collapse of volcanic fragments (i.e., pumice). From the Italian, fiamma (flame).

fissure vent—An elongate crack in the earth's surface from which lava or pyroclastic material has erupted.

fluvial—Deposit a sedimentary deposit transported and laid down by a stream.

formation—A mappable rock unit, consisting of one or more types of rocks deposited essentially without interruption and distinctive from rock units above and below.

gastrolith—A rounded, polished pebble or stone from the stomach of some reptiles, including dinosaurs, thought to have been used in grinding up food.

gastropod—A mollusk characterized by a distinct head with eyes and tentacles, and, in most cases, a single, unchambered shell of calcite. Modern-day gastropods include snails and abalone.

gneiss—A foliated metamorphic rock, formed by regional metamorphism of igneous rock (like granite), in which mineral grains are aligned in distinct bands, often of alternating light and dark minerals.

graben—A downthrown fault block bounded on either side by normal faults.

group—A formal rock unit combining two or more formations.

grus—The weathered fragments of disintegrated granite.

gypsum—Calcium sulfate ($CaSO_4$)

hematite—An oxide of iron (Fe_2O_3). May be an earthy, red color or a silvery metallic gray.

hoodoos—The informal term for erosional landforms that resemble spires, pillars, and columns, and which form through the differential weathering of horizontal sediments, often in arid landscapes.

hydrovolcanic—The general term for volcanic features that form as a the result of interaction between magma, gas, and water at or near the earth's surface.

igneous—A rock that has formed from molten material. Igneous rocks can crystal lize at or near the surface or deep beneath the surface.

ignimbrite—The term for a volcanic deposit that results from a pyroclastic flow; includes ash-flow tuffs and welded tuffs.

intrusive—Referring to igneous rocks that are emplaced and cool slowly at depth beneath the earth's surface—for example, granite.

karst—A type of typography that forms generally in limestone terrains and is char acterized by subsurface dissolution features (caves and sinkholes) and an absence of surface streams.

laccolith—A domed igneous intrusion, generally with a flat floor, which is concor dant with surrounding rocks.

lamprophyre—A variety of porphyritic intrusive igneous rocks (typically dikes) in which the phenocrysts are primarily composed of mafic minerals and the groundmass includes both mafic and felsic minerals.

lava—Molten rock (magma) that erupts at the surface is known as lava; it hardens into a volcanic rock such as basalt.

lava tube—A subterranean hollow tunnel or cave in lava, which forms in a variety of ways as molten lava escapes from an eruptive vent.

limestone—A sedimentary rock composed chiefly of calcium carbonate (calcite). Limestone can form by either organic or inorganic means.

maar—A low-relief volcanic crater formed from numerous shallow steam and magma explosions.

mafic—The term applied to igneous rocks composed chiefly of dark colored ferro magnesian minerals (rich in iron and magnesium).

magma—Molten rock beneath the earth's surface. Once it erupts onto the earth's surface and hardens, it is referred to as lava.

malpais—Spanish for "bad lands," usually applied to the rough surfaced areas covered by basalt.

massif—A massive topographic and structural feature, often in orogenic belts, commonly formed of rocks more rigid than those of its surroundings.

mesa—A flat-topped erosional landform bounded on one or more sides by a steep cliff.

metamorphic rock—A rock that has formed from pre-existing rocks at depth, without melting, in response to changes in heat, pressure, stress, and the chemical environment.

minette—A variety of porphyritic igneous rock.

monocline—A single-limbed fold.

mudstone—A hardened sedimentary deposit made up of particles of clay and silt.

orogeny—Mountain building episode, generally involving large-scale faulting, magma intrusions, uplift, volcanic activity, and deformation.

pahoehoe—The term for basaltic lava flows that are characterized by a smooth, billowy, or ropey surface.

paternoster lake—One of a chain of small lakes that occupy rock basins in a glacial valley, connected by streams or waterfalls and resembling a string of rosary beads.

pedogenic carbonate—Secondary carbonate that forms through the processes responsible for soil development. See *caliche*.

pegmatite—Coarsely crystalline igneous rock that typically occurs as irregular veins or dikes in finer-grained intrusive igneous rocks. Pegmatites represent the last portion of a magma to crystallize and often contain concentrations of otherwise rare minerals.

pelecypod—A bivalved, bottom-dwelling aquatic mollusk. Modern examples include clams and mussels.

phenocryst—A relatively large, conspicuous crystal in a porphyritic rock.

phlogopite—A magnesium-rich variety of mica.

piedmont—A flat to gently sloping surface formed at the base of a mountain. In the Albuquerque area, piedmonts are thick alluvial aprons.

placer—Mineral deposit formed by mechanical concentration of heavy mineral particles, such as gold, from weathered debris.

plagioclase—A sodium- or calcium-rich feldspar.

playa—A dry, flat, vegetation-free area at the lowest part of an undrained desert basin, typically filled with evaporate deposits and sometimes occupied by ephemeral lakes.

pluton—A deep-seated igneous intrusion.

porosity—The percentage of a rock or deposit that consists of open spaces.

porphyry—An igneous rock containing two distinctly different sizes of crystals, typically large crystals (phenocrysts) in a fine-grained groundmass.

pressure ridge—An elongate wrinkling of the crust of a lava flow, apparently caused by the viscous drag of lava moving beneath a solidified crust.

pyroclastic—The general term for clastic rock material ejected during a volcanic eruption.

resurgent dome—A structural feature that forms following the collapse of a caldera when magmatic material beneath the surface creates an uplift or dome on the floor of the caldera.

rhyolitic—A compositional term that refers to (generally light colored) igneous rocks that are rich in quartz and potassium feldspar.

rift—A long, narrow trough that is bounded on either side by normal faults.

sabkha—A supratidal sedimentary environment, which often forms in arid or semi-arid climates, characterized by saline evaporate deposits.

salina—The general term for a place where crystalline salt deposits form, such as a salt pan or playa.

sandstone—A hardened sedimentary deposit consisting of grains of sand-sized rock materials. Most sandstones consist largely of quartz (SiO_2).

sauropod—A large plant-eating dinosaur with a long neck and tail.

sedimentary rock—A rock that results from the consolidation of loose sediment that has accumulated in layers, either clastic sediments (as in the case of sandstone) or chemically/organically precipitated sediments (as in the case of limestone).

scarp—A line of cliffs produced by faulting or erosion, or both.

shale—A finely laminated, hardened sediment composed of silt and clay or clay-sized particles.

siderite—An iron carbonate mineral, typically yellow-brown or red. It often is found as nodules in sedimentary deposits.

silt—Unconsolidated grains ranging in size from 1/256 to 1/16 mm.

siltstone—A hardened sedimentary deposit consisting of silt-size grains.

slickenside—A polished fault surface that shows lineations or striations caused by friction due to fault movement.

strata—Layers of rock, usually sedimentary but may include volcanic flows.

syncline—A trough-like fold in layered rocks; the core of a syncline contains the youngest rocks.

talus—A sloping heap of rock fragments at the foot of a cliff or steep slope.

tarn—A small glacial lake.

terrace—Relatively flat bench on a hillside, generally remnants of former stream valleys.

terrane—A general (and somewhat outdated) term for a body of rock or group of rocks of regional extent that are characterized by a geologic history different from that of surrounding terranes.

tholeiite—A basalt characterized by the presence of orthopyroxene and, in some cases, low-calcium pyroxenes.

travertine—A dense form of limestone formed from the deposition of concentric layers of calcium carbonate from solution in both surface and ground waters, typically in caves or around the mouths of hot springs.

trilobite—An extinct class of marine arthropods having a flattened segmented body covered by a dorsal exoskeleton divided into three lobes.

ultramafic—The term for an intrusive igneous rock that is formed primarily of ultramafic minerals, i.e., hypersthene, augite, or olivine.

unconformity—A surface that separates older and younger rock units and represents a gap in the geologic record. It may represent a time during which deposition was interrupted by a period of erosion, or a time of no deposition.

vesicular—Refers to the texture of a lava characterized by an abundance of vesicles or cavities, formed by the expansion and entrapment of gas bubbles as molten lava approaches the surface.

volcaniclastic—A general term for all clastic volcanic materials.

volcano—A vent in the earth's crust from which molten lava, pyroclastic material, volcanic gases, etc. issue.

welded tuff—A pyroclastic rock in which the volcanic deposits have been indurated through heat and the pressure of overlying deposits.

xenolith—A fragment of country rock within an intrusive or volcanic igneous rock.

Contributors

Paul Bauer is a principal geologist and associate director at the New Mexico Bureau of Geology and Mineral Resources at New Mexico Tech, and has spent 30 years enjoying the sublime geology and landscapes of New Mexico. He has co-authored a series of geologic quadrangle maps of north-central New Mexico, has published a variety of books and articles on the geology of the region, and has led a multitude of field trips, both for professional geologists and the general public. Paul received a B.S. in geology (1978) from the University of Massachusetts, an M.S. in geology (1983) from the University of New Mexico, and a Ph.D. in geology (1988) from New Mexico Tech.

Sean Connell is a field geologist with the New Mexico Bureau of Geology and Mineral Resources. He has 21 years of consultant and research experience in geomorphology, engineering and environmental geology, sedimentology, and stratigraphy of semiarid regions in southern California and New Mexico. During his 13-year career at the bureau, Mr. Connell has contributed to regional mapping and geologic studies of the Rio Grande rift in central and northern New Mexico. Mr. Connell received his B.S. in geology from the California State University at Northridge, and his M.S. in geology from the University of California at Riverside. He is currently finishing his Ph.D. in geology from the University of New Mexico.

Larry Crumpler is research curator of volcanology and space sciences at the New Mexico Museum of Natural History and Science in Albuquerque. Primarily a field geologist interested in volcanoes, his research focuses on the physics and dynamic processes of volcanoes as recorded in the structure and morphology of young volcanoes and volcanic features. He also specializes in the geology of the terrestrial planets, with an emphasis on planetary volcanism. He has mapped over a dozen 7.5-minute quadrangles in young volcanic terrains, and has participated in NASA Viking and Pathfinder Mars missions, the Magellan synthetic aperture radar mapping mission to Venus, the Russian Mars 96 mission, several Mars rover field tests, and (most recently) the Mars Exploration Rover mission as a Science Team member.

Nelia Dunbar is a geochemist and associate director at the New Mexico Bureau of Geology. She also manages the electron microprobe laboratory at New Mexico Tech. Nelia completed a B.A. in geology at Mount Holyoke College (1983) and then went on to a Ph.D. in geochemistry at New Mexico Tech (1989). She has worked for the Bureau of Geology since 1992, focusing on geochemistry of volcanic rocks, particularly volcanic ashes and other explosive eruptions, mainly in New Mexico and Antarctica. In addition to research, Nelia teaches a graduate class on electron microprobe analysis and is involved in outreach activities for New Mexico teachers and students.

Adrian Hunt was born in the United Kingdom and came to New Mexico almost thirty years ago to go to graduate school at New Mexico Tech and the University of New Mexico. Subsequently he worked at colleges and museums in New Mexico and Colorado and conducted extensive fieldwork in the Southwest, principally related to fossil reptiles and amphibians of the Mesozoic, as well as fossil footprints and feces of all ages. He has published over six hundred scientific articles and is currently executive director of the Flying Heritage Collection in Everett, Washington, where he still publishes a paper or two a year.

Shari Kelley earned a B.S. in geological sciences at New Mexico State University and a Ph.D. in geophysics at Southern Methodist University. Shari has spent most of her professional career studying the uplift and erosion history and tectonic evolution of mountain ranges in the southwestern United States. She currently works for the New Mexico Bureau of Geology and Mineral Resources, where (among other things) she composes material for the bureau's Frequently Asked Questions and Virtual Geologic Tours Web pages. In addition, she is a field geologist working with geologic mapping teams in the Jemez Mountains, the Sacramento Mountains, and on Mt. Taylor.

Dave Love is a principal senior environmental geologist at the New Mexico Bureau of Geology and Mineral Resources, where he has worked since 1980. His work has focused on a great variety of topics, including impacts of surface and subsurface mining; shrinking, swelling, collapsing, and corrosive soils; behavior of arroyos; geology of archaeological sites; movement of contaminants in the shallow subsurface; faulting, earthquakes, and earthquake education. He has been involved in geology outreach for teachers and students, has worked as a geologist for the Southwest Institute, as a sabbatical replacement at Washington State University (1976–1978), and as a seasonal interpreter for the National Park Service. Dave holds a B.S. from Beloit College (anthropology and geology), and an M.S. and a Ph.D. in geology from the University of New Mexico.

Spencer Lucas is curator of geology and paleontology at the New Mexico Museum of Natural History and Science. He has a B.A. from the University of New Mexico and a M.S. and Ph.D. from Yale University. Lucas is a paleontologist and stratigrapher who has undertaken research on New Mexico's Phanerozoic fossils and strata for more than 30 years.

Bill McIntosh is a senior volcanologist/geochronologist at the New Mexico Bureau of Geology and Mineral Resources. He also co-directs the New Mexico Geochronology Research Laboratory at New Mexico Tech. Bill completed an A.B. in geology at Princeton University (1976), then went on to an M.S. in geology at University of Colorado, Boulder (1980) and a Ph.D. in geology at New Mexico Tech (1989). He has worked for the New Mexico Bureau of Geology and Mineral Resources since 1989, focusing on geochronology of volcanic rocks in New Mexico and other areas of the western U.S., South America, and Antarctica. In addition to research, Bill teaches a graduate class on argon geochronology and is involved in outreach activities for New Mexico teachers and students.

Virginia (Ginger) McLemore is a senior economic geologist with the New Mexico Bureau of Geology and Mineral Resources and has spent nearly 30 years studying the geology, mineralogy, and environmental geology of mineral deposits and geology of the state parks in New Mexico. She has written numerous articles and books on the copper, uranium, gold, silver, industrial minerals, and other mineral resources of the state. Ginger received a B.S. in geology and a B.S. in geophysics in 1977 and an M.S. in geology in 1980 from New Mexico Tech. She received a Ph.D. in 1993 from the University of Texas at El Paso.

William Muehlberger was on the faculty of the Department of Geological Sciences at the University of Texas at Austin for 38 years. He and his students have mapped large areas of northern New Mexico. For years he has worked with NASA in northern New Mexico teaching astronauts about geologic processes. In addition to his many professional publications, he is the author of a number of popular volumes on geology, including *The High Plains of Northeastern New Mexico: A Guide to Geology and Culture*, which was the recipient of the 2007 New Mexico Book Award.

Greer Price is the deputy director at the New Mexico Bureau of Geology and Mineral Resources, where he also manages the publishing program. His varied experience includes eight years as a geologist in the oil patch, ten years with the National Park Service, and four years with Grand Canyon Association. He is an adjunct member of the faculty in the Humanities Department at New Mexico Tech, as well, where he occasionally teaches. He holds a B.A. and an M.A. in geology from Washington University in St. Louis.

Geoff Rawling is a field geologist at the New Mexico Bureau of Geology and Mineral Resources. His main interests are geologic mapping, hydrogeology, and structural geology. Most of his geologic mapping has been in the Ruidoso and Capitan areas of the northern Sacramento Mountains. He is also involved in a multidisciplinary hydrogeologic study of the southern Sacramento Mountains. He has a Ph.D. from New Mexico Tech, an M.S. from SUNY Stony Brook, and a B.S. from Penn State, all in geology.

Adam Read has been a geologist with the New Mexico Bureau of Geology and Mineral Resources since 1998. During that time, he has produced several geologic maps in and around the Sandia Mountains, the Santa Fe area, and Ladron peak (among many other projects). He also manages the bureau's Web site. He has a strong interest in structural geology, particularly in ductile deformation and breccia formation. His M.S. from the University of New Mexico in 1997 focused on the Rincon Range north of Mora, New Mexico. He lives in Los Chavez north of Belen with his wife, Beth, and daughter, Erin.

Steven Semken is assistant professor of geoscience education and geology in the School of Earth and Space Exploration at Arizona State University. He is a geoscience education researcher and ethnogeologist who works at the intersection of earth science with cognitive science and cultural geography. His research is centered in the Southwest and includes studies of sense of place in place-based geoscience teaching, American Indian and Chicano ethnogeology, informal geoscience education in national parks, K-12 teacher preparation, and Cenozoic volcanism and environmental geology of the Colorado Plateau. He taught at Diné College, the Tribal College of the Navajo Nation, in Shiprock for 15 years. He has a Ph.D. in materials science and an S.B. in geology from MIT, and an M.S. in geochemistry from UCLA. He is a past president of the National Association of Geoscience Teachers.

Acknowledgments

Thanks first and foremost to our authors, who provided the framework on which we built this volume. Special thanks are due to Nelia Dunbar, Paul Bauer, and Shari Kelley, who in particular worked very closely with us to develop captions, photos, and graphics, not only in their own chapters but throughout the book.

I am grateful to Peter Scholle, our director and state geologist, for his ongoing support of what turned out to be a massive project, and for his patience while we worked so hard to make it a reality.

Special thanks to Christina Watkins, who (as always) went way beyond her role of designer, sharing our vision and our hope, and helping us to share hers. And to Gina D'Ambrosio, who dedicated herself to this project, worked closely alongside me every step of the way, and in a very real way made this book happen.

Leo Gabaldon and Tom Kaus took primary responsibility for producing or finalizing the maps and graphics, but I would also like to thank Kathy Glesener, Glen Jones, Mark Mansell, Dave McCraw, Brigitte Felix, and Phil Miller for their cartographic expertise and cooperation.

Many people generously provided photos or graphics that we adapted for use in the volume, and we gratefully acknowledge their help—in particular Ron Blakey, Fraser Goff, Kirt Kempter, Grant Meyer, and Gary Smith.

Without the expertise and cooperation of the many professional photographers who provided images for this book, we would not have been able to communicate our message so effectively. In particular I would like to thank Adriel Heisey, Gary Rasmussen, and William Stone, all of whom worked closely with us for several years to provide so many of the images we needed.

Many bureau staff offered help in reviewing manuscripts and helping us to develop photos and graphics. Among those I am grateful to are Doug Bland, Sean Connell, Robert Eveleth, Gretchen Hoffman, Shari Kelley, Bill McIntosh, and Maureen Wilks.

Special thanks to Bruce Heise and the National Park Service for their generous support, financial and otherwise, of this project from the beginning. Thanks also to Steve Cary (New Mexico State Parks), Pat Hester (Bureau of Land Management), Michael Linden (U.S. Forest Service), and Vince Santucci (National Park Service) all of whom offered advice and support on behalf of their organizations and facilitated review of the individual chapters. We wish to thank Lisa Madsen and the board of Public Lands Interpretive Association for their support, financial and otherwise.

We are grateful to New Mexico State Representative Mimi Stewart, who for many years has championed the cause of the publication program at the bureau. Without the support of Mimi and others like her, we could not continue to publish these kinds of books.

Photo and Illustration Credits

 Unless otherwise noted, all maps and illustrations were produced by the staff of the New Mexico Bureau of Geology and Mineral Resources. When modified from existing maps, original creator is credited below.

Page	Credit
Front cover	George H. H. Huey
iii	Adriel Heisey
9	After Christopher Scotese
12	After Eugene Humphreys

PART I

Page	Credit
18	William Stone
22	Steve Cather
24	Adriel Heisey
29 bottom	U.S. Geological Survey
30 top	U.S. Geological Survey
30 bottom	Nelia Dunbar
31	George H. H. Huey
32	Laurence Parent
33	William Stone
35, 38	L. Greer Price
41	William Stone
43	National Park Service
44	Adriel Heisey
45, 48	Gary Rasmussen
51	Laurence Parent
53–56, 59	Larry Crumpler
61, 63–66	Larry Crumpler
68	Adriel Heisey
72	George H. H. Huey
73–75	William Stone
76	David W. Love
79	William Stone
82	Brian Brister
84	Adriel Heisey
89	Gary Rasmussen
90 bottom, 91	L. Greer Price
93	George H. H. Huey
95	Gary Rasmussen
96, 99	Bob Sullivan, Pennsylvania State Museum
97	Ronald Blakey
98	University of Utah Press (Carel Brest van Kempen)
101, 104	Gary Rasmussen
102, 105	L. Greer Price
107, 112	Gary Rasmussen
116, 120	Shari Kelley
121	Gary Rasmussen
122	L. Greer Price
12 (both)	Gary Rasmussen

PART II

Page	Credit
126	George H. H. Huey
129	After Smith, Bailey, Ross
132–133	Kirt Kempter
135	Nelia W. Dunbar
139	After Fraser Goff
140–141	Kirt Kempter
143	Fraser Goff
144, 149	George H. H. Huey
147	After Kenneth Wohletz and R. McQueen
150	Nelia Dunbar
151 top	Gary Rasmussen
151 bottom	After Stephen Self
153, 155	L. Greer Price
156	Adam Read
158	Gina D'Ambrosio
159	William Stone
161, 163	Gary Rasmussen
164	William McIntosh
167	William Stone
168	From an original map by Will Moats
169	Peter Scholle
170	Steve Cather
173	Gary Rasmussen
174, 177	L. Greer Price
179, 180	L. Greer Price

PART III

Page	Credit
182	Adriel Heisey
185	After Gary Smith
188	William Stone
193, 195, 196	Paul Bauer
197	Adam Read
201	Grant Meyer
207	Adam Read
209	NPS photo by Luke Fields
212 (both)	Shari Kelley
213	U.S. Geological Survey
214	Shari Kelley
215	National Park Service

PART IV

Page	Credit
218	Mike Butterfield
223, 225	Paul Bauer
224, 226	Ronald Blakey
227	Mike Butterfield
228	George H. H. Huey
231 top	Steve Cather
231 bottom	L. Greer Price
233, 244	Mike Butterfield
235	Winifred Hamilton
237	Mike Butterfield
240	William Stone
246	Paul Bauer
248	Gina D'Ambrosio
249	Bovay Engineering, courtesy of R. Young
250	Mike Butterfield
251	Museum of New Mexico
252	L. Greer Price
253	U.S. Geological Survey
254	Laurence Parent
258 top, 260	Mike Butterfield
258, 259	Gina D'Ambrosio
261	Colorado Historical Society
262	Laurence Parent
265	William Stone
267	Paul Bauer
270, 271	Mike Butterfield
273, 274	L. Greer Price
275	Paul Bauer
277, 278	L. Greer Price
280	After Brian Ohlmsted
282	Adriel Heisey
283	Courtesy Palace of the Governors (MNM/DCA), cat. no. 67161.11-15
286	William Stone
288 (all)	Geoffrey C. Rawling
289	George H. H. Huey
291	Gary Rasmussen
295	L. Greer Price
299	Paul Logsdon
303–306	Geoffrey C. Rawling

PART V

Page	Credit
308	William Stone
313	Adriel Heisey
317 (both)	L. Greer Price
319	Adriel Heisey
321	Ronald Blakey
322	John Sibbick
323	William Muehlberger
325	Gary Rasmussen
328	After Brian Ohlmsted
331	L. Greer Price
335	George H. H. Huey
340	L. Greer Price
341	William Muehlberger
344	New Mexico Bureau of Geology archives
347, 349	L. Greer Price
350	Ronald Blakey
351	L. Greer Price
353	U.S. Army Corps of Engineers
Back cover	George H. H. Huey

Index

Index